MORE BY THE AUTHOR

SPECIAL AGENT KIM KUPAR NOVELS

Jade Eyes
They
The Why Files

THE TSCHAAA INFESTATION

Book 1: The Gathering Storm
Book 2: The Tsunami
Book 3: Typhoon of Steel
Free Range Protocol: Tales of the Tschaaa
Beyond the Great Compromise: Tales of the Tschaaa
Survivors: Escaping the Tschaaa

ANTHOLOGIES

Monstrosity (Unnerving Anthology)
Descent (Unnerving Anthology)
Wicked (Unnerving Anthology)
The Mighty Pen
Unconditional
Cascadia
Tales of the Slug
Super: Unexpected Heroes Arise

COLLECTED WORKS & MORE

Inhumanity: A Year of Stories
The Island (The Haunting of Orchard House)
Shane (Angels of Anarchy)

GAME WORLDS

MARSHALL MILLER

BLUE FORGE PRESS
Port Orchard ✺ Washington

Game Worlds
Copyright 2024
by Marshall Miller

First eBook Edition July 2024
First Print Edition July 2024

ISBN 978-1-59092-906-3

For information about film, reprint or other subsidiary rights, contact: blueforgegroup@gmail.com

Blue Forge Press is the print division of the volunteer-run, federal 501(c)3 nonprofit, Blue Legacy (EIN 83-4307421), founded in 1989 and dedicated to supporting artisans marginalized due to race, age, disability, economics or other factors. We strive to empower storytellers from all walks of life with our four divisions: Blue Forge Press, Blue Forge Films, Blue Forge Gaming, and Blue Forge Sound. Find out more at www.BlueForgeGroup.org

Blue Forge Press
7419 Ebbert Drive Southeast
Port Orchard, Washington 98367
blueforgepress@gmail.com
360-550-2071 ph.txt

GAME WORLDS

MARSHALL MILLER

PART ONE

WESTERN WORLD

CHAPTER 1
THE CAMPFIRE

Reylie King looked up at the bright new star in the evening sky. To say the light was brilliant would be a disservice to the distant future generations that have only the written record to explore this moment of discovery. It seemed a small thing from the vast distances of outer space, but Reylie knew the source had significant influence. With this vessel, a light of hope returned to the people.

Reylie brushed back her long bronze hair. She had found a grey strand just this morning. Reylie smiled as she realized that even in these days, time and aging marched on.

Reylie heard the back screen door open, then lightly shut and knew it was her Mother Jeanie coming to join her late-night observations while careful not to wake Reylie's children.

"Are the kids asleep, Mom?"

"Yes, dear. Although the twins kept whispering

about sneaking out to their treehouse."

Her mother linked arms with her. Reylie saw the grey in her mother's hair and felt the pang that someday she would be gone, passing like Granddad and Grandma. There was a double feeling of loss as, without the man known as the Tinkerer, the light in the sky would not exist.

"If Granddad could only see the Sky Tunnel on its first use," said Reylie.

"Oh, trust me, my daughter. He is looking at it from an alternate reality we call the afterlife. This project proves that other dimensions and universes exist, one of which must be Heaven." Her mother patted her arm. "But had you and your brother Ron not fiddled with that game he built, and disappeared, then came back, we would never be at this point in history."

Reylie tried to smile but could not. Whenever she thought about that time in her life, she remembered both the joys and fears and regrets. She had left this reality at age fourteen and returned at age nineteen. Her oldest, Marianne, was the result everyone tried to conceal. Now, as Reylie was nearing forty, she often mused, 'what if.' Then the reality that Marianne would not exist had not everything happened 'just so' would poke her in the heart. Her daughter was away at college, studying to follow in her step-father's footsteps.

Jeannie looked towards the large family home

which had once been Grandad and Grandma King's house.

"I had better check on those two grandsons of mine, Jack and John. Who would have thought in your late twenties you would have more kids—twins, even!—after…" Jeanie trailed off, leaving the rest unsaid. Reylie coming back, pregnant from some other reality, was shock enough. Adapting to a time out of mind after her violent adventure was not smooth.

Then she met Michael Mann. Twin boys soon followed. Now age ten, they were double joys in her life. The thought of her husband made Reylie look up again. "Funny how I met and married a man who would help complete Grandad's final dream."

Her mother patted her arm. "Mike will come back after they fire up the Sky Tunnel. Then I'll guarantee he'll never leave."

"Mom, I just worry some of them will get sucked into the vortex as I and others were with Grandad's game."

"That was then, Reylie; this is now. They know what they are doing."

Jeanie kissed her daughter on her cheek. "You stay out here and watch. Try to use some of that telepathy to talk to Mike."

Reylie finally smiled. "Wished that rumor was real. Ron and I only brought back some out-of-sync artifacts. And memories, of course."

Reylie's mother smiled and walked to the back door. Reylie looked again at the bright new star; it seemed to flicker a bit like a flame. To some, it was a flame of hope for a dying Earth. To Reylie, it was a flame from a campfire that introduced her and Ron into a strange new existence. Once again, her mind wandered to a time past when she and her brother were in a campfire—literally.

Five male figures hunkered down around the campfire in New Mexico Territory. The five would have been called highwaymen, road agents, or bushrangers, in different places and times. In the Southwest, desperados or banditos would be more appropriate. The oldest one, nicknamed by some as Greybeard—but known as Uncle Jake to the group—looked across the campfire to the massive shape cleaning an oversized revolver. Uncle Jake was taller than most and robust in build, but he looked very average compared to his nephew, Barnabas McCain. Due to the bearded and dark-haired man's size, the name Bar, as in bear, was used as a shorthand.

"Bar, I don't know why you don't get a cartridge version of those Coult Root revolvers of yours. It would make loadin' and cleanin' a lot easier."

Bar kept wiping his revolvers as he spoke. "As your brother James said, if it ain't busted, don't fix it."

Uncle Jake snorted. "Yes, he did say that. And you are as stubborn as he was. You are your father's son."

Bar held up the pistol to the campfire light. "These two caps and ball Coults designed by friend Root have seen me right good service for some nine yar. When you shoot something with their forty-four caliber bullets backed with sixty grains of black powder, it stays shot." Bar glanced over at his uncle.

"And they have better steel than that old Coult Walker you have. You still need to get that busted cylinder chamber fixed from that overload you used. That won't happen with these newer sidehammer ones."

The eighteen-year-old Olsen twins, both boys athletic and toe-headed, tried not to laugh. They heard near-duplicate discussions between uncle and nephew at least once a week. The year the Olsens had spent with the group had also taught them that it was best not to joke or interfere with such family interactions. Bar's sense of humor was limited.

The fifth person sharing the campfire looked up from sharpening his stiletto. Cajun Armand Bergeron had been with the McCains for some two years. The tall and lanky former resident of New Orleans first met them at the Second Battle of El Paso Del Norte in December 1865. Just over a month later, and the Second Mexican-

American War officially ended. However, not for the McCains. And thus, it had not stopped for those who rode with them. A small smile formed on Armand's mustachioed mouth. The Cajun had often marveled at the rough way the elder and younger members of the McCain clan demonstrated their affection for each other.

"I'll get my Walker fixed when we have the time and wherewithal to do it. It's not like we have been able to spend a lot of time in towns. Hells Bells, it's been a good month since I had a young resident of a bordello wash my—"

A bolt of energy exploded into the campfire, sending a metal coffee pot perched on its edge flying. Hot coals and small flaming sticks landed around the five campsite occupants, sending them leaping and scurrying from their seats.

Then two figures seemed to drop into the remains of the fire from out of thin air.

"What the…" Bar yelled out as he grabbed his huge Bowie knife. The two figures stumbled from the once center of the campfire, yelping and screaming as they slapped at their smoldering clothes.

"Reylie! Are you okay?" a young male voice called out.

"Yes, Ron," the female voice answered. Then a large bellow froze them in their tracks.

"Stop right there and reach for the sky," commanded Bar. "Who the Hell are you, and where in Hell did you come from?"

Bar saw a young woman jerk her head in his direction. He noticed Reylie had long bronze hair and was wearing some kind of skirt and stockings. A familiar face from his past flashed from his memory. He shoved it back and away from his consciousness.

"She's my sister Reylie, buddy," the young male called Ron tried to growl out menacingly. The dark-haired boy, soon to be a man, started to reach for something in a slung pack he wore. Ron found out just how fast the big man could move as Bar put Reylie's brother on his back with a swipe of a bear paw-sized hand. Bar then stepped on the young male's chest.

"Easy, boy. Take that pack off slow and careful—"

A screaming Banshee slammed into Bar's side. The surprise and force of the attack knocked Bar off balance and forced him to stumble back. A red rage began to take over until the massive man saw it was a bronze-haired young lady who had slammed into him.

"You stay off my brother, you big-assed bully!"

Everything seemed to freeze in time and space. Then Uncle Jake began to laugh and yell. "Whoooweee! We just had a spitfire fall into our campfire."

Tom, one of the Olsen twins, found his voice.

"Did you see that? They rode that lightning bolt down like a couple of demons."

"Are they Haints?" asked his twin Tim.

"We'll find out," growled out Bar. "First, don't hit me again, girl or I will hit back." The tall and wide beaded man watched as Ron slowly regained his feet.

"Hand the pack here, boy. You have a Coult Navy aimed at your spine." He nodded towards Tom as he spoke.

Ron's face flushed, and his mouth set in a stubborn line. Armand was a good student of human reactions and saw that youthful stubbornness led to bloodshed. He stepped up to Reylie, slouch hat in hand. "*Ma cherie*, no one means you and your brother harm. Please just follow Bar's requests. You must admit falling from the sky into a fire is far from normal."

Reylie examined the Cajun and made the snap decision that he was the least violent of the five men around the campfire. Her Granddad had given her some advice based on his secretive government service. '*If you are a stranger in a strange land, make a friend.*'

Reylie forced a smile as she spoke. "Yes, I can see us knocking over your coffee pot could be upsetting." Reylie then addressed her brother. "Ron, please give Bar your backpack; I'll give him mine. We are in his camp."

Ron glared at his sister and Bar. He looked at the large Bowie in the man's hand and grunted as he shoved the pack towards him. "Here," he spat. "If you take anything, I'll call the cops."

All the men but Armand chuckled at the attempt of defiance.

"If you mean a sheriff or marshal, the nearest one will be in Mesilla or Las Cruces," said Uncle Jake. "Both are miles away."

Bar grabbed Ron's school backpack and unceremoniously dumped the contents in the light of the damaged campfire. "Huh. What do we have here?" Bar held up a stainless steel pistol. "Now I know what you were trying to grab, boy."

Armand had taken it upon himself to examine Reylie's backpack more respectfully. As he did, Uncle Jake called out to Bar. "Toss me that revolver. It looks nickel or silver plated."

His nephew complied, then finished pawing through the contents of Ron's pack. "A box of bullets here, Uncle. Label says 357 Magnum. What is that? You're the odd gun guy."

Uncle Jake answered with a frown as he tried to use some bifocals to read the lettering on the three-inch barrel revolver.

"Something like, maybe Ruger? That looks German. Magnum sounds French. And it has some weird swing out cylinder." The grey-bearded man looked over the top of his glasses at Ron.

"Where'd you get this, son?"

"I was holding it for somebody," Ron grumbled back.

"Holding sounds like stealing. Someone else owns this gun, right?"

"It's a prototype, a test gun," Reylie blurted out. She knew Ron and her were in danger of even more trouble if she did not think on her feet.

"My Granddad made it. He is known as the Tinkerer, as he is always building weird things."

"And he knows you are here, with this hogleg?" asked Uncle Jake.

"No," answered Ron. "Look, it is all one big mess and accident that you would not believe even if you could."

"Well, you did fall into our campfire from God knows where," interjected Bar. "It's getting late, and the five of us have an important task in the morning. So my Uncle and I are going to have a short powwow and decide what we are going to do with you two youngins."

The two men stepped out of earshot into the darkness as Armand handed Reylie back her pack. "You have school books and many-colored drawings," said the Cajun. "You are studying to be an artist?"

Reylie smiled as she answered. *Stranger in a strange land*, she reminded to herself. "Among other things. I wanted to study medicine also." The young lady glanced into the darkness. "Now, I don't know. I don't even know where we are."

"New Mexico Territory," answered Armand. "We are in the foothills of the Potrillo Mountains. Las Cruces and Mesilla are not that far from here. Maybe a day's ride or so."

Reylie was always good at history and geography. She quickly racked her brains for details as she looked at her brother. He was standing sullen, arms folded on the other side of the dying campfire. Right now, Ron would be of little help. "Fort Bliss Texas is what, about fifty miles away?" she asked.

"Yes, Reylie—is that your name? Fort Seldon and Fillmore are closer. All the forts are near to protect people from the Apache and the occasional Comanche."

"And Mexican bandits," an eavesdropping Tim, the other Olsen Twin, commented.

"That is true," said Armand. "However, since the Second Mexican War and the Treaty of Sante Fe, we are supposed to be on friendlier terms and giving common cause against raiding Indians."

Reylie was trying to rack her brain for a means to ask questions about times and dates without arousing more suspicions when Bar and Uncle Jake stepped back into the dim campfire light.

"Okay," said Bar, "you two stay and travel with us in the morning. No way am I gonna have the death of a young lady on my conscience. We Texans don't work that way. But you will follow *my* orders. Got it?"

"Yes, sir," answered Reylie. Ron grunted and nodded his head affirmatively.

"Where's you say you youngins are from?" asked Uncle Jake.

"Seattle, Washington." Reylie chose the most significant city she figured the men would know in this strange place. It was all so confusing.

"Washington Territory? You folks missionaries or something? After the Negro Relocation Act, I heard the only people wanting to stay there are rough sailors, fur traders, and nigger-loving missionaries."

"My family does work with Black people," Reylie carefully replied. She would usually never tolerate his language but she knew she had no power or influence around this waning campfire. "They work with the church people but are not missionaries."

No way could Reylie explain a divorced mother who worked as a teacher at the local parochial school while her father was an auto mechanic and sometimes over the road truck driver. Would the explanations be meaningless to this band of outlaws?

"*Black people.* Huh," growled Bar. "Bible thumpers. No John Brown abolitionists among you, are there? Hear tell some fled up towards Canada."

"John Brown's body lies a-molding in his grave,"

Ron interjected, having found his voice.

Bar spat. "He does. But some of his bitches—excuse me, some of his *followers*—escaped Montgomery and the Mexican War. I shot 'em on sight." Bar examined the two siblings more before speaking again. "There's a spare horse we took off a dead Mexican who was trying to bushwack us. It's tied up with the others. You ride, yes?"

"She rides the best," replied Ron.

"Okay. In the morning, you saddle up and ride double. There," Bar pointed to a pile of a saddle and bags. "There are blankets and such. Make yourselves a bed. You can do that, right?"

"Yes, sir," the siblings answered in unison.

"Go easy on the waterskin. It has to last us another day."

In a few minutes, Ron and Reylie had laid a blanket on the ground and used another threadbare companion as their cover. Reylie pulled off her tights and folded them up into her backpack. She put her running shoes back on and used her light windbreaker as a pillow. Reylie had made a quick trip to a nearby bush to relieve herself under the watchful eye of her brother. She thought she saw Uncle Jake maneuvering the others away from Ron and her to give them some privacy. Reylie surmised, the older man knew the two siblings would not run off into an unfamiliar night.

"I'm hungry," whispered Ron.

"Well, if you hadn't hidden in Granddad's workshop and screwed with his game, we wouldn't be here," scolded Reylie as she made air quotes around the word *game.*

"I had to. Raymond and the others ratted on me. Here I was hiding the pistol for them and then *bam!* They gave me up to the cops."

"I told you not to trust them. But what does your little sister know."

They lay in silence for a moment, then Ron whispered again. "I didn't mean to twist that dial in the middle of that table. I was just—"

"Scared. And angry. Right?" asked his sister.

"Yeah. And now, look at us. In some science fiction movie. Time travel!"

"Yes and no. This past is different. I don't think Bar and the others had a Civil War. Those pistols looked like the 1860s but no mention of the Confederacy, Blue, and Grey."

"Well, they had two Mexican Wars. And John Brown."

"Negro Relocation Act." Reylie shivered a bit as she spoke. "Just like they did to the Native American tribes. Forced them to move when they wanted the space."

"So they stopped slavery without a war, but still

treat African Americans as scum," said Ron.

Reylie let out a long sigh. "My head hurts."

Just then, they heard a growling voice. "My pa said he'd tan my hide if I didn't sleep when he told me to," said Bar.

"Yes, sir," the siblings answered.

They lay quiet, and then Reylie snuggled up to her brother. "Goodnight, Johnboy," she said with a trace of a giggle.

"You're not funny, Reylie."

Uncle Jake and Bar set out their bedrolls and readied for sleep. "What do you think, nephew?" Uncle Jake asked.

"I think we have to be careful so we can still hit the stagecoach tomorrow. We need the Mexican money your friend said was on it to keep us going."

"If Hank says the Butterfield Stage carries Mexican Gold, it does. He was a Texas Ranger too, you know."

"It's a question of doing on our part, not what is on the stage. All coaches out here carry people, goods, and money." Bar looked towards the now quiet siblings.

"The big question is those two getting in the way of us doin' what we aim to do. As I said, I don't want to dump anyone out in the middle of nowhere."

"Especially a young girl who reminds you of someone," said Uncle Jake.

Bar grunted. "You saw that, too, huh? She does look like my younger sister Judith—not to mention my wife, Rebekah."

Both men stood silent at the mention of the two deceased loved ones. Uncle Jake finally broke the silence. "I don't remember your father and my brother, James, ever having to threaten you with tanning your butt for not going to sleep."

"They don't know that, Uncle. And he always worked my ass off anyways."

Uncle Jake chuckled. "I think the fact you were always big for your age gave him pause."

"Whatever the reason. Now, time for us to sleep. Bleary eyes ruin good shooting."

"Right as always, Nephew. Right as rain."

A light firearm report woke Reylie and Ron.

"Sounded like a little twenty-two," opined Reylie. The two siblings rose to their feet and looked around; The Sun was beginning to poke up over the eastern horizon. Uncle Jake came walking into the camp with a grin on his face and a massive jackrabbit suspended by his left hand.

"Quick rabbit breakfast," said Uncle Jake as he walked towards the campfire. Someone had stoked it with fresh pieces of wood.

"That is one big rabbit," said Ron.

"They grow them big around here," replied the greybeard. "You two get over here and help me cut up this meat. We need to eat fast and get moving."

Reylie stepped closer and examined the carbine held by Uncle Jake.

"Winchester?" she asked.

"Got your guns mixed up, missy. Smith and Wesson made these lever actions Volcanics. Their rocket ball ammunition is weak, makes for an excellent rabbit killer, not much more."

"I thought Smith and Wesson make pistols," stated Ron as he walked closer.

"They also do. Smith and Wesson now make stouter Wesson Repeaters in thirty-two and larger rimfire. Not to mention centerfire guns starting this year."

"1867?" Reylie quickly asked,

"No, this year. Not last year."

Uncle Jake did short work of skinning the large Jack without a blade by yanking the fur and skin up over the head. He then produced two sharp tomahawks.

"Here. You two do know how to cut up game?"

"Yes, sir," replied Reylie. "Our granddad and dad showed us how."

"Well, cut this Jack up, find some sticks for spits and roast it. Times a wasting. Everyone works."

As Ron and Reylie watched the roasting meat,

they held a low-volume conference. "1868? Who was president then, Rey?"

"Andrew Johnson or Grant. However, no Civil War, so Lincoln could still be alive."

"But then why no Emancipation Proclamation?" asked Ron.

"Lincoln originally thought of sending all the former slaves back to Africa or a third country. He did not believe Blacks and Whites could live together."

"This is so screwed up. This group is so hateful and racist and we're stuck with them."

"For now, Ron. Until Granddad finds us."

Ron snorted. "Oh, sure. Just like that. Across time and space."

Bar walked up to them with his slouch hat in his hand and looked at the roasting meat.

"You ain't burning breakfast, are you? "

"No, sir," replied Reylie.

"Good. After we eat, you saddle up. We have a ways to go before Noon. And we have to be at a special spot by then. If you two can't keep up, you get left behind. Got it?"

"Yes, sir," the brother and sister answered in unison.

"And, boy. Uncle Jake will hold on to your pistol for now." The oversized gunman paused for a moment, then asked, "What is your family name?"

"King," answered Reylie.

"As in King Ranch in the lower valley of Texas?"

"Distant cousins."

"Huh. Interesting. Maybe after we're done, we'll get you on a stagecoach, send you there. Better off than up in Washington."

Bar turned and went back to talk with Uncle Jake. Ron looked at his sister. "Quick thinking, Reylie."

"From here on out, I hope being fast on our feet will be enough. This is not a world for the weak and slow."

Bar walked over to his uncle. "Just thought to ask those two their last name. They say it's King. Distant cousins of the Texas Kings."

"Huh. That still don't explain where the two came from, how they fell into our camp, Bar."

"Right now, Uncle Jake, I have more important things to think about. Let's break our fast and hit the trail. We need to be in place, or all this is just so much cow flop."

They were about ready to join the road a half hour later. Uncle Jake divided the rabbit meat and gave the two young people a corn dodger, straight out of a well-known cinematic classic from their world. Then it was hop to it, saddle the horses, and break camp. Reylie could tell Bar was surprised about how quickly she and Ron bridled and saddled the strange Mexican pony.

Reylie had just enough extra time to ask Bar if she could look at his horse pistol as he loaded the twin weapons.

"Coult's Root Patent," Reylie said as she read the inscription just below the thick cylinder on the left side. "I thought he spelled his name C-O-L-T."

"Nope," Barr replied. "He added Root's name on these side hammer pistols to let people know they were different Coults from his Dragoons."

Reylie met the eyes of the bear of a man as he finished loading the last cylinder chamber.

"You've used these—Coults—a lot."

"Since I got them when I joined the Texas Rangers in 1859."

"Why did you join?" asked Reylie.

"To join my uncle in fighting Comanche and Mexicans. Then the Montgomery Seige started, and off we went to kill negros and Brownites."

"Brownites?"

"John Brown family and friends. Lincoln gets the Great Compromise passed to free the slaves in ten years, but John Brown takes Montgomery, Alabama, and holds it for ransom." Bar spit into the New Mexico dirt. "Give'em an inch; they want a mile. Come on. Time to hit the trail, young missy."

Several minutes later, the five men and two young adults mounted. Ron rode double behind Reylie as she was the better rider. Bar moved his mount up and down the line, checking the riders, and paused near Reylie and Ron's mount.

"How'd you two become so involved with guns?" he asked.

"Our Granddad and Father," answered Reylie.

"Granddad was the Tinkerer," added Ron. "He took us shooting so he could tinker with new ideas for guns and machines."

Bar grunted. "I'd like to meet him. Now, it's time to leave."

Bar led the file of slouch hated riders in a fast walk down a well-used trail. The Sun was poking up over the Organ and San Andres Mountains to the east. Uncle Jake had fashioned some Admiral hats from a leftover newspaper with no other hats around, providing some protection from the hot New Mexico sun. As the Sun rose in the sky, the trail widened. The band was soon moving at a trot; all rode in silence, other than the occasional horse sound. Reylie and Ron managed to keep their cell phones hidden as they had been in their pockets, not the backpacks. There was no telling what the five armed riders would have thought or reacted had they seen an active cell phone. Witchcraft might have been the accusation.

Reylie had an old windup wristwatch that could pass as something familiar to Bar and Company, so they left it alone. It was set at Pacific Standard Time, so she added an hour for being in New Mexico. Thus the young lady figured it was 9:00 AM as they worked their way out of the foothills.

Bar called a halt once, signed for silence, looked, and listened. Five minutes later, they started moving again. Uncle Jake noticed Reylie's puzzled look and nudged his mount close enough to whisper.

"Watching for Apaches. They sometimes sneak around and raid."

Reylie nodded and then began to try and remember her history. Apaches were nasty at times but not the horsemen the Comanche were. The Washingtonian did not want to run into the 1860s versions of either.

The band kept moving as the Sun climbed higher in the sky. Reylie and Ron shared lukewarm water from a canteen, sipping tiny amounts based on Bar's comment that it had to last another day. The horses let out a snort once in a while, flicked flies away with their tails when they slowed down in the descent.

Reylie figured it was about 11:00 AM when the trail leveled out, and she glimpsed what looked like a wide dirt road about a half-mile ahead. Bar halted the group and waved the riders up to his lead spot. When they were close enough to hear his low voice, Bar pointed to the roadway.

"Butterfield Stage Route. The Butterfield

Overland Mail Line has operated since 1858. There is at least one Concord stagecoach heading West and one East each week. Occasionally a cheap mud coach is added if there are enough cheaper paying customers or some buffalo hunters need a ride."

"Why a separate coach for buffalo hunters?" asked Ron.

Bar and Uncle Jake laughed.

"If you were ever around any hidemen, you'd know," replied Uncle Jake. "You think we get ripe smelling from no bath. Buff hunters kill, gut and skin the buffalo on the plains. They do not change clothes, do not bathe until they finish filling up some hide wagons, which usually takes a month or two. When they are finally done with the slaughter, they burn their clothes and pay someone a goodly sum to bathe."

Reylie's mind flashed back to tales her Granddad had told about rendering plants in the Southwest. She imagined the smell was similar.

"Yes, buffalo hunters are a different lot," continued Jake. "Now that the Second Mexican War is over, more and more former soldiers are turning to hide collection. People back East love a good buffalo blanket, rug, or coat."

Bar spit and sneered.

"Let it be over for them. Not fer me."

The huge man pointed to a slight rise on the

north side of the roadway.

"Uncle Jake, recognize that clump of rocks and boulders? That hill is a couple of hundred feet high and is set back from the road about three hundred yards. That should be a good spot for your Sharps."

"What about the youngins?" Jake asked.

"Take them with you. It'll keep these two out of the way if things get hot."

Bar looked at Ron and Reylie with stone grey eyes. "You two do what Uncle Jake says. If you do something to screw this job up, I'll take a horsewhip to you."

"What—" Reylie started to question what was happening when Ron squeezed her arm. Now was not the time to ask about what had to be a stagecoach hold-up.

"You three," Bar gestured towards Armand and the Olsen twins, "head west and parallel the stage route. When it passes, birddog it, stay a mile back. You'll know when it's time to act."

"It would be nice if we had some newer repeaters instead of these old Hall breechloaders," griped Tim Olsen.

"When you get shot with a half-inch bullet from that Hall, you stay shot," replied Bar. "Just hit what you shoot at. If not, use your Coult Navies."

"Hell, they are still cap and ball—" Tom Olsen

stopped mid-sentence when he saw that look in Bar's eyes. The former Texas Ranger glared at the Cajun. "You got a bitch now, too?"

"Last shell for the Maynard, my friend. Then I'll use my pinfire."

Bar grunted, "Okay, let's get moving. If things go right, we may have some new shootin' irons to play with."

Reylie followed Uncle Jake's Mount as Bar turned his horse East. Some fifteen minutes later, Reylie and Ron secured the two Mustangs as Uncle Jake set up a sniper's perch between two large rocks. Reylie watched the Texan use a thick blanket to create the rest for the large Sharps rifle. Uncle Jake set up six fifty caliber Sharps shells in a row, then took off his wide-brimmed hat. From a saddlebag, Uncle Jake produced a large bottle and a long cylindrical object. A quick twist and a pull, and viola, it became a ship's spyglass.

"Ron, come over here."

The young man walked over to where Uncle Jake lay.

"How old are you?" Jake asked.

"Fifteen. Reylie is fourteen."

"Older brother, huh. Here. Take this spyglass and keep an eye out west for a Concord Stagecoach."

"Is that one of the bigger and fancier coaches?" Reylie asked.

"You got it, young lady. Now, have a seat behind this boulder here so no one can see you."

Reylie sat down as Ron scanned the Butterfield Trail.

"Hey, this is powerful. Like a small astronomy telescope."

"You like stargazing, huh? Well, son, I got that off a sea captain in a poker game in Mobile, Alabama. He said he had it specially made."

Uncle Jake turned where he lay and looked at Reylie. "So now. Tell me your story. How'd you get to our campsite."

Reylie blushed as she tried to formulate an answer. "I don't know… if you will understand or believe me."

Uncle Jake snorted. "You see our rough ways, rough speech, and think we are uneducated louts, don't you?" Uncle Jake said.

"Now, I don't mean to—"

"Missy, I have twelve years of schooling, plus some class time at Baylor Christian College in Independence, Texas. I managed to have Bar stay in school for eight years, despite my older brother dragging him off for ranching and farming in Van Horn, Texas. I also have read everything ole Willie Shakespeare wrote. Can you say that?"

Reylie quickly realized that she had

underestimated this grey-bearded man. Just because someone seemed rough around the edges did not mean they were necessarily unintelligent or uneducated. "Please accept my apology, Uncle Jake. I did not mean to disparage your abilities. It is just, well, our story is so strange and unbelievable."

"Well, young Reylie, we have a bit of time here. Ron can keep an eye out for the stagecoach while you tell me your story."

The images of what had occurred just the previous day flashed from Reylie's memories. Ron snuck into Granddad's workshop in the back of the house as a police cruiser pulled up in front. Reylie immediately went to intercept her older brother. "Ron," she asked, "what happened? The police are here."

She and her brother stayed with their grandparents for a week as their mother spent time with her new boyfriend at some timeshare condo. The grandparents lived close enough to the kids' school to attend even with their mother away.

"I'm holding a pistol for Raymond, and the guys and someone ratted them out. Now they ratted me out."

"I told you they were trouble," said Reylie.

"Yeah, well, I needed to get a rep, a reputation. I'm not going to be a nerd my whole life." With that statement, Ron has stomped over to a long and wide table that contained Granddad's newest project.

"Like this game Granddad says he is building. A tabletop combined with a video. That screams loser nerd."

Ron gave a large dial in the middle of the new creation an angry spin...

"So let me get this straight," said Uncle Jake. "Your Granddad was fooling around with electricity and such, did something new and strange, you were—sent here."

"When Ron spun the dial, yes."

Uncle Jake paused in thought, scratching at his chin beard. Then he spoke. "Well, there is some Frenchman named Jules Verne writing about long trips in a balloon and trips to the center of the Earth. People say his tales are possible, so, why not a machine that zaps people and sends them like a charge down a telegraph pole."

"Somebody's coming down the trail," interrupted Ron. He handed the spyglass to Uncle Jake. The older man aimed the vision device down the western part of Butterfield Trail. He chuckled.

"Yessiree. A nice large dust cloud. That's the Concord style coach on the move, all nice and big." Uncle Jake stated. He looked at the King siblings.

"Alright. Stay out of the way, do not bother us. We have a job to do."

"Which is?" asked Reylie.

"Revenge."

Bar managed to pull a lone Alligator Juniper over and onto the Butterfield Trail Route using his rope and horse. It wasn't a large tree, but with a few tumbleweeds arranged around it, the downed tree was enough of an obstruction to make the stagecoach stop and at least inspect for a way around it. The former Texas Ranger then trotted his Mustang east down the stage route a couple of hundred yards, swung off the road, and behind a pile of boulders. He could see Uncle Jake's rifle perch from his concealment and waited for the signal that the Butterfield Stage was near. Bar would meet the stagecoach on the road, the opposite side of the fallen Juniper Tree. Hopefully, he could get the drop on them, and there would be no gunplay. If there was, well, it would not be the first nor the last that Bar had to be a pistolero. The Texan had become quite good at it.

He took a sip of warm water from his canteen. The stagecoach should have some additional waterskins as the road across New Mexico Territory was long, hot, and dry. Bar thought about just how strange this 'job' was becoming. Having to set up a robbery on one man's word only to have two unfamiliar youngsters drop into camp did nothing to improve Bar's disposition. He spits some chewing tobacco onto what looked like a nearby anthill, then disposed of the rest of the chaw. Having something in your mouth when things got rough and tough could lead to a choking fit at just the wrong moment.

Bar looked up at Uncle Jake's perch. He was about to dismount and stretch when he saw the directed flashes from a small hand mirror. The stagecoach neared. With a grim smile, Bar checked his Kentucky flintlock squirrel rifle. The .36 caliber gun was no buffalo killer, but Bar could hit a man consistently at some three hundred yards from horseback. Again, Bar had never replaced it with a percussion weapon as, if it ain't broke, don't try to fix it. Bar nudged his mount onto the road and started a slow walk towards the approaching stagecoach.

Reylie looked at the approaching stagecoach through the powerful spyglass. She thought she could make out two figures with rifles riding on top, with another riding the typical 'shotgun' position. The young lady had already examined the debris Bar placed on the Butterfield Trail to stop the coach and saw Uncle Jake load his Sharps rifle. Reylie lowered the spyglass, turned towards the greybeard man, and asked: "Why?"

"I told you why. Revenge. Mexicans with money, some Alcalde with a hacienda sent some charros up to Van Horn the day they signed the peace treaty in 1866. They killed my brother (his father), Bar's mother, Bar's wife Rebekah, and Judith, his little sister. They are all connected. The ones traveling in that Concord coach are the same breed."

"But they weren't there, in 1866, were they?" asked Reylie.

"I don't have time to argue. My nephew wants this done, so we do it. Now, be quiet why I line up a shot."

The stage driver saw the tree in the road and pulled hard on the six-horse team's reins. The stagecoach came to a halt some twenty-five yards from the road blockage. One of the guards on top and the shotgun rider clambered down from the stagecoach and moved clear the road. Then they saw the slowly approaching Bar.

The remaining guard on top of the coach did a most unfriendly thing. He fired a warning shot over the large man's head.

"Hey, asshole! You don't own this road," Bar bellowed out as he readied his Kentucky rifle. He was near a hundred yards away when he stopped his mount.

"Please—" Reylie began to say, but Uncle Jake cut her off.

"Shut up," he growled, then the Sharps boomed. The half-inch in diameter bullet struck the armed guard on top of the coach as he was readying to fire once more. The man toppled off the stagecoach as the two men clearing the tree dashed back to the conveyance. The shotgun man clambered back up to his place next to the driver just as Bar shot him in his right collar bone with his squirrel rifle. The guard fell into the driver's boot as the driver wrapped the reins around the brake and leapt from his seat.

Bar slung his rifle over his saddle horn, yanked out a horse pistol, and rode in screaming like a Comanche warrior. The other top guard grabbed up his cohort's long-gun from the ground and aimed it at Bar. A shot sounded from the rear as the three other gang members came galloping up. Armand's Maynard carbine bullet struck the man in the back. The guard toppled over as his rifle discharged into the air.

Arms with hands holding pistols poked out stagecoach windows, firing both front and rear. One of the Olsen twins fired his Hall breechloader, the bullet smashed into the left side of the coach and sent splinters into the face of one of the shooters; the man screamed and dropped his pistol as a woman's screaming emanated from inside the coach. Bar's Coult Root boomed as a new shooter leaned out a right side window of the coach, the hefty .44 caliber slug smashing into the left bicep of the man. As the pistol fell from the man's hand, another shooter lept from the stagecoach and snapped a shot at Bar. The former Ranger shot the man in the chest as he swerved his horse towards the left nondriver side of the coach.

An additional shooter clambered from inside the

stagecoach on the left side. As he did, the second Olsen Twin's Hall carbine spoke, taking the cowboy hat off his head. The shooter swung around and fired a wild shot at the three approaching riders. Bar's Coult Root boomed again, and the shooter's brains were splatter over the Concord coach and the New Mexico landscape.

"Driver!" yelled Bar. "Tell the passengers to stop shooting, or my Sharpshooter on the hill will sieve your coach."

The stagecoach driver rose from his hiding place under the stage and raised his hands. "Don't shoot no more," the driver cried out. "They are killing us all!"

"Have them drop their guns outside the coach. Now."

Within five minutes, the stagecoach driver had everyone sans their pistols and outside the coach. A woman passenger cried as she tried to tend to the wood splinters in her husband's face. Face covered with a bandanna, Armand examined the wounds under cover of Bar's horse pistols.

"His eyes are okay, ma'am," said Armand. "He will have a scar or two for tales to your children."

The driver managed to help his shotgun rider down from the front boot and worked on stopping the bleeding. The Olsen twins pulled a strongbox from the front driver's boot, then set about throwing down all the other luggage. Bar shot the massive lock off it, and

Armand examined the contents.

"There is little here for such a large box, Boss."

"Alright. Where is it? The gold," Bar demanded.

"You scum won't get it," snapped the one male who had not tried to defend the coach. He was a well-dressed middle-aged banker with a Yankee demeanor. Bar spurred his mount to bump into the insulting man, knocking him onto his rear end.

"Wanna bet, Loudmouth?" Bar asked.

"Please, no more violence," cried out the young wife. "They put the gold and valuables in our steamer trunk in the rear boot."

Just then, the Sharps rang out again.

"What the..." Bar said, then yanked out a pair of binoculars from a saddlebag. He looked towards the West and swore.

"This coach has a mounted guard following it. And I think our Sharps just took out one of the riders."

Bar pointed to the two Olsens.

"Grab the trunk. See if you can carry it between you and head for the hills. We'll meet you at the pre-arranged spot."

He pointed at the banker. "Empty your pockets, take off your clothes. Jackass. Now."

Five minutes later, the Olsen twins suspended the steamer trunk between them as they trotted off. Jackass banker was standing nude, all his clothes and valuables, to include a .32 Rimfire Coult, stuffed in an emptied mailbag. Armand and Bar had recovered two like-new Smith and Wesson .44 Long carbines. They also took two Coults Army pistols from the shooters and a Starr double action cap and ball pistol from the coach driver. A Coult Navy and the stagecoach shotgun rounded out the gun booty. Any weapon they did not want, they threw in the sagebrush. Bar gave the stagecoach passengers a warning.

"If any of you come after us, we will shoot you and leave you for the buzzards. Had the Mexican Guards not started shooting, we would not have shot either. We just wanted the Bank of Mexico gold and silver."

Then Bar and Armand were off in a different direction from the Olsens.

It was dusk before all seven met up. This time the group met in the foothills of the Black Range Mountains. Bar was the last one to make it to camp.

"I was beginning to worry, Nephew," Uncle Jake commented as Bar rode into camp. They were by the remains of some settler's covered wagon, which didn't make it. No one knew the story as to why it was there.

"I separated from Armand and went back to get some steaks off that horse you shot. Sure enough, the rider broke his neck, and they just left him there. I guess the money was more important."

"Well, after I got Little Missy here to stop complaining about me shooting people, I took out that Mexican guard and that rider."

Reylie was silent. The day's events were sinking in. She had seen people shot and killed for something called revenge.

Bar dismounted his horse and approached Reylie.

"Did Uncle Jake explain to you about our family?"

"That doesn't change the fact more people are dead," Reylie replied.

Bar paused and looked at her. Then he spoke. "Someday, when some pieces of crap take people you love from you, civilians not even soldiers, maybe you'll understand. If nothing else, perhaps some Mexican will think twice about coming across the Border to mess with us."

"Does anger and revenge help you, Bar?" Reylie asked.

"It keeps me warm at night when the ghosts visit me." Bar turned and went to the campfire; He was soon roasting horse meat steaks.

Ron walked over to his sister. "Sorry I got you into this. If I hadn't been trying to act so tough—"

Reylie waved his apology away. "We can't change that. Now we have to figure out how to survive in a world where everyday violence is real and close up. This is no video game or TV news reporting happening in some poor neighborhood."

"They gave me the pistol back, Reylie. Said I'd need it to protect you."

"You're going to do that?"

"Hell, yeah. That's what older brothers are for, right?"

Reylie hugged him and kissed his cheek. "Ready to try some horse meat?" she asked.

"Smells like beef to me."

The two siblings walked to the campfire, knowing that the coming days could be as rough as strangers in a strange land.

"Coming to bed, dear?"

Her mother's voice snapped Reylie back to the here and now. "Sorry. Just woolgathering."

"I know. You're still thinking about what could've been."

Reylie turned to her mother.

"Mom, Ron and I have never told the entire story. There was way too much violence and bloodshed for people not to hold us responsible."

Her mother patted her arm.

"Without the Sky Tunnel technology you helped discover, we would not have the chance to get off of a dying Earth. Magnetic pole shifts, massive solar flares, crops dying, it's almost as if someone is trying to force us to move—or die."

"I know. But that still does not help with all the memories."

As mother and daughter walked back into the house, Reylie could not tell her mother about some real sadness. For someplace in an alternate time and space, there was this giant bear of a man that she had shared so much with, to include everlasting love. Reylie felt guilt about the death she helped cause, but the love she had experienced? Never. And there were so damn many more stories she could tell. Reylie mentally shrugged. Maybe someday.

And it all started with a meeting around a campfire.

CHAPTER 2
ATOMIC INTERLUDE

John King sat in the interview room—actually an interrogation room—at the Homeland Security Investigations local office. The Special Agents brought him a cup of coffee with cream and sweetener. John knew this was an attempt at the Good Cop routine, to be followed by the Bad Cop if they thought he was bullshitting them. The near sixty-year-old man with slight touches of grey in his hair smiled. John's connection with Area 51 in the Nevada Test Ranges meant at one time or another, the man also known as the Tinkerer had been grilled by the best. When you worked on projects so highly classified that Top Secret seemed mundane, circumstances led to you being on the hot seat when the bosses thought someone leaked sensitive information to the outside.

Only this time, the investigating Agents had a specific target: John King and his Game.

This situation began after John did a stint in the Marines during Desert Storm and then an assignment in the Bosnian War before someone pulled him aside. The 'someone' had been this tall, silver-haired woman whose employer always seemed vague. Yeleanah Moon was the name she went by, but John always felt the name was a chosen one, not a family name.

The six-foot-tall woman strode up to him while he was pulling Embassy Security in Bucharest, Romania, after a period with the Fleet Marines. He was sitting in the day room on break, doing what he loved to do; tinkering. Whenever something was busted or not working right, one of the embassy staff would say, "Hey, give it to Corporal King. He loves to tinker and fix things." He soon had the handle of The Tinkerer.

John was tinkering with a brand new laptop computer that the Staff could not boot up and work. The local tech guy gave it to John as the last resort. The next step for it was sledgehammering in the parking area or giving it to the Marines for target practice. John, intent on his work, did not notice Yeleanah standing over him until she cleared her throat.

"Oh, shit! Sorry, ma'am," he exclaimed as he tried to stand up. "I did not see—"

"You are the Tinkerer?" asked the statuesque woman as she sat down at John's table. Men took bets as to her age when she first appeared two months prior.

She exuded this ageless sensuality but had been around the block. John was a healthy, hard-bodied, and traditionally handsome Marine who was not afraid to 'hit' on attractive women. However, the Embassy men, and some of the women, saw Specialist Moon as out of everyone's league.

John sat back down as he answered. "Yes, ma'am. A nickname I picked up."

"Because you like to tinker, figure things out and repair equipment," Yeleanah said with a hint of a smile on her lips.

"Yes, ma'am. I guess so."

"How are your math skills?"

John shrugged. "I had Advanced Calculus in high school. Math and physics come easy for me."

John felt like Yeleanah was looking deep into his soul with her jade eyes. Then the woman took a business card from a pocket in her fashionable blue jumpsuit. "Take and keep this. I'm an excellent judge of talent and hidden abilities. Do not be angry if I try to have you re-assigned."

"Why would you want to do that, ma'am?" John asked with a frown.

"Because your abilities are wasted in your current position in the Embassy. And call me Yeleanah when we are talking privately."

The tall woman stood up, turned, and walked

away. John stared as she exited the dayroom.

"Weird," he mumbled and went back to working on the laptop. He had it rebooted and operating a half hour later.

A week later, his Gunny Sergeant and the Embassy personnel officer told John King he was assigned to a particular classified assignment and a promotion to Staff Sergeant. When he tried to ask questions, Gunny Ray fixed him with his steely gaze as he spoke.

"Don't look a gift horse in the mouth, Marine. Just go where the Corps says."

Three days later and Staff Sergeant John King was on a military airlift aircraft headed stateside. He landed at Andrews Air Force Base in the Washington, D. C. area. As he was collecting his B-4 bag and rucksack, he heard someone clearing their throat behind him. John turned to see Yeleanah standing behind him in a high-end business suit.

"Follow me, please, Marine. We have a long trip ahead of us."

John started to protest but saw a look in her eyes that she would explain things as necessary. The Marine grabbed his gear and followed her long strides. An hour later, they drove in a nondescript rental vehicle headed West. As they left the District of Columbia area, she handed him a file.

"Start reading that. After you are done, you may ask questions. However, everything you hear, see, read, or think about is so highly classified that one could quickly be buried in the Nevada Desert if the information was leaked."

"We are driving to Nevada?"

"You listen and reason. Good. The answer is yes. Now, read the file."

They drove for some twelve hours before Yeleanah exited off the Interstate and directly to a small ancient motor hotel. As she parked in front of the lodging office, a middle-aged man with the military bearing stepped out and nodded to the Specialist. Yeleanah caught thrown sets of room keys as she nodded back to him. As John stepped from the rental car, Yeleanah tossed a set of keys to him.

"Two rooms with a connecting door. Keep that file with you until I retrieve it. Get settled for the night, and I'll contact you with dinner."

They had made only a couple of short pit stops along the way for bathroom breaks and some fast food. John went to his room and stowed his gear. He kept the file with him as he relieved himself of some of the fast-food in his intestinal tract. John then sat as patiently as possible in the old stuffed armchair. The Marine wondered what the connection was between Yeleanah and this motor lodge. It had seen better days.

A quarter of an hour later and there was a knock on the connecting room door. John went to the door and said. "I hope that is you."

"It is I, John King. May I enter?"

He unlocked the door and stepped back. Yeleanah had changed into a loose-fitting t-shirt and some running shorts. John could not help but notice the woman's shapely legs went all the way up.

"I'll relieve you of that file so you can shower and relax. We have room service en route."

"Ma'am, Yeleanah, what connection do you have with this place?"

"Again, excellent observation. The U.S. Government owns this place. It exists to prevent any foreign or criminal surveillance, including satellite. Mike, the manager, is a retired Delta Force Member who lives here with his wife. His children are grown, so it's no problem for him to live here, with excellent compensation, of course."

"That bespeaks of a high need to protect the— particular project mentioned in the thick file."

Yeleanah smiled as she answered. "You are about to enter into the world you probably have heard hints about over the years."

"Then, why me? I'm just a Grunt Marine. I was on the team who rescued the F-16 pilot in Bosnia, had some rounds shot at me in Desert Storm, but that was it."

"As I said before, John King. I am an excellent judge of hidden capabilities. Your intelligence quotient is off the charts, with an innate ability to fix things, tinker with them. Plus, that K-Bar blade you have concealed under your shirt tells me you also have the ability of controlled violence when need be."

John laughed. "So, I'm going to be a spook? An intelligence type?"

"No, John King. You will be doing something much more important. You will be dealing with the spooky side of science."

There was a knock on the outside room door. John saw the frown on Yelanah's face and went straight to the door with his K-Bar in his hand. He looked at the Specialist, who nodded 'yes,' and John yanked the door open amidst a second knock. An attractive young woman jumped back in surprise.

"Shit! You scared me, mister."

"Can I help you?" asked John.

"I saw your car, and it's the only one here. So I thought I could get some gas money," the cute brunette said with a seductive smile. "My car is out of gas." The woman turned to point down the access road, her noticeable bosom heaving as she gestured. John was briefed on all the possible scams overseas to take out service members, so he saw the figures trying to hide in the shadows.

"You can tell your friends to step out of the shadows, young lady." As John spoke, one of the two male figures stepped out with a large pistol in his dirty hand.

"Step back, asshole," the scruffy-bearded man commanded.

John grabbed the woman and hugged her to him. She yelped, and the second man yelled, "Hey! Let her go."

Actual assassins would just shoot through the female. However, John recognized the three as ne'er do wells looking for a quick score.

John heard the 'pfft' sound of a suppressed weapon and watched the man with the pistol collapse to the ground from a headshot. Then a thin green beam from the room passed by John and struck the other man in the forehead. That would-be robber toppled backward as John stifled a scream from the woman with a hand across her mouth.

Mike, the manager, stepped from the darkness with a suppressed MP-5 in his hands. "Sorry, people. These three snuck up on me."

Yeleanah stepped up and looked at the wide-eyed woman. The female tried to say something through John's smothering hand but failed.

"You can take care of these three, Mike?"

"Yes. Yeleanah."

The Specialist struck the woman in John's arms at just the right spot on her temple. The seductress collapsed, and Mike threw her upon his shoulder and turned towards the motor lodge office.

"Shut the door, John."

"Don't we help—"

"No, John. Situations like this rarely happen. When it does, people like Mike are paid to—handle it."

John did as he was told and sat back in the overstuffed chair.

"You did not see that beam of green light, John."

"What beam?" John asked with wide-eyed innocence.

Yeleanah chuckled. "I judged you correctly, my newfound friend. You are a fast learner."

The two made it to Dreamland on the Nevada Test Ranges without further incident. During the trip, Yeleanah briefed John King on his new assignment and life. For it was a new life involving a level of secrecy and technical expertise John never in his wildest dreams thought existed. The first month he lived at Site Four. Then, John was allowed to establish an apartment in Las Vegas. He kept it sparse as he was only there on days off.

Yeleanah knew everything about John King, but the Marine knew little about his mentor. Her nickname was the Mystery Woman, as no one knew her back story.

Other than one day, years ago, she just—appeared. Rumors were she appeared at one of the access gates, but people laughed down that story. The one thing everyone knew was she was tall, sexy, brilliant, and mysterious. Yeleanah recruited many a person for Dreamland over the years. Other than other recruiters, she never failed in picking people who fit into the 'spooky side' of things.

Rumors were she and John were an item, especially after John was 'released' from Active Duty with a pension and rehired as a civilian specialist, just as Yeleanah. John, at one time, thought about trying to develop something along the lines of at least a physical relationship. Then he met Joan Williams. The bronze-haired beauty came to Dreamland as a personnel expert to handle all the necessary paperwork in running a classified operation. People had to be paid, transferred, granted security clearances, etc. She was a former U.S. Airforce Security Force Member who, as a woman, had seen action in Iraq and Afghanistan after 9/11. John, by that time, could not be released for active military duty. He was too integral to Project String. Joan made it to Dreamland, John met her, and they fell in love. Then they married and started a family.

John worked on the project as Yeleanah's second banana for years as the U.S. Government tried to locate the doorway to one of the many String Theory

Universes. Someone up the chain of command knew that Yeleanah had an inside track into how to breach the 'spooky wall' between the universes. Some officials threatened personnel if they repeated that the Mystery Woman came from another reality. Some higher-up people did not like the story at all.

Then one day, Yeleanah dropped off the face of the Earth.

John King had been in the hot seat of interrogation after Yeleanah disappeared. The scrutiny he had received in the past when there was an alleged leak was nothing like what happened when the Senior Specialist disappeared. Thus, dealing with Homeland Security? This would be a piece of cake.

The two Special Agents returned to the interrogation room. Rachel Jones, a thirty-something attractive larger Black woman, and her partner was a red-headed tall and lean James McNabb. They sat down opposite John as he looked at the two-way mirror, which was standard in every room. Of course, the Agents had notepads, a recording device, and a thick file that most likely came from John's previous employer. They had already given John his Miranda Rights. The Former Marine had not demanded a lawyer as he knew that would just mean they would drag his daughter Jeanie and wife Joan onto this mess. Thus, he smiled at the two agents and sipped his coffee.

"So, Mister King," Rachel said. "You have acknowledged your rights and agreed to speak to us."

"Yes, ma'am," replied John.

"So, we had this spectacular burst of energy that set off some nuclear detection sensors. You know from working in the Nevada Test Ranges that various federal agencies track possible local nuclear threats, like missing Russian suitcase bombs."

John sat and smiled.

Jones frowned. "Does your smile mean you do not know from your days at Area 51—"

"Sorry to interrupt, Agent Jones. But to cut to the chase, unless I get a release from my previous employer, I cannot discuss anything about what I used to do near Nellis Air Force Base. I have signed numerous nondisclosure forms. I am not released from those restrictions until my former employer says I am. Plus, unless told otherwise, you have no need to know what I did or allegedly did."

"You're kidding us, right?" said McNabb.

"No, sir, I am not."

"You realize a spike in what is believed is nuclear energy occurred in your workshop?"

"So you say. All I know is that my two grandchildren are missing. Something flashed while the local cops were looking for my grandchildren. You and some other federal personnel responded and seized my shop and a game I was working on."

"What type of game was it?" asked Rachel Jones.

"A combination board and an electronic game. I had a spinning wheel in the middle. You spin it, and videos would appear within the game. Or so I hoped. I was not finished with the design yet."

McNabb pulled a paper from the thick file. "Have you had recent contact with Yeleanah Moon?"

"She disappeared two years before I retired. That file says that I assume."

"So, no contact?"

"Not that I know of, Agents. Any more questions on what she did require—"

"I know, a release, a need to know. Sheesh."

"There is a piece of equipment in that game believed to be government property," interjected Rachel.

"I would not know that, agent; I received a box in the mail a month ago. A unique device was in it."

"You claim it did not come from your previous employer nor Yeleanah Moon?"

"I don't know. It just came. And I tinkered with it. That is what I do."

"You are the Tinkerer."

"Yes, ma'am. That is what I do. And if it caused my grandchildren to disappear, I will never forgive myself."

A tall woman wearing a hijab stood across the street from the Homeland Security Investigations office building. Her friend, John King, was in there because of her. That was unacceptable to a Thinker First Class. Yeleanah Moon used the work in Dreamland to return to her world and time. Now she must make amends for the problems she wrought.

Or die trying.

CHAPTER 3
DONA ANA

Reylie King looked at the large airlock door of the decontamination and isolation facility. She kept willing it to open so that she could run up and hug her husband, Michael Mann. He had been in the farthest reaches of the solar system for over a month, two weeks in a relatively high-speed craft back to Earth, then another two weeks in quarantine. All this scientific advancement and exploration and the powers that be were paranoid about germs from space.

Her oldest child, Marianne, was wailing in a loading zone near a back exit gate to the Space Force Launch Base near Tucson, Arizona. The plan was to grab her husband and hustle him out of the rear exit before the media types and paparazzi inundated him with questions and photos. Then a high-speed escape to a remote cabin they had located. Reylie's mother, Jeanie, was already at the hideaway with Jack and John, their younger twin sons.

Finally, the moment arrived. The large airlock wheel began to turn. Reylie immediately pushed her way forward, flanked by Space Force Security Police. They and others saw her as almost a patron saint; because of her and her brother Ron's adventures and survival, the human species could travel to the stars and new life. No one dared to interfere with Reylie's progress to get her husband.

Michael Mann swung open the heavy door and was immediately wrapped up in his wife's arms. Reylie had stopped being hesitant in her actions years ago, so she slapped a lip lock on Michael to the applause of the crowd who watched.

"Let's get out of here," she whispered in Mike's ear. "I have a vehicle standing by for our escape,"

"Of course you do, my own Lara Croft," he replied. "Lead on."

The Media was soon trying to glom onto the rest of the crew, so Mike and Relie could slip behind the phalanx of Space Force Security Police. Within minutes they were in the dark-tinted windowed SUV with daughter Marianne and hauling butt towards the Mount Lemmon Ski Resort. Like most other vacation and recreational spots, the ski resort was almost vacant as humanity hunkered down and tried to survive the all too often upheavals of Mother Earth.

"Any more earthquakes?" asked Mike. "We did not get much news in quarantine. I think they like to think of us like mushrooms."

"Keep you in the dark and feed you bullshit, right, Dad?" said the dark-haired and stately Marianne. Mike laughed as Reylie smiled. Marianne had only known Mike as her father but knew she took after her biological father, Barnabas McCain of Alt Earth. It was also called Game World as a spin off of a game dial created by Reylie's grandfather, who opened the first Tunnel to another universe. Mike had raised her as his own, and mother and daughter loved him for it.

"Once again, it looks like California is about to slide into the Pacific Ocean," answered Reylie. "Mount Saint Helens is rumbling again."

Mike grunted in reply. "Well, I guess a lot of Californians will be among the first to relocate through the Sky Tunnel."

"All went well?" asked Reylie.

"More than well. I'll give you more details later, but suffice to say we have identified at least six worlds for habitation. Only one, Reylie's World, is almost exactly Earth norm...."

"You didn't! The crew did not name a planet after me."

"Yes, they did. I had no say in the matter, with another named Ron's World. I agreed with the idea; did not fight it."

"Face it, Mom. You're Saint Reylie, and Uncle Ron is Saint Ronald."

Not for the first time was Reylie frustrated by her fame. She told people many a time she was not a hero, just a very fortunate young lady who had survived a bizarre situation thanks to luck and an extraordinary man. Reylie looked out the window so that her family could not see the tears of frustration and sorrow in her eyes.

Reylie's world... and she could not share it with Bar McCain, the man who saved her.

The group was up and moving the following morning. The night in the foothills of the Black Range Mountains was uneventful after everyone was sufficiently satiated with broiled horse meat. Up at dawn, as they were saddling the horses, Reylie asked Uncle Jake what the next destination was.

"We head out of the mountains to Dona Ana. We nose around, pick up another horse for you, youngins with the money from mister stagecoach bigshot now with no clothes."

"You know people in Dona Ana?"

Uncle Jake grinned as he answered. "I got around a lot. I know people in most places. But mostly in Franklin, on this side of Texas."

"El Paso?"

"Mexican side is called El Paso Del Norte. U.S side was Franklin; now some people call it El Paso. I guess living in Washington Territory, you schoolin' in geography is limited."

"You about ready?" Bar called out.

"Yep, Nephew."

Ten minutes later, the band of seven rode. They had a quick breakfast of corn dodgers and coffee before swinging up onto their saddles; Ron again mounted behind Reylie. The seized trunk from the stagecoach robbery provided extra and more appropriate clothing for the pair. The group rode in silence for the first half hour, then Bar maneuvered his horse alongside the sibling's horse.

"If'n you cooperate, I'll see to it that you two get a grubstake and coach ride to the King Ranch. You'll go in with Uncle Jake and Armand; I'll go in separate with the Olsens. You two youngins will throw off anybody looking for stagecoach robbers."

"Think the local authorities will be watching for us?" asked Ron.

The big man shrugged. "If someone took the effort to telegraph what happened, maybe. Most towns of any size now are getting what Injuns call talking wires."

"Telephones are next," said Ron.

"Never heard of no tele—phones. Just do what we say, and I'll help you out. Alright?"

"Yes, sir," the two siblings said in unison.

The sun was setting as the now two groups entered the town of Dona Ana. Reylie's nose caught the smells of authentic Old West Living, outhouses, and horseshit in the street, mixed with sweaty and unwashed bodies. Uncle Jake led them to a small cantina as Bar, and the Olsens trotted further down to a dive saloon.

"I can stand Mexicans in small amounts, and I like their food," said Uncle Jake. "Bar has trouble being around them at all."

"That's a lot of hate."

"When you lose those dear to you for no real reason other than just pure meanness, you'd understand. A sister and wife killed and abused—well, it is what it is."

Uncle Jake spoke sufficient Spanish to get them a table, tortillas, and salsa. Reylie and Ron surprised the young serving girl when they began to converse with her, using more respectful terms and pronouns. The girl looked to be barely a decade in age but acted as if she had been working for years. Uncle Jake and Armand smiled at the King siblings.

"Hiding more skills from us, I see," the grey-bearded man said.

"Did not mean to, sir," replied Reylie.

"Where'd you two learn Mexican?"

"School," replied Ron.

"Well, you speak it better than me. I'll let you two do the talkin', just don't say anything about who we are," directed Uncle Jake.

The young girl soon had rice and beans for all. Ron asked if they had any arroz con pollo, and the girl replied yes, but it cost more.

"Uncle Jake, what's our budget?" asked Ron.

"You mean what we can spend on vittles? Here." The man took several silver dimes out of his pocket and added some copper coins to them. The young girl's eyes widened, as did her smile. She swept the money from the table and hurried to the back. Within a quarter of an hour, all four travelers had plates full of chicken and Spanish Rice, with a large dulce roll with each dish. A small bottle of wine and a quart bottle of beer also arrived, and Uncle Jake divided both among the group.

"Water around here and in Mexico can give you the grips. Best stay with something a bit fermented."

They were soon all stuffed. Uncle Jake produced a homemade toothpick and used it to remove pieces of chicken from his teeth.

"That was right, good. I was tired of rabbit."

"Yes," added Armand. "Those horse steaks last night were a welcome change also. I have some meat wrapped up in my saddlebags."

"Smart man. Learn from that, youngins. Always have a stash of food. You never know when you can get your next meal while on the trail."

Uncle Jake dug some pesos out of another pocket and put them on the table.

"That young lady can probably spend pesos easier than we can, at least until we reach Franklin," said Uncle Jake.

Just then, an angry adult male's voice emanated from the cantina kitchen. The young girl tried to answer but was interrupted by yelling. Then there was a loud slap followed by another.

"Huh. Family—" Uncle Jake started but Reylie was up out of her chair before he could finish his statement.

"She is not a bitch!" Reylie yelled in English as she dashed towards the kitchen. The young girl almost ran her over as she fled the angry man she referred to as Tio—uncle in English. Reylie began to dress him down in Spanish as Ron scrambled to intercede. The Mexican man raised his hand to strike Reylie but a short and thick length of rope with a large end knot smacked the man on his jaw before he could initiate his blow. Uncle Jake moved fast for someone with a grey beard.

"Y'all don't hit no white girl, Poncho."

Two male youths appeared behind Tio as the

man stepped back, rubbing his face.

"I suggest we leave," Armand stated in a firm voice, his right hand concealed under his vest.

"Yep. Time to go." Uncle Jake gave Tio and the two men his best shit-eating grin and stepped back.

"Grab your and your sister's stuff, Ron."

"Got it, Uncle Jake."

The man known as Tio cursed in Spanish and English. Uncle Jake displayed the butt of his Bowie. "Keep that up, Pancho, and I'll gut ya."

Tio stopped and seethed with a red face. The four travelers walked quickly out of the cantina to their horses.

"Reylie, a man can discipline his young family members around here," Uncle Jake advised. "Now, you and Ron ride double as we can't stick around."

Tio burst from the eatery with a pistol in his hand. Armands hand was a blur from under his vest. A short-bladed throwing knife buried itself in the neck of the Mexican Uncle. The man stumbled back, the firing of the revolver forgotten. The Cajun strode forward, twisted the gun from Tio's hand, and shoved him to the crude plank sidewalk. He covered the two advancing young men with the pistol as he recovered his blade.

"I suggest you stop, hombres," Armand stated with an evil smile. The two dropped the knives they had brought to the conflict, seeing the error of bringing stabbing weapons to a possible gunfight. Uncle Jake maneuvered his mount so he could cover the cantina occupants with his Coult Navy. With one smooth move, the Cajun was on his horse just as Reylie helped her brother mount behind her.

"Vamos as they say around here," said Uncle Jake. As the band nudged three horses into trots, Uncle Jake began to curse.

"Damn it, and we need another horse. And I hope we can meet up with Bar and the others before the law shows up."

"I think the man will live, Jake," advised Armand. "The blade is short for discouraging, not killing."

"We still hurt a local business owner, Armand."

The four were near the end of the main street when Uncle Jake noticed the livery stable with a lit lantern in front. The reason for the light appeared to be a young rider with two horses in tow talking with a man who must be the livery owner, at least judging by the examination he was performing on the spare mounts.

"Hold up, people," ordered Uncle Jake. "Hey, mister. You selling those horses?"

The two extra horses' possessor was a handsome male not much older than Ron but wearing a two-gun rig. The young man had the clothes of a cowhand, but the two pistols said otherwise to Jake.

"Yes, I am," the young man replied. Uncle Jake

looked at the livery owner, who stepped back to say, go ahead, the horses may be trouble. They both had Mexican Vaquero saddles and bridles. The horse equipment and the two gun rig told Uncle Jake that the two mounts' previous owners were probably no longer breathing. The new 'owner' clearly wanted some quick cash and then get out of town.

The former Texas Ranger reached into an inside pocket and produced a twenty-dollar gold piece. He flipped it to the alleged cowhand as he dismounted.

"Pick of the pair, young man," said Jake as he started to examine the two horses.

"I was wanting to get something for the saddles also," said the young man.

"That might be arranged. Both horses look in good shape."

Uncle Jake did a quick examination of the horse flesh and pointed to one.

"We'll take that one. Now, let's dicker for the saddle."

"The dickering will have to wait," said a new voice. Walking down the street was an older thin man with a male in his late teens behind him. They both had long guns pointed in the group's general direction. The pistolero cowhand called out as a hand moved closer to a pistol.

"I don't want no trouble, Marshal."

"You just sit on your horse while I deal with these four. I don't like strangers cutting up our business owners."

"Is that an old Coults Ring Rifle?" asked Uncle Jake with a wide grin. "My God, I thought most of them disappeared after the First Mexican War."

"Your palaver won't distract me," said the town marshal. "I'm as old as you and not easily buffaloed. So, let's see everyone's hands and then tell me who stabbed Mister Nunez...."

A booming voice interrupted the marshal's questioning. "Hey, lawman. Can I have that little filly up on that horse after you're done with her? She's a lot purtier than the whores in town."

Bar had come to the party, his massive broad frame and bellowing voice demanding the lawman's attention. The younger man turned to intercept him.

"Stand back, mister," the deputy said with a shake in his voice when he saw the size of Bar. "We have business with these people—"

Bar put on his best-drunk imitation and stumbled towards the deputy. "How about I buy us all a drink? Then we can all sit down and talk nice-like."

Bar was on top of the young man before he could react. Large hands grabbed the lever-action rifle in the deputy's hands and yanked it from his grasp as Bar spun the teenager around and to the ground.

"What the—" Before the marshal could finish his statement, the butt of the lever-action caught him on his jaw, and the older lawman toppled over backward. Luckily, the Coult rifle did not discharge. In a flash, Bar had the marshal's weapon in his hands also.

"Leave you alone for an hour, and you four get in trouble," growled Bar as he threw the lever-action to the center of the dirt street,

"Young missy here got into it over a man slapping his niece and cursing her," said Uncle Jake.

Bar pointed the Coult rifle at the stunned deputy. "Just lay there until we leave. Pull a hideout hogleg, and you'll be a-singin' Soprano."

"Uncle, can we go?"

"Just as soon as you get your horse, Nephew."

"I'll ride for it," said the young pistolman.

"Up the street, by the saloon. It's the large bay."

"Got it," said the young man as he spurred his horse.

"Trusting, ain't ya?" said Uncle Jake.

"He's in this mess with the rest of us now. He'll perform."

The unnamed rider was back with Bar's mount in less than a minute. Ron had swung up on the saddle of the horse Uncle Jake picked out. The older town marshal began to moan as he came back to the living.

"Time to go," Bar said as he did a quick legless

saddle horn mount. His strong arms made it easy despite his size. He looked at the young pistolman. "What's your name. son?"

"Jessie. Jessie James."

Ron and Reylie's mouths dropped open at the name.

"Who'd you ride with during the War? You carry yourself like a man with some history."

"First Missouri Mounted. With Quantrill."

Uncle Jake laughed. "Ole Crazy Bill. Made his name hanging all a'them fellows by their thumbs in Montgomery."

"My brother Frank was there. I was too young. I was at the Battle of El Paso Del Norte in '65."

Bar grunted and nodded his head. "Time to hit the road as the marshal is waking up. People will start looking for him in a minute."

"Let's ride!" Uncle Jake called out. "The Olsens will have to catch up."

The five riders began to gallop out of Dona Ana, Ron getting a quick review on how to stay aboard a fast-moving horse. Jessie James drug the spare horse behind him and soon had it galloping along.

Ten minutes out of town, and Bar reined up. "Hope the Olsens saw us leave," he said as everyone as they bunched around him. "They have all the supplies."

"You trusted them with your money?" asked

Uncle Jake.

"They have to learn someday. And I'm afraid my size makes me too noticeable walking around in some general store."

"How was Ana's Saloon? I remember it as being pretty quiet but with cold beer."

Bar let out a barking laugh. "Is there any place you did not visit in your younger days?"

"Hey, First Mexican War gave me a thirst and a wanderlust."

"I think I see the Olsens approaching," interjected the Cajun man.

Bar looked at the young Jessie. "Well, son, what's your pleasure?"

"Well, sir. I hope you would take this other horse off my hands. Don't take it wrong, but I think I can do better on my own."

"Yes, I think this group just created another story."

Bar fished out some more coinage and tossed it towards Jessie. "You watch your back, young man. Some relatives of the vaqueros who owned those horses will come looking."

"Well, they shouldn't try to take some beeves which don't belong to them. I told the owner I'd get them beeves back or the hides of the thieves." Jessie smiled. "I got their pistols and sombreros in my saddlebags."

The young man named Jessie James tipped his hat to Reylie as he nudged his horse into motion. "Ma'am," he said. Reylie smiled and nodded her head in response. Jessie spurred his horse into a trot and looked back at Reylie, then had the mount in a gallop.

The Olsens, Tim and Tom, rode up on their overloaded horses.

"Who was that?" asked Tim.

"Jessie James," replied Ron.

"Who the heck is that?" asked Tom. Reylie and Ron smiled knowingly at each other.

"Come on," said Uncle Jake." Load up that spare mount we have now. He'll be our packhorse. Night's about here."

Hours later, the five companions made a cold camp as they watched for pursuers. None appeared.

"We'll make a fire in the morning," said Bar. "I had the twins pick up some extra bedrolls. You two youngins wrap up nice. Reylie, we need to talk."

Bar and Reylie moved to the hobbled horses. "So, you started a fight?"

"Bar, no young girl needs to be called a female dog. Not even by her Uncle."

The oversized man grunted. "I tend to agree. My pa and Uncle Jake would never use such language. But remember. You start fights; you better be able to end them."

"Yes, sir. You didn't shoot the marshal. Nor the deputy."

"No need. And those two ain't Mexicans or Negros. Now, make your bed."

Ron and Reylie tried to lay as close as possible—without being too awkward—to share their body heat.

"Someday, I may understand Bar's mindset," said Reylie.

"Well, right now, I wished his mindset was to make a campfire. I thought New Mexico was hot."

"Desert cools at night, Ron. Remember?"

"Okay, smarty-pants."

"Hey, we met Jessie James."

"The *here*-Jessie, not the Jessie from our history. Now get closer. It's cold here."

CHAPTER 4
THE CROSSES

Reylie King-Mann sat and stared at her computer screen. She thought the story was all organized and planned in her head. Reylie had written about the beginnings of her adventures in Alternate Earth. Now, however, the bronze-haired woman needed a way to put it all on paper. A way to explain how Marianne's biological father fit in with the father the daughter only knew; Mike.

The now Gang of Seven was up before dawn after a cold and sans campfires night. As they attempted to get moving, Barnabas McCain walked in from the shadows.

"Alright. No one came after us. So, let's get moving onto Las Cruces."

"Do you think that town marshal in Dona Anna will try to contact law enforcement in Las Cruces?" Reylie asked. The oversized man known as Bar shrugged.

"He could. But I doubt he wants to share his getting knocked on his butt and his rifle taken. We did not steal anything, so other than a Mexican business owner getting cut over a fight he had with a white girl; there is no reason for a posse."

"A guy getting cut is no big deal?" Reylie's brother Ron asked.

"A greaser cut for messing with a white girl? Nope."

Not for the first time did Reylie realize her time's racism was nothing compared to this reality.

"I spent many a day in Las Cruces," Uncle Jake interjected. "There is a disorderly house run by a nice woman, Susan James. She always kept her visitors in line, made sure any lady of the evening was clean and—"

"Uncle," Bar growled as he gestured towards Reylie with his grunt.

"Oh, sorry, missy. Just ignore me. It's early, and I need a good strong cup of coffee to get my brain parts working."

"Disorderly house. A brothel. Right?" Reylie's question caused stares and some laughter from the Olsen twins.

"Ain't she the smart one, knowing about whores and all," said Tim Olsen.

"You use that word around her again, and you'll be spitting teeth," Bar said through gritted teeth. Both

Tom and Tim clamped their mouths shut. Bar never warned twice.

"They call them sex workers where I come from," added Reylie. "Prostitutes, call girls—"

"Okay. We get the point, Reylie," said Bar. "You know all these growed up words. But places like brothels or parlor houses are not fit for young ladies. Now, less talking and more moving."

The band left the cold camp, with Cajun Armand Bergeron bringing up the rear.

"He does best as the rear lookout," said Uncle Jake. "The Olsen boys get distracted much too easily."

"They're not much older than I am," said Ron.

"True, But you have to grow up fast around here. Especially if you make a living with a gun."

The group made time, and Ron was getting the feel of his new mount. They entered the outskirts of Las Cruces, New Mexico Territory, some two hours after breaking camp.

"Alright," said Bar. "Olsen twins, you go in separate again. Reylie and Ron, you're with me. Uncle Jake, you and Bergeron bring up the rear five minutes behind us. Look for a place to stay and dodge the law."

A half hour later and Bar helped Reylie and Ron stable their mounts. The three carried their saddlebags and bedrolls up a side street as Bar scanned the area, shifting his 'squirrel rifle' to his off-hand.

"Okay. Start looking for signs of hotels, boarding houses. We just need a place with hot meals and places to sleep."

Just then, a loud whistle echoed from across the street. The three travelers looked up.

"Well, damn me," said Bar. "Uncle Jake is at it again."

Across and up the street was Uncle Bar, standing next to a buxom and flashy dressed woman.

"Is that Susan James, the Madam?" asked Reylie.

Bar grunted. "I bet on it. My Uncle cannot stay away from the women. Come on."

The three crossed the street and walked up to Uncle Bar and his female companion.

"Howdy. This here is—"

"Susan James," interjected Reylie. "Pleased to meet you, ma'am."

The brassy blonde laughed and presented her hand to shake like a man.

"And who is this comely young lady, Jake? A relative, long lost daughter of yours?"

"Reylie King," said Jake. "We—found her on the trail with her brother Ron here. They were separated from their people by Injuns."

"What a tale of adventure, young lady," said Susan as she linked arms with Reylie. "You must tell me all about it."

"Ah, ma'am. We are looking for a place to stay," stated Ron.

"And Reylie ain't staying at yer bawdy house," said Bar. "She's too young for any of those activities."

Susan stopped in her tracks and glared at Bar. "You must be the same nephew with the reputation of hating Negros and Mexicans. Well, my doorman, Jim, is as black as night. And better than half the white men in Las Cruces, and all the Mexicans."

"Ma'am—" Bar started to say, and Susan Jame bowled right over him.

"No way did I think of introducing this fine young lady to house visitors," said the madam. "I can tell by looking at her; she is a lady. I'm a damned good judge of character. Now you keep a civil tongue in your mouth, Mister McCain, or—"

Uncle Jake burst out laughing. "Same ole, Buffalo Susan," the older man said. "Still buffaloing men who anger her." Jake leaned over and stole a kiss on the cheek from the lady of the night.

Susan giggled like a young girl. "Stop that, Jake. We're in public."

Bar removed his hat and spoke. "Beggin' your pardon, ma'am. I'm just a little protective of Reylie. She reminds me of—kin."

Susan pierced Bar with her gaze. Then she smiled. "Barabas, I think Jake said was your name. I apologize for losing my temper. I just get tired of people making assumptions about me and mine. I'm not no street-walking whore, pardon my language, young Reylie. But I have pride also."

Reylie looked at the strong woman and imagined her in the 21st Century. Some businesswoman, a CEO, having to live and work in a man's world. And the young girl, soon to be a grown woman, smiled. Reylie liked this strong female.

"Ma'am, I can tell you run a tight—ship," said Reylie. Buffalo Susan grinned and hugged her.

"You could tell my Daddy was a sea captain, can't you? I think you and I are going to be fast friends, my dear." The madam looked at the other three. "Well, business has been good to me. The War and a couple of Cattle Drives to Sante Fe have kept my place busier than a one-armed buckaroo."

"John Chisum, still around?" asked Uncle Jake. The name caused Reylie and Ronald to perk up their ears.

"Yep. Chisum should be coming down this way in a day or two; he ran his third cattle drive to Sante Fee for the army and the haciendas that still exist. Most people with ties to Mexico are gone due to the Second Mexican War."

"And rightly so," growled Bar.

"Now, their money spends just as well as any

white man's. I even have a couple of Mexican Girls working for me. But I'm distracted. Come with me, please."

The four followed Susan James down to the southern end of Mainstreet. Some people smiled and nodded at Susan, and others tried to act like she did not exist. Reylie knew some houses of prostitution garnered respect in her universe along with the madams, depending on the community. Here in Las Cruces, there appeared a mixed bag of feelings.

Susan stopped in front of a storefront with a 'CLOSED' sign in the window. She pulled a ring of keys from her large and colorful handbag and searched for the correct one. A quick insert and turn of the key, and they were inside.

"Who owns this?" Bar asked.

"I do. I told you business was good." The voluptuous woman grinned like a Cheshire cat as she continued. "I invested my money in real estate. This place was a photography studio."

"What happened to the cameraman?" asked Ronald as he looked around.

"He, his wife and son, went off to photograph the War around El Paso—called Franklin for you old-timers, like Jake here." Susan wiped some dust from the front counter before answering.

"Got a letter saying they were all killed by some

raiding Mexicans and Comancheros who didn't like people taking pictures of them. Mister Black helped me make postcards of my girls and sell them for a good bit of coin, so we stayed in touch. Somebody found my address in his things, so a Texas Ranger sent me a letter."

Ron mumbled, "Porn," under his breath just loud enough for his sister to hear, which prompted a stink-eye at him.

"I'm sorry to hear that, ma'am—"

"Susan or Sue to you, Reylie. But their loss was my gain. I bought this place from the Bank." The madam looked at the others. "Banks don't care where your money comes from as long as it's good. They did not want to screw with finding a family to take care of the personal items left behind."

"What did you do with leftovers?" asked Uncle Jake.

"Put it all in a closet in the back. Come, I'll show you the kitchen in the rear, water pump and all. "

"So the idea is we stay here," said Bar.

Susan grinned at him. "Dollar a day for the lot of you. Until I find a new photographer, those French postcards are very popular. You get it cheap if you keep it nice and neat."

They made the deal, and Uncle Jake paid for a week. Susan talked to them as Bar went to find Armand

and the Olsen twins.

"Can we get baths, Susan?" Uncle Jake asked.

"I'll set up a tub in my suite for the young missy here. You men can pay full price for a bath with front and back scrub."

"...Back scrub?" asked Ron.

Buffalo Susan grinned. "The first roundup, I see, young man. My girls want a clean man the first time they meet them."

"Meet? With...?"

Jake began laughing. "Yep. First time alright. No, no need to blush. We all had to start somewhere."

Reylie began to giggle, then laugh. Ron blushed even more as he knew his sister knew what was going to happen. "Quit that," Ron stammered out. "It's not funny."

"It's all part of being a man, Ron," said Uncle Jake. "You want to be a man. Yes?"

Ron sputtered, and Reylie went to the front room to sit down as she laughed—hard.

Bar came in with the others a few minutes later and began to assign sleeping areas. "I'll have Jim bring a mattress for the bed in the back," said the madam. "That is if it's for Reylie."

"Of course," said Bar.

When Uncle Jake told him about the bath arrangements, he angered and pulled his Uncle aside.

"What are you doing talking about that in front of Reylie? She is still just a girl."

"She's a lot more grown-up than you think, Nephew. I can tell by the way she acts and talks," Uncle Jake replied.

"Oh yeah?"

"Yes. Reylie knows how a whore house runs. And Susan won't let anybody bother her. Susan is acting like a brood hen around Reylie."

"Better be that way, Uncle. Or I am going to be very angry."

As Armand and the Olsens examined their new temporary home, Ron pulled Reylie aside. "Hey, this is weird. A sex worker is going to be bathing me? Where we come from, sex with someone less than 16 is rape. I'm still fifteen. This is not funny."

"Hey, brother. Sorry, I laughed, but you were blushing up a storm."

"Well, what would you do, Reylie? Do I do this to fit in like something at school?"

It dawned on her that she did not realize the consequences as Ron was male. People talked about the 'double standard' at home between girls and boys concerning sex. Sex with an older woman supposedly was something about which young men/boys fantasized. But what if you didn't?

"Ron, we need to survive here until we find a

way home, to our time and place. But, I don't want you sacrificing your morals or your body."

Ron was quiet for a minute, then asked, "You're going to try to stay a virgin, Reylie?"

"Yes, Ron. But I can get pregnant. You can't."

"Still, if you feel pressured into it—"

Bar chose that moment to walk to the pair. "Reylie, I need to talk to you about something. Excuse me, Ron." Bar led the young lady into a side room chosen to house her bed,

"What is it about, Bar?"

"Here. I think you know how to use this."

Bar handed Reylie the .32 caliber pistol taken from the banker on the stagecoach. "Single action rimfire, five cartridges. You—"

"Cock the hammer, pull the trigger. I know. My dad, uncle, and granddad taught us how to shoot." Reylie looked Bar in the eyes. "Why this now?" she asked.

"Lots of bad men hang around bawdy houses. So if one decides you are one of the girls—"

"I jam this in his gut, cock it, and pull the trigger."

Bar frowned. "You catch on fast, for someone who grew up with some bible thumpers in Washington Territory."

Reylie shrugged as she answered, "Ron and I

learn fast as we read a lot about places, things. It helps."

The big man grunted. "Well, I'll keep an eye out, so hopefully, you won't have to gut shoot someone."

"Jim's here with the mattress," Uncle Jake called out.

Reylie walked to the front entrance and saw a Black man, muscular but wiry, and almost as tall as Bar. He carried two mattresses and went straight to the room chosen by Susan for Reylie. There was a set of bedsprings on a frame in the corner of the room. As Jim placed both mattresses on the bedsprings, he remarked, "Missy, I brought two of these as they ain't very padded."

Bar grunted from the bedroom doorway. "I thought the Negro Relocation Act was in effect."

Jim turned and looked Bar in the eye. "It applies to the States, not here in New Mexico Territory."

"So, they let you have jobs here," Bar added. "I didn't know nigg—"

Reylie saw where this was going and cut him off. "These springs must have cost a pretty penny."

Still looking at Bar, Jim replied, "Previous owners bought them, and Madam Susan kept them."

"Well, thank her, Jim, for letting me use them," Reylie continued.

"She'll be here in a minute, with some refreshments. You can tell her in person."

"Well, let's go meet her, Jim, Bar." Reylie smiled and walked out towards the front. "Come on. She may need help carrying something."

Jim followed her as Bar glowered.

Susan appeared at the front door with two comely young women in tow carrying trays piled high with meat and sandwiches. Tim and Tom Olsen grinned and quickly introduced themselves to the two ladies of the evening.

"Welcome committee," one of the women introduced themselves. "I have a couple of bottles of libation and some lemonade also."

Jim excused himself as Bar watched. As the others grabbed food and drink, flirted with the working girls, Reylie walked up to Bar. "You know, Jim is not your problem."

"He's one of 'em, isn't he? The same people who sacked Montgomery helped the greasers fight us, the same Mexicans who killed my kin."

"You are so damned full of hate, Bar, and it's eating your insides."

"I don't need some little girl from some strange place schoolin' me on who I am." Bar turned on his heel and stomped out.

Reylie was so angry she had to blink back tears. How could a man who one moment would help strangers the next moment treat others with such hatred just because of the color of their skin?

"You are poking the bear, missy," Uncle Jake said behind her.

"Someone needs to tell him that the people around here had nothing to do with the killing of his family."

"Well, maybe if you found your wife Rebekah and little sister Judith raped and dead, along with your Pa, your Ma, and the whole homestead, you'd understand. Mexicans and others declared war on our family, and Bar wants vengeance."

"Then find those responsible. Not strangers. Why aren't you so angry?"

"Because I'm older and dealt with more crap over the years. But I'm still here for my nephew."

"Killing strangers," Reylie finished.

"Missy, look. Have something to eat, drink. Then a bath—"

"I need some air," said Reylie and then walked out.

Why was it men were so hardheaded, stupid? *God*, Reylie thought, *this must be Hell.*

"Mademoiselle, may I walk with you?" It was Armand the Cajun.

"I'm not good company right now, Armand."

"You should not walk alone in a town you do not know. Thus, I will walk with you. Your arm, please. And on the inside of the street. Walking on my outside may mean to some that you are—available.”

Reylie, as angry as she was, could not help but smile. She remembered a history teacher talking about 'Old World Chivalry' and thought this must be an example.

“Why are you with the McCains, Armand? Do you have anything to do with this revenge thing?”

The Cajun sighed, then spoke. “I first crossed paths with them at the Battle of El Paso. As a French speaker, I helped these Texas Rangers to interrogate some captured French Officers. They remembered me some six months later.”

“What happened then?”

“I was in a bad state, a total drunkard. While I was at war, my wife ran off with a close friend, taking my son and daughter. I was drunk, being beaten by some town constables in Texas. Bar and Jake stepped in and broke some faces, freeing me.”

“So, you hooked up with them?”

“They fed me, cleaned me up with some help from some soiled doves Uncle Jake knew. They helped me to climb out of the bottle. So, I am loyal to them.”

“Loyal to the point of killing people with them?”

“They saved me. I owe the McCains my life. So I help Bar with his Vengaza, as the Spanish say. Although I have nothing personal against Negroes.”

Reylie walked in silence as she tried to process everything she had heard and seen. Times were raw in her and Ron's world, with people splitting families and friendships over presidents and politics. And, of course, there would always be racism and sexism. But she had never been exposed to this level of hate and violence.

"You are quiet, Reylie," said Armand.

"Just trying to figure this all out." Reylie stopped walking, turned, and kissed Armand on the cheek.

"Thanks for listening, Armand."

The Cajun grinned. "For a kiss on the cheek from a pretty young lady, you may have my ears at any time."

Reylie went back to the band's new accommodations and ate some of the plenty that Buffalo Susan had brought. Bar had not returned yet, which was probably just as well. His presence would only make her angry. After about a half hour, Susan latched on to Reylie and said it was bath time.

"What about us?" asked Tim Olsen with a grin.

"Show me some silver, and I'll get you a bathing partner," Susan snapped back.

Them madam's suite was spacious and comfortable, with all manner of feminine accouterments. Reylie soon sat in a massive tube with Susan's maid, fetching pitchers of hot water as needed. The hot water leeched out all the dirt, sweat, aches, and pains from Reylie's body. Susan gave her a scented bar of soap and a soft washcloth. After the events of the past few days, the young lady thought she had died and gone to heaven.

Susan came in and washed Reylie's as the fourteen-year-old told her the family 'history.' At least, Reylie told her the made-up one. If she had told Susan what had happened due to the spin of a wheel on a game, Reylie knew the madam would kick her out as crazy.

"So, you don't know if any other people from your group survived?"

"I don't think so, Susan; those, ah, savages were pretty thorough. Ron and I escaped in the dark and confusion as my father and the others fought them."

"Oh, I am so sorry, my dear; well, you can stay here as long as you like."

"I appreciate the offer, but Ron and I are limited in funds. Barr and Uncle Jake have been more than generous. However, we will need money to make it down to the King Ranch."

"Well, if you change your mind, let me know. I think you could help me run my businesses."

Reylie's eyes widened. "Susan, I know nothing about running a whore, I mean bawdy house!"

"You're smart; I can sense it. Besides, I have other businesses. I am about to obtain a livery stable.

Plus, I still plan on bringing a photographer back. Those French Postcards were quite the money maker."

Reylie sat for a moment as she tried to frame an answer without offending their possible benefactor. After all, the story of King Ranch was a total fake. So if she and Ron stayed here, closer to where they had arrived in the Alternate Earth, it might be better.

"Can I talk to my brother first? I can't separate from him."

Susan grinned and patted Reylie's arm.

"Of course! I know Uncle Jake would just as soon stay here as long as possible. Now, soak some more, and then Mary will help you dry off. I'll get you some clean, not too flashy clothes to wear. We always have spares left over for when girls leave. Many even find a husband."

An hour later and Reylie met Ronald down in the back parlor of the establishment, which was for private 'conversations.' She noticed he was bathed and clean with new clothes supplied by Susan. Ron seemed calm and satisfied.

"So, your sister has to ask, Ron. Did you—"

"Not really... although, gentleladies should not ask."

Reylie laughed. "So a bit of help at masturbation—"

"Reylie!" Ron yelled out as he blushed. "I would never dream of talking like this if Mom and Dad were around."

Reylie sighed. "Well, they aren't here, and I need to discuss a proposition with you." Ron gave her an odd look at the word 'proposition,' but Reylie explained Susan's proposals and the pros and cons.

"What would I do?" asked Ron.

"Help me run the businesses, other than this place."

"I don't know, Reylie."

"Well, if we make it to King Ranch, I doubt they will be very accepting. They'll know we are not relatives. You and I know some underlying technology we could use to make money in the 1860s of our world. We can do the same here."

"Yeah. Uncle Jake asked for one of my pistol shells. I said if he used it to make smokeless powder or anything, he would owe us."

"What did he say?"

"He laughed, said I was a smart boy, and no, he would not rip us off. Or words to that effect."

"He'd better not. I'll get even, and he knows it."

Loud voices interrupted their conversation, and three dusty cowboys walked in as one of the working girls tried to keep them in the front parlor.

"This is the third time I've been here, and by

damn, I'm going to find out what is back here—well, *hello*, sweetkins." The cowboy speaking was a raven-haired man with a large mustache. "Come on over and visit with a real man, not peachfuzz over there."

"Sorry, I am not one of the girls," Reylie said with a pleasant smile.

"The Hell, you say!" a dirty brown-haired companion to Mister Mustache butted into the conversation. He was heavier with a long scar on his right cheek. "You just don't like cowhands," he accused.

"She's my sister, buddy," Ron replied as he reached under his shirt for his Ruger.

"Your sister is a whore?" Scarface said.

Ron stood up quickly from the table. "Come over here and say that, *punk*."

"Ron," Reylie saw this was about to get out of hand. Scarface was a lot beefier than Ron, and Reylie knew he was probably an experienced brawler.

"Take yer hand off your pistol, boy," said Mustache. "You feel tough; take Louie on man-to-man."

Reylie pulled her pistol from her handbag under the table. She would not let these thugs hurt her brother or her.

Scarface, clearly already in his cups with cheap alcohol, walked up and grabbed Ron and cocked his right arm for a blow. The young man planted a textbook front snap kick into the manhood of Scarface. The cowhand began to fold as Ron grabbed the grasping left hand of the loudmouth and used a wristlock and arm-twist to take the man to the floor.

"Want some more?" Ron said as he placed a foot on the neck of Scarface.

"Fight like an Injun, huh?" said the third man, a dirty blonde-haired tough who advanced on Ron.

Reylie stood and aimed her pistol at the cowhand. "Stop right there, mister."

Mustache had a large frame revolver in his hand and aimed at the siblings. "You want a shoot-out, missy?"

Jim came up quick and silent behind the cowboys. He grabbed Mustache's gun and effortlessly yanked it from his grasp, then buffaloed the man with his pistol to the floor. Jim was on the dirty blonde man in a flash, using the same revolver to smash across the man's face. The man fell to the floor.

"You okay?" asked the Black man.

"Now we are, Jim. Thank you."

"You two need to leave. Please. These are Chisum men. He will not be happy."

The siblings left out the back and were soon back at their temporary home. The other group members were still out.

"Now what?" asked Ron.

"We wait for the others, tell them

what happened."

"Were you going to shoot, Reylie?"

"If I had to, yes. Thanks for fighting for my honor, but we might want to reconsider next time."

"Just trying to adapt to this crazy place,"

A half hour later, Uncle Jake and Bar entered the residence. Jake had a wide grin on his face.

"Heard you got into a tussle with some Chism boys."

"They called my sister a whore," said Ron with his chin thrust out in defiance.

Uncle Jake chuckled. "You have more sand than I thought you did. Though Black Jim clubbed two of them." The greybeard looked at Reylie.

"And we have the makings of a pistolero, missy."

"I will not let them beat down my brother," Reylie replied.

"Well," interjected Bar, "we'll lay low tonight. If John Chisum wants to have a row, he'll probably come over in the morning with the town marshal."

"Why would the marshal care about what happens in a bawdy house?" Reylie asked.

"Money. Chisum and his men spend a lot of money in Las Cruces, not just at Buffalo Susan's place. So if'n he grouches, the city fathers listen."

"Sorry," said Reylie. "I didn't—"

"Don't be telling your sorry for standing up for

yourself and kin, young lady. If you don't stand up, you get run over. In your case, you could be besoiled and abused." Bar looked at Ron. "Keep your pistol handy. The next time they'll call you out for gunplay."

The Olsens and Armand came back later, the Olsens with a bottle of whiskey and Armand with some fresh fruit and cheese for all, plus a bottle of wine. Uncle Jake went back out and brought back some bread, beans, beef, and beer. The band sat around and swapped tales into the evening. Reylie, after seeing Bar had a couple of beers under his belt, broached the subject of his past.

"You had a wife."

"Yes, Reylie, I did. Just four years older than you."

"Any children?" At that question, Bar stood up and grabbed the whiskey bottle from the Olsens. The bear of a man took a swig, then another. Then he passed it back.

Bar sat down, facing Reylie. "Since you are so— inquisitive is the four-bit word—let me tell you. Rebekah was my wife. I married her in 1865 in between chasing Mexicans, Brownites, and Comanche."

"Nephew…"

"No, Uncle Jake. Time to clear the air with this one." Bar leaned closer.

"We had a short honeymoon, and she was with

child when I left. We both knew it. I went back to the War, and she stayed at my family's ranch and farm near Van Horn. Someone hand me a beer."

The Cajun handed Bar a mug of beer, and the big man gulped it down, then slammed the pewter mug on the nearby table. "January 31st, 1866, they signed the Southwest Peace Treaty in El Paso, and the War ended. February 2nd, I and Uncle Jake arrived back at the McCain place."

"Groundhogs Day," whispered Ron.

"Our family had been dead one, maybe two, days. My wife and sister, also named Susan, were—abused. The greasers stole the horses, shot the stock, tried to burn the house, but were bad fire makers."

"Bar—" Reylie interjected.

"No, let me finish, goddammit. You're gonna ask how we know they were Mexicans, the ones who did this. Right?"

"Yes," mumbled Reylie

"Because we tracked those sons of whores back across the Rio Grande. We killed every one of them. But not before we found out what Alcalde ordered this murder. Then we kept moving until we found the hacienda, the plantation they lived on." Bar quickly stood up. "But I'll give you all the gory details some other time. Everyone up! And to bed. We have to be fresh if Chisum comes a-gunnin' for us."

The men knew not to question Bar and went to their respective bedrolls on the floor. As Reylie walked to her private room and bed, Bar bellowed. "Anyone trying to visit Reylie in the night, and I'll make you a gelding. Got it?"

Reylie went to bed and had a fitful sleep.

The group was up and eating breakfast when Bar said, "Here comes Chisum and the town marshal."

Reylie watched as the five men plus Ron all made sure they had their pistols belts on and their rifles within reach. Bar had his massive Coults in cross-draw holsters. The gun's weight seemed to have little effect on him. He and Uncle Jake stepped out onto the small porch area in front of the former photography office. "John Chisum hasn't changed, has he, uncle?"

"Nope."

Chism walked slow and deliberate, twisting the ends of his thick black waxed mustache. He had the slender but wiry and robust look of many a cowboy. Large men like Bar did not make good cowboys as they wore out the horses with their weight during the long cattle drives. Walking just behind him was a young man, blonde-haired tall, and slender with a badge on his chest.

"Howdy, Jake," Chisum called out.

"Howdy back, John, Marshal."

"Is that Bar with you?"

"Yes, sir. All grown up."

Chisum laughed. "Bar never was small."

"No, sir. But you came here to talk about a couple of other youngins."

"Marshal Linden here," John Chisum said as he gestured to the younger man. "Nearly appointed as the last one got himself shot."

"Yep. New Mexico Territory is rough on town marshals and constables."

"Well, Jake. He and I have a couple of questions. See, I have three men who aren't up to snuff to work right now because—"

"A certain young man and lady kicked their asses," interrupted Bar. John Chisum laughed.

"Bar is as blunt as ever, Jake. Yes sir, Bar. One of my men was kicked in the privates by a young man. Then he had his trigger finger broke. If not, he'd be here calling the young man out."

"And the marshal would allow that," said Bar.

"If they did it on a side street," answered the young marshal, "and it was a fair fight, no one else shot."

"Are the two Jim busted up going to come lookin' also?"

The marshal looked at Chisum.

"Well, Bar," the cattleman answered, "not right now. Since Black Jim did it at Susan's, probably not.

Once that busted finger heals and his swollen privates heal, I can't guarantee anything from Joe Blume. He's still mad about his scar."

"How'd he get it?" asked Bar.

"Fight in a whorehouse."

Bar laughed. "He has lousy luck around the ladies. He ought to quit."

"Be that as it may, I have three men who can't do a full day's work right now."

"How much?" asked Jake.

"Twenty. In silver or gold."

Jake took a gold piece from his pocket. "This ends it, John."

"Yes, sir." Chisum caught the twenty-dollar gold piece.

"Thanks, Jake. By the way, some Mexican boys were asking about you and Bar."

"Yeah?" said Bar. "What are they saying?'

"Asking about a damn big gringo and a greybeard. Oh, and I saw a Pinkerton in town."

Jake swore under his breath. "Thanks, John. What else can we do for ya?"

"Can I see the young lady the fuss was all about?"

"Only if she wants to," growled Bar.

Chisum held his hands up in surrender. "But of course."

Bar turned to call out, but Reylie and Ron were already there. John Chisum let out a short whistle as he took off his hat.

"Well, hello, young lady. You are good-looking. But not one of Susan's girls."

"No, sir, I'm not."

"You'd a shot, my men?"

"Yes, if they tried to hurt my brother Ron and me."

The cattleman looked at Ron. "When you and she are done with these reprobates, look me up. Son, you could be a cattleman. And your sister here, I'd find a job for her. I like grit."

John Chisum put his hat back on, tipped it to Reylie. "Jake, Bar, good to see you. Hope the Mexes and the Pinkertons don't mess with you."

"It will be their mistake," replied Bar. Chisum laughed and left with the town marshal.

"Do U.S. Marshals come around here?" asked Reylie.

"Sometimes," said Uncle Jake. "This being a territory and all, they are the official law. These towns run things loosey-goosey, just enough law to keep too many dead bodies from appearing in the streets."

"Chisum, huh?" said Ron.

"You know of him?" asked Bar.

"I saw a mov—a, uh, a story of him once. Said he

was as tough as nails."

"You have to be, to move cattle, boy. Now, inside. We need to talk and plan."

The band sat over cups of hot cowboy coffee as Bar laid out the situation. "We have Pinkertons and some nosey Mexicans looking at us. They are most likely connected. The banks hired The Pinkerton to see who's been harassing the money shipments and transfers."

"So the stagecoach we saw you rob was not the first," said Ron.

"It was our second coach but our sixth money shipment. The others were small horseback robberies. The most were for a thousand dollars and some pesos. But it all adds up."

"So, now what?" asked Reylie. "You have detectives on your trail. Where do you go?"

"El Paso, Texas. Formally known as Franklin," replied Uncle Jake. "We have a lot of friends there, including some Rangers. They're not going to care if we have been stealing from Mexican Banks."

"And we can arrange for coach travel from there, to the King Ranch," said Bar.

Reylie paused, then spoke. "Susan asked me to stay here, help her with her businesses. And Mister Chisum offered us jobs."

Bar laughed. "You two greenhorns won't last a month. You faced down one or two scum, and you think you have it all figured out. Driving cattle and whores are both tough jobs. And Reylie. That palaver from Susan about not using girls your age? Pure cow flop."

"But she's been so helpful."

"Madams and pimps are all the same. They always have an ulterior motive, as my uncle here will say. You'd be on your back in a month."

"Hey, that's kind of harsh talk," said Ron.

"Time to get truthful. It would be easy to leave you both here. But the ghost of my Rebekah would never let me forget."

Silence filled the room; everyone was lost in their thoughts. Then Reylie spoke. "So, you want to be stuck with Ron and me."

"Until you're on a safe trail, yes," Bar replied.

"Okay, then now what?"

"We leave before sunrise in the morning. Tim and Tom, you're in charge of getting the horses here. Armand, you get to go and snoop around the town and use your Cajun charm. Bring us back some grub. Any questions? Good."

"What about us?" asked Reylie.

"You stay away from Buffalo Susan. We can't let on we are leaving; she might sell that information. Rest. We'll be moving fast to Texas."

It was still dark out when Reylie woke with the sounds of someone in her room. She started to call out when she heard a loud thud, then the sound of something heavy hitting the floor.

"Fucking Mexican," growled Bar.

"Bar, what—"

"Get up. Greasers know we're leaving."

Survival instincts took over, and Reylie was up in a flash. She had remained dressed, so all she had to do was put her boots on. She had a momentary thought of regret as Susan had bought the boots for her to replace the shoes from the 21st Century. She grabbed her shoulder bag and small case and stepped over the body of a Mexican. A glance told her the man had somehow opened and snuck through the bedroom window. But Bar heard him when she did not.

Tim and Tom had the horses at the rear door within minutes. Just as they went to their mounts, a voice echoed down the alleyway.

"Pinkerton Detective Agency with a warrant. Surrender, and no one will be hurt."

"We have youngins with us," Uncle Jake called out as he slipped a revolver from the saddlebag opposite the voice.

"Don't stall. Put your hands up—"

Bar was a blur as he raised his sizeable Coult

Root pistol and shot at the man behind the voice. How he cleared his cross-draw holster so fast would always be a mystery to Reylie. Then everyone scrambled to mount their horses as Bar and Jake stepped towards the far end of the alley and shot at the others who came with the Pinkerton.

"Ride!" Bar commanded. Reylie slapped the ends of her reins on her mount's rump, and the horse leaped into a gallop. Someone yelling in Spanish tried to grab her, and Reylie back-handed him in the face. The grasping hands let go, and Reylie crouched low on her horse as she dug her boot heels into the mount. The bay horse took off like a rocket as a bullet whizzed by her face. She didn't have time to notice where Ron was.

Then a Mexican rider spurred his horse directly in front of Reylie. She tried to rein in her horse and failed. The equines collided and went down in a tangle of legs and screams of animal fear. Somehow Reylie rolled free from the collision. The Mexican was not so lucky. His cry cut off when a horse hoof crushed his head. Reylie scrambled to her feet and pulled the pistol Bar gave her from her bag.

"Reylie!" It was Ron. He spurred his horse up to where she stood and reached a hand down to pull her up behind him.

The large-caliber rifle bullet hit Ron's mount in the head. The horse collapsed to the dirt, dead as Ron jumped free.

"Shit," Ron said, and he yanked his Ruger revolver free from his belt.

A man walked up with a Sharps rifle in his hand and yelled in accented English.

"Children. Raise your hands or—"

The Mexican never finished his statement as Ron shot him. The modern .357 Magnum round punched a hole in the chest, going in, and an even larger one going out. The dead Mexican toppled over. Ron and Reylie jumped to their feet, and Ron grabbed the Sharps.

"Round in the chamber," he said.

"We need a horse," stated Reylie as she moved down the side street. "Here, Ron. The dead man's horse."

The two siblings now noticed the loud booms of Bar's massive .44s as Ron mounted the horse behind his sister.

"We need to help," Reylie said.

"Damn," said her brother as the young woman turned the horseback down the alley they were fleeing. Reylie trotted the mount down the backstreet as she kept to the dark side.

Armand leaped from the shadows. "You are alive."

"Yes. Armand," said Reylie. "You need a horse."

There was a final loud report, a scream, and then

silence. Armand led Reylie's mount slowly down the alley.

The Olsens suddenly appeared with several horses. "Where's Bar and—"

"Here," said Uncle Jake. "time to go before the law shows up."

Bar wore a bandoleer Pancho Villa style across his chest. In his hand was a Remington rolling block rifle.

"Let's git," the big man said.

On the way out of town, Reylie and Ron recovered their possessions from the dead horses. Then, all seven riders were hellbent on Texas.

An hour later and with no visible pursuit, Bar ordered a stop to rest the horses. They found a clump of low trees to hide in as they watered the horses as best they could.

"Well, we lost three mounts and gained four," Uncle Jake stated. He looked at Ron.

"You shot someone, didn't you?"

"Yes, sir, I guess I did."

"Is he dead?"

"Yes," stated Reylie. "He did it after they shot the horse from under us."

Bar walked up and grunted. "You did what you had to do.No shame in that, son. Just don't get to enjoy it like me." The massive man walked off to behind a tree and was soon urinating a river.

Uncle Jake shoved a liquor bottle in Ron's face. "Here. You and Reylie take a slug. Helps relax you after your first gunfight."

The two teenagers drank the rotgut and kept it down. They both laid back and dozed off from the booze and the worn-off adrenaline.

Reylie awoke to the voices of Bar and Uncle Jake. "That Pinkerton had a bunch of coin on him," said Bar.

"Bribes. You know, Nephew, I have done a lot in my life. But I just don't understand singing like a bird for money. A man gotta have some honor, say things to be right, not for money."

"Well, it's ours now. Plus, some silver pesos from those Mexicans."

"We are well-heeled now, Bar. Keep this up, and the stash in the hills of New Mexico will stay there."

"I ain't doin' all this for money, Uncle. I'm doing this in memory of our family. And to make sure all the greasy Mexicans think twice before they cross the border again."

"I know, Bar. Now let's get these two new ruffian members of our gang up. We have a long trip ahead."

Reylie stopped typing. She realized now this history was as much about her and her brother Ron as it was about

Bar. Things were so damned intertwined. But for the sake of Marianne, she would continue. Bar's daughter needed to know about her father. And now, Reylie realized Marianne required to know about her mother also. Warts and all.

For someday, Marriane may have children. She needed to know no mother was ever perfect.

Reylie saved the file; now time for some loving from Mike. That always made hard memories so much more bearable.

CHAPTER 5
EL PASO: PART 1

Reylie King rode out the trembler minor quake in the kitchen of her and her husband's house. It was near Fort Bliss Armed Forces Base in El Paso, Texas. She and her husband Mike Mann had chosen El Paso as it was not far from the various Space Command Launch and Recovery Sites in New Mexico, Arizona, and Texas. Thanks to all the seismic activity in California and the rest of the West Coast, aviation, space, and military operations moved inland towards the Mid and Southwest. That included all the former Nasa and USAF Missile Launch Facilities at Vandenberg Air Force Base. Plus, Reylie had a bit of history with the area, even if it technically was in a different universe.

The trembler was no doubt started from a shockwave in California. Hunks of shoreline were falling into the Pacific Ocean, and the scenic Coastal Highway was shut down. As things worsened, the Sky Tunnel

Project became more important. It had been decided the survival of much of humanity depended on escaping an Earth, which seemed hellbent on destruction. Massive earthquakes and volcanic activity seemed in danger of tearing the Earth asunder. Star travel to Earth-like planets found through the Star Tunnel technology was the hope of transferring humans to new homes.

"Everything okay, Mom?" Her tall, dark-haired daughter Marianne walked into the kitchen from the dining area.

"Just another minor shockwave from the coast. Turn on the news, please, and we'll see how much damage is in California."

The two women were able to connect with a satellite feed broadcasting real-time information. Reylie and Marianne sat and watched the reports for a good half hour. The bottom line, the reports showed more hunks of ground and buildings around San Francisco and the areas south sliding into the Pacific Ocean.

"Well, Mom, this will speed up the evacuations," said Marianne.

"Yes. Sad that so many people will have to leave their homes, the countries of their ancestors."

"Change always happens, Mom. We humans are tough. We'll adapt and survive."

When Marianne spoke like this, Reylie saw the heritage of her biological father in her only daughter.

Mike Mann was the only father Marianne knew, but he was not her sire. A man lost in an alternate timeline was her true father, Bar McCain. Whenever Reylie saw Bar's genes and mannerisms in Marianne, she felt pangs of remorse and remembrance. Reylie took a deep breath, then exhaled. Reylie had discussed the matter with Mike. Now, she knew it was time.

"Dear, do you ever think about Barnabas, Bar, your father?"

"Of course I do, Mom. Mike is my Dad, and we love each other to bits. He raised me and is the reason I am in astrophysics. But, well—I feel Bar—inside me. He is part of me. And I feel he is still alive, somewhere."

"Mike told you what the technology of Sky Tunnels might mean about... Bar."

Marianne paused and looked at her hands. Then she looked up at her mother. "I know you, or I, or us together, could be sent to that time. Before I was born, even conceived..." Marianne stopped speaking. Then she said again. "Mom. I have a tough question."

Reylie thought she knew what was coming next yet did not let on. "Go ahead, honey; you know I love you."

"Were you—abused? Were you forced, you know..."

"Was I raped? No. Not no, but *Hell no*. Bar was not like that. And he was so protective of me..." Reylie blinked back tears.

Marianne moved over to the sofa they were on and hugged her mother. "You loved my father, didn't you?"

"And he loved me. He loved me so much that he waited until my eighteenth birthday before asking for my hand in marriage. He refused to touch me before that, despite my—I wanted him to. I was in love with him and had all the feelings and hormones of a teenage girl." She looked into her daughter's eyes. "You were not an accident. I thought I would be in that time, that Alt Earth forever. As did your Uncle Ronald."

"So, I was conceived on your wedding night?"

"Or shortly after that. Then the Emergency Rescue Team showed up. They came through the first tunnel between realities created after Ron and I were spun into that version of the American West. And I had to come back."

"I was never really told why Mom. Why did you have to return?"

"The government was threatening Granddad because of how he had come to build his 'Game.' He had taken something from Area 51 he was not supposed to have. Other people were also disappearing. Finding us proved others could be recovered."

"If they were not, Granddad the Tinkerer would have been held responsible?" asked the daughter. Reylie nodded yes, wiped her eyes with a napkin she had found.

"Plus, we found my other older brother, your Uncle Maxwell, was not Missing in Action. He was yanked by some—*beings* from their side, their reality using similar technology. They swore me to secrecy about that but, screw. It's been twenty years, and we have the Sky Tunnels."

The two women sat quietly for a few minutes. Then Reylie said, "Time for lunch. Your dad won't be home for a while."

The two made and ate lunch as they felt the bond a mother and daughter can develop due to shared problems.

As they ate, Reylie explained more. "Your Uncle Ron and I did things which should result in jail time. The authorities know some of them, but not a lot of them. However, they wanted to take us back so much; the records were wiped clean. We were the guinea pigs that had to prove the technology that would save people in our world. The Problems began about a year after we were 'spun' into Bar's world."

"There were rumors the creation of the first 'tunnel' with The Game upset the universe, that it caused our Earth to become unstable," stated Marianne.

"Yes, I know. But the creation of the other passageways by the 'small Ones' as they called themselves disproved that idea. Their universe seems to have no instability."

"What happened to them after Uncle Max returned?"

"That whole story is buried in Area 51. I think there is an open link. But that tale is so deeply buried we may never know. Especially if we all leave Earth."

Marianne looked at her mother. "You need to write your story, your tale before it is lost and buried forever. I think you owe it to my father, Bar."

Reylie stared off into space for a few moments. Then she spoke. "I kind of started that already. But I wanted to talk to you first and after the first Sky Tunnel was successful."

Marianne took her mother's hands in hers. "I want you to. I want to read the complete story. Especially if we never go to meet Bar."

Another deep trembler hit El Paso, shaking the house and its furnishings.

"They never had these quakes in Bar's El Paso, did they?" asked Marianne.

"Not earthquakes. But it was a rough town when it was known as Franklin. We share a cemetery with Alt Earth. The connection between the two realities is closest there. Which is one reason I was able to return."

"And why you moved here, Mom?"

"Yes, dear. I feel close to the people I left

behind here."

Marianne walked over and hugged her mother. "You'll have my support. Always. I'll turn the television back on, see what the trembler did."

"Alright, Marianne." Reylie stood over the sink as she cleaned up from lunch. She looked out the window at the Franklin Mountains, and some memories stirred.

Yes, she thought. *I must write my story for the sake of Marianne. And for Bar.* Reylie smiled. *He would be so proud of our daughter.*

Reylie could have sworn she heard a familiar voice whisper in her ear. "I am, my love. I am."

Reylie King-Mann pulled the sedan over to the side of Interstate 10. She and her daughter Marianne were on the outskirts of El Paso, Texas, and en route to Fort Bliss to meet Mike Mann, Reylie's husband, and Marianne's stepfather.

"What Is It, Mom?" Marianne asked.

"Call it a flashback. To when I first rode into El Paso in another—reality."

"With my father, Bar?"

"Yes, dear. Writing my memoirs is giving me feelings of déjà vu. With our world falling apart and us planning to relocate via Sky Tunnel, thanks to my and your Uncle Ron's trip down the rabbit hole, I get this feeling of unreality when I see something—that takes me back to that Old West world. We thought that was our permanent new existence."

"Care to talk about it, Mom? "

Reylie took a deep breath, then let it out. "Yes, why not? There is no hurry to get to Fort Bliss. Ron and I were with Bar and the bunch when we came down a trail from the Franklin Mountains foothills to an El Paso, a helluva lot different than the El Paso of today…"

"There she is," said Uncle Jake McCain. "The edge of El Paso formally called Franklin."

"El Paso Del Norte is the Mexican side?" asked young Reylie.

"You got it, missy. I know a lot of people in El Paso. The Second Mexican War is making it grow like a bad weed. People are pushing to put the railroad through here."

"Hope there are fewer Greasers," growled Bar McCain, nephew of Uncle Jake.

"The truce stopped the war and blamed on the French and Europe, but there are still a lot of hard feelings, so I expect there will be fewer Mexicans crossing. But some have family on both sides."

"They can just stay away from me. Any Alcalde types had better tread lightly."

"Those are the upper class?" asked Ron,

Reylie's brother.

"Yep. They own the haciendas and use peons to work them. I hear the peons have to get permission to leave the hacienda, move to another town."

"Indentured servants," said the Cajun Armand Bergeron.

"We have Irish indentured servants in the King family tree," said Reylie.

"A lot of Texans are Scots-Irish. The Celts were warriors," Bar said.

"Where's we gonna stay?" asked Tim.

"Not in a bawdy house or brothel," stated Bar. The oversized man shifted in his saddle. "We had enough of that in Las Cruces."

"Well, we had our ashes hauled," Tom said with a wide grin. "And, I think Ron also did."

Ron began to blush at the reminder he had been a virgin until Buffalo Susan's whore house.

"I'd go easy on Ron," said Uncle Jake. "He shot that clean Mexican through, killed him dead. One Bullet Ron. Yessir, he has a new name."

"Well, we need none of that in El Paso," said Bar. "We need to lay low for a few days, watch for the Pinkertons. Then we'll send a telegraph to the King Ranch, tell them we have two kin to put on a stage to them."

Reylie glanced at Ron. The day was fast

approaching when they would have to disburse people of that story. But not just yet,

"So, Pinkertons will still try to apprehend you in El Paso?" asked Reylie.

"Yes, missy, they will try," answered Uncle Jake as he scratched his greying beard. "But the local Rangers and Marshals, not to mention the Sheriff, don't much like the Pinkertons. They are always sneaking around without contacting the local law. We are the Independent State of Texas. We're different than the other states."

"But you're in the United States," said Reylie.

"Yes, missy. Up there in Washington Territory, you probably don't hear much of our goings-on. However, Texas cuts its own trail. Our Governor-General confers with the U.S.Congress, the President, about dealings with other countries. Ole Sam Houston set Texas to be independent as possible from the start. So when we joined the U.S. after the First Mexican War, we did away with the President of Texas but created a superior governor position in our Governor-General."

"Who is it today?"

"Sam Walker."

Reylie and Ron looked at each other. "Of Walker-Coult fame?" asked Ron.

"Yes, the same. How'd you youngins know so much about Coult Firearms?"

"Our grandfather and father," said Reylie. "They taught us a lot about firearms. Grandfather had a replica—a Walker Coult. I shot it once. It almost knocked me on my rear end."

Uncle Jake laughed.

"You two are full of surprises. I'll have to help you shoot mine when I get the cylinder fixed."

"Um, we heard Sam Walker was shot and killed in the First Mexican War," added Ron.

"The Mexicans shot him but did not kill him. He is one tough hombre. He gave me my Walker."

"You served with him?"

"Hell, yes. I left the farm in 1842 to join the Rangers. Farming bored me, but not Bar's father, William."

"It bored me too," interjected Bar. "Which is why I left to join the Rangers, joined up in '59."

"How old were you?" Reylie asked.

"Fifteen. Born in '44, like the caliber of my Root Coult."

"He was already big for his age," said Uncle Jake. "Some of the Rangers said his size would wear out the horses and eat up all the vittles."

"You joined up at sixteen, Uncle. What's the difference?"

"Lied about my age also. I was born in 1826. My father fought at the Battle of San Jacinto in 1836 for

Texas independence. He took some gold off a dead Mexican officer. That helped buy the spread up on the Colorado River north of what became Austin, Texas."

"How did you wind up near Fort Stockton?" asked Reylie.

"That was my brother William's doing. Our father put some gold aside and helped William, as the eldest son moved to the Fort Stockton area after the First Mexican War. The Fort itself did not happen until 1859 when people got tired of fighting Comanches, Apache, and others in the area. Us Rangers had taken care of the fighting until then."

"Less jawin', more ridin'," Bar said. "When we enter the town, Uncle Jake, you take Reylie and Ron with you; no flirting with the ladies. I'll find a livery stable for our horses while Armand, you ride herd on the two Olsen brothers. Go buy a beer or something, but no getting drunk. Stay on El Paso Street, and I'll find you."

Everyone grunted or mumbled their agreement.

"I'll take these to our friends El Paso Guns and Leather," said Uncle Jake. "That way, they can watch me wheel and deal for some more shootin' irons."

"Just stay low, Uncle. And watch out for Pinkertons. I'll ask at the livery for places to stay."

Five minutes later, as they neared the town limits, Uncle Jake handed a pistol to Armand. "Here. A Coult Army in .44 rimfire. That Frenchy pinfire ammunition is too hard to find these days."

"I will acquiesce to your expertise, Jake," the Cajun said with a smile.

The band broke up into the pre-planned groups. Bar cantered ahead as the others went to opposite sides of El Paso Street. Despite the dust and smells of horseshit and other noxious odors, Reylie was fascinated by the hustle and bustle of 1868 El Paso, Texas. It was growing as the bad weed Uncle Jake mentioned. Other substantial side streets connected to El Paso Street. Reylie looked down one and saw the signs of at least one bordello. The town was rapidly becoming a city.

Reylie also saw Mexican Vaqueros on horseback, with some of the locals giving them the stink eye, while others tried to attract their attention and wallets. Saloons and cantinas seemed plentiful, as were the street vendors. A young Mexican boy ran up to Reylie, displaying roasted corn on the cob of the colorful Mexican maize variety. Uncle Jake swore at him in Spanish and threatened him with his boot spur.

"Keep them back, Reylie. Half of them are pickpockets, and the rest will sell you what they just stole."

"They're just kids," said Ron.

"Kids who will offer you their sisters and then rob you blind. You're a *gringo*, easy target."

Uncle Jake finally reined in his horse. "There, on

the right. El Paso Guns and Leather. Come on. We'll do some wheeling and dealing with that Magnum cartridge while we wait for Bar."

The three tied their mounts on the rail in front of the establishment.

"Bring your saddlebags in if you don't want them rifled."

"Yes, Uncle Jake."

"Some places hire young boys to keep others away. There is a lot of poverty around. A lot of Mexicans and a few Americans lost everything during the War. If you see a veteran soldier missing a leg, you'll understand."

Reylie did not mention both her grandfather, father, and uncle were all military veterans. It would be too confusing.

The double doors into El Paso Guns and Leather were wide open, and Uncle Jake let out a bellow.

"I hear tell a fat old border rat, a former Ranger by the name of Kolster, runs this den of iniquity."

A bellow came from a back room behind the long shop counter. "That must be Jake McCain. Only he uses his tongue like a five-dollar whore."

A large man with an equally large belly and mustache pushed through a curtain and greeted Jake with a wide grin. "Jake—oops, you have a young lady with you. Sorry about the rough language. Is she kin, Jake?"

"Nossir, Bar, and I are just helping her, and her brother make it to their family. Reylie, Ron King, meet Greg Kolster. We Rangered together."

The big man put out a paw of a hand to shake. Reylie and Ron both shook it as the gunshop owner kept talking. "Business has been good in the repair, not so much the sale of guns—too many surplus military smoke poles."

"Mexicans still making all those cartridge revolvers?"

"Yes. The Mexes take all the cap and ball pistols from the War, bore out the cylinders, and make them take rimfire and the new centerfire shells."

"What about the Smith and Wesson patents and copyright?" Reylie interjected before she knew what she was doing. Both of the older men stared at her.

"You used to be in the gun business?" Greg Kolster asked.

"She reads a lot," said Ron. "She also has a photographic memory."

"What is that?" asked Uncle Jake.

"It means," interrupted Reylie, "when I read something, it's like I have a photo of it in my mind. You both have photographs of your family and friends, yes?"

"I have some French Postcards from up Las Cruce's way," replied Greg.

"Don't show those, Greg. Missy here gets the point. To answer your question, it won't do any good to sue a Mexican gunsmith or worker at some hacienda. Who's going to collect the fine? The military."

"Yeah, Jake," said Greg. "We should have invaded Mexico when we had the chance, made it ours. The Campesinos and us would both be better off. Mexico, even without the French meddling, is still a cesspool."

"What is the quality of the guns?" asked Ron.

"Some are good, and some are shi—uh, junk. I have some guns people brought in as they needed cash."

Greg pulled several examples out of storage cabinets and laid them on the counter. "Mostly Coults. A couple of Remingtons."

"You don't sell Smith and Wesson pistols?" asked Ron.

The store owner sneered. "Nigger and John Brown guns. Forget that. Let the Mexicans buy them."

Uncle Jake handed Greg his Walker with the blown cylinder and gave it to Greg. "Overload?" asked the gunsmith.

"One too many," Jake said with a laugh.

"Want a new cylinder?"

"If you can find or make me one, yes."

"I can modify a Root Coult cylinder.

Better steel."

Uncle Jake put a five-dollar gold piece on the counter. "This cover it?"

"Hell, Yeah. Bought some Army surplus for pennies on the dollar."

Jake laid another coin on the counter. "Need some.44 Short, .44 Long, a full powder horn, and some lead we can cast for bullets. Oh, and some .32 and .38 rimfire also."

"Pick stuff up tomorrow, Jake?"

"That'll be fine. Oh, one other thing.

Uncle Jake pulled out the Magnum bullet from Ron's Ruger pistol. "I have something to show you, Greg."

The shop owner took the silver-colored shell from his friend.

"The shell casing is nickel," said Uncle Jake.

"It's pretty, that is for sure," said Greg, then he frowned. "What is this 357 MAG stamped on the base?"

"Young man says It stands for three fifty seven Magnum. That is the bullet nomenclature. Now, pop the bullet out and take a look at the powder."

Greg found some pliers and managed to pull the bullet from the casing. He poured the powder on the counter. "That ain't black powder," he said.

"If you soak high-quality cotton in a mixture of nitric and sulphuric acid, get gun cotton, then gelatinize it in an alcohol-ether and stabilize it with amyl alcohol, you will get something similar to that; smokeless powder."

The two men frowned at Reylie. "What is smokeless powder, missy?" asked Greg.

"It is a fast burning powder which leaves little burning powder signature in the air, low smoke. It was developed by the French as Poudre B or Poudre Blanc. "

"Is this your picture memory at work?" asked Uncle Jake.

"Yes, sir."

The gunshop owner rummaged in some drawers, talking as he looked. "Let me find a pencil and paper and write all this down. I have a chemist friend at the pharmacy."

"Guncotton is very unstable," added Reylie. Ron poked her and tried to give her the 'shut up' sign.

"I heard of that, Reylie," said Uncle Jake. "You two must have had some interesting conversations with your kin."

"Yes, we did."

Despite Ron's silent protests, Reylie repeated what she said. As she was finishing, three men in long dusters walked through the front double doors.

"Be with you in a moment, gentlemen," said Greg. "Now, Reylie is this like nitroglycerine, the explosive."

"Yes, sir. It's related—"

"Jake McCain." The voice from behind the trio was loud and official.

"Never heard of him," Jake said as he shifted his stance by the counter, his right hand going under his trail jacket. As he grasped the handle on his chopped barrel .44 Coult Army, the voice sounded again.

"You pull a hogleg from your belt, and you'll be whistling through your chest."

"Mister, whoever you are, I'm just here with my friend Greg to get a new cylinder for my Coult Walker. It blowed up, and I carried it for years in the Texas Rangers—"

"We have a warrant for your arrest out of California," another voice spoke. Reylie turned and looked at the three figures as she slipped her hand onto the pistol in her oversized handbag.

"Sir, I do not see any badges. Are you U.S. Marshals?" she asked while presenting her best young lady smile.

"Pinkerton Detective Agency hired by the Bank of Mexico," said the tall, dark man with the first official-sounding voice.

"Well, Mister. This ain't California, and it sure as Hell isn't Mexico," said Uncle Jake. "So why don't you all just wait outside till we're done here, and then we can talk."

As he spoke, Uncle Jake straightened up and took his hand off of his Coult. Greg Kolster slid a Remington .46 cartridge revolver into Jake's left hand on the shop counter.

"What's the charge?" asked Ron.

"None of your goddamned business, boy," said the man. "Are you going to come peaceable, or do I have to shoot you in the back?"

Reylie and Ron looked at the three men as they both shifted away from the counter. They saw the three men in dusters looking as if they stepped out of an Old West movie from their world.

"One of you isn't named Wyatt Earp, are you?" asked Reylie with the smile still plastered on her face.

"Who?" The third man finally spoke through a bushy beard.

"Take it outside, boys," said Greg. "This is my establishment, and this is Texas. We do it differently here."

All three men pushed their trail dusters back to reveal large holstered revolvers.

"If those two youngins get shot," said Man Number Two, "it will be on your head."

"Leave us alone," replied Ron as his hand moved towards his Ruger.

"One more inch, boy, and you'll—"

A massive fist smashed into the side of the head

of Man Number Two. Bar's blow drove him into the tall and dark first speaker. The third bearded Pinkerton tried to spin around and draw his pistol at the same time.

"*No!*" Reylie screamed, letting her handbag drop to the floor as she pulled her gun and cocked the hammer in a blink. Reylie fired before she realized she had. The .32 slug struck the bearded man in the groin. His pistol dropped to the floor as his mouth opened into a silent scream. Bar slammed him into the other tangled pair, and all fell in a heap. His Root Coult appears in his hand as he began to curse in a red rage.

"Fucking Pinkerton pieces of shit, gunplay on young women—"

"Bar! *No!*" Reylie yelled as she lowered the pistol in her shaking hand. "Please. They are down and out."

Reylie's voice had an instantaneous effect on Bar. He glanced at her, then reholstered his Coult. Uncle Jake stood over the heap of humanity on the shop floor and kept the Remington trained on them as Bar disarmed the three. The groin shot Pinkerton joined the one struck by Bar in unconsciousness. Bar yanked some folded papers from the tall, dark man and read them.

"Warrant for you out of California, based on crap from Mexico. Just you, Uncle. Oh, and unnamed— accomplices. Ten cent word, ain't it?"

"You all better leave," said Greg. "I'll handle the law. The Rangers and the rest do not like Pinkertons in El

Paso. They got swelled head after protecting Lincoln from those death threats by the Frogs and Mexicans."

"They don't have authority in Texas?" asked Ron as he put his arm around his shaking sister.

"Nope. U.S. Marshals are supposed to talk to the Rangers before doing anything in Texas," Uncle Jake answered. "The Independent State of Texas still means something."

"Okay. We leave," said Bar. "Reylie, you can put your pistol away."

"Oh. Sorry."

"We'll pick up the things tomorrow, Greg, plus a .38 Coult Police for the pistolera here," said Uncle Jake as he laid a wad of Mexican paper pesos on the counter. "You can probably get more from these than I can. Just remember where you got that there smokeless powder shell."

Greg laughed. "Come back tomorrow. Hope to have more fun, keeps me young."

Uncle Jake laid the borrowed Remington on the counter, and the four left. "How'd you come up when you did, Bar?" asked Greybeard.

"I saw those three talking to a bunch of the Mexican street boys. They had Pinkerton written all over them. Those dusters were too clean for cattlemen who work for a living."

"Damn, Bar. I'm famous."

"You need to shave that beard. Change the way you look, Uncle."

"I guess so." The four mounted up, and Bar led the way to a livery stable a few blocks down. As they checked their horses in, Bar watched for signs of lawmen looking for them. He saw none.

"I guess Greg Kolster tells a good story."

"He used to Ranger in El Paso. He knows everyone. They'll take those Pinkertons to the state line with New Mexico Territory and dump them off after the law patches them up."

Bar walked over to a still shaken Reylie. "You did good, missy."

"It happened so fast. I was on auto-pilot."

"Well, I don't know that means, but you did what needed doing. And you kept me from splattering the Pinkertons' brains all over the gunshop."

Reylie took a deep breath, then let it out. "Well, I guess I'm a pistolera like Uncle Jake said."

Bar put his massive arm around her. "Come on. We'll find a good hotel, and you can have a hot bath with no soiled doves around."

Reylie smiled. "Yes. That would be nice. And no Pinkertons, either."

"So, did he die?" asked Marianne.

"You mean the man I shot?" replied her

mother, Reylie.

"Yes. You shot the Pinkerton in the groin. Did he die?"

Reylie and Marianne waited in the parking lot of the Space Force local command building on Fort Bliss, Texas. Even though Fort Bliss was a traditional U.S. Army Base, many Space Force operations moved to the interior of the United States since the beginning of the Problems. Earthquakes along major fault lines on the West Coast, tsunamis, massive shifts in weather patterns led to the federal government moving primary functions and projects to more stable areas. El Paso, Texas, was one such place. Tremblers made their way to West Texas but nowhere near the massive coastline shifting earthquakes of California. Much of Los Angeles and San Francisco now sat beneath a fathom of water and increasing by the month.

Now, Reylie and Marianne waited at the Space Command building for Mike Mann, Reylie's husband, and Marianne's stepfather. Mike had been the only father she had ever known, so she considered him Dad. Marianne had two half brothers, the twins, who were with Reylie's mother at the house in West El Paso. Jack and John had inherited a slight permanent tan from Mike due to his mixed-race heritage. Marianne's skin was lighter, with some of her mother's freckles but her biological father's dark hair instead of Reylie's bronze.

"You know, I am not sure," replied Reylie. "I know he probably had trouble siring children, as they called it back then."

Marianne chuckled. "That must have been a sight," said the daughter.

"Well, we did not stick around and wait for the law to show up."

"Well, come on, Mother. We're here early, and Dad usually runs late. Tell me more."

Reylie smiled at Marianne. She was so much like Bar McCain. Once she got her teeth into a bone, there was no letting go until Marianne got what she wanted.

"So, that was your adventure in El Paso, Mother?"

"Half of it. There's more as we spent some time in Texas, which is why I have a soft spot in my heart for the state."

"You were, and are, quite the woman, Mother."

Reylie looked at her daughter. "I did what I had to. I'm proud of some of it. Other things—not so proud."

Marianne patted her mother's arm. "Well, I'm glad you did it all. I would not be here if you hadn't."

Reylie kissed her daughter. "That is what has kept me going. You gave me hope. You still give me hope. When you have children, you'll feel the same."

"Until then, Mom. Let's get Dad. Then you can tell me the rest of the story."

Hours later, Marianne and Grandma Jeanie put the twins to bed in a suite at the ski resort near Reyadosa, New Mexico, to allow Mike and Reylie some alone time. She lay in bed, his strong arms wrapped around her. Reylie was glad the rumors of telepathy were not valid as Mike might not understand how this moment reminded her of one well before she had met her current husband.

Mike kissed her forehead. "Missed me?"

"Couldn't you tell? I may not be a randy young college student, but I still appreciate an old fashion roll in the hay."

"Yeah. You did seem to be very appreciative of certain parts of my anatomy."

Reylie slapped his broad chest and tried not to giggle like a young schoolgirl. She looked at his permanent tanned arm, the result of mixed ancestry. His skin color would have been a problem in the Game World Reylie and Ronald had spun into thanks to The Game. Now, Mike, who would have been a second-class citizen in that world, was using Game technology to help humanity survive.

"Well, there is something I need to pass on that involves your previous—adventures," Mike said.

"What is that?"

"Since that chance attempt which located you and your brother in what we can call, the Sky Tunnel has led us to find unique targeting systems."

Reylie frowned.

"What do you mean?" she asked.

"In a nutshell, we can send people back to the time and place you left some years ago."

Reylie sat up and stared. "Wait a minute. There was a time difference between this Earth and that Earth. Now, with some twenty years past, there is even a bigger time difference. And when the rescue mission found us by as much chance as by skill, we were lucky another doorway back could be opened. Then the connection with my grandfather's device in the game shorted out and stopped working."

"Yes, and it took us almost twenty years to discover how to do it again. But with a special twist."

"Mike, I thought the Sky Tunnel was for star and space travel."

"Which also involves time. Remember, time and space are connected."

"Alright, dearest. Cut through the B.S. What are you saying?"

"The Sky Tunnel can send you back to within a month of when you and Ron left."

In the middle of the night, Reylie went to the bathroom. She washed her face and then looked in the mirror. Her mind seemed to see a fourteen-year-old Reylie staring back at her as she appeared to be transported back to the first week of her meeting Bar, all those many years ago.

"Would you go back to see Marianne's father? Would you find Bar?" Reylie said to her reflection; she so wanted Bar to know he had a daughter. God, if only he could see her. Bar would be so proud of his daughter; would see the fantastic young lady she had become. Marianne had so much of Bar's genetic makeup that his better characteristics had bred true.

Reylie sighed. She would have to discuss this matter with her daughter once again—soon.

Two days later, the powers that be dragged Reylie and her husband into a media event about the actions, both recent and past, around the Sky Tunnels. After all, people were afraid of the Earth trying to tear itself apart. The idea of Reylie's adventures led to the science of Sky Tunnels and would allow humanity to be rescued from their home planet and set to a New Earth was the subject of the day. Survival in the face of worldwide catastrophe would always be subject number one.

The Public Affairs officers for NASA and Space Command set up a controlled 'presser' to spread information without Reylie and Mike being beaten to death. Mike started with a detailed explanation as to what the Sky Tunnels found. Classifying information about inhabitable planets during a time of threatening death was asinine. It was also counterproductive and could lead to riots.

"Yes, we have at least six 'Earths' in range of our probes," said Mike. "And yes, the crews on the star probes named two planets in honor of Reylie and Ronald King. Let's face it; without them falling down a rabbit hole through the Tinker's Game, we would not be here."

"Jason Thomas from International Science News. Are these planets actual Alternate Earths like in Reylie King's case?"

"They are Earth-type planets, but only one seems to have an alternate timeline existence for similar primate species. On that Earth, the timeline divides after the last ice age, which lasted much longer. Humanity is still in a tribal environment, just about to enter the Copper and Bronze Age. What we call Neanderthals and Cro Magnons intermarried to such an extent that the shorthand name for humanity is Crothals. Our human explorers have yet to make contact with some one million individuals."

"Valentina Aguilar from Azteca News. So, no other Earths with two Mexican Wars."

Someone always returned to the wars and violence of Bar McCain's world. There were times Reylie wished she had never given any details about her and Ron's adventures and challenges. People always concentrated on racism and violence as if today's world was that much better.

"Not that I know of," answered Mike.

"Rumors are that scientists and the government have the capability of sending people back within weeks of Reylie King's timeline on her Alternate Earth. Could we thus send people back to right the wrongs of that society?"

Reylie tensed up. Invariably, someone brought up the idea of 'what are we to do about all that racism and injustice' as if it was a moral imperative to change that Earth's timeline. So far, science had not found a way to send people back in time to this America's Civil War. Reylie imagined what would happen if someone could. It would be a horrendous mess. She stood up. "Since we are talking about an Earth I have intimately associated with, please let me answer."

"So, Ms. Aguilar, at what point in time would you wish the timeline of what is called Gameworld Earth be changed?"

"Well, stopping the deprivations of the First and Second Mexican Wars would be a start. So, say, 1845 would be a good start point."

"But slavery was established by then. Thus, your focus is only on Mexico."

"Having Mexico in control of the Southwest and California would be an excellent start. Those areas would be non-slavery areas."

"But then what? The Mexican government was at war with the local native people. How would that be improved?'

"I submit the proven racism of the Northern Europeans would be limited."

"But the peons in Mexico, the Indios put to work on the Catholic Church property, how would their lot improve?"

"Through time enlightened rulers in Mexico—"

"And who would that be? The foreign governments who came and took over parts of Mexico demanding payments of debt? Foreign troops pushed innocent Campesinos into war. You don't think the foreign officials would be any more understanding than they were, do you? Debt and power were all they cared about, not helping the average peasant."

"Well, maybe someone would have killed your precious racist Bar McCain before he killed more Mexicans and Blacks," sneered the reporter.

"Which means Ron and I would be dead. The drones sent out would not locate us, so the development of the Sky Tunnel technology may be delayed decades as it would be assumed to be automatically deadly. Thus, we would not be having this conversation about escaping a self-destructing planet."

Just then, a ten-second trembler shook the

building. After it ended, Reylie said, "I think Mother Nature just proved my point. Attempts to change timelines in any past may have unintended consequences, whether the intentions are noble. I never claimed Bar and others were saints. They were who they were, and they helped me get back here. For that, our society should be grateful."

The reporter sat down angrily. Reylie saw she was a Social Justice Warrior who wanted someone punished for wrongs in the past, like killing Hitler before World War Two. Yet no one mentioned Stalin or the various empires of the day, which were not known for POC civil rights.

A half hour later, Reylie and Mike made their escape. The couple went to their home in West El Paso, Texas. Recently the federal government purchased a house nearby for permanent security detail. As more and more information on 'West World' as some called it came out, more and more upset people tried to contact Reylie and Ron. There was enough conflict in the world due to the rapidly deteriorating status of Earth that Reylie never could understand why people felt a need to yell and scream about events in the past of an alternate Earth. Reylie thought some of the more radical critics felt she and Ron should have died just because they did not fight for social justice enough. Their survival and return led directly to the Sky Tunnel method of rescuing humanity. That fact became lost on the social warriors. In recent weeks, the protests became more violent.

Reylie's mother lived with Reylie and Mike full-time, which helped out keeping the twins under control. Before The Troubles, as people came to call the earthquakes and other disasters, West El Paso had grown out towards Las Cruces, New Mexico, so it wasn't easy to see where one city started and the other ended. With the Troubles came abandoned homes and closed businesses. The two towns became more separated. When Reylie compared the current cities and towns in the area to what she experienced with Bar in his world, it was two different universes.

The early Fall in El Paso was a much more pleasant time than the summer's oppressive one hundred degrees heat. Mike was out in the backyard near the pool and grilled while the twins splashed around. The history of relatively lower housing cost compared to other areas meant that the purchase price of a two-story four-bedroom home with a pool was half of that in other areas. Of course, places like California and the major fault systems were basket cases from where people fled, not approach.

Grandmother Jeanie brought the side dishes out to the picnic table set up near the pool. She smiled at the twins cavorting in the pool.

"To be young again, with few cares," Jeanie said.

"Which is why we got the Hell away from the West Coast," said Mike as he flipped some burgers, ribs, and chicken breasts. "All the earthquakes, fires, and sea storms were just too stressful."

"True, Mike. An occasional trembler here is not a big deal." The older woman looked at her daughter's husband. "Before she and Marianne get here with the additional drinks, I am forever grateful she met you. Missing over four years from her life because The Game yanked her from here is bad enough. Then for her to feel like she is stuck married to a man in another universe—that would be just too tragic."

Mike smiled at Jeanie. "I'm glad I met the love of my life also. But I do owe Bar the fact he kept Reylie alive in a world of violence and mayhem."

"What if the powers to be decided to yank him here? I heard that is possible."

Mike shrugged. "Over eighteen years have passed in Reylie's life. She is not the woman Bar would remember. I don't think it would be a problem."

"And Marianne, his biological daughter?"

"She treats me as Dad. But I think she has a right to meet her father, Bar. And he has the right to see her if we could physically do it."

"So, what are you talking about?" Reylie said as she walked in with a box full of various bottles and cans. Behind her came Marianne with a cooler full of ice.

"Solving all the problems of the world while I finish with the meat," replied Mike.

"Well, I hope you are all done, as my daughter and I are hungry," said Reylie. Then she put her fingers to her mouth and loudly whistled as Bar taught her.

"Out of the pool, young men. Soups on."

That evening the twins were playing video games as the adults sat around the large dining room table. They watched the excerpts from the press conference. Reylie watched Marianne frown as the press asked the questions about somehow changing the conditions in an alternate reality often called Westworld.

"Why do they have to judge people and demand they change when it is all in the past? Don't they understand the ripples in time, if they could affect the past, may cause unforeseen consequences?"

"People want to feel in control, to right wrongs," said Reylie. "The problem is trying to right wrongs that occurred a century ago, and in this case, in an alternate reality."

Marianne looked at the only father she knew, Mike. "So what if we could snatch my biological father and bring him to this universe. Would you be okay with that?"

Mike smiled. "As I told your mother earlier, I owe Bar for keeping her alive. He may have racist opinions towards me; a person in his time like me may be classified as a half-breed or mulatto, so if he came here, there might be a period of education. But putting him on trial for past wrongs in an alternate universe? Where would it end?"

"That is very understanding of you, Dad. But I could see people demanding reparations for alleged descendants in the name of fairness for that universe."

"Which, in my opinion, would solve nothing. Even today, there are areas of slavery and racism. How about we deal with today instead of beating people over the head for sins committed by grandparents, long since dead."

"That sounds logical to me, Mike," interjected Reylie. "But our shakey Earth is causing a lot of fear and anger. We nasty monkeys seem to need a lashing out to fight off the fear and anger."

"Which is why the people I am working with want to start sending people through the Sky Tunnel system as soon as possible. That will reduce some of the pressure."

Space Command gave Mike some time off to depressurize as well as exercise under full gravity and not behind anti-radiation shielding. While Marianne took classes at the University of Texas, El Paso (UTEP), Reylie began running and working out with her husband.

"The four years plus in an actual Old West made

me used to hard work and lots of physical activity," said Reylie. "I miss it sometimes."

"So you wanted to punch cattle along with Ron on the McCain spread?" Mike asked with a grin.

"That term came into use here when the railroads became the go-to method to move lots of cattle," replied Reylie. "Chisum called his people cattlemen, range hands; cowboys came a bit later."

Mike shook his head as they jogged. "I still find it unbelievable that you and Ron wound up in the one alternate reality discovered with a direct connection to our history."

"In all the discussions I have had, in all the debriefings, no one there could explain why only we wound up in Westworld. Except for the search and rescue personnel who came looking for Ron and me, the others wound up in the other unique Game Worlds."

The couple slowed to a walk as they cooled off. "You plan on writing about the other Game Worlds?"

Reylie sighed. "I'll get permission first, but I need to get all the stories recorded while actions are fresh in the minds of the participants. As the granddaughter of John King, the Tinkerer who led to all this inter universe comings and goings, I feel a family responsibility to record the correct and true history."

Mike smiled and put his arm around his love. "You know," he said, "you have an overdeveloped sense of duty for a non-military type."

"Guilty as charged. Now, let's get to the gym, finish our workout, then a nice big lunch at some restaurant. I'm hungry."

The trouble arrived as the couple went to their car. As Mike unlocked it, Reylie sensed then saw four figures approach the vehicle in a spread formation.

"Astronaut Mann?" an attractive female with a lovely smile said as she made a beeline towards Mike. Four years plus of life in an Old West environment, Comanche raid and all, gave Reylie a heightened sense of danger that never went away. She reacted automatically, grabbing the snubby revolver in her gym bag.

"Yes, can I help you?" Mike replied.

Two large males lunged and grabbed at Reylie as the female pulled an object from her purse. Reylie had the pistol out and shot the nearest man in his genitals. He screamed and fell against his partner. The collapsing body prevented the second man from getting a good grip on Reylie as she jabbed the barrel of the revolver into his right eye. This blonde man yelped in pain and grabbed at his damaged eye, stumbling back.

A gunshot from across the parking lot turned the lovely female's smile into a red mess as an aero spray can fell from her grasp. The redheaded woman collapsed to the parking lot pavement, dying. A Space Command

Security Agent began yelling commands as she CQB moved towards the situation. The remaining male tried to turn and run. He was grabbed and slammed to the ground by a now enraged Mike.

Within moments an additional Security Agent appeared and began placing zip ties on the miscreants. Sirens blared as police and medical personnel responded.

"You okay?" Mike asked as he stood next to his wife and watched the police deal with the problem. The shot redhead was dead; the groin shot male was alive but fading fast.

"As people in the Old West say, this is not my first rodeo, Mike."

Mike hugged Reylie as he spoke. "I keep forgetting you are a trained and experienced pistolera. Another thing we can thank Bar for after some eighteen years."

The Space Command Agents debriefed the couple, and the local police took statements. It seemed the group of four was intent on kidnapping the couple, the aerosol can containing a sedative spray. The man Mike slammed to the ground sang like a bird after he saw the dead redhead and bleeding companion. They were members of some Truth Squad who wanted to use Mike and Reylie's bargaining chips to attempt history revision in Westworld. Now, the surviving fanatics would spend years in prison; or would disappear. Nothing must interfere with the Sky Tunnel Project.

The Space Command upper echelon was a bit miffed that Reylie shot the guy instead of an Agent.

"You'll get over it," said Reylie to the voice on the telephone and then hung up.

"My wife; how to make friends and influence enemies."

"Fuck them, Mike. I had to survive for some four years with no Space Command. They just have to realize I can still do it. They owe the King family, and you, Colonel Mann. We are the basis for Sky Tunnel. Next time, security can shadow us closer if worried."

"Hmmm. That female agent did look like someone we could shower with—"

"You are about to get walloped."

Space Command added security to the entire King and Mann families. A press conference reiterated the importance of the Sky Tunnel Project and the debt owed to Reylie and her family. A particular reporter from Azteca News received grief when she tried to blame the death of the alleged female kidnapper on Reylie and Mike as if their mere presence in public was a problem.

Two days later, Mike, Reylie, and Marianne shared lunch at a small Mexican Restaurant in Dona Ana, New Mexico. An extra team of Space Command Agents spent money in the restaurant to the pleasure of the owners.

"I know there is a reason you wanted us to eat here, Mom," said Marianne.

"This is close to the exact location where I caused a kerfuffle. A Mexican uncle called his niece a bitch and slapped her in 1868 Westworld, and I stepped in, or into it if Uncle Jake was here to express his opinion."

"So you stood up for what was right then, and today people say it isn't enough?" asked Marianne.

"Some people are never satisfied," interjected Mike.

"What did you eat?" Reylie's daughter asked.

"The best Arroz con Pollo I ever ate. Of course, your Uncle Ron and I were scared and hungry after a day of riding with some real desperado stagecoach robbers." Reylie looked around the restaurant as if expecting Bar or Uncle Jake to appear.

"Uncle Jake let us do the talking as he said our Spanish, or Mexican as Bar often called it, was better than his."

"You had some—fun—leaving, right?"

"Yes, Marianne. Armand had to cut the uncle a bit after he threatened to shoot us. Then the town marshal came after us. Bar got us out of that arrest."

"How, Mom?"

"Well, you can read the full details in my

completed stories, but suffice to say it was and combination of what they would call palaver and some application of just the correct amount of violence. Then it was on to Las Cruces and then El Paso."

Marianne fixed her gaze on her mother. "Did Bar, my father, kill anyone here?"

"Nope. Over time I also helped him control his temper, his violence."

Reylie looked at Mike, then her daughter. "Bar was far from perfect, but down deep, he was a good man. The prejudices of their world shaped Bar and Uncle Jake. I tried to re-educate them whenever I could. But the violence visited on his first wife and his sister—I know how I would feel if the same assholes who tried to grab Mike and I harmed you and the twins. So I understand that kind of thirst for vengeance, even if I did not condone it."

Marianne reached across the table and grasped her mother's hand. "Mom, I know you always tried to do what was right." The young lady then grasped Mike's hand.

"You're my Dad; you raised me. But Bar is my father; he is the reason I am here. I hope Mom delving into the history of her first husband, my father, never hurts you, Dad. I love you; I always will."

Mike reached over and hugged Marianne, then hugged Reylie. "Never worry about my feelings being hurt. As I have said many times before, Bar kept your mother, my wife, alive. He never abused her nor your Uncle Ron. He may have a problem with the color of my skin, but I still owe him."

Reylie blinked back tears, then waved for the waitress. "Time to test 21st Century Arroz con Pollo. And I could do with a beer."

That night Reylie laid in bed with her husband. She and Mike had made love after all the kids were asleep. However, Marianne was no longer a kid; she was a young lady. Reylie never quizzed her about her love life other than making sure she knew how not to get pregnant. Reylie trusted her daughter, saw Bar's streak of common sense in her. And, Reylie saw his toughness in her. She knew that inner strength would serve Marianne well in the coming days of the trembling and self-destructing Earth.

Reylie looked at her sleeping husband. A better spouse and father she could not hope for in a man. Most women were lucky to have two great mates in their lives. Reylie knew the gods smiled on her to give her two such men. Reylie also thought about life on the other side of the Sky Tunnel system. She knew that they would have to leave this Earth for another world. Reylie's Planet named after her? That may be a new reality.

Reylie looked at the ceiling as she considered

another option she never discussed with anyone. From what Mike, NASA, and Space Command said, there was a way to transport people to the reality of Bar's Westworld. It was an unspoken idea that 21st Century refugees from a dying planet could force a 19th Century civilization to accept them. After all, the Old West of Bar's world had expanses of unsettled land just like in the history of Reylie's America. However, there would be a bitter push back if the deprivations of the Native Tribes became part of this history. Were they wiping out massive herds of buffalo just to accept millions of people with superior technology? That could lead to another civil war. Of course, it sounded like the people of her Earth could send people two decades after the expansion of Manifest Destiny. However, that still begged the question of forced settlement. Reylie and her immediate family relocating near the McCains is one thing. Millions of people from all over the globe are something else.

The other Game Worlds provided alternate choices. Yet, there was still the problem of forced settlement into someone else's backyard. The more Reylie thought about it, the more it seemed that settling a world without a hominid population was best. Reylie's World reportedly had no such people. However, living on a planet named after you would be weird.

Reylie looked at Mike, sleeping blissfully. He had

never voiced these concerns to her despite being on the cutting edge of Sky Tunnel. Reylie smiled. He was waiting for her to express her ideas and concerns. After all, she had been the one with experience living years on a different planet, not him. She spooned up to Mike's muscular body and closed her eyes. She would finish writing the history and stories as soon as she could. Reylie thought it might be conceit, but her stories and the experiences of the others connected to the arcane game created by the Tinkerer, her grandfather John King, might help the people of her Earth decide.

Reylie King could only hope as she fell asleep.

CHAPTER 6
EL PASO: PART 2

Reylie King-Mann looked at her computer.

"Ron and my adventures in El Paso, Part Two," she said out loud.

It still caused a bit of an almost out-of-body experience when Reylie King-Mann, then called Reylie King, thought of the El Paso of 1868 Western World as she sat in her dining room in El Paso, Texas, 21st Century on her shaky Earth. The surrounding landscape looked a lot the same if you took away all the human habitations. However, when Reylie sat and thought about it, there was this feeling of connectivity, like not all of her had returned to this universe.

"Bar," Reylie whispered. "Over time and space, we still connect."

She and her brother Ron's trip to a Game World as some called them (thanks to Grandpa King's table Game he created, spun people into other realities and proved String Theory) led to the Sky Tunnel system and salvation from a world-shaking itself apart. Reylie still needed to document the experience of hers and others. After all, people needed to know the trials and tribulations of members of the King family and others who seemed to be yanked down Alice's rabbit hole. Without those trips into other universes and successful returns, the Sky Tunnel Project would not be a reality. Instead of expanding into other universes to save humanity, there would be some colonists on Mars racing against time for a new home for Earthlings.

Reylie cracked her knuckles. "This won't type itself, Bar," the mother of three said. "Now, where was I? Oh yeah, Bar showed up at just the right moment and got Ron, Uncle Jake, and me out of the gun store."

Bar saw a decent hotel after stabling his horse but had been distracted when he noticed the three Pinkerton Agents snooping around. Now he led Uncle Jake, Ron, and Reylie to the El Paso Royale.

"Come on, let's get some rooms. Uncle Jake, you're the youngin's Pa. Got it?"

"Got it, Nephew."

The desk clerk was a rather arrogant young man who saw the trail dust on their clothes and thought he could chase off the uncouth foursome. That was until Uncle Jake threw some silver coins on the counter, and

Bar put his face inches from the mustached man.

"Is our silver good enough? Or do I have to do something to convince you to give us some room keys?"

They soon had four rooms, one private one for Reylie despite her protests. "Ron and I—"

"You get your own room, missy. Young ladies need their privacy for—female matters." Bar spoke with a tone of authority, which told Reylie it would do no good to argue.

"So, you six men have to divide three rooms—"

"No. I'm having the Olsens split up with us. Uncle Jake will give them a large poke to live on until we meet up six months from now. Those Pinkerton's showing up so soon tells me a lot of people are looking for a bunch of hard cases of our description."

"What about Armand?"

"We'll see what he wants. And we have to get you two on a stage or wagon to the King Ranch."

Reylie had to bite her tongue. She was going to have disbursed him of the story she and Ron had a connection to the King Ranch in Texas. But not now, as Reylie had not figured out how she and Ron would survive in this world of the Old West.

"Here, room keys and money. Go to your rooms while I find the Olsens and Armand.

Bar turned to leave, and Reylie spoke. "Can you check on the man—you know."

"Not close up, Reylie. Wait for things to calm down, then I'll find out."

"Up to the rooms," said Uncle Jake. "I feel a need for a hot bath."

Reylie soaked in a large tub an hour later. The El Paso El Camino Real Hotel was a definite four-star establishment. She sipped a lemonade with honest to God *ice* in it. She read in a history book once that by the 1860s, people created ice houses by storing ice from the mountains in basements, warehouses, and covered with sawdust. The ice was sold to those who could afford it. Apparently, their band could.

Reylie was beginning to think either Uncle Jake kept more money from the stagecoach robbery than initially believed, or else the people they had shot in Las Cruces had a lot more money on them than Reylie imagined. Either way, the group seemed to have plenty of money.

There was a knock on the room door.

"Yes?" Reylie called out as she reached to a small end table set next to the tobe. On it was her .32 pistol.

"It's Bar. You about done?"

"I'm getting there. Is there a hurry?"

"Nah. Just let me know, and I'll show you how to clean your new pistol. Uncle Jake is back with a bunch of stuff."

"Okay. Just a few more minutes until the water cools down."

"Okay. Come next door when you're ready."

Reylie slid back down in the water until just her nose was above the surface. She had tied up her hair into a bun for the bath. She'd have to see if there was such a thing as a female barber or salon around El Paso and have her bronze hair correctly washed and combed out. *Another pistol,* she thought. *I'm turning into quite the gun moll of all those very old movies.*

Five minutes later and Reylie was out of the tub and drying herself off. She used a fine horsehair brush she had bought in Las Cruces to brush her hair. Then she dressed in the local nineteenth-century clothes Buffalo Susan had helped obtain for her. In the back of her mind, Reylie still wished she could have worked things out with the woman, business-wise. Some 21st Century CEOs could learn a thing or two from the madam and brothel owner.

Reylie finished with her ensemble and pinned her hair up. It made her look a bit older. The young lady knew she was growing up faster than she had ever imagined. Being thrown into this strange and rough world did that.

Reylie put her pistol in her oversized handbag and made her way to Bar's room. She knocked, and Bar bellowed, "Come in."

Uncle Jake and Bar had their various pistols disassembled on a large tarp spread atop the room's table. It took Reylie a moment to recognize a beardless Jake. She tried not to laugh but failed.

"What's so funny?" demanded Uncle Jake.

"Your face looks so pale without that bushy beard," replied Reylie with a smile. "At least you kept a bushy handlebar mustache. They gave you a nice haircut also."

"Call it what you want, but I miss my beard, missy."

"Had to go, Uncle Jake," said Bar. "I'm next for a cutting. The Pinkertons are looking for some bushy-haired hard cases. New city clothes and shined boots, no one should recognize us.

Uncle Jake scratched his newly shaven chin as he spoke. "Suit of clothes, huh? We'll have to buy Missy here a new dress, also. She'll need some extra duds for her and Ron's trip to King's Ranch."

Reylie's stomach tightened a bit upon hearing about her impending departure. "Well, Bar. You said Uncle Jake had a new pistol for me."

Bar took a spare bed cover from a hotel chest and wrapped it around Reylie. "We don't want to get your dress all messed up. Now, take a gander."

Bar held out a smaller version of a .44 caliber Coult. "Here. They call this a Coult Police, but Cooper

Arms made it in double action."

"So, it's not an original Coult?" asked Reylie.

"Based on it, but by making it double action, they dodged the patent restrictions. It's converted to .38 rimfire Smith and Wesson cartridge, and holds five shots."

Bar showed Reylie how to disassemble the pistol. Cooper Arms added a loading gate to the design so Reylie could reload it without breaking it down. The old-style double action was surprisingly smooth, in Reylie's opinion.

"Like it? Uncle Jake and I will take you back to the gunshop at sunset for some target practice in the shop's basement."

"This will fit in my bag. Thank you both. Though, I never imagined I would need a pistol up until—a few days ago."

"Well, missy, if you are going to take a long trip to the King Ranch, you'll need an Evenizer," said Uncle Jake. "God created men, but Colonel Coult made them all equal."

"That should apply to women also," added Reylie.

Bar demonstrated with his oversized pistols the art of cleaning black powder pistols with hot water with some brushes and rags.

"No gun solvent or oil?" asked Reylie.

"Don't know about any special solvent," answered Uncle Jake. "We use tallow, linseed, or whale oil for lubrication. Tallow's the cheapest, along with bear fat."

Reylie used a short brass rod to clean the bore of her new pistol, then loaded it. Jake had a small sheath holster for it. The young lady slipped the gun into a side pocket in her oversized handbag.

"Bar, did you find out about the man I shot?"

The broad man shrugged. "He went to the local doctor."

Reylie frowned as she replied, "It was so—automatic. I thought that man was going to shot you, or Uncle Jake, or Ron—"

"No worries, Reylie," said Bar. "You did right. Those Pinkerton's ain't real lawmen. They're just hired guns."

"I never hurt anybody like that, Bar."

"Don't worry. There is no chance you'll turn out like me, missy, if that is what worries you."

"We'll get you safe and sound to your relations in South Texas," interjected Uncle Jake.

Reylie took a deep breath, then let it out.

"Something else bothering you?" asked Uncle Jake.

"I—think we need to talk about this King Ranch—thing."

"Let me guess," said Uncle Jake, "they are not your kin."

"How'd you know?"

Uncle Jake looked at Bar, and the big man nodded. "We had talks while you slept," said Bar. "That Ruger revolver and ammunition is not like anything made in America. You just popped out of nothing at the campfire that night. You talk about things we have never heard of."

"And I am educated more than most," interjected Uncle Jake. "I figured that if lighting and electricity exist, why cannot some other power?"

Reylie sat silent. Their reaction was so unsuspected she had no idea where to go next. "So, where does this leave Ron and me?"

"You come with us to the family spread near Fort Stockton," replied Uncle Jake. "We can't let two tenderfoots go wandering around, no matter how quick with a smoke wagon you are."

"Why? You don't owe us anything. We have caused you a lot of trouble."

"We are rough men, used to rough ways," said Bar. "But that does not mean we are beasts. Only a sick bastard would leave some young woman to rot along the trail."

"I have to get Ron, see what he wants to do."

"Well, skedaddle and round him up. He should be

with Armand."

Five minutes later, with her brother Ron in tow, they were talking with the two McCains.

"So, what would we do on your ranch?" asked Ron.

"You'd learn how to be a wrangler. We deal more in horses than cattle," Bar said. "And we have some farmland if you like to work corn or wheat. My aunt Shar, Uncle Jake's younger sister, runs it right now with her husband, Adam."

"Would you stick around?" Reylie asked Bar.

The big man shrugged. "At least until you get settled. Uncle Jake and I will have to meet the Olsen twins and Armand in six months to split the strongbox money."

Brother and sister looked at each other. Ron nodded yes.

"Okay," said Reylie. "It's a deal. I'll have to be a wrangler also as I ride better than Ron."

"I was going to ask you to help the local schoolmarm," said Uncle Jake. "You know a whole bunch about a lot of subjects."

"Well, I can help out. But I refuse to be a second-class citizen. I may not be able to vote as a woman—yet—but I will someday."

Bar snorted. "A little firecracker, ain't we?"

"She does know how to handle a

pistol, Nephew."

"Well," added Bar, "Let's get to Fort Stockton first. Then we'll make sure everyone gets a share of decent living."

Reylie convinced the two McCains that they wanted to say goodbye to the Olsen twins. Tim and Tom came to Bar's room with hats in hand, slicked-back hair from a good haircut and bath.

"I hear you two are splitting up with us," said Reylie.

"Yes, ma'am. Uncle Jake thinks it's best we split up for a while. Throw the Pinks off our trail," said Tim, the 'older' of the twins.

"Will we be seein' you two again?" asked Tom, the younger.

"I think so. We are going to be staying with Bar and Jake for a while."

"Well, in case you take off, it's been right nice riding with you two," said Tom. He stuck his hand out to Ron. "I thought you might be too much of a Sugarfoot to hold your own, but the way you kicked that cowhand in the brothel—you can back me up any day."

"And you handle a gun real nice, for a good-looking filly," added his brother Tim.

For a moment, Reylie felt like she was stuck in a bad Western movie, then realized people talked and felt this way at one time, alternate timeline or no.

Tom elbowed Tim. "Mind your manners, boy."

"Who you calling, boy?" Tim snapped back.

"You start fussin' in my room, and I'll kick both your butts," growled Bar. "Now, finish with your goodbyes, and Uncle Jake will give you a poke to last you until we meet up on August thirty-first. You can find where we buried the strongbox, right?"

"Yes, sir," the twins answered in unison.

"Just don't get any ideas of visiting that place early," said Uncle Jake. "You'll get your fair share."

"We know better'n that, Uncle Jake," replied, "We ain't no gutter trash who'd try to rob pardners."

Reylie surprised the twins by hugging and kissing their cheeks. "You two, be careful until we can meet again."

"Will do, ma'am," Tim said with a bit of a blushed face.

Uncle Jake saw them out of the room.

"He'll pay them now?" Ron asked Bar.

"Uncle Jake will give the twins five hundred each plus some paper Pesos they can spend on the Border. They said they're heading to visit some family in San Antone."

"What about Armand?" asked Reylie.

"He's going to travel with us to Fort Stockton, then heads to New Orleans. The plan is to meet him here, in El Paso, then travel to the stash in New Mexico during August." Bar pulled a gold pocket watch out and checked the time. "Okay. I'm going with Uncle Jake to get a bath, a haircut, and a shave, and then I'm going to buy some new suit clothes. Can you two stay out of trouble?"

Reylie smiled as she answered. "We promise we will not get into a fight in a brothel like Las Cruces."

Bar grunted. "See that you don't. Now, I'm out of here for a couple of hours."

Bar turned and left. Ron and Reylie went to her room and locked the door. Reylie laid down on the bed as Ron sat in an overstuffed chair. "So, how do we make a living for the rest of our lives, Sister? I don't see us working on a ranch for fifty years."

"I have my school books, including history, math, and science. I also have some artistic talent, so I could work for a newspaper or publisher just with that while learning the business. You were always good at telling stories. Plus, the Information in the books gives us some options."

"Like making things years before they would appear naturally?" asked Ron.

"Yes. I assume we can do that with the smokeless powder in your shells. We need to have a written contract made for developing this so-called Powder B. Maybe we can file a patent application in

Washington, D.C. So, we get a piece of anything produced."

"Well, then we could set up a factory as Coult Firearms has in the Northeast. Or, maybe we could sell the formula to Coult, or Root, or whoever is in charge."

"Anyways, we have options until someone comes and gets us."

"Come on. Reylie. Do you think someone is coming to get us? How? And why?"

"The 'how' is Grandpa or someone else will figure out how that game he created works. 'Why' is that we are minors, and someone will want to find us if for no other reason but to prove the thing Grandpa made works."

Ron snorted. "Yeah, right. We'll probably be old and grey when that happens."

"You're wrong. Grandpa and Dad will never give up. Neither will Mom." Reylie's face flushed with anger. She did not need to hear the idea that they would be stranded forever in a place where the 'N' word was acceptable. Reylie knew their disappearance would be significant, even if it were to the so-called powers that be in the 21st Century.

"Fine, Reylie. Believe what you want. I plan on living as if this is it, and this is our life. Time to make the best of it."

"Well, I will never give up hope. I'll work hard to

survive, but I will never give up hope that someone will come after us."

Ron did not argue after that last statement. In his sister's eyes and the set of her jaw, he saw that further discussion would go nowhere. Ron changed the subject to discussing possible products in which the two siblings could develop and profit. Reylie pulled out a notebook and soon had a page full of ideas on making a living in the 1860s with 21st Century knowledge. The sun began to set as their brainstorming continued.

There was a knock on the hotel room door. "Bar is back with Armand and Uncle Jake," the voice reverberated through the door. Reylie went and opened the door, and her eyes widened. Bar stood in the doorway attired in a new suit of clothes that would not be out of place in 21st Century Seattle. On his head was the current form of a Stetson western hat. Uncle Jake had a similar outfit for new clothes plus the same hat. Armand rounded out the trio with a fresh suit coat, vest, and pants. All three had wrapped bulky packages that must be their old train clothes.

"My, aren't we the fashion plates," Reylie said with a wide grin. "And I see you, Bar, have added a bath, excellent haircut, and beard trim. Not to mention Armand has had his mustache newly waxed."

"I am not sure what fashion plate means, missy, but I will take it as a compliment," replied Uncle Jake.

"We all have nice new boots which will need breaking in to prevent blisters."

"Tomorrow will be your turn, Reylie and Ron. We'll get you some decent work clothes for both of you also."

"Where is all this money coming from?" asked Reylie. "Ron and I will owe you for the rest of our lives."

"We have plenty of coins," said Uncle Jake. "You earned it by helping us get out of Las Cruces and the El Paso Gunsmith store in one piece."

"Besides," interjected Bar. "You two became family not long after falling in our campfire. Things like that happen with a purpose."

"Well, when we make our first million," said Ron, "we'll pay you back with interest."

"First million?" asked Armand.

"Reylie and I have figured out a bunch of stuff we can design based on the knowledge we have, which some people like Rothschild, Vanderbilt, Trump, and Edison."

"Trump? Edison? Never heard of them," said Uncle Jake."

"While we are on the subject of making money, Uncle Jake, we need a contract for the smokeless powder Ron gave you," stated Reylie.

Uncle Jake laughed. "Your family will be rightly proud of you, missy. I can see why Buffalo Susan thought you would make a good business partner."

"Well," interjected Ron, "we do need to come up with some profit-sharing documents."

"We can discuss this over at the gunshop," replied Uncle Jake. "Reylie needs to test fire her pistol, and I need to pick up my repaired Walker."

The five friends made their way to the gunshop. Greg Kolster was waiting for them. He put a 'CLOSED' sign on the door and locked it as the five entered.

"Come on down to the basement. It took a bit to dig this through the thick band of clay that a lot of El Paso sits on, but I managed it, with some help from a bit of nitro."

"You know about nitroglycerin?" asked Reylie.

"Yes," replied the gun store owner. "I had to make a small batch here with my chemist friend as its transport is strictly controlled. They had some bad explosions while trying to build the railroad around these parts."

"That's the same chemist who is examining the smokeless powder?" Ron asked.

"Let's stop with the jawing and get to the shooting," interrupted Bar. "Reylie, test your pistol on that target yonder, at the end of this room."

Reylie looked at the kerosene lamp-lit area in the long and thin basement room. Greg had strategically placed some shined curved pieces of metal to help concentrate the illumination towards the end of this indoor range. She estimated the two targets tacked up at the end of the room sat fifteen yards away.

"Ready?" asked Bear.

"Yes. I'll shoot at the right target."

After putting some cotton in her ears, Reylie slid her new pistol from a pocket in her handbag. She let the bag slip to the hard dirt floor as she assumed a two-handed combat stance.

"Squeeze the trigger," she whispered as she obtained a decent sight picture. At least this double-action four-inch barrel pistol had a separate rear sight, not just a notch in the cocker hammer. The trigger squeeze was smooth for such an ancient design. Reylie achieved a surprise shot, so she did not jerk the pistol off target. The black powder discharge was not as sharp and violent as smokeless cartridges from her world.

"Damn. Bullseye," exclaimed Greg.

"I told you she is quite the pistoleer," said Uncle Jake.

"Fire the remaining four shells," directed Bar.

Four more shots resulted in four more hits, all in or touching the center ring.

"I think she likes that smoke wagon," Uncle Jake said with a wide grin.

"It does shoot nice," replied Reylie.

"Okay, my turn," said Uncle Jake. "You have my

repaired Walker?"

"Yes, I do," said the gunsmith. "I used a slightly used Root cylinder I modified to take .44 Extra Long Rimfire. The hammer I also shaped so it will discharge the new centerfire cartridges if you load them. Forty-five grains of black powder should be enough for you. Remember, the cylinder is like new, but the barrel and the rest are original."

"I understand. You should not abuse a twenty-year old pistol."

Greg handed Uncle Jake his pistol. "Loaded and ready to go. Six fresh factory shells."

Jake called out, "Watch yer ears," as he bladed his body a bit, cocked, and aimed the horse pistol one-handed. There was a satisfying *Boom!* and Jake put a hole in the bullseye of the virgin left side target.

"Yep," said Greybeard, "shoots right on." He turned his head a bit. "You youngins want to try?"

"Sure!" replied Ron. Uncle Jake handed him the larger than the standard revolver. Ron at first tried to aim it one-handed like Uncle Jake, and then he realized discretion was the better part of valor. Ron switched to a two-handed grip combat crouch.

"You two like that two-handed style, I guess," said Bar.

"We are not as large as you are, Bar," stated Reylie. The nephew grunted as Ron cocked the piece, aimed carefully, and fired. A satisfying boom, and he put a bullet hole next to Uncle Jake's.

"It kicks, but not as bad as a Magnum," opined Ron as he handed the pistol to Reylie. No one said anything as Reylie lifted the rather massive Coult, cocked the hammer, aimed, and fired. She absorbed the recoil of the big horse pistol, and the reward was a bullet hole next to Ron's.

"*Sacre bleu*," said Armand. "You shoot that Coult as if you were born to it."

"Maybe we were, Armand," answered Reylie as she handed the pistol to Uncle Jake. "I think such native-born skills will do us well in this strange land."

"Care to empty it, nephew?" asked Jake.

"Sure." The pistol seemed reasonably sized in Bar's bear paw of a hand. The man did not hesitate, but from a low crouch, cocked and fired one-handed, using no sights. All three rounds joined Uncle Jake's in the center of the bullseye.

"And the pistolman speaks," said Uncle Jake.

"Definite lite kick compared to my sixty-grain loads."

"Keep the reloads under fifty grain, Boys," said the gunsmith. "Or you will be back here crying for a new pistol."

"Not me," said Uncle Jake. "If it blows up, I'll leave it. Then maybe I'll buy a cartridge version of Bar's.

They started making .44 Extra Long cartridge guns the last couple years of the war."

"I like loading my own cylinders," said Bar as he handed Uncle Jake back his repaired Walker. "Then I know I have a full sixty grains of powder behind a hundred and fifty round ball or Minie round."

"Not a heavier bullet?" asked Greg.

"Lighter bullets shoot flatter and faster."

"How fast?" asked Ron.

"Twelve to thirteen hundred feet per second on a good day."

Ron whistled appreciation. "Magnum loads."

"And with that comment, Gentlemen," interjected Reylie, "we have a business to discuss. Mister Kolster, I have a rough contract written up for shares in Powder B, as we shall call it. That is if your chemist friend can make powder like he mixes nitroglycerin."

The gun shop and smithy laughed loud and hard. "Missy, I think you must be older than you look to have this business sense. So, upstairs, please. We will discuss our partnership with some drinks. I think we will all be happy with the financial results."

Reylie was careful and sipped at the whiskey as the group discussed a partnership. Intoxication would lead to poor decisions, which she and Ron could ill afford. A half hour of discussion as Reylie made changes to her draft contract, and it looked as if there was an agreement.

Greg and his chemist friend would start producing sample batches of Powder B. A patent in Reylie's and Ron's names were sent to the U.S. Patent Office. They would then send the patent samples to various gun manufacturers to drum up interest, along with a copy of the patent to disburse anyone from stealing the chemical makeup of the powder. Greg Kolster would make small batches of ammunition with brass cartridge cases used, not drawn copper.

"That will take some time. It would be better to use cheap copper."

"Brass stretches and gives, less apt to stick or crack under pressure," said Reylie.

"Smart girl," said Bar. "That is the reason I stay with my cap and ball Roots. I saw many a cartridge swell and jam."

"Well, brass will help with that problem, especially under the higher pressures generated by this smokeless powder. You can also use steel cases."

Greg scratched his chin. "Well, it's your idea, so we'll get it done. Just do not expect a quick result."

"We have some time," said Ron. "I don't see us leaving Texas anytime soon."

"Well, I feel a steak dinner calling me," said Bar. "I'm buying, so who is with me?"

"I'm hungry also," replied Reylie. "I'll tag along."

Armand, Uncle Jake, and Ron nodded in assent, and Jake asked his friend, "You too, Greg?"

"Sorry, I have a wife waiting at home with our firstborn."

"You got married?" Uncle Jake asked with wide eyes.

"Yessir. It surprised me also. Two years this month, Jake. You'd already taken off for places unknown after the Battle of El Paso."

"Yes, we have been busy," said Bar. "Well, I'll owe you a steak dinner. We should be back through in about six months."

"I'll hold you to that, Bar. Stop by before you leave town."

They all shook hands, and the five left the gunshop.

"Shaking hands is losing favor at home," said Ron.

"Why's that, young man?" asked Uncle Jake.

"Lots of viruses, sickness going around."

"You can gauge the mettle of a man—or woman—by how they shake hands," said Bar. "Bowing like some Chinese or Japanese, just don't hack it."

The group made their way to a steakhouse named The Longhorn. It was busy, but as usual, Uncle Jake knew the owner, and they were soon seated, with

Bar's back to the wall. Ron whispered, "Like Wild Bill Hickock," to Reylie, and Bar heard him.

"We knew Wild Bill. How'd you know him?" asked Bar.

"There was an article in *Harper's Magazine*," replied Reylie. "I think last year."

"There's that photographer memory you mentioned," said Uncle Jake. "That article was a bunch of buffalo chips. He was a fine Scout against the Mexicans and the Brownites, but he didn't go around getting into gunfights at the drop of a hat."

"He shot Tutt in Missouri, right?" asked Reylie.

"He shot the man because Tutt had run off with an Army Payroll. Hickock was in Springfield snooping around and spying on some of John Brown's alleged kin. Tutt tried to desert from the Army, taking the payroll with him. Wild Bill shot him dead with a Coult Dragoon when the idiot attempted to shoot him as Bill told him to drop the money bag. Killed him deader than an Injun with smallpox."

"Where did you and Bar meet him?" asked Reylie.

"Our company of Rangers was sent down in the Valley after the U.S. Army under General Taft tried to invade Mexico near Del Rio. He lost nigh to five thousand men out of twenty thousand and got himself killed. March 1962 was the First Battle of Del Rio, and the last time idiots lined up their men like they did in 1776, out in the open and blasted away. Kit Carson and Wild Bill, both scouts, tried to warn them the Mexicans don't fight that way."

"What happened?"

"A thousand Campesinos shot from behind rocks, in ditches, from some short trees in the area. Then they ran. They killed Taft, and the second in command had enough sense to retreat across the Rio Grande before the French Army showed up."

"French Army?" asked Ron.

"Napoleon III installed Maximillian to rule Mexico as they owed Europe, especially France, a ton of money. The French, Limeys, Belgians, Austrians, and Spanish were behind the Slave Revolt in Montgomery. The Mexican upper class and the Catholic Church were behind it also. They wanted to stir crap up, maybe get back some land lost in the First Mexican War. Don't they teach you anything—oh, I forgot. Different place and time."

Armand's face displayed a quizzical look, but he held his tongue.

"Anyways, we Rangers, Bill, and Kit helped to get the Army straightened out. Then the French and Austrians, some twenty thousand strong, crossed the Rio Grande and tried that old-fashioned way of fighting when everyone had muskets. They learned what repeating horse pistols and breach loaders could do, especially when Texas Rangers and U.S. Dragoons had them. Some photographers spent a week afterward, making photos of ten thousand dead French and Austrians, a few hundred Mexicans. The Army lost a hundred, and the French commander retreated."

"So, what was Wild Bill like?" asked Reylie.

Bar shrugged as he answered, "He was alright. You could tell when he was angry. His eyes got a steely look to them."

"Good pistol shot?"

"Yeah, he was as good as me but with those smaller Coult Navies. I think he carried that Dragoon pistol he killed Tutt with for show."

Their steaks with vegetables came, and the five quickly discovered how much hunger they had. Reylie ordered a Buffalo steak, and Ron opted for some venison.

"They should call this place The Meat Market with all the different types of flesh they serve," said Reylie between mouthfuls.

"Longhorn cattle started this all, so they kept the name," said Bar.

Armand ordered a beautiful Madeira after the main courses. Uncle Jake had everyone try thick blackberry syrup over crushed ice and oatmeal with a splash of thick cream. "I don't know what they call this, but it tastes good," said the older man.

"It's not ice cream," said Reylie.

"No. This is a lot easier to make."

"We'll just call it Uncle Jake's Dessert from here on."

Jake laughed, then spooned another portion into his mouth.

The five companions took a stroll down the major streets around the El Paso Royale to let their food digest. In this different time and place, the Five Star Hotel had indoor plumbing, which was a welcome relief to Reylie. She did not ask where along the Rio Grande, the sewer system emptied. When they arrived back at the hotel, Reylie freshened up and then went looking for Bar. He was seated on the edge of the smoker with what could only be a Cuban cigar and a glass of bourbon and branch water.

"May I join you, Bar?"

"Of course, young lady." Reylie could tell the meal and drinks had given him a comfortable glow. He motioned to a waiter and had an iced lemonade delivered. When the staff brought him another glass, Reylie asked for a liquor and watched it delivered with nary a bat of the eye.

"You're not planning on trying to drink me under the table, are you, missy?"

"No, of course not. I like the smell of a good cigar, which makes me strange where I live. My Dad and Grandpa used to smoke them outside in the back of the house."

"You miss them, don't you? You miss your end of the rainbow?" asked Bar.

"Yes. It is sinking in Ron, and I may never get back to our side of the rainbow. But we are lucky we fell into the campfire of people who can—understand."

Bar set his cigar down and sipped his drink. Then he spoke. "You came down to ask me something, didn't you?"

Reylie swallowed a large draught of her drink. "Yes. This is why a fourteen-year-old in what my place calls an underage teenager is drinking alcohol. I need some liquid courage."

"You? Need help with guts? You are one of the bravest girls I know."

"I have to ask you something, Bar, if Ron and I are going to be members of your family, live with you and yours, well, I need—"

"The whole story as to why I am who I am. This hardcase, a rough man."

"Bar, I do not want to make you angry, upset you. I know it's hard—"

"My wife's name was Rebekah. My little sister was Judith. Rebekah was with a child when those charros killed them. Jake lost his brother James, my Pa. And my Ma, Ruth. Then there was my cousin Charles; they slaughtered him also."

"Bar—"

"No, you're right. You and Ron are going to be family. So you need to know how we got here." Bar motioned the staff for another drink and placed a gold coin on the table. After he had another bourbon, he finished the last one off in a gulp and then began to sip at the new drink as he talked.

"Uncle Jake and I were in Mexico, a mile into El Paso Del Norte. The other Rangers and we had pushed in further than anyone else during the Battle of El Paso. We had no idea as to what was about to happen…"

Bar looked around a bit of rubble left after an old Napoleanic cannon shell strike. The building was a former cantina with attached rooms of brick and mortar. The Avenida De El Paso Del Norte, where the two Texas Rangers hid, connected El Pas Del Norte, Mexico, and El Paso, Texas. An attack led by General Sherman from Fort Hancock across the Rio Grande distracted the French and Mexican forces long enough for five hundred Texas Rangers and U.S. Cavalry Dragoons to thunder across the full street bridge connecting the twin cities. With a quartet of four armored plow horses in the lead, the five hundred not so light brigade was among the Mexican defenders before they could shoot at many equestrians. Then horse pistols decimated the Mexican defenders, and the survivors broke and ran, abandoning the plan to blow up the bridge.

Bar and Uncle Jake were off their horses and worked their way up the side streets and alleys as fast as possible. Bar had his Kentucky squirrel rifle slung across his back as Uncle Jake has slung his Sharps. They had moved so quickly that they soon realized they were alone among the rubble. The Federal troops had softened the Mexican city up with several hundred rounds of cannon fire, driving most civilians into the countryside. Now the two Rangers were alone, except for possible Mexican defenders. They were also low on ammunition.

Bar had searched the body of a dead soldier and recovered a Smith and Wesson .32 revolver.

"Greaser gun," said Bar with a curse.

"Beggars can't be choosers, Nephew."

"Well, I've seen them with Coults, British Adams, and French pinfires. Why couldn't this Mexican have one instead of this Negro pistol?"

"Look around some more, Bar. I have one round left in my Sharps, but my Walker and Coult Navy are without."

"My Root horse pistols are empty up also," replied Bar.

A rustling and the sounds of boots on gravel came from a few yards away. Bar snapped a shot off using the Smith and Wesson and was rewarded with a cry of pain.

"I'm surprised this little pistol could hurt a mouse."

"Well, you hurt a Mexican. Let's move and look for—"

They both heard the unique bugle call.

"Is that a recall tattoo?" asked Bar.

"That it is; we are about to be left even more alone. Let's move before we become the only two Rangers in greaser jail."

The two began to hurry back towards the bridge.

"Made it over a mile into Mexican land, and we get recalled," grumbled Bar.

"Well, ours is not to reason why—hey, Nephew. Is that a body with a musket?"

The unlucky Mexican soldier had lost the top of his head to a well-aimed bullet. The Enfield rifle-musket was still loaded. A quick search of the body produced a small powder horn, a tin full of percussion caps, and a small bag of various-sized Minie bullets. The two Rangers grabbed the munitions and found a hut to hide in as they tried to reload their weapons with limited supplies. They soon had two loaded chambers in their horse pistols, and Uncle Jake had a light load in his Navy revolver.

"Take the Enfield, Uncle. You're a better rifle shot than me."

"I still wonder why the Limeys are supplying the French and Mexicans," said Jake. "They are friends with neither."

"They all hate us, Uncle."

"You mean the U.S. Who could hate Texicans?"

Bar guffawed.

"The Mexicans. You kicked their ass in '48, remember?"

A half an hour later and they were at the connecting city bridge. They saw one barricade sentry on the Mexican side.

"Yankee Doodle," called out Bar.

"Is that a Texas accent I hear?" the sentry replied.

"You got it, Rangers Bar and Jake coming in."

They were soon behind the barricade with the loan sentry, a blue-uniformed Federal. "You the last two?" asked the Corporal.

"I think so," replied Uncle Jake. "Why the recall? We had the greasers licked."

"The French are suing for peace. President Lincoln is taking it."

Bar spit. "Old Speechifying Abe strikes again. The man did not like the first Mexican War, and now he is ending this one with a draw."

The two Rangers made their way across the bridge and went to rally point. As they walked up to a makeshift corral, someone called out.

"I told you Captain Jake would make it back. With the Sergeant also." It was Corporal Johnny Hardwick calling out their approach.

"Making bets about our demise, I see," Uncle Jake said with a wide grin.

"We have to do something, Cap'n. You and your nephew took off so fast we lost track of you."

"We gonna have to learn ya how to keep up, you lazyass cowboys," replied Bar.

Jake, as ranking officer, soon took a report from the surviving members of Company B. The fifty-man Company had three dead and five wounded. The Company recovered the wounded and dead.

"So ole Abe is going to smoke a peace pipe," said Uncle Jake.

"Yes, sir," answered Private Callahan. "We were told to wait here in case things went bad."

"Huh. Well, boys, let's get some barbecue going and clean your gear; see to the horses. We might as well make ourselves comfortable while we wait."

The word came down that a Ceasefire and Peace Treaty was to take effect on January 31st, 1866. On January

28th, the Governor of Texas told all Texas Militia and Rangers to make their way back to their home areas. Uncle Jake completed a report on their last affray into Mexico.

"I do not know why we just do not take Mexico," Uncle Jake told Bar. "If it were part of the United States, things would be better for everyone."

"Not part of Texas?" asked Bar with a grin.

"We're big enough. And we have enough Mexicans running around Texas as it is."

Then word came that the Comanche were raiding and stealing horses around Fort Stockton, with just a skeleton U.S. Army unit at the Fort. Hearing that, Uncle Jake called Corporal Harwick over to him.

"Corporal, Bar, and I are going to leave in the morning and high tail it to our spread near Fort Stockton. Can you get the men to the Ranger Station at the Fort?"

"Yes. Captain. No problem. I'll wait for you at the Fort."

Uncle Jake did not realize he would not see Hardwick for several years.

It was January 30th, 1866, when Uncle Jake and Bar left El Paso.

The two men pushed their mounts but had to rest them some or they would break down. They had some 250 miles to cover, so they could not just walk the horses. They were in the saddle some twelve hours a day, then wiped down, rested, and fed their mounts. They had no extra horses, or they could have ridden day and night. They also had to be wary of running into a band of raiding Comanche or some wayward Apache. Thus, it was dusk when they approached the family ranch located a few miles north of Fort Stockton.

"No lights," said Bar. "Looks like a small campfire near the back of the main house."

"Somebody should still be up; it's not that late," said Jake.

Bar swung wide to the south of the main house and slid off his horse some one hundred yards away. He had his matching Coult Root horse pistols out with his Kentucky squirrel rifle across his back as he snuck up to the house.

Uncle Jake slow-walked his horse up towards the front of the house and called out. "Hey, Uncle Jake and Bar are home. You all went to bed early or something?"

That was when Jake saw the first body, Cousin Charles. Jake was off his mount in the blink of an eye, his Coult Walker in his hand. He whistled a warning to Bar. The bear of a man sprinted and burst through the back door.

It was the only time Uncle Jake heard him scream like that.

The two men took the bodies to a haystack near the barn and lay them together. Neither would mention the condition of the women. However, the images of the abused bodies burned into the men's brains, especially Bar's. He lost his mother, sister, the young wife of less than a year, and an unborn child.

Jake's brother James put up a fight but had died, shot once in the head. The attackers hacked Cousin Charles to death with machetes.

They found some coal oil the attackers had left behind after a failed attempt to burn the house. They turned the haystack into a funeral pyre, watching the cleansing fire engulf the bodies.

"No time for burial," said Bar.

"You want to go after them now? You don't want to rest—"

"No." Bar stared at the funeral pyre. "I found some tracks and a blood trail. They did not attempt to hide they were here. Rebekah has not been—dead for more than an hour. We just missed them."

Uncle Jake held up a small ornate single-shot pistol.

"Someone dropped this target pistol. It's French but has an inscription in Spanish to a Pedro Valdez. Some Frenchie must have worked with a Hacienda down Ojinaga way."

"Good. We'll make sure the owner gets it back. With interest."

The two Rangers did not bother to stop at the Fort. Rebekah's family were settlers at Fort Stockton, ran the post store and canteen. That was how she and Bar met. Bar would have to break the news of her death later after he had served justice and revenge. The young widower pushed his horse hard. Uncle Jake thought the horse, Midnight, would give out at any moment. However, the stallion seemed to sense his rider needed an extra effort that night.

They saw the glow of a solitary campfire some twenty miles southwest of the Fort. Coyanosa Draw, the path of an intermittent stream, formed a natural pathway down through Texas towards the Mexican Border Crossing at Presidio, Texas. The Mexicans made camp as if not expecting any pursuit. That was a fatal decision.

Bar had his horse pistols strapped to his waist, a difficult feat for a smaller man. He also took his Kentucky Rifle as he started to sneak towards the distant firelight.

"Nephew, use my Sharps," whispered Uncle Jake.

"No. You keep it, follow me twenty-five paces back. When the shootin' starts, cover my back."

Jake looked at his nephew, started to say something, then held his tongue. He had seen Bar in this cold rage a couple of times. Once the big man had his mindset, it was time to watch his behind and make sure he survived.

Five Mexican Males passed a bottle of alcohol around the campfire as the youngest one took a saw to a leg wound on one of his companions. Bar could see a body strapped to a horse at the edge of the firelight. Someone at the McCain homestead had made the group pay for their evil.

Bar spoke and understood Mexican Spanish; he just refused not to say it unless forced. The three sitting closest to the campfire were cursing the fact their companion was dead, and a bronze-haired beauty had stuck a butcher knife in poor Paco's leg. The Paco they spoke of yelped as the youngest of the group, Manuel, tried to be a doctor. One of the men laughed at Paco's misfortune, saying he did not even get a taste of the women before being stabbed. One man stood up, and Bar noticed the Mexicans had set their guns and holsters aside. The standing Mexican began to express his need to drain his bladder when the young Ranger stepped into the edge of the campfire light.

"*Quien es?*" someone said as Bar used his rifle to shoot the standing male between the eyes.

Bay let his squirrel gun drop as he yanked his Root Coult .44s from their holsters and began to shoot. Caught flat-footed and before they could react, Bar gut shot the other two murderers and rapists. He then rounded on young Manuel, who was on his knees by the wounded Paco.

"*Por favor,*" Manuel said as he raised his hands in supplication. Bar laid the eight-inch pistol barrel alongside the youngster's head. The Texas Ranger then stomped on Paco's leg wound, which elicited a scream.

"Behind you, Nephew," said Uncle Jake as he walked into the firelight.

"We got ourselves a couple of pinchy *pendejos* to question, Uncle."

"I see that Bar; oh, do I see that."

A half hour of intensive interrogation (a red hot knife blade had its own persuasive powers) and the two Rangers knew the original half dozen Mexican vaqueros crossed the Rio Grande the week prior. They were angry the French military was suing for peace along with the other Europeans and wanted to obtain some payback and trophies in celebration of an upcoming birthday for the Alcalde of the Vazquez Hacienda, near Ojinaga, Mexico. The oldest of the group, now dead, had been to Fort Stockton in his youth and remembered some rich *gringos* had property nearby. Who better to suffer some acts of revenge?

The two Rangers tied the surviving charros to a tree, placed the holsters and pistols of the Mexicans in their saddlebags, and threw four of the five long guns into the brush. Bar kept a .45 caliber Kentucky-style rifle.

"This will be of use against the hacienda," Bar said.

"Why don't you finish those two Mexicans?" asked his Uncle.

"I'll let God decide. If'n he wants them to, they will get loose. Though I think the one Rebekah stabbed may bleed to death. His wound opened under during our conversation."

"The young one, Manuel? What if he follows us?"

"He'll be limping a lot on his carved up feet. Also, I don't think he will be in any hurry to get back home and tell everyone he begged for his life and then flapped his gums about how to get to the hacienda."

The Texas Rangers took the largest Mexican mount as well as a broad sombrero and serape. They scattered the other horses, including the one bearing the corpse, and left the bodies of the three Bar killed where they lay. After some cowboy coffee, they hit the trail. The pair had about one hundred fifty miles to travel.

They slept on horseback, stopping only to care for the horses. The Rangers crossed the Rio Grande downriver from Presidio, Texas, and slowly approached the area just south of Ojinaga, Mexico. Even during the recent War, no one paid much attention to a couple of riders passing through. They quickly found the Vasquez Hacienda.

Bar put on the oversized sarape and sombrero and mounted the former hacienda horse, the seized Kentucky rifle in his hands.

"Sure you don't want me to go in with you, Bar."

"No, Uncle Jake. You are my ace in the hole. If I get pinned down, start blasting with your Sharp and my squirrel gun."

"Be careful, Nephew."

"Of course. I'll be back shortly."

Bar saw through Uncle Jake's spyglass that one old man guarded the main gate. As in feudal times, the upper class kept loyal older workers on to perform jobs so the rulers could enjoy themselves on special occasions. El Patron Vasquez, the Alcalde of the area, was the subject of a massive birthday celebration. No one would dare to interrupt the party this far into Mexico.

The older man at the front gate was dozing off when the approaching horse stirred him to action. He looked through the dim torchlight to see a familiar horse, sombrero, and sarape.

"Juan?" asked the man as he stood up, a worn flintlock musket in his hands. A good-sized thrown rock to his head interrupted the questioning. The elder toppled over without a cry as Bar slid from the borrowed horse. He strode to the stunned old man and picked up the flintlock. There was no good reason to leave a loaded weapon behind him. The sentry could recover before Bar left. Keeping to the shadows, the Texas Ranger strode towards the large main house. Bar looked and found the outside stairway, which circled to the various entrances of the massive mansion. Bar slung the Kentucky rifle and checked the flash pan of the musket by torchlight. The gun was still primed and ready to fire. As Bar began to climb the stairway, a figure staggered on a side door onto a stairway landing. A drunk vaquero prepared to relieve himself in the dark.

Bar slammed the musket barrel into the temple of the Mexican male, and the man fell over. As Bar strode past, he smashed his boot down on the vaquero's face. The Ranger continued up to the next doorway. Just as he reached it, two laughing figures stumble through. A young male partier had managed to push a senorita out from the light-filled interior to the more subdued lighting of the stairway. Before the man could make good on his conquest, Bar jammed the barrel of the musket into his face.

"*Callete! No se mueve,*" Bar growled as he cocked the musket and considered his next move. The decision was taken from him when the women let out a scream.

"Shit," cursed Bar as he pulled the gun's trigger. The musket blast sent skull, brains, and blood splattering all over the stairway and the *senorita*. Some of the detritus wound up in the young lady's open mouth, choking off her scream. Bar butt stroked her to the ground.

Yells and cries came from the ballroom as people noticed the screams and gunshot over the music and party. Bar stepped to the side of the doorway and readied to swing the musket like the 21st Century home run king. He smashed the first figure exiting the party across the face, an ornate pinfire pistol the man carried discharging into the night. The man fell back onto the Mexicans following him as Bar turned and dashed up the stairway. He ducked through the next doorway and found he was right where he wanted. This doorway led to a small balcony that overlooked the festivities. Bar unslung the borrowed Kentucky rifle and drew a bead on an older man standing at the head of a long table.

"*Patron!*" Bar yelled, and the man in the fancy clothes looked up. Bar fired the rifle into the chest of the patriarch of the Vasques family and watched with satisfaction as he toppled over. A quick pivot and he smashed a small wall-mounted coal oil lamp. The flammable liquid soon was burning on a wall hanging tapestry.

"*Asesino!*" The cries came loud and often as Bar dropped the empty rifle and ran back to the stairway and searched for an exit. He found a stairwell that went down towards a door in the back of the warehouse-sized mansion. The Ranger pulled a horse pistol from his belt as he scrambled down the stairway. As he reached the bottom, a figure burst through the door, gun in hand. Bar fired first, and the person toppled out the way he had entered. Bar stepped by the body and saw it was of a young lad no older than fifteen. Bar scooped up an ornate Coult revolver lying next to him and ran towards the darkness.

Bar yelled, "*Asesino!*" a couple of times as he ran, still in the sarape. The Ranger made it to the stables and pulled from his pocket a box of matches. He threw open each stall door and then lit a pile of hay afire as he heard people yelling and running towards the stables. Two horses burst out the stable doors, bowling over men. Bar ducked into a vacant stable and crouched in the shadows. The flames began to spread through the hay, the rest of the horses bolted, and Bar followed them out. People screamed and ran around like chickens as more smoke swirled around. The Ranger made a break for it. A horse with a saddle on it ran across the open courtyard, then stopped dead still. Bar sprinted, caught the bridle of the horse, and was upon it in a moment. Then Bar was breaking for the main gate. A bullet whizzed by, and then he was through. He stayed low in the saddle like a Comanche and was out into the night.

"And the rest is history," said Reylie.

"I and Uncle Jake made it out alive if that is what you are saying."

"You killed the patriarch you blamed for the deaths of your family. Why continue after that?"

"Because the Mexicans kept at it. A week later, four *vaqueros* were trying to pass as cattlemen bumped into some of our Texas Ranger Company. They thought I was with them and shot first out of stupidity. One survived and said they were looking for me as part of a blood feud. The Patron dies, as did his eldest son, the man I beaned with the musket."

"But you feel they started it, Bar, and you will finish it."

"Yep. I never killed women and children for fun. They did."

Reylie sat and sipped at her liquor as Bar stared into his drink.

"Missy, you make me think more than I have for two years," the Ranger finally said. "I and Uncle Jake are on Extended Leave Without Pay until we get our family matters settled. My Aunt and Uncle and their children are watching the homestead. When Uncle Jake and I show back up, we take over again."

"But, you will still be a Texas Ranger when needed."

"Yes, Reylie. Comanches and banditos still cross the border, raid, steal, and kill. I am good at what I do, which is killing when necessary. And, before you jump in when I am angry enough. I never claimed to be perfect."

Reylie sat quiet, lost in thought. How do she and Ron live in a time and place where an entire region was like living in drive-by shootings in Chicago on a July Fourth Weekend. That was *not* their background.

But maybe what she and Ron needed to survive was a Bar McCain. A hardcase. The man had his sense of honor; he was not a psychopath. However, there were psychopaths out there. The slaughter of Bar's family proved that fact.

"Okay," Reylie finally said. "I understand where you started. Ron and I just ask you to help us survive until our people come looking. Which they will. I feel it."

Bar smiled. "Reylie, you remind me of Rebekah. Always looking at the positive side."

"Glass is half full, Bar, not half empty."

The massive man laughed. "Yes, ma'am. She always pointed out the good things. And she made me laugh. Like you do." Bar suddenly stood up. "Come on. You need to get some sleep. I need to buy you some more clothes tomorrow if you are going to live with us."

"Keep track, and we'll pay you back, Bar."

"Young lady, a family, does not pay family back. You just 'do' for them. Uncle Jake kept half our money from the various actions we have taken. We trust the Olsens, but not that much."

"So if there is nothing in New Mexico when you go back—"

Bar shrugged as he answered, "We have plenty of money, extra stuck away here and there. It was never about the money anyway. It was about justice, with revenge thrown in. I want people to think twice before they do something like they did to me and mine."

Reylie smiled. Bar was so much more complicated than she and Ron imagined. As was this world in which they fell. Now all she had to do was try and educate Bar about racism. "Okay, Bar. But I still may push back about buying a bunch of —stuff."

"Won't do no good. My mind is made up."

Reylie laughed. "Yes, Bar. And it is a great mind in that large head of yours."

"Now you get it, missy. Now you get it." Bar offered his arm to her, and Reylie took it. Funny how now, after being told what started all this, she felt safe.

She and Ron would make it. She knew it.

CHAPTER 7
RESCUE PARTY: PART 1

Once again, Reylie King-Mann, known to all by her maiden name on this Earth as Reylie King, fidgeted as she waited for the interview to begin. Space Command and NASA demanded more and more televised interviews as preparations for the first migration through the Sky Tunnels neared. Humanity all over the unstable planet Earth wanted reassurance. They wanted certainty that transporting through these tunnels or holes in space and time would get them to a safe place in one piece. More fanatics came out of the woodwork every day, claiming this or that god or belief would save the Earth as the tremblers and seaquakes worsened.

Reylie did not understand all the science. She just knew what had happened to her on a very personal level. She knew her brother Ron, and she fell through a hole in time and space to the Alternate Earth called Western World. By pure chance, they landed in the camp of Bar and Jake McCain. In some other place, the two teenagers might be killed immediately. Instead, the McCains helped the strange brother and sister to survive. However, survival was not easy. Due to the racism and violence in the alternate thread of history (or was it an entirely different universe?), there existed groups of people who became upset that Ron and Reylie did not do more to change the racism and inequality in Western World. Yet no one seemed to have any ideas about how two teenagers arriving in a strange world could affect substantial change even over a four-plus-year period. A general comment of the critics was, "You should have tried harder."

Reylie shook her head. She was beginning to accept some would always hold a grudge over imagined injustices to them and their families, forgetting Western World was *not* from their history or universe. As usual, significant upheavals as the world experienced every day caused people to lash out from fear.

"Fear?" Reylie mumbled. "Go to Western World. That'll show you fear."

The 'Talking Head' interviewer Carson Tainter approached Reylie in the Green Room while yapping with the Space Command Information Officer, Captain Fields. 'Talking with Tainter' was the catchphrase used for the weekly broadcast. Tainter specialized in interviews with people involved in the attempts to deal with the rampaging Earth. Tainter had a wide grin on his face as he stuck his hand out to shake.

"It is both a pleasure and an honor to meet you, Reylie King. Or should I call you Reylie King-Mann?"

Reylie smiled as she shook the talking head's hand. "Everyone knew me first as Reylie King before I met and married Mike. However, they know I am married, so let's use my married name, King-Mann."

"Any subject off limit?"

"Marianne, my daughter. She does not need to be dragged into conversations about her biological father, Bar McCain."

"She has never had the chance to meet him."

"Not yet. But you know as well as I do, Mister Tainter, the powers that be are getting better at moving through the Sky Tunnels first breached by my grandfather, John King."

"Do you believe that someday she and Bar McCain may be united for the first time?"

"Yes. And dragging that possibility out for perusal by the various tabloids, I will not allow it." Reylie fixed Tainter with a glare that Barnabas McCain knew was an invitation to be gelded.

"Okay, Mrs. Mann. I guess I can agree to that limitation. Now, you know the drill. Let's get some last-minute make-up and off to the races."

INTERVIEWER TAINTER: "So, there were attempts to contact you in the universe we now call Alternate Westworld."

REYLIE KING-MANN: "Yes, there were actual attempts to locate and rescue my brother Ron and me. Although, we had found some local people who helped us survive, so the need for a rescue disappeared after a few months."

INTERVIEWER: "What was the first attempt to send someone through euphemistically called the Rabbit Hole, and now is officially the Sky Tunnel System?"

REYLIE KING-MANN: "His name was—is—Bartholomew Carson."

Bart Carson went into an airborne forward roll as he popped into existence a few feet from the ground. The tall, lean but muscular man was warned that "dropping" into what was named Western World could be a matter of inches or feet. The phasing between the two planes of existence was tricky.

Bart stood up and looked around. It looked like the New Mexico of his Earth, but he knew it was not. Bart was nude except for a leather jockstrap designed to double as a throwing sling because of its unique design. The powers that be decided additional metal objects, even clothing, might affect their ability to place Bart in the correct time and space. As it was, Bart knew he could be months or even years off from the King siblings.

It had taken months of working with the Game the Grandfather, known as the Tinkerer, accidentally created to figure out what happened. The how, what, and where the two teenagers went was another matter. The scientist thought they had determined the correct spatial coordinates. But as Bart's grandmother used to say, the proof was in the pudding.

Bart reached into his mouth and removed two unique items he had secreted in his cheeks. One was a razor-thin piece of steel, the other a sharp piece of flint. The fact he had those items was unknown to the people who sent him on this rescue mission. However, his survival training told him he needed flint and steel for fire-making. The scientists might send thousands of miles or years off course with the new technology. A rough-sounding voice told Bart he landed close to his mark.

"Looky here. Hank! A nekked asshole."

"I told you I seed a flash of light, Johmmy! Watch for a smoke wagon. Something caused that flash."

Bart turned to watch two men in dirty U.S. Cavalry uniforms approach, one holding a Remington revolver issued to many a Civil War horseman. Only in this universe was it the Second Mexican War. At least, that was the limited information he had.

The Special Forces trained warrior knew that just two cavalrymen out in the New Mexico desert at night was odd. There were still Apache and Comanche raiders about if Bart had landed close to 1868 as planned. Bart felt his 'spidey sense' tingling.

"What the hell are you doing out here, Boy? Nekked and all."

For a moment, Bart had an urge to reply, "Washday, nothing to wear." He restrained himself as these two would have no concept of that theatrical dialogue. Instead, he kept it realistic.

"Got away from a pack of Injuns. They was about to skin me." Bart used his best semi-literate patois to appear as unassuming as possible.

"That a fact?" said scruffy shave needing Hank. He held the pistol while Johnny came armed with a regulation saber. Bart knew the Old West was rough, but these two looked as if they had not been in a Unit Inspection for quite some time. Their demeanor did not bode well.

"Could be he escaped from that crazy house I heared they were building around Sante Fe," suggested Johnny. "May he has a bounty on him."

"And in our situation, we are just gonna march up and collect it," retorted Hank with a sneer. "We'll take him back to camp in case he is crazy and hogtie him. And keep an eye out for Apache and Comanche." Hank stepped up and jabbed the pistol at Bart.

"Come on you. We'll get the true story out of you, one way or another."

Bart had slipped his two small blades into his jockstrap as he stepped towards the two soldiers. The near-naked man also walked as slow as possible.

"Hey, get moving," ordered Hank. He poked Bart in the back with his Remington.

"I don't have any shoes on, and there are cactus needles and sharp rocks."

"That is your problem, boy, Get—"

Bart knew from extensive training and experience that the worst thing you can do is get so close to a man that he can grab your pistol. Poking him with it does just that, as well as lets your prisoner know precisely the location of the weapon. In one swift and practiced move, Bart spun around, knocking the gun in his back aside. Bart obtained a wristlock in the blink of an eye, twisted and both felt and heard the snapping of bone as he relieved Hank of his pistol. A further twist and Hank was on the ground with Bart standing, holding the revolver.

Johnny was quicker with the saber than Bart imagined. The dirty man slashed at Bart with the long blade. The warrior used the Remington's eight-inch barrel to parry the deadly cutting edge and then stepped into Johnny past the sword swing's arc. Bart slammed his left forearm under Johnny's chin as he clubbed the sword hand with the pistol's barrel. Bart laid the eight-inch heavy revolver barrel across Johnny's forehead as the saber fell to the dirt. The soldier went down, stunned. Bart bent over, scooped up the sword with his offhand, and impaled Johnny's throat. The former Special Forces member was taught never to let someone who just tried to kill you get a second chance.

Bart turned towards broken wristed Hank. The man laid on the ground holding his right arm up with his left.

"You broke it!" Hank yelped.

"Yep. And I'll do worse if you try something or don't answer my questions."

Bart marched the surviving Hank to the nearby campsite. Bart found a lariat and tied Hank up to a boulder to safely examine the deserters' saddlebags and personals. There were two Spencer repeaters, another saber, as well as a large Bowie knife. Bart transferred every item he thought would be helpful to the saddlebags, then saddled up the best-looking horse. Some of his preparation for the assignment had involved judging horseflesh. The black mare seemed better and accepted new ownership with no fuss.

Bart knew the two cavalrymen were deserters within five minutes after hogtying Hank. He also knew they deserted with Army payroll destined for Fort Stockton and Fort Davis in Texas this fine February of 1869. A glance at an older EL Paso, Texas newspaper found in the saddlebags told Bart Ulysses S. Grant ran against Lincoln for POTUS and won. George A. Custer was the Army Chief of Staff after using his political pull to curry favor with Grant. African Americans were being 'removed' from the States to the Washington Territories. Slavery was to end in 1870, although it sounded like some form of indentured servitude would still exist to help with the cotton, tobacco, and other crops. What in Old South vernacular classified as mulattos and 'High Yellas" would be allowed to exist south of the Washington/Canadian Border with some social limits. All other People of Color were extremely limited in their abilities to live and function in the United States.

Bart found some hardtack, cheese, and a few sausage bits as food and added that with a spare shirt. Bart paused long enough to find a pair of civilian trousers and another shirt to cover his nudity. A pair of moccasins that just fit worked well for his feet. The deserters had a near full waterskin, which Bart added to his booty.

"Hey, Hank, this pistol I took from Johnny, is this some Smith and Wesson pistol?"

"Yeah. We took that Wesson off a nigger we killed. He got too snoopy." Bart grimaced inwardly at the word, but kept his face unreadable. He could readily see Hank was a bigot who was not afraid to speak his mind.

"Only Brownites and his type bought them." It was an odd medium frame four-shot forty-one caliber tip-up.

Bart spent many an hour researching the history of post-Civil War era weapons in his universe. An examination of the pistol made him think about a prototype and limited sales model in his reality but obtained in this Old West. "Ole John Brown. Well, he is of no concern today."

Hank spat. "I can tell a Bushwhacker like you never fought in the Montgomery Alabama Resurrection, or you would be cursing John Brown's name."

Limited drone surveillance through the Rabbit Hole had told the mission organizers a little about society in this alternate Earth. No Civil War but a Slave revolt pushed by foreign interest, to include French-controlled Mexico and other European Countries pushing back on the Monroe Doctrine. Mexicans and Blacks were despised by many.

Bart smiled at the captive. "Who tried to bring who back at gunpoint? Who stole an Army payroll? And I am a Bushwhacker. That's a hoot." Bart swung upon his horse.

"Hey, you going to leave me here?"

Bart tossed Hank's saber near the man's tied-up

feet. "Figure out how to cut yourself loose. I left you your unloaded Spencer; I took the other. Follow me, and I'll shoot your horse and then you." Bart nudged his mount with his heels, and the horse slowly made its way down the crude game trail. Hank began to swear loud and hard until he realized all he would do would be to draw the attention of any passing Apache or Comanche. Bart figured the man could use the sword to cut himself loose in a half hour. He had taken most of the payroll, sans the Army marked bags, and left Hank a small amount to use. Bart was not an easy man, but he was not entirely cold-blooded.

The special forces warrior made his way North towards what a crude map found in the deserters' possibles, and his prior intelligence briefings reported was the Butterfield Stageline trail. Based on the information he had obtained from Hank and intelligence briefings, Bart was sure he had come to rest very near the spot Reylie and Ron had 'landed' when they had traveled to this West World. Now the man was working his way from the West Potrillo Mountains down into Las Cruces, New Mexico.

Bart took his time, not pushing his new mount as he had no idea how hard the original owner had ridden the horse. Bart stopped, looked, and listened about every quarter-hour for any pursuit by Hank or some random Indian. The specially trained operator knew all the effort spent sending him on this mission was a waste if somebody bushwhacked him within the first hours. Bart's training and experience enabled him to free himself of the two deserters. However, now was not the time to push his luck.

As he nudged the black mare into a trot, his mind replayed the pattern of events, which became his mission.

Bart Carson had just turned thirty years of age days before passing through the portal created by The Game. Eleven years of military and special operations experience began at age nineteen with an enlistment in the U.S. Marine Corps. Bored after a quarter spent in College, Bart went down to the local bank of recruiters' offices. The Marines promised him quick access to the 'action' he requested, so off to Paris Island, he went. As Bart enlisted, there was a policy to send people to the Coast farthest from their homes. It was all about divorcing a recruit from their civilian home. It did not matter to Bart.

Bart Carson had never been close to his brothers and sisters, which he had two of each. As the middle child, Bart had developed a 'loner' mentality. His parents worried that his lack of bonding with others pointed towards a sociopath or psychopath personality. Bart did not care. He was the person who always marched to the beat of a different drummer. So some thought him joining the regimented Marine Corp was bizarre. What people did not know was Bart's internal discipline and toughness were to an extreme. Some said he inherited his ancestors Kit Carson's ability to survive the harshest situations. To Bart, the reasons did not matter. His powers were just there.

Bart knew how to work with others, so he had no difficulties in the Marine Corps. However, he always kept a particular part of himself secret. Some said Bart had a hard, sharp edge to him. Whatever it was, it served him well when he needed it. He excelled at individual sports and martial arts. People soon noticed a wiry strength in his slender less than a six-foot frame that seemed more fitting to a bulkier person in his world. Thus, when Bart applied to the SEALS and later the DELTA FORCE, it came as no real surprise to those who better knew him.

Sometime during this first decade of service, a two-person team from some odd alphabet-named agency appeared. They recruited Bart on the spot to become a 'Ghost.' The man and woman did their homework before approaching him, knew his affirmative answer was a foregone conclusion. Bart whisked out of existence for a year within forty-eight hours from the meeting.

Bart spent time in secret installations in

Romania, Poland, and an unnamed country in Africa. The Forner Marine trained in 'wet work' well past even the SEALs and DELTA FORCE. During the training, Bart completed missions. The ancestor of Kit Carson found himself eliminating various targets as if it was just a walk in the park. Bart soon found himself working on assignments where it seemed he was in a test rather than achieving the desired result.

In an unnamed African country, two so-called backup operators disappeared, and Bart spent a week trying to survive and escape. When he made it to a safe house, it was no big deal. Had the operator disappeared, Bart would have been a writeoff. A month later, on another mission, one of the two previous 'no-shows' as backups vanished. Bart never let on that he watched the man die. Bart was not about to stick his neck out for someone willing to let him die as part of a test.

For the first year of these activities, Bart lived in agency provide quarters, mainly on a hidden installation. He once counted the number of continual days of training and mission work. There were two hundred days when he had maybe four hours to himself. At the end of the year, the two original recruiters, contact agents, showed up and gave him a massive amount of funds and precious metals. They then told Bart to find a place to live, receive a cover job, and wait for future instructions. Bart received no 'attaboys.' It was as if this was all expected.

Bart moved far enough away from any family or past friends to derail any detailed questions about his employment. He received documentation for a cover position as a minor bureaucrat in the State Department. Thus Bart could travel to various embassies as necessary. The actual people he worked for stayed in a nebulous realm of government reality. For an entire month, Bart had no contact with anyone about work. Bart found a dojo and a gym to work out at, set up his household in a three-bedroom, two-bath ranch house from the 1950s near Kingman, Arizona. With more money than he knew what to do with, Bart bought furnishing and began a firearm and weapons collection he always wanted. A lot of Arizona Desert to shoot in, so Bart kept up his skills as a marksman. Thirty-one days from the last contact, and he received an assignment.

Bart was sent to San Luis, Rio Colorado, and helped with a 'snatch' job. A team of operatives grabbed a person of interest in Mexico and transported her to the United States. Bart iced two local gangbangers who got too close to the operation. It was the first of many such 'days in the office,' as Bart's co-workers liked to call it. Bart Carson soon had a reputation as one who stayed calm under pressure, took no unnecessary chances, but was not afraid to ice anyone who got in the way. He soon received the nickname, Iceman.

Bart also received the reputation of an operative who preferred to work alone. His employers trusted him to be a single 'overwatch' who always made sure the other employees made it out, even if they never met him.

One night as Bart sat drinking fifty-year-old single malt Scotch, alone of course, he started pondering just how many fellow humans he had damaged in his line of work. While on active duty military, Bart knew he had killed a dozen 'enemy,' wounded at least another dozen, some of whom may be dead. Since his new vocation as the 'Iceman,' Bart counted fifty dead, six injured. Ten of the deceased were during his year of training.

During the same period, the descendant of Kit Carson received credit for preventing a dozen other employees from being killed or injured and the same for six 'civilians' under his employer's care. However, did he make friends? Not really.

Bart made a couple of trips up the roads to Las Vegas, Nevada, and utilized the services of some high-maintenance escorts for the release of sexual tension. Bart never was much of a gambler as he did not like the House Odds. He did find the twenty-four-hour activity of Lost Wages stimulating.

Bart approached the end of the third year of his unique employment when rumors circulated about an unusual assignment. No sooner had Bart heard the stories than the word became 'SHUT UP!' Something leaked that should not have leaked. This 'leak' was the first time Bart saw such an occurrence and such a reaction. The leak had also mentioned the term 'volunteer.' Bart knew that once you agreed to the employment he was in, everything else was a non-volunteer situation. You did what they told you.

Bart bided his time for a month. He had a suspicion they would come to him. Bart knew that he had less baggage, personal connections with his family or society than all the field personnel. The man knew they wanted him or his clone. He could feel it.

A month later and one more 'snatch' job in Asia and the two original contact agents met him at the airport in Tuscon, Arizona.

Tall Blonde Female said, "We have an— opportunity for you."

Short Fire Hydrant Black Man said, "It's volunteer. And it may be—permanent."

"As in dead?" Bart asked.

"No," answered the Blonde. "As in—gone."

The three went to Bart's home, which someone in authority swept for electronic bugs while Bart was on assignment. There the contact agents laid out the deal after Bart signed a Non-Disclosure Agreement, with Death as punishment for violation.

"So, I am sent down this—wormhole—to test the technology and locate the original victims of this Game. And the brainiacs may be able to bring them back, along with me."

"The 'maybe' is a big one, Carson," said the Black Man. "You may become stuck in a world similar to Post Civil Way America, but with no Civil War."

A small smile formed on Bart's mouth.

"So that is a reason a person like myself, Heinz 57 but look like a paleface, is needed."

"You've got it," Tall Blonde Female answered. "If you need time—"

"I'm your Huckleberry, as that character in the western movie said."

The two contact agents exchanged glances, then the Black Man spoke.

"That was quick."

Bart shrugged.

"Why not? I'll be one of the first travelers between universes. Someday, I'll be in the history books. If it works out."

"Or forgotten if it does not."

Bart's smile broke into a grin.

"I'll make it work."

The next day, Bart began his unique mission training. He went to a special annex on the Federal Training Center at

Marana, Arizona, outside of Tucson. Bart received every bit of intelligence the U.S. Government had on Project Gameworlds in a secured lead-lined room. Gameworlds were plural as the head shed were sure there was more than one 'world' universe opened by the Game created by the Tinkerer. The creator and his family were 'sequestered' as someone sorted out the whole mess. It became a mess as more people disappeared, down the Rabbit Hole, the slang used for what happened. Drones sent in transmitted first for seconds, then up to a full minute.

Bart looked at every piece of usually hazy video, audiotape, still photo, and intelligence report. Next, he asked for and received briefings by experts on the Old West of his universe. Even with the ending of Slavery after the Civil War, the Old West was a violent racist mess in many areas. The Gameworld Old West, soon called Western World, was even worse. Wars with Mexico, forced transport of African Americans as Slavery supposedly ended, Ron and Reylie King, the young brother and sister grandchildren of the Tinkerer, fell into a special kind of Hell.

Bartholomew Carson volunteered to find them and then connect with a way to bring them back.

Bart owned an original Coult Peacemaker. He began to practice with it in his spare time until he realized the pistol was not invented yet in the period he went. 'Coult' as it was spelled in the Gameworld West had an entirely new line of massive Root sidehammer horse pistols, as well as the familiar Navy and Army models. The Winchester/Volcanic designs remained with Smith and Wesson and were used in the Second Mexican War, 1861 to 1866. During the Second Mexican War, the government suspended the Smith and Wesson copyright and the patent on the cartridge revolver for the 'duration.' During the American Civil War, in Bart's reality, that had not happened. Thus, black powder caps and ball designs were much sooner converted to various cartridges in this alternate universe.

Bart went and bought every black power replica arm he could find from the American Civil War Era. Then, when he was not at classified briefings or classes about life in the Old West or this version of it, he was practicing with Nineteenth-Century firearms.

Six months after accepting the assignment, the powers that be contacted Bart. He was on a one-week notice to D Day.

Bart made sure his affairs were in order also to include an updated will. His employers found a retired government employee and her family to stay in his house with an option to buy if he never returned. He secured personal items in a long-term storage facility, with his Will stating who received what if he was declared legally dead. After a round of immunizations,

Bart relaxed at home with some single malt Scotch. He had no partner or companion to share this panned journey even if he could. His decision not to obtain a dog had been the right one.

Bart ate a high-protein Fighter Pilots breakfast of steak and eggs at a safe house the morning of the journey near the Tinkerers home where the Device, the Game, resided. The operative then hydrated himself with two glasses of water. Stripped down to just the jockstrap/sling, he stepped into the lead-lined small blockhouse constructed around the device. The only other object in the room was the infamous Tinkerer's Game, modified by the alleged best of the best in scientific knowledge. A short countdown, and he zapped through the Rabbit Hole.

Hours later and Bart sat on the former cavalry horse overlooking the Butterfield Stage Trail in New Mexico Territory. Some things stayed the same in this alternate Earth. Bart watched as a Butterfield coach went by with two mounted escorts. Bart gave them a friendly wave as the riders and stagecoach guards stared suspiciously at him. Bart did not need the hassle of explaining himself to curious strangers. Luckily, the riders agreed and stayed with the stagecoach.

Bart watched the dust settle from the passing of the coach, then nudged his mount forward. Bart headed at a slow trot towards Las Cruces. He started this trip well before sunrise, so the Sun was setting when he guided his horse off of the trail. Some half-mile from the Las Cruces city limits. Bart stripped the saddle and bridle off the mare. He rubbed the horse down, fed it some oats from a saddlebag, then slapped its rump. As it trotted away, Bart stashed the cavalry saddle in some brush but kept the other tacking. He decided riding into a strange town on a cavalry horse and rig may cause too many questions. Bart put on the duster found in the Hanks saddlebag, adjusted the saddlebags and bedroll on his shoulders, and then began walking.

Barely five minutes later, a wagon came out of the waning light. Bart stopped on the side of the road as the wagon driver pulled on the reins.

"Lose your horse?" the bearded beefy suntanned man asked.

"Yessir. Snake bit, bad. I had to put her down." Bart noticed the wagon piled high with odds and ends, plus two horses tied on the rear. A small side banner proclaimed, "JONES' MERCHANDISE AND SALVAGE. SAM JONES BUYS AND SELLS MOST EVERYTHING.

"Well," the man who must be Sam Jones spit some chaw on the road. "If you have some money, I can make you a deal on one of the Widow's horses here. And there is a nice cattleman saddle in the back."

"Widow?"

"Yes, sir. The Widow McKenzie. I just bought her out, lock, stock, and barrel. Except for the pigs. Her neighbor bought those."

"What happened to her husband?"

"Consumption. The McKenzies moved out to this dry country as a cure two years ago. It didn't work. She and her youngins are going to California; she has relatives there. I gave them a fair price on their goods."

Bart looked at the man, then shrugged.

"Sure. Why not? Let's start at dickering."

A half hour later, Bart had a good bay mare, a near-new saddle, a pistol, belt, and holster. The dead husband had a Coults Dragoon converted to .44 Extra Long Rimfire and bobbed to a six-inch barrel in a cross-draw rig. For some extra nickles, Bart had a loaded cylinder for the .44. He figured he could pick up some extra ammunition in town.

"New Mexico Territory is still rough. You'll need to let people see you are well-heeled."

"Yes, Mister Jones. I can see that."

Bart did not mention the Remington pistol in his saddlebags nor the tip-up Smith and Wesson hide-out gun.

"Call me, Jonesy. Everyone else does. It's getting dark, so head towards Buffalo Susan's hotel and bawdy house. She'll get you a room, no questions asked."

"With a bit more for—companionship, right?"

"Yes. But like I said, this time of night—"

"A little extra cost, no big deal."

Sam Jones grinned, spit some more tobacco juice.

"That's the spirit. Stop by my store tomorrow. You can pick up some more supplies."

Bart knew Jonesy was the observant type, had noticed Bart was traveling lite. However, the man was wise enough not to pry into a stranger's business as night fell.

"Will do. See you then."

Bart heeled his horse into a canter towards town. It was easy to find Buffalo Susan's establishment. There were extra lit lamps out front and a balcony with some comely women hanging over the railing. Bart smiled. It looked like Las Cruces was a wide-open town when it came to late-night activity. He walked the mare up to the hitching post in front and dismounted. Before he could tie her up, a dirty-faced boy ran up to him and rattled off in Spanish, then English, "I'll take your horse, Mister. Give me a dollar, and I'll take him to Manuel's stable. I'll pay him for the night, bring you back the change."

Bart grinned. *Quite the young entrepreneur,* he thought.

"Here, take this coin and bed her down, hang up the saddle. Keep the change and tell your family member

I'll pay him in full in the morning."

The young man grinned.

"Si, Senor!"

Bart took his Spenser carbine in with him. A rather large black man met him at the entrance.

"Hello. I'm Black Jim. What's your pleasure?"

"How about a room for the night, with some companionship, of course. Maybe a bath in the morning."

"That can be arranged. Follow me."

Bart followed the combination greeter and bouncer across the main floor. A dozen cowboys enjoyed the attentions of the ladies of the establishment as well as the food and beverages. Black Jim escorted Bart to the sweeping staircase up to the second floor. A young dark-haired woman met them, flashed a smile.

"Room, Jim?"

"Yes. And I think the man could use some food and a beer or two."

"Hi. I'm Eve," said the young woman, which Bart estimated was barely eighteen years of age.

"Pleased to meet you, Eve. My name is Bart Carson."

"Any relation to Kit Carson, the mountain man, and Indian Fighter? I've read a bunch of dime novels about him."

"Distant cousin, Eve."

"Sorry to hear he died last year."

"Yes, it was a sad day."

Kit Carson's death was another odd confluence of people between the two alternate timelines, or was it alternate universes? Figuring out that was above Bart's pay grade.

"I need two dollars upfront for the room."

Bart paid with a smile and made sure that Eve and Jim saw the small quantity of cash in his pocket. If they realized he had the lion's share of an Army patrol in his saddlebags, there would be hell to pay.

Bart had the room and Eve for information, not for fun. A drone had recorded a hazy picture of what Bart realized was the bawdy house. So, he started with Eve, some cold beer, cheese, and meat. As Bart relaxed, he talked with Eve about Reylie and Ron.

"I heard about them from Buffalo Susan," said Eve between mouthfuls. (Apparently, she had trouble finding time to eat.) "She was upset the young girl, Reylie, took off. I came to the house a month after Reylie and the others left. The other girls told me all about a big shootout they had with some Mexicans and Pinkertons."

"Anybody say where they went?"

Eve paused for a moment, then answered, "Something about the King Ranch in Texas. Susan would know." Eve took another large bite of cheese and beef. Bart grinned, then drank his beer. Ten minutes later, the young Eve daintily wiped her mouth, gave Bart her best coquettish smile.

"You want some—fun?"

"Sure, why not."

Before sun-up, Eve left with several more dollar bills. Bart had also picked her brains about a place to buy some clothes, besides at Jones's. Taking the saddlebag of money and Remington pistol and his Spencer rifle, Bart was up and walking downstairs for shopping and reserve a room for another night when Black Jim braced him.

"Buffalo Susan wants a word, stranger."

Bart could have protested, taken the large man out before he knew what hit him, but decided an audience with Buffalo Susan could provide some first-person testimony. Black Jim escorted him to Susan's office but did not ask for Bart's large pistol. The man was confident in his protection ability.

The office of the owner and madam was large and ornate, as was Buffalo Susan. The buxom blonde wore silk vestments with coiffed blonde hair. She intently examined Bart with her eyes as Jim escorted him in.

"Would you care for something to drink, Bart Carson?" the proprietress asked.

"Coffee would be nice, ma'am."

Susan rang a small handbell setting on her large desk. A comely lass wearing little more than a smile came in with a tray containing a silver service within moments. The young lady prepared cups of coffee for Susan, and Bart smiled at Bart and then left. Buffalo Susan sipped her coffee then asked, "You any relation to Kit Carson?"

"Distant cousin, ma'am."

"I met the man once. He was a lot shorter than I imagined. He had steel in his gaze, though. Had iron in his handshake."

"Like I said, a distant cousin. My part of the family was taller."

Susan gave Bart her version of steel in her gaze as she asked, "So why the questions about the King youngsters?"

"I was hired by her family to find them, help them get home."

"So, you're not a Pinkerton, working for a bounty?"

"No, Buffalo Susan, I am not. But then, now I have to ask you why you are concerned about Reylie and Ron?"

The woman smiled as she answered, "You could be seen as pushy as this is my place, Bart, and I ask the question."

"Well, then, I guess this conversation is going

nowhere, "replied Bart. "I'll get my things and find a different lodging."

The office door opened, and a third person entered.

"Is this the man you were talking about?" the man with a two-gun rig and a badge asked.

"Yes. Marshal Linden," answered Buffalo Susan. "He says he is working for the King family to locate the brother and sister."

Bart stood up slowly, transferred the coffee cup to his left hand as he presented his right for a handshake.

"Bart Carson, Marshal. The family hired me to find the two younger family members."

The lawman declined the handshake.

"You have any papers or documents stating that?"

"Sorry, lost in a gullywasher in Arizona Territory on my way here. Along with my boots and most other things."

"You're going to have to come with me. The Kings and the McCains they traveled with had a shootout on the way out of town last year. We had dead Mexicans and Pinkertons all over the place. The King Ranch family in Texas said they never heard of a Reylie and Ron King."

"Texans won't help us even if they had," said

Susan. "Jake and Bar McCain are examples of just how onery Texans are to the outside world. And I consider Jake a friend."

"So, Marshal, what can I possibly do if I don't know where Reylie and Ron are staying?" asked Bart.

'You can put me in touch with the real King family."

How to explain such contact was impossible as the non-Texan King Family was across time and space? Bart knew there was no way.

"Well, Marshal, if you have a telegraph here. I might just be able to do that."

"Then, let's go," said the Marshal. Bart set down the coffee cup and smiled at Buffalo Sally.

"Thanks for the excellent coffee. It tastes like it's from Columbia—"

One of Bart's martial arts instructors had taught him something he called the Six Strike Escape. It was actually five blows and a Front Mule Kick, with an optional takedown throw. Bart flattened the Marshal in the first few seconds, then had to work on Black Jim. The operative left the large man lying over Susan's office desk, stunned. The madam and business owner tried to get a Coult Baby Dragoon into play. Bart did a quick weapon take away and shoved the barrel of the smaller pistol into her left nostril.

"We are now leaving this establishment and

fetch my horse. I will shoot you at the first incident of gunplay. Understand?"

"You are no Sugarfoot," said Buffalo Susan.

"My business is that of kidnap and assassination on a typical day. With the Kings, I am on a rescue mission. Don't press your luck."

Bart escorted Susan to recover his horse and saddle; the Baby Dragoon stuck in her ribcage. The young Mexican lad met him with a smile, and Bart tossed him a five-dollar gold piece wrapped in a paper dollar.

"That should cover the board and care for my horse," said Bart in Spanish.

"Of course, Senor. I will saddle it and bring it to you."

"Thanks, Amigo." Bart then turned his attention to the madam.

"Where would these McCains be taking Ron and Reylie?"

"Jake said they had a spread outside of Fort Stockton."

"It's been about a year. If they made it, Reylie and Ron should still be there."

"They must be paying you a lot, Bart," opined Susan.

"In potential fame and fortune, yes, Buffalo Susan. But you wouldn't understand. The easy way for you was just sitting and talking to me, not call the marshal."

"That shootout caused us all a bunch of problems. I had to help clean up the mess Uncle Jake and Bar left me."

"Well, boohoo. Sit on that bucket while I mount my house. I'll drop off your pistol on the edge of town."

Bart was up on the bay mare just as soon as the young Mexican brought it to him. Bart gave Susan a three-finger Boy Scout salute and called out, "Don't take any wooden nickels."

As he prodded the horse into a canter, a four-man U.S. Cavalry patrol entered the edge of town. They had a prisoner in custody. As Bart passed the group, he saw the prisoner was Deserter Hank.

"That's him! That's the guy who took the payroll."

Bart had the former Army Remington pistol out of the saddlebag and blasted away at the horses before the four troopers could react. He hated killing innocent beasts, but it was that or shooting innocent soldiers. In seconds there was a mass of screaming and dying horses as well as yelling troopers. Bart pushed his mount to a gallop and lit out of Las Cruces towards Texas. He dropped the empty Remington on the outskirts of town. If Bart ever saw Buffalo Susan again, he'd have to apologize for not dropping her pistol off as promised.

Bart swung his path wide up into the foothills of

the Organ Mountains to throw off pursuit. He stopped once to rest the mare and discovered someone at the stables had placed some oats and tortillas in a small bag tied to the saddle. They had also refilled the waterskin. Someday, he'd have to repay Manuel's stables.

After a night of a cold camp, he pushed his horse to cover the remaining miles to El Paso, Texas. He entered the main streets of the growing city late in the afternoon and quickly stabled his mount. He paid the owner some extra coin to have his daughter give the mare a good rub down. Bart then went looking for a place for him to stay. He found an average hotel on El Paso Street and checked in. The special operator stowed his Spencer and bedroll in the room but kept the saddlebag with the army payroll. Now it was time to purchase some needed supplies for his continued search.

Bart found a small clothing and sewing store and purchased some spare clothes, including longjohns and a decent coat. Bart next went looking and found a leather goods store still open for some boots and chaps. He bought a decent slouch-style hat off of a street vendor. Now it was time to expand his ammunition supplies. He found El Paso Guns and Leather just before the owner, Greg Kolster was about to close for the evening.

"I'll be quick, I promise," Bart said.

"You'd better. My wife is awaitin'.""

Some .44 Extra Long for the modified Dragoon, .41 for the S&W hide-out, and 56 Spencer for his carbine rounded out his initial purchase.

"You open tomorrow?"

"Yessir. Since 1860 I've had the store."

"I'll be back for a Sharps or Remmington rifle. I may be taking a long trip."

"Your money's good, Mister. Come back anytime," Greg Kolster said.

Bart found an open Chinese restaurant and bought a large to-go order, along with a bottle of plum wine. He went into a cheap saloon and bought a shot plus a large bottle of beer. Then it was back to the hotel for a bath.

As Bart soaked in the tub in his room, at an extra charge, of course, he pondered his next moves. Things had exploded since minute one, it seemed. The Kings had been traveling in a rough group, which may have helped them survive. However, their group seemed to cause some problems and bad feelings. Thus, he had to be careful about who and how he asked questions. The owner of the gun store would probably know about those who used firearms in their travels. Bart would feel him out tomorrow.

Bart sighed as he felt the bathwater cool. He had been in worse situations. After a good night's sleep and a decent breakfast, then it was back to work. The sooner he found Reylie and Ron, the sooner he could try and return them all to home. If that was an impossible task, well, he had the skills to exist here comfortably.

Someone always needed an assassin.

John King walked into his home's backyard. The federal government decided to allow his assistance on the now named Operation Rabbit Hole since he had somehow built The Game. After all, he was The Tinkerer and creator of the odd device, even if the mysterious Yeleanah Moon gave him a unique piece of equipment called the heart of machinery.

Once John's workshop was now a twice the size lead encased building with a hidden two-story basement. The same federal agencies who allowed his help also bought up the houses for a two-block radius square using proxies; the one holdout threatened with eminent domain seizure by some Men in Black as well as some unspecified pain. Examining the nuclear energy pulse from the two 'events' convinced the government scientists there was no serious threat of an atomic detonation or radioactive contamination once the lead-lined walls were in place. At least, that was the official mantra. The two-block barrier was to keep things secret there was radiation leakage. The scientists involved were afraid to move The Game until they figured out how it worked and if this the only place on Earth where it did work. The possibility of inter-universe transport was much too significant to chance.

A guard camouflaged as a gardener nodded at John as he went to the security door, presented both his iris and palm print to gain access. John King was the Tinkerer, so even if he was not an official advanced degree scientist, he was a 'go-to' man. John shut and secured the door behind him and then repeated the process on the inner door. In an emergency, the two-door access could become a sealed airlock.

"How are things going, Doc Deeneka?" John asked the twenty-something whizz kid Donald. The toe-headed youngster kept staring at his computer screen as he answered.

"Our agent made it through, it seems. We are trying to squeeze another drone to find him. So far, sir, no luck."

The younger scientists gave John significant levels of dispensation and respect despite his lack of formal scientific training. Many came from Area 51 and knew of his background, not to mention his connection with the legendary Moon Lady, Yeleanah Moon. Her name was still spoken in hushed tones in her former work areas. Plus, the Tinkerer had put The Game together. No one else had been able to accomplish what he had in interdimensional travel.

"How about Jasmine Wright? Any information

about what happened?"

Donald turned away from his computer and spoke to John.

"All energy indications are she went down a Rabbit Hole. However, it is a different hole. We can't find enough information about the hole's location to send a drone into it. The tachyon and Higgs Singlet traces are not enough to obtain a good lock on her path."

John shook his head.

"If I had known creating a game from some mechanism I received in the mail would cause all these problems, I would have created a card game instead."

"If that had happened, we would not be on the cutting edge of a scientific breakthrough. One which could open this universe and others to human transportation to the stars."

John snorted.

"Yeah, but it's my friends and family who have suffered so far. Maybe if some of you people from Dreamland had got yanked from this Earth to God knows where it might be more personal."

"I know, sir. It's easy for eggheads like me to spout platitudes. But trust me when I say we will solve this puzzle and get people home. These pathways *are* two-way roads. Our tests and math prove that."

John sighed.

"I wished I had your youthful certainty. Well,

until we have the highway built, what can I do to help you with The Game?"

A couple of hours later, John went back into his house to have dinner with Joan. Their daughter Jeannie, mother of the two missing grandchildren, stayed with them full time now but had a night shift as a nurse at the local hospital. Her ex-husband Christopher "Chris" Hawkins drove a long-haul truck and was on the road. When Reylie and Ronald first disappeared, accusations about who was responsible did not help the relationship between the divorced parents. John always hoped his daughter would reunite with Chris as his son-in-law, a veteran also, was like a second son to him. So far, that was not in the cards. At least the smartass Kyle, the stockbroker, had disappeared from Jeannie's life. The fact he left without any goodbye did not help Jeannie's state of mind. Only the hope the government scientists and officials gave (classified, of course) by stating Reylie and Ron arrived in the new world alive and were seen alive in fuzzy pictures transferred through time and space kept Jeannie sane.

Joan placed the meal on the table and said little. She was still getting over that their son Maxwell was MIA in the Middle East when the grandchildren disappeared. As with her daughter, the government assurances kept her hoping Joan would see her grandchildren someday. Jasmine Wright had been a sore spot in her life as she returned from the Mid East and not her Battle Buddy Max. However, her 'spinning' by The Game into another reality showed Joan the highways between the universes were still open.

"Any news?" Joan finally asked and broke the silence.

"The rescue agent they sent arrived safe and sound. Now the eggheads hope he activates the beacon they sent with him. Then, they can locate the grandkids and start working on bringing them back."

"Think it will be in our lifetime?" asked Joan.

"I have hope and confidence in the abilities of the people from Dreamland. They are the best of the best, just like most were when I worked at Area 51."

Joan stood up, having eaten little.

"I wished now you had never worked there, never met that Yeleanah," said Joan.

"Then I would never have met you, dearest," John replied. "Then we would have no children."

"Maybe that would have been better," Joan said as she walked towards the kitchen.

"No children, no pain from loss."

John let the comment go. It would do no good to argue. John knew his wife; his love was fighting depression. He fought the clouds of depression by working with The Game. She had no such release.

John was still up reading when his daughter

Jeannie returned from the late shift. John met her at the door and hugged her.

"How was work, Jeannie?"

"The same. Nothing too serious, no gunshot wounds."

She went to the refrigerator and found a beer.

"How about out in the back?" His daughter motioned with her chin in the general direction of his former workshop.

"They say the rescue agent landed safely in the general area in which the kids landed. The question is the timeframe. How close to Reylie and Ron's time is he? They hope at the most months later. However, there is the worst-case scenario of years later."

"No chance of arriving before my kids did? "

John shrugged. "Theoretically, yes. However, the technicians and scientists prefer later as then they have a better idea of their location. Too early, and it's harder to match up the limited drone data they have on the area Reylie and Ron are in now. Or at least, 'now' in Western World."

Jeannie sipped her beer. "Dad, any idea when they are going to let the public in on this? The neighborhood noticed all the nearby homeowners suddenly sold and moved."

John chuckled. "Doctor Mankaweitz complained to me that some neighbors try to hide behind their drapes when they see any of the Project personnel and their families walk down the street. The various cover stories are wearing thin in spots."

"Well, at least they have their kids and spouses." Jeannie took a slug of beer. "Some of us have neither."

Father and daughter stood silent in the kitchen. Then John spoke. "Any chance you and Chris will get back together?"

"Hell, after the accusations back and forth about the fault in the disappearance, then the security crackdown, talking is difficult." Jeannie finished her beer, took two more from the frig, and handed her father one.

"I hate to drink alone, Dad."

"Thanks."

"Mom is really depressed, isn't she?"

"Yes, she is. Your Mom likes you here but not under these circumstances. When the kids return, please think about living with us for a while."

"If you'll have me, yes. The plan of Kyle and I have a house together fell apart when the bastard up and disappeared. So keeping Chris and my former home with no kids around makes no sense. I'm glad he did not raise a stink when I said I wanted to sell it. "

"You know that house was for you and the kids."

"I know. You and Chris got along great. Somewhere along with life, we just started fighting all the time. Our work schedules did not help matters." Jeannie took a drink of her beer. "Kids love Chris, wanted us to stay together. Our breakup led to this—mess."

"No, daughter. My stupid tinkering with that Game did. You had nothing to do with it."

"They were here because of the divorce and my trying to hook up with Kyle. Without those actions, someone else would have activated it."

"Yeah, like you dear old dad." John drank from his beer. "That is what should have happened."

"No, Dad. If that happened, your expertise would be lacking; Mom and I would not be in this house as there was no reason for the Men in Black not to seize everything. They need your happy onsite help to understand this—thing."

Jeannie walked over and hugged her father.

"Things just happen sometimes. At least Reylie and Ron are alive; they figured that out. Hopefully, the rescue agent will find them in record time, activate the beacon, and then the head shed will find a way to get them back."

John kissed his daughter on her forehead.

"I love you, Jeannie. Always remember that."

"I will, Dad. Do you ever think about Maxwell?"

"All the time. I sometimes hope Max fell down a Rabbit Hole rather than being grabbed by Islamic

Radicals and killed. "

Father and daughter stepped apart and finished their beers.

"Time for bed, daughter. I need to keep an eye on the goings-on in the workshop."

"Okay. Night dad."

"Goodnight to you, Jeannie. Sleep tight, don't let the bed bugs bite."

Jeannie laughed as she went to her room.

John stayed up a few minutes more and looked out the back windows. The scientific staff kept the workshop operated twenty-four hours a day, with two backup personnel in the double-storied basement under the lead-lined building. They were afraid that if a hole in space and time opened up unexpectantly, they might make a mistake and miss the whole shebang. When they sent the rescue agent through, the first time a controlled transfer event was attempted, not even John was allowed in the former workshop. The excuse was if something went bad and the wrong people were sucked through the Rabbit Hole, the original creator could not be one of them. John thought the Men in Black just wanted him out of the way.

He thought about his missing son Maxwell. He assumed he was dead. But then, that thought about— what if he fell through a similar hole in time and space? If Yeleanah Moon could create a device to bend time and space, there must be others.

John grunted and made his way to bed. Best to stick with this Sci-Fi reality sitting in his backyard than imagine something else. His machine sent three people to an alternate reality. That was a problem enough.

A man in a Brooks Brothers suit stumbled through a humid jungle, cursing as he tried to gain a good cellular connection. Kyle Whitney, late of Earth and one time possible fiancé of Jeannie King, cursed loudly and often. He *knew* he shouldn't have nosed around that workshop of old man King, especially after the cops asked all those questions about the missing kids. He'd escorted Jeannie there when the report of the possible runaways after some problem at school with the little punk Ronald. Like father, like son had been his thought. Ex-husband Chris was a loser truck driver type; his son was on the same path.

Kyle nosed around the workshop when the cops were not looking, and *Zap!* A flash of light and he was in Jungle World Theme Park.

"Goddammit, there's got to be away out of this place!" Kyle cursed loudly as his silk shirt stuck to his body.

He failed to notice the painted humanoids sneaking up on him until they grabbed him.

CHAPTER 8
RESCUE PARTY: PART 2

art Carson checked out of his hotel room and collected his horse from the stable. He ate some leftover rice from the Chinese takeout the night before. The Chinese in America had helped create takeout food by using early versions of thick paper cartons for rice and other not too liquid dishes. Here in the 1869 Alternate Earth, it was the same. A gulp of plum wine and a cup of coffee from the hotel pot round out Bart's breakfast.

Bart walked his mount over to the 'EL PASO GUNS AND LEATHER SHOP.' He needed a heavy-duty rifle and some information. The proprietor Greg Kolster seemed like a man who kept his ear to the ground and knew what happened in the community. It was still early in the morning, yet there were already people bustling between the various businesses. Bart worked his way between the moving humanity until he could tie his horse in front of the gun shop.

Greg Kolster had just opened his business when Bart walked up.

"So you did make it back, Mister Carson."

"Call me Bart. You have a newer cartridge Sharps in there?"

The big man grinned.

"More than one, Bart. Come on in; I have a fresh pot of coffee brewing."

Greg soon had Bart examining a brand new Sharps breech-loader.

"Brand new .50-70 sent to me as a sales model. It is not a conversion. I'll sell it at a premium price if you need a new rifle for your travels. Otherwise, I have some conversion models—"

"How much?" asked Bart,

"Forty dollars."

"Thirty. You know there are tons of surplus weapons since the War."

The two men haggled back and forth until Bart agreed on paying thirty-five dollars for the rifle, plus fifty rounds of newly manufactured cartridge centerfire and a cleaning rod. Bart dug out thirty dollars in bills and five silver dollars.

"Throw in a few hand loads?"

"You make a hard bargain. Five for two bits."

"Okay."

"By the way. Bart Carson, I have to ask—where you headed and why? "

"I was going to bring it up if you didn't, Greg. I'm looking for two youngins, the last name of King."

Greg paused for a few minutes as he examined the man who stood before him.

"You don't look like a Pinkerton," said the gunshop owner.

"I'm not. I've been hired by the King Family from near Seattle to find Reylie and Ronald King. I think you probably have heard of them passing through."

"Well, what do you know about them, Bart?"

The special operator told Greg about the problems in Las Cruces, and the shop owner laughed.

"Yeah. Bar and Uncle Jake McCain told me about it. They and the two young ones took out some other Pinkerton's in this very place."

"I heard they headed to a spread in Fort Stockton."

"Yessir. The McCain ranch. I understand they are not related to the Kings in Texas."

"Will the McCains take good care of them?" asked Bart.

"Yessir. The McCains treated them like family. I say they became adopted family." Greg chuckled. "Those two were quite the pistoleros—damned fine shots."

"Well, I thank you for the information. It sounds like the McCains kept them alive in a rough country."

"They'll be in good shape at the McCain spread, barring catching a sickness. Bar and Uncle Jake would not let anyone hurt someone's children. I've known them for years—that is against their nature."

Bart shook hands with the gunshop owner, picked up his new rifle, and went to his horse. After a couple of quick stops at local shops and Bart thought about his next moves, he slowly rode out of El Paso, Texas. Bart stopped some three hours later at the small mission town of Ysleta, Texas. It was still a stronghold of people of Mexican descent, even since the last War. Bart thought he might obtain some more information about some Gringos traveling with a brother and sister on the young side. It was also a spot to pick up some more food supplies for his journey. Eating jerked beef, hardtack, and cheese for the next week was not his idea of a preferred diet. Some Mexican beans, spices, and chiles would add some variety.

He stopped at an adobe cantina with an attached Tienda/store. He left his new Sharps concealed in a wrapped blanket on his mount and walked in with Spencer carbine. Bart let his eyes adjust to the dim interior and then walked to the general store side. The man and women behind the county gave him the once over as he clearly was not a local Mexican. When Bart spoke Spanish like a native, their faces brightened with expressions of a pleasant surprise.

The man and wife proprietors of store half of the establish soon provided him with a bottle of ginger beer, corn and wheat tortillas, chili beans, onions, pan dulce, and barbacoa for his journey. They did not remember two Jovens traveling with older men, but they may have visited the bar. Bart thanked the couple, paid for his goods, and placed them in a flour sack for transport. He then walked into the bar side.

The bartender was a large dark-skinned Mexican who watched Bart as he walked up to the bar railing.

"*Cerveza, por favor*," Bart said with a smile. The barkeep grunted and filled an old and scratched up but clean mug from a barrel behind him. The typical lukewarm concoction of many a frontier drinking filled the glass of an establishment too crude to be called a saloon or tavern. Bart chugged the beer down, munched on some stale tortillas as he waited for his refill. Bart placed four bits on the bar top so the man would know he would pay. He then struck up a conversation in Spanish about the Kings.

"You speak our language well," the bartender Jorge said in English. "You a Huero, light-skinned Mexican? Or maybe a Spaniard who stayed around after the last war with Mexico."

"No. Just a man who worked with people from a

lot of countries. So, do you remember the young man and lady passing through?"

Jorge spits in a spittoon behind the bar.

"I only got a glimpse of the two young ones. I remember the bronze hair on the girl. What I do remember are the two *gringos* they traveled with, especially the large one. He hates Mexicans."

"How do you know?"

"As a bartender, you know when somebody hates by the look in their eyes. The large one, I heard him called Bar, came in with Greyhair to buy wine and beer. The water around here is not good. Bar took exception to a comment a Mexican male made about the girl. The two men exchanged words, and the one called Bar busted the other man's head wide open. Then he broke the jaw of another. Greyhaired Viejo threw some gold my way, grabbed the bottles they bought, and got Bar to leave before shooting began."

"Sounds like the people I am looking to find. The King family hired me to find a brother and sister."

"Well, the two young ones did not seem to be going against their will as they walked freely outside."

"The two young ones separated from their family during a fight with some Indians. The McCains seemed to protect them, so I do not quarrel with them. I just need to return them to the King family."

"Another *chingada gringo* I see," came a voice

from across the bar. A drunk man wearing the trappings of a vaquero stood up from a table on unsteady legs and walked towards Bart.

"You friends with the *Hijo de puto* who broke my brother's jaw?"

"Sorry, *amigo*. Never met him."

Two slightly more sober vaqueros joined their friend near Bart.

"Hey, guys. I'm just passing through. How about I buy you all a drink?"

"How about you *vamos*, you *gabacho*—"

Bart smashed his fist into the nose of the speaker. The blow knocked the man back into the arms of his companions. Bart had the chopped down Dragoon out of the holster and aimed at the trio in a flash.

"I was trying to be sociable, but you just had to ruin the moment. The next person who tries to brace me will have a .44 slug in their gut. Now, sit down!"

The two still conscious Mexicans moved their friend back towards their table. Bart threw a dollar coin on the bartop.

"Thanks for the conversation, Jorge. However, I think it's time to leave."

"Stop by anytime—what's your name again?"

"Bart Carson. I doubt I'll be passing by here again, but thanks for the invite."

Bart had his goods loaded on his horse and

headed out of the small town within five minutes. He knew he would be looking over his shoulder for some miles as the Mexicans looked like the 'vengaza' type. Thus, as the sun set, Bart rode off the trail into some low hills north of the small settlement of San Elizario, Texas. He passed through the village without stopping as he wanted no more trouble this day. Bart was unsure of the population around San Elizario, so the warrior decided to camp in the scrub brush. After wiping down his bay mare and feeding her some oats he had obtained from the stable, he tied her to a lead attached to a low tree.

Bart built a small campfire, then removed the new Sharps from the concealing bedroll. He found the five reloaded shells and walked a ways from his camp. There was still enough light for him to see the giant jackrabbit munching on some greens approximately a hundred yards away. Bart loaded his new rifle, sighted in on the shadowy figure, and squeezed the trigger. The large shell was overkill on the rabbit, taking off its head and shoulders. At least the shot proved the rifle functioned well and was accurate.

Bart walked out and collected the rabbit's two rear legs and soon had them roasting on the fire. In a cast-iron skillet he procured in El Paso on his way out of town, the former soldier fried up some tortillas and old cheese as crude grilled cheese sandwiches. Bart added some chilies and spices to the rabbit meat and the cheese-filled tortillas. He sat down on a small boulder and ate. Bart liked his own cooking, which was suitable for a Batchelor. He washed it all down with the bottle of ginger beer.

Bart chuckled. This part of his mission was not bad. He always liked solitude in the outdoors, so this fits his personality. Bart cleaned up the skillet and put it back in his saddlebags. He then found an El Paso Newspaper he bought on the way out of town and went to locate a log or boulder to use while he took care of his necessary bodily functions. He took his Spencer repeater with him. *It would be best if you never were without a firearm in this turbulent world,* Bart thought.

Bart was finishing his business when he could a muffled curse in Spanish. Shit. Those assholes had come looking for him after all.

Bart dropped down behind some bushes and began a low crawl in the direction of the curse. He saw a figure a few yards away moving towards the light of his campfire. Bart heard his bay mare voice a nervous whinny as the horse sensed strangers approaching. He made out two other figures coming to his campsite from further out. Ascertaining the three men could not see each other well, Bart snuck up on the nearest Mexican. In Bart's right hand was a good-sized rock, which he quickly used to knock the man out. Bart took the pistol from the Mexican's limp hand and stalked the other two men.

Bart was some seven yards behind them when the two remaining would-be attackers began whispering and cursing between them as to where was the pendejo Gringo?

"Here, hombre," Bart called out as he used the first man's Remington Pistol to shoot the two companions. The first dropped like a rock as Bart fanned the revolver at the human targets. After the third shot, the cylinder bound up. Bart dropped the jammed pistol and swung his Spencer into action. The second man fell, then sprung back up like a bunny rabbit. Bart began to aim in when the man fell again. This time he lay twitching for a few moments, then lay still. Bart went to both dead men, removed their guns, belts, and money pouches. He then walked back to the unconscious Mexican.

Bart stripped the third man's belt and used it and the two others' belts to bind him. The two dead men had Coult Navy revolvers converted to .38 rimfire cartridges. Bart placed those in a saddlebag for later resale. Bart took a length of rope from a saddlebag and used it to hobble the unconscious man to the trunk of a short desert tree. Then, he went back to his camp to rest. The bay mare would fuss and wake him up when the Mexican tried to free himself.

Sure enough, four hours later, the mare began

moving around and snorting. Bart was up immediately with his Dragoon pistol and walked to where the Mexican was tied up. The man managed to stand up but had trouble figuring out how Bart hobbled him to the tree. The man was working on freeing his hands with a piece of flint rock.

"That won't do you any good, Jefe," said Bart. The man jerked his gaze to Bart and saw the short-barreled Dragoon pointed at him. The former attacker proceeded to urinate in his pants.

"Oh, I won't kill you. You just sit down while I break camp. Then you can finish freeing yourself after I'm gone."

When the man did not move, Bart bellowed, "Sit!"

He sat.

Bart had his horse saddled up and ready to go in a quarter of an hour. He kicked some dirt on the campfire, then urinated on it. The warrior walked his horse the fifteen yards to the bound man still seated on the ground. Bart smiled at him as he walked by and spoke.

"I'm leaving now. Your friends are dead. I usually give people just one chance to harm me. You, I'll make an exception." Bart paused in his walk and fixed the man with his stare.

"Follow me, and I see you again; I will gut shoot

you. Understand?"

"*Si*—yes."

"Good. Your pistol is jammed up and near the campfire. Adios."

Bart swung up onto his horse and continued his journey. He found the Mexican's mounts a little more than a mile from his former campsite, about a mile off the main road. Bart took the saddles and bridles off of two horses and slapped them on the rump to move. He used the third mount as a packhorse, affixing the saddlebags and rifles from the Mexican horses. Then Bart was off. If the surviving Mexican freed himself soon, he might be able to catch one of the mounts. It not; he had a long walk before him.

Bart rode all day, only stopping to rest the two horses. Ten hours later, Bart camped near some nondescript village that did not seem to warrant a formal name. Again, he kept to himself, saw to his horses, ate, and turned in. Bart was up at daybreak, fed and watered his mounts. Then he hit the road once again. The special operative hoped to make it to the stagecoach waystation near Sierra Blanca Pass that day. He passed a coach-headed El Paso Way, but the driver did not seem to have any desire to stop and jaw. Bart kept up a steady pace and made Sierra Blanca by nightfall.

The sizeable German station keeper was glad to

have a new face to commune with and made sure Bart's mounts had a spot in the Butterfield and Wells Fargo coaches' stables.

"Yah, sure, the Apache and Comanche still try to steal and kill along the trail when they get a chance," Dutchy Muller, the stationmaster, said over a hot cup of coffee and pie baked by his wife. "Since the end of the Second Mexican War, President Lincoln and then Grant have added cavalry to patrol the trails to the West and California. Did you have any trouble after leaving El Paso?"

"Not with Indians, just with some Mexican Vaqueros." Bart relayed an essential telling of the conflict but left out the detail of him killing two of them and leaving the third horseless.

"Yah, sure, you betcha. Many Mexicans are still angry after the War. The Rangers check in with us from time to time and ensure we are not bothered."

"They have Texas Rangers at Van Horn?" asked Bart as he sipped his coffee.

"Yes, Cavalry, Second Mounted Dragoons, also. Van Horn is growing from a small outpost thanks to the War and then the Indian raids. You headed there?"

"Fort Stockton is my final destination. I need to catch up with a brother and sister, about fifteen years of age. They were separated from their family in an Indian Raid. Have you heard about a couple of youngins named

King? They are traveling with Bar and Jake McCain."

Dutchy laughed.

"Anybody with any dealings with the Rangers knows about the McCains. They are legends as Texas Rangers. They can be your best friends or your worst enemies. Bar, the young nephew. He is legendary with a Root Coult horse pistol."

"So if the King children are traveling with them, they're in good hands?"

"The McCains won't let anybody harm them. But sometimes, trouble follows the McCains."

Dutchy had Bart stay in a bunkhouse for layover stage drivers and such if storms stopped the stage. The stationmaster had not seen the MaCains nor the King siblings, so he assumed they bypassed Sierra Blanca. The good news was everyone who knew the McCains said they would be like mama bears protecting their cubs when it came to the Kings. The fact trouble followed them was worrisome, however.

Mrs. Muller fed Bart an old-fashioned farmer's breakfast; thus, the searcher left with a very full stomach. Bart gave Dutchy some extra silver for his hospitality and then hit the trail. Dutchy said if Bart followed the Stage Route, he would have to go South from Van Horn and through Alpine, Texas, then back to the Northeast to Fort Stockton; there was a rougher and unimproved trail direct East from Van Horn, which was shorter. Bart decided to take the harsher of the two routes when he left Van Horn.

By the end of the day, Bart was at Van Horn, Texas. He could tell it was once just a small trading outpost that expanded due to the last war and settler's headed West. Bart found a rooming house attached to a small stable for his horses and himself. There was a small bar next door where Bart obtained a hot meal of stew and some chilled beer. Someone had access to ice, it seemed. Bart decided he would get a good night's rest after a full stomach and contact the Ranger Station in the morning.

The former Marine was getting ready for a good night's sleep when someone knocked loudly on the room's door. The .44 Coult was in his hand in the blink of an eye as he asked. "Who is it?"

"Jack Williams, Texas Ranger. I need to talk to you."

"Okay," Bart said as he opened the room door. He held the Coult Dragoon behind his right leg as he let the Ranger in. Ranger Williams met all the stereotype images of a Texas Ranger. Tall, broad-shouldered with a ten-gallon hat on his head and a large revolver in a cross draw holster, Jack Williams stepped into the room as if he owned it.

"Y'all not going to shoot me with that horse pistol, are you?"

"I don't plan on it. That looks like a Ranger badge on your chest, made from a Mexican silver Cinco peso."

"Huh. You know about it then?"

"Yes, sir, I do. I can offer you some rotgut whiskey I picked up on the trail if you wish."

"No, thank you, Mister Carson. This won't take long. I heard you are looking for the McCains."

"Actually, Ranger. I am looking for the King brother and sister, Ron and Reylie. I heard the McCains took them under their wing."

The Ranger looked at Bart, sizing him up as Bart had done with many people in a far-off country.

"You don't look like a Pinkerton man," said Jack Williams.

"No. sir. I'm just a man used to going into rough countries and sometimes taking people back with me. No badge, no warrants. Just entered into a covenant with the family to retrieve their young kin."

"Well, I can assure you the young kin are safe with the McCains. They passed through Van Horn some months back and are now at the McCain ranch near Fort Stockton."

"Well, Ranger, this information saves me from bothering you in the morning." Bart laid his pistol down and offered his hand in friendship. The Ranger shook it, then went to leave.

"Just be warned, the road you are traveling on is

not safe right now. I stopped by tonight as tomorrow I need to collect together a Ranger Company to chase some Comanche. They decided to come down from the Llano Estacado and do some horse stealing. That means some settlers will die."

"Thank you for the warning. However, I gave my word I would find Reylie and Ronald."

"What if they don't want to go back with you?"

Bart smiled.

"As people say. I'll cross that bridge when I get to it."

"Well, be careful. Vaya con Dios, Bart Carson."

"Thank you, Ranger; I will."

Bart lay awake for a while after Ranger Williams left. He knew this mission was potentially dangerous when he accepted it. However, it was as if his mere presence in this universe had upset the scheme of things. Military Deserters, vengeful drunk Mexicans, and now Comanche on the warpath. What was next?

Bart mentally shrugged. *No use to worry now.* He was in the thick of things and thus needed to focus on his mission. With that last thought, Bart rolled over and went to sleep.

Bart Carson was up at daybreak. He grabbed some biscuits and gravy at the local greasy spoon, washed it down with some strong Cowboy Coffee. After collecting his horses and equipment at the stables, Bart rode out of town and took the northern route to Fort Stockton. As Dutchy had stated, it was a rougher trail than the one used by the stagecoaches through Alpine, Texas. However, the over hundred-mile trip was a lot shorter than the one through Alpine. Bart needed to bring this assignment to a close, one way or another.

Five miles outside of Van Horn. Bart heard a rifle shot. Then he heard other booms and cracks from various firearms coming from behind a rise in the road. He spurred his horses into a canter. The small hill on the route climbed to a peak about a mile in front of Bar. He reined up short and stood up in the saddle. Bart looked down into the gully on the other side just as he heard an unmistakable war-whoop. The ex-special forces member had found the band of Comanche spoke of by Ranger Williams-or at least part of it.

Two open wagons traveling together were pounced on by what Bart saw were at least half a dozen Indians. Bart quickly surmised two local farm and ranch families had been traveling (maybe temporarily relocating) together for safety due to reports of marauding Comanches. They were the first victims of the raiders, it seemed.

Bart placed the rains of the packhorse in his mouth, pulled the Sharps rifle from the bedroll, and spurred his horse into a gallop. One entire month preparing for the mission, Bart had ridden day and night at a secret training base, practicing shooting and horsemanship. Bart used historical reports of Texas Ranger and Comanche riding skills as the basis for his exercises, learning to shoot from all types of positioning while on horseback. He may not be as good as the Rangers or Comanches, who spent years in the saddle, but he was close to it. Learning sniper skills from the SEALS on how to shoot from a rocking vessel at sea helped also.

The Comanches used the traditional 'wagon wheel' attack after shooting the lead horse from the first wagon. Bart saw more than six of the Comanches as he neared, as they rode round and round the victim's wagons, shooting arrows and bullets. The Caucasian settlers tried to hide in and around the wagons as the second wagon driver attempted to keep his horses from bolting.

Bart's first shot took the horse out from under a Comanche with a buffalo horn headdress. The rider managed to roll from the horse as it slammed into the dirt. The shot was from a good four hundred yards, and Bart slung the sharps on the sling as he yanked the Spencer repeater from its scabbard. Bart was galloping hellbent for leather as he began firing his repeating rifle. Because the shooter had to cock the hammer after a person fired every new round, it was not as fast in operation as a Winchester or Henry repeater. However, it was fast enough.

Bart used the Ranger Tactic of close fast and hit hard as he bore down on the Comanche. To stand back was to invite an arrow shirt. Thus Bart started hitting targets from two hundred yards out. The sudden attack caused the Comanche to sit up and take notice. Two braves toppled from their horses as the just over a half-inch in diameter bullets struck home. Another horse and rider went down as the bullet hit the mount in the head. Then Bart galloped past the tableau at full speed, screaming like a Banshee with the horse reins in his teeth.

Such a vicious attack by a lone rider had stunned the Comanche warriors. As Bart flew past, various Comanches began to yell out in their language. Bart reined in his mount whipped the bay mare around, and replaced Spencer's tube magazine with a loaded one. Three Comanche warriors came galloping at him with war lances raised. Bart stood up in his stirrups and shot all three down. Had they been smart, they would have made him a pincushion with arrows. Youthful exuberance had been their downfall.

The farmers and ranchers fired a steady stream of rifle and pistol fire as the Comanches' fatal attention was taken from them. The remaining warriors then performed a standard retreat tactic; they broke off the attack, helped horseless and wounded fellows onto other mounts, and fled over the rise in the terrain from whence they came and out of temporary sight. Bart galloped up to the wagons.

"Who the hell are you, Mister?" the driver and senior male of the second wagon called out.

"Someone who is trying to get you out of here," Bart yelled back. He saw the oldest male of the first wagon laid next to the wagon with an arrow through his chest. A teenage boy, white as a sheet, stood in shock with a long gun in his hands. Bart spurred his mount to the boy and jabbed him with his carbine barrel.

"You! Cut the dead horse loose, get the others under control." Bart looked at the wife/mother holding her dying mate. "Get him in the wagon; you have other children to save. MOVE."

Bart did a quick count of the people. He saw five adults; three were women; one of the males was dying. There were two males and two females of teenage status and six more minor children. Bart called to the driver of the second wagon.

"What's your name?"

"Tom O'Reilly."

"Who can shoot and who can handle horses?"

"I can shoot." The voice was from a tall red-headed woman who stepped next to Tom.

"Get a repeater rifle. Get in the back of the

wagon. Tom, you handle the horses. Can your son there shoot? Good. He gets in with, what's your name?"

"Shannon. I'm Tom's sister."

"You two have to help me keep the next wave of Comanche from running us over. Yes, they will be back. Their warrior ability is in question. The war leader can't go back to the tribe without some horses, scalps, or captives. There are probably some other small groups out, looking for good targets. These just stumbled onto you and became impatient."

Bart maneuvered his horse up to the first wagon. The teenage boy had cut the dead horse loose and maneuvered the remaining three horses and wagon to the side with his siblings' help. Bart slid off the bay mare and quickly helped the wife load her soon-to-be-dead husband into the wagon. Before remounting, he unslung and reloaded the Sharps rifle. He looked at the teenage boy.

"What's your name, son?"

"James. James Polk."

"Load the breechloading shotgun with a slug round. Shoot at the Indian horses. If they have no mounts, they can't follow us. Who can handle the team?"

"I can—now," said the soon-to-be widowed Mrs. Polk' "My daughter Sarah took a bullet."

Bart saw a teenage girl with a bleeding arm in

the back of the wagon. He pointed at what had to be her Twin.

"What's your name?"

"Susan."

"Tie a strip of cloth around Sarah's arm to stop the bleeding. Then, find a gun. Got it?"

"Yes, sir."

Bart swung back onto the saddle. Then he called out.

"Listen up—those who can find a gun. Aim for the horses. Without horses, the Comanches cannot follow us. Let's get moving."

"What's your name?" asked James.

"Bart. Bart Carson."

"Any relation to Kit Carson?" asked Mrs. Polk.

"Distant Cousin. Let's head towards Van Horn. It's about five miles away with Rangers and some Cavalry there. I am surprised the Comanche are raiding this close unless they have something to prove. But they are, so Van Horn it is."

Bart spurred his horse and galloped ahead. Luckily, the Comanches had retreated in a different direction, so he found his packhorse. The two muzzle-loading carbines (cut down old Brown Bess rifles converted to percussion cap) he took from the dead Mexican horses were loaded but needed percussion caps. Bart remedied that lack and then road back to the two wagons. He tied his packhorse onto the back of the O'Reilly wagon, then handed one of the ready-to-go rifles to the people in the rear of the wagons.

"Wait until they get close and shoot the horses."

Bart then moved to lead the two wagons. He soon had all the horses at a trot to eat up the distance as he watched for the Comanches Ten minutes later, four mounted Comanches appeared on their right. Based on his pre-mission research, the man knew they came to draw their attention from the actual attack. One he recognized as the Buffalo Headdress warrior, whose horse he had shot with the Sharps. Bart realized the Comanches he killed with the Spencer, he should have just killed the horses, and Buffalo Headress would be on foot.

He glanced over to the left, and sure enough, six Comanches came riding hellbent for leather, thinking they had the element of surprise. Bart yanked on the reins and faced his horse to the six Comanches. Up came the Sharps, and he shot the lead horse at five hundred yards. Through a lot of pre-mission practice, Bart was excellent with the Sharps rifle. Five shots in fifteen seconds, five dead horses. The last horseman peeled off his attack, and Bart turned his attention to the right group.

There were a series of loud reports as the settlers fired their weapons. Bart watched as Buffalo

Headdress signaled to the remaining Comanches to retreat. The soldier decided to leave any other action against the raiders to the Rangers and Cavalry.

An hour later, and the wagons were at Van Horn. Words spread fast. Ranger Williams met Bart at the edge of town. "You ever thought of being a Texas Ranger?" Williams asked.

"Maybe someday. I have some grandchildren to find for a certain family."

"I think the Polk and O'Reilly's want to thank you for saving their hides."

"More luck than skill—and overconfident Comanche. Had they waited until nightfall, they might have snuck into the outskirts of Van Horn while you were all beating the bush for them. They were close by."

"Yes, sir. Time for another 'punitive expedition' I think the Army calls it."

"Well, I still need to make it to Fort Stockton sometime this year. I'll be heading out."

"Don't think the Comanche will be waiting for you?"

"Nope. They need to find some more horses first. They'll be hitting any homestead nearby for mounts."

"Hmmm. Time for us Rangers to hit the trail. Catching a group with few horses would be just fine."

The two men shook hands and parted ways. Bart

pondered if there was a comparable person in his universe's timeline. He hoped there had been.

Bart kept his eyes open as he worked his way east. His ideas about the actions of the Comanche were proven correct. He saw no other signs of a war party.

Four days later of hard riding and Bart reached Fort Stockton. He checked in with the local Ranger Company and received directions to the McCain's Ranch. Bart spent a night in town to have a bath and a good night's sleep. Bart figured the powers that be in his time and place would understand. Besides, he thought he deserved it after saving the people from the Comanche war party.

The following day, Bart rode towards the McCains. It was some five miles north of Fort Stockton with good water from the Pecos River's small tributary. Bart stopped on a slight rise a mile from the combination ranch and farm. The main house spread out like a so-called Ranch Style house in the 20th Century. Two sets of corrals were within twenty-five yards of the house. One contained several horses, the other a few cattle. Bart looked beyond and saw a fenced-off pig slop pit with quite a few porkers of all sizes, ages, and shapes. The was a tall windmill that Bart assumed provided the pump action on a well. Smoke came from a double chimney towards the back of the ranch house.

Connected to the horse corral was a double barn

with a hayloft. A man who looked like a professional wrestler was forking hay into a large wheelbarrow. He must have sensed Bart's presence as he looked up. As soon as he saw Bart, he whistled. Two large dogs that looked like some form of Great Pyrenees came out from the house, sensing Bart and his horses. They made a bee-line to the special-ops warrior, so Bart nudged his mount forward.

An older grey-bearded individual stepped onto the porch of the ranch house with a rifle in his hand. Bart realized these two men must be Bar and Jake McCain. Bart talked to the two large canines as they escorted him in, with the knowledge a command from Bar would send the two dogs attacking him and his mounts. This area was a rough and lonely country, violence often just around the next hill.

"Can I help you, mister?" the immense Bar called out from the barn. A lever-action rifle appeared in his hands, concealed prior in the hay wheelbarrow.

"I take it you are Bar McCain, and the greybeard man with the Sharps is your Uncle Jake."

"You guessed, right. Now, what do you want?"

"I, Bart Carson, have been hired by the King Family from Seattle, Washington Territory, to locate Reylie and Ronald King. The family wishes them back."

Uncle Jake walked up to his left. "Well, Reylie is due back with my sister Helen and her husband William and their four youngins any time now. They went shopping yesterday in Fort Stockton, spent the night so everyone could enjoy a real bath. Reylie was treating them with her money."

"And Ron?"

"He's due back with an antelope. No antelope, he better brings in a stray beeve or two."

Bart smiled. "Sounds like they adapted to the rough and tumble."

Bar fixed Bart with a steady gaze and asked. "You ride the lightning here?" the huge man asked.

"They told you, did they?"

Uncle Jake laughed. "Hell, they didn't have to. King youngins exploded our campfire the first time we met!"

A few minutes later, Bart was sitting on the porch with the two McCains, sipping bourbon and branch water. They even had ice, a luxury Reylie had arranged.

"Got us to dig a small ice cellar," said Uncle Jake. "Then, she went and sent a telegram to Denver. Offered two hundred dollars to anyone who could bring down a wagon of blocks of ice. Some fool did just that." Greybeard laughed. "That young lady can wheel and deal with the best of them."

"Next, she said something about—refrigeration," added Bar. "She has a lot of ideas from your—place."

Bart sipped his drink. "She gets it from her grandfather, the Tinkerer," he said. "The man has a way of building and doing things."

"I'd like to meet him sometime," said Uncle Jake. "He raised Ron and Reylie right."

Bart smiled. "We'll have to see if that's possible."

The wagon with the other McCains and Reylie appeared an hour later. Bart saw the family resemblance between Helen and Uncle Jake as she and her husband, William, herded four kids, ages eight to fifteen, into the house. Reylie walked up to Bart and stood in front of him.

"You came for me, didn't you?"

"How'd you know?"

"You have a—look to you; you're from home."

"We'll leave you two alone," said Bart. "Ron should be back anytime."

Reylie helped Bart take his horses to the barn, a dog escorting them. Reylie smiled as she scratched the dog's massive head.

"I belong to Brutus here. The first day I came to the ranch, he was a year old, decided I was part of his pack."

"Dogs do pick people. We think we chose them, but they seem to make us choose them."

"You have dogs at—home?"

"I have, at times. But all that is on the back burner right now."

Reylie helped take the saddles off the horses and rubbed them down. Bart saw she was turning into a full-bodied young lady under West Texas outdoor life. Her file said she was just a fourteen-year-old middle schooler when she 'left,' interested in medicine, art, cell phones, and being a young girl. In this place, she was a young woman.

"So, they sent you down the Rabbit Hole after Ron and me?" asked Reylie.

"Yes, ma'am. Your grandfather's tinkering has opened possibilities once thought to be science fiction. I am the guinea pig sent to see if he can control his Game."

Reylie stopped brushing the bay mare and looked at Bart.

"There have been others, hasn't there?"

"Yes, there has."

"Ah, shit." Reylie went and sat down on an old milking stool.

"Hey, it's not your fault."

"In a way, it is. Ron and mine, screwing with that Game in Grandpa's workshop."

"I can tell you that if it hadn't been you, it would have been somebody else," Bart stated. "The machine Grandpa King tinkered together has a bit of a mind of its own."

"Artificial intelligence?"

"It may not be artificial."

Bart brushed the packhorse as he let Reylie ponder the situation. As he fed his mounts some hay, Reylie spoke. "What is the next step? Can you take Ron and me back?"

"I'll need your help. It involves activating a homing beacon and see if it works. Then, we see if the bigwigs on our Earth can snatch us back through the Rabbit Hole."

"If they can't?"

Bart smiled as he replied. "Then we star in our very own perpetual Western movie."

Ron showed up an hour later with four stray Longhorns, including a cow and her calf. Uncle Jake and Bar met him and congratulated him on not getting gored by one of the Longhorns.

"Only one has a brand, boyo," said Jake. "The other three, including mama and baby, are wild."

"I fed them some sweet grass and corn," Ron said. "They came all peaceful like."

Bart saw a rapidly muscled young man. Western life seemed to suit the King's children. Ron gave the man a once-over as Reylie stepped up to him.

"Private conference time, brother."

"Okay."

As Bart, Reylie, and Ron walked towards the barn, Bar followed them with his eyes.

"They may leave us, Nephew," said Uncle Jake.

"I know. That's just the way things can be."

Jake paused, then spoke again. "You'll miss her."

"It's not like she'll be dead, now will it?"

"That's true."

In the barn. Ron asked, "So, what's next?"

"You two help me activate a beacon. Then we see if it works using Tachyons, or whatever the head-shed figured out."

"Then we get pulled back through the Rabbit Hole?"

Bart shrugged. "I guess. That's the plan."

"What if I don't want to go?" Reylie blurted out.

Bart had broached this idea before they sent him. What if the Kings said no? Or were dead? Those in charge had hemmed and hawed. Dead was easy. No one wanted to bring back a body. However, out and out refusal was not part of the plan. Thus, the bosses said, "Who wouldn't want to come back?"

"Your decision," said Bart. "I will not Shanghai you, even if I could."

Ron and Reylie looked at each other. Finally, Ron nodded his head.

"Okay," Ron said. "What do we do?"

Bart removed the small piece of the razor from his dental work. The selection of super metal Reylie attached to the equivalent of a toothbrush handle. Then, with some skill gleaned from her previous studies, she slit open a spot on Bart's left arm. She used a set of tweezers she found in town weeks ago and deftly removed an inch-long metallic capsule. Bart had her hand it to him.

"Okay. Now, the highest point around is the windmill tower, yes?"

"Yep," replied Ron. "It's pretty flat around here."

"Okay, Quick bandage on that spot, then up I go."

Bar and Jake watched the special operator easily climb the windmill.

"I guess he is trying to call the lightning," said Uncle Jake.

"Yep. Bart Carson may just fry himself."

Bart surveyed the area from the top of the tower. It was a lovely clear view from up atop the structure. No pollution, no signs of internal combustion engines, no war machines.

"One could do worse than living here," he mumbled, then carefully pressed the metallic capsule.

He secured it in a small slit he fashioned with his Bowie knife and quickly descended.

"Now what?" Bar asked him at the bottom of the windmill. Bart shrugged.

"Your guess is as good as mine. If this works, somebody or some machine will arrive to help Reylie and Ron. Someone rides the lightning, as you say. Then maybe, the two Kings can go back. This operation is all new to me also."

"So, you have no idea how long this takes," said Reylie.

"No, sorry. It may be days. It may be years. Mine is not to reason why; mine is just to do or die."

"So, that is why you volunteered? It is no big deal to you?"

Bart looked at her. "I want success. That is what I strive for, especially if it means a rescue for you two. For me—*machts nichts.*"

Bart was well fed by Helen and William that night, as they, the Kings and the McCains and all the young brood, asked him about the stories they had heard for the telegraph operator in town.

"So, you did fight off a bunch of Comanches?" asked the youngest, Emily.

"In a fashion, The Polks and O'Reillys helped."

"Those are the freight haulers," said William.

"They had quite the business."

"Not with Mister Polk dead," said Helen. "Damned savages."

"Comanches do what they do," said Bart. "They have for decades."

"You kill a bunch?" asked William Junior, who was Ronald's age.

"I shot five Comanche and about seven horses. That made the rest leave."

"You're a bit of a hero," said Reylie. "You saved two families."

Bart shrugged again. "It's all in the training, with some luck thrown in."

Bart sat on the porch as Helen and William put the young ones to bed. Bar walked out and handed him a bottle of homebrewed beer. "You plan to wait around here?"

"No, Bar, I won't. If that beacon works, there will be others to pick Ron and Reylie up. My job was to find them, see if they were still alive."

Bar frowned. "But how will you be picked up, returned if they come here and—"

"And I'm not here? I'll worry about that later."

"You can stay if you want. There is plenty of work to do, ways to earn money."

"Yes, I guess you, Uncle Jake, and Reylie has figured out ways."

"So have you, Bart, on the way here."

Bart smiled. He had a large chunk of the military payroll he took from the deserters, plus a small amount from the vaqueros. He still had their pistols in his saddlebag.

"I think, Bar McCain, you and I are a lot alike. Except for one specific difference."

"What is that?"

"You want and need family. I do not."

Bart left a small sack of coins on the dining table with a thank you note. He then snuck out. Brutus escorted him to the barn, where Bart quietly saddled and packed his horses. He patted the dog who owned Reylie and then walked his horses as quietly as possible away from the ranch. Brutus made sure he left, then returned to the house.

If Bart stuck around, he would seem like a third wheel. And as he said, he needed no new family attachment. Bart helped people when needed, treated people with respect as long as they respected him, and was kind to children and dogs. However, he had a skill set desired in specific situations.

There would always be a need for an assassin.

In the blockhouse used to be the Tinkerers Workshop, young scientist Doctor Don Deneeka had the night watch. A minimum of one scientist/technician was on duty twenty-four hours a day, with backup crews housed in the added two-story basement. In addition, two square blocks of the neighborhood were now inhabited by additional technicians, scientists, and security, families included. Those in command decided long ago a nuclear explosion was so remote as not to warrant undue concern. Thus, families of Project Alice (as in Wonderland and magic rabbit holes) were settled close for a response and provide operation security coverage. The families came and went like typical U.S. suburban families, with those assigned the Tinkerer Workshop duty sometimes leaving early in the morning to travel to an offsite office. They reviewed information gleaned from the sensors and drones connected to The Game and figured out how to build a duplicate. No one wanted to think about the day The Game shut down.

The U.S. Government treated Project Alice like the original Manhattan Project but with one difference. They had to build the project around the existing device, not create a location first, then make the mechanism for travel between universes. No one wanted the world to know a hole in space and time sat smack dab in suburban living until they knew all its workings and felt secure in moving it or replacing it with a device at a more remote location, like Area 51.

Doc Deneeka wheeled himself over in his well-padded office chair to the high-end coffee maker and poured himself another cup of espresso. The extra caffeine kept him awake and alert on the shifts when there was no one to talk to unless he called someone on the telephone. The man watched three oversized computer screens connected to sensors he did not fully understand. They tracked tachyon and Higgs Singlet energy signatures which flowed in and around the 'hole' connecting two universes. Don understood the mathematics behind it all and the theory based on Quantum Physics. However, how the technicians and engineers were able to build the sensor and drones? He had no clue.

Just as Don finished pouring his cup of stay awake, he heard an unusual tone from one of the computers. It took him a moment to recognize it, then dropped his coffee on the carpeted floor as he scrambled back in front of the set of computer screens.

"Shit, shit, shit," the young scientist said as he pushed keys and flipped a couple of old-time toggle switches. His eyes widened as the full realization hit him.

"My God. The Bart Beacon works!"

John King forced his way into the control room, which was his former workshop. No one dared to keep him out as many felt he had a unique 'touch' that kept The Game functioning. Others whispered it was a psychic connection. Whatever the reason, the creator of the unique device was allowed total access to the area and the collected data.

"So, how long has the beacon been transmitting?" John asked.

"Our time, one hour," replied Don.

"You understand," began Doctor Von Richter, the chair of the Physics Department from Stanford University, "the passage of time here and in Western World do not precisely coincide, do not match. Thus, we can say one hour of our time, which may be days, weeks, or months to Bart Carson and your grandchildren."

"How long will it take before you can send a team in and arrange transportation back?"

Von Richter, Daneeka, and the rest of the technicians and scientists glanced at each other as if hoping the other guy would answer and not them. Finally, Don spoke.

"We had trouble sending Bart Carson to the Western World reality. I can tell you it was as much about chance as it was about science. Quantum Physics and the related uncertainty factors are hurting our abilities to find specific pathways to the other string theory universes."

"So," replied John, "you are getting a lock on where my grandchildren are but have no idea how long it will take to retrieve them."

"I'm sorry, sir. The beacon gives us a general

location but a natural pathway through which to send humans? We were lucky to get Agent Carson to New Mexico Territory in one piece. His survival expertise did the rest."

John stayed in the control area for a while longer, then went back into the main house. He needed to update Joan and Jeannie.

The children were so close yet so far. John just hoped they would be recovered in his lifetime.

In a different reality, Reylie King sat on the front porch of the McCain residence. She looked at the top of the windmill pump tower where the activated beacon sat, expecting any minute for a figure 'riding the lightning' as Uncle Jake termed it to appear. Reylie sipped the iced coffee she prepared (no one else in the Western World seemed to like the concept of ice-cold coffee) and pondered the situation.

She and Ronald had resigned themselves to growing old around the McCain family, making their fortunes from 21st Century knowledge they could turn into profitable products in a world of late 19th Century society and technology. The smokeless powder developed from Ron's pistol ammunition had led to royalty checks from two separate ammunition manufacturers. The owner of El Paso Guns and Leather, Greg Kolster, helped the siblings with some excellent contacts and the manufacturing of two slightly tweaked types of 'Poudre B' which could be sold under separate patents. Brierfield Ironworks in Alabama used an in-depth examination of Ronalds Ruger pistol to start the manufacture of superior steel. Jonathan Browning, the father of John Moses Browning, offered his gun-making services located in Ogden, Utah, to produce Ruger pistols with the fine steel from Alabama. With a name change to King Model Pistols, excellent copies of the original design soon were made. The first pistols were to be offered on the open market in a month. Royalty checks arrived every week.

Reylie was already communicating with some medical schools about information from hr school books and her photographic memory. Hopefully, she could obtain wider acceptance of germ theory, help to develop vaccines and inoculations for the late 19th Century diseases, which killed thousands. Maybe she could help head off the misnamed Spanish Flu and save millions. Of course, if no World War One happened, the spread of the disease may be lessened.

There was so much she could do to /better this timeline if given a chance. However, she missed her family. Her mother and father must be worried sick about her.

A large figure stepped out onto the porch. "Mind if I join you, Reylie?" Bar asked.

"Your company is always welcomed, Bar," the young lady said with a grin."

Bar sat down, sipping at an iced drink. The two humans from different universes sat in silence until Reylie broke it. "It may be a long time before Ron and I leave Bar."

"You're no bother, Reylie. Stay as long as you like."

"You sure about that? We seem to attract trouble.

Bar laughed. "After all you know of Uncle Jake and me," he said, "you think you attract trouble? He and I have lived on the edge of a dark star for years."

Reylie looked directly at Bar and felt the combination of butterflies and warmth in her stomach. She kept thinking thoughts around the word 'love' and its meanings. Before she could speak again, Bar did.

"You are fifteen years of age."

"Yes, Bar. I will be eighteen in some three years."

"Ron said at eighteen in her home you become an adult, can vote, drink, and own property."

"Yes, Bar. Why do you ask?"

"Just wondering." Bar sipped his drink. "You'll maybe want to be married then. Around here, twenty-five and some people think you're an old maid.

"I'll cross that bridge when I get to it. I may be—gone by then. I may ride the lightning back home."

"True. Just remember you can stay as long as you like."

"I will, Bar."

Silence. Then Reylie spoke again. "Will, you— miss me, Barnabas?"

"Yes." The bear of a man stood up and walked back into the house.

Reylie looked at the setting Texas sun. The warmth in her stomach seemed to grow into a nice comfortable campfire. It all started with Ron and her falling into a campfire. Maybe, she pondered, this story would end with a falling into something else. Something called love.

John King woke up with the felt presence of his granddaughter Reylie. As he listened to the even breathing of his wife Joan lying next to him, the Tinkerer knew his granddaughter was safe, and he would see her again. John looked upwards and said, "Thanks, Lord. I owe you."

He went back into a restful slumber, not knowing what else the Creator had in store. John just knew it involved hope and love, a good combination in any universe.

Western nineteenth-century saloons were traditionally identified as single bit or two-bit saloons: i.e., they either charged a single bit (12.5 cents) for a beer, a glass of whiskey, or a cigar; or they charged twice that amount—25 cents for each. Customers at a single-bit establishment could pay with a quarter, and they would receive a "short bit"—or a dime—in change, which could then be used for the next round. In his essential book on Rocky Mountain saloons, Elliott also talks about half-bit establishments, but that would have been offering a product for too low of a price for most communities.

Dan DeQuille (William Wright), in his 1876 book The Big Bonanza, tells a story about a customer who came into a two-bit saloon, drank a glass of whiskey, and then offered a short bit in payment. The bartender objected at explained that it was a two-bit establishment at which the customer said that this was his understanding until he tasted the whiskey, which seemed to warrant only a single bit.

On this, see Kelly Dixon's work, Boomtown Saloons, or Ronald M. James, Virginia City: Secrets of a Western Part (2012).

PART TWO

WARWORLD

CHAPTER 9
WORLD AT WAR

Reylie King sat at her computer and pondered her next step. She looked out of her study window in El Paso, Texas. Reylie wrote about hers and her brother Ronald's experiences in the trip down the rabbit hole created by The Game to explain the development of the Sky Tunnels. The combination board and computer game created by her grandfather, John King, the Tinkerer, led to the technology which made the Sky Tunnels the new hope of humanity. The throes of systematic destruction by earthquakes, volcanoes, and extreme weather gripped Earth, and The Sky Tunnel system enabled society to flee to other planets and universes.

The trip to the alternate Old West Reylie and Ronald endured for over four years was challenging. However, falling into the campfire of the McCains meant they soon had two older and experienced protectors ensuring their survival. Other victims of The Game were not so fortunate.

Luckily, the friend and now family member, Jasmine Wright, had been a Battle Buddy Marine to their Uncle Maxwell, now her husband. Thus she survived her trip down the rabbit hole.

"Sorry we got you into this, Aunt Jasmine," Reylie mumbled. "But, you did help us recover Uncle Max."

Stranger became the Game Worlds stories. And Reylie began to write another one.

Jasmine Wright drove her compact car up to the King's home and stopped. In front of the Ranch style house were two police patrol cars. Jasmine frowned. The King family was not one to have police problems. The light chocolate-colored woman grabbed a box and stepped from her car. She still had her International Delivery Service dark blue uniform even though she was driving her car. As Jasmine left the warehouse, she noticed a package that had fallen off a previous delivery. Instantly recognizing the address, she told the supervisor she'd drop it by on her way home.

"They're friends, Boss," she said to the supervisor. The man grunted and went back to checking his paperwork. Jasmine took the grunt as an acknowledgment of her plan. Out the door, she went and was soon driving her red compact to the King's home. Jasmine knew the family well as she had been the one to tell the parents, Joan and John King, the details of their son being MIA. Jasmine Wright, a Sergeant at the time, had seen her Battle Buddy Marine Sergeant Maxwell King drive off in a HUMVEE en route to deliver a Private with appendicitis to the field hospital some five miles away.

Max and the Marine had vanished. The story was the Taliban, or some other enemy of the U.S. presence in Afghanistan, had grabbed them. Patrols sent out, people questioned, and still no idea what happened to Max. Six months later, Jasmine rotated out and went to the King's home. Joan, the mother, was bitter that Jasmine came home, and Max did not. John, a Former Zoomie (Air Force), welcomed her with open arms. Jasmine rotated out of the Marines, stayed in the Reserves, and found a job with IDS. Her mixed-race parents wanted her back home, but she was used to being on her own. She wanted a job with simple routines and some human contact. Jasmine did not want a job that required her to supervise others and no need to carry weapons. Working as a bonded driver was right up her alley. Once she realized she lived within a mile of the Kings, she arranged to add them to her route. After a year of delivery, she got to know the King family well.

Thus, she frowned as she walked up. Jasmine

hoped no one in the family, including the two Grandchildren, were injured. John 'Grandad' King saw her approach over the officers' shoulders and pointed her out.

"Hey, talk to Jasmine here. Maybe she saw them on her delivery route."

"What's up, Mister King?" Jasmine called out.

"Do you know their Grandchildren, Reylie and Ronald King?" a female officer asked.

"Why, yes."

"Have you seen them today?"

"No, ma'am. I just drove by their school on the way here, no kids around at all."

John saw the large box in her arms and motioned to Jasmine. "Why don't you go ahead and put that on my workbench? The officers already checked out the Tinker Shop."

"Okay. Then I can help look. I know where all the kids hang out on my route."

The two police officers nodded affirmative, and Jasmine went through the backyard gate. The Tinker Shop, all wood, and home-built, perched on the back of the acre lot. John King's shop was an all wood and home-built shop, no prefabricated stuff for him. Jasmine had been in the shop numerous times, often arranging her route to take a break and visit with John King in the shop. The wood and oil smells gave Jasmine this nice homey feeling, something she missed with no family around.

Jasmine stepped thru the open door, saw the footprints from the police officers' shoes in a light dusting of sawdust. Then the former Marine noticed the Tinkerer's recent project. On the long worktable sat a giant board game with a large central wheel. Jasmine sat the box down next to the worktable and examined the game. As Jasmine looked, a bluish light came on in the main wheel.

"Hmmm. What turned that on?" Jasmine wondered as she leaned over the table.

The large flash from the shop was seen in the front yard by John and the two police officers. They found no one in the backyard.

One second, Jasmine leaned over the worktable; the next second, she was falling. Jasmine had a momentary vision of landing on top of a figure. Then she crashed to the ground. Marine-trained reflexes enabled her to go into a roll and absorb the hard impact. She lay stunned for a few moments, then realized she was in wet mud.

"What the Hell?" she exclaimed as she slowly stood up. She saw the person who had broken her fall; a young male dressed in a greatcoat, like those worn on the Russian Front in two World Wars. Jasmine cursed as she noticed the young man's head twisted at an unnatural angle. A quick check of his pulse told her the soldier was dead.

"What happened?" Jasmine said. Then she realized the weather was cold and wet. She was no longer in Washington State during the Summer. Survival training took over. She did a quick squeeze and patdown of her body to make sure nothing was severely damaged. The former Marine then stripped the deadman of his greatcoat, slouch hat, tunic, equipment belt, trousers, and boots. Jasmine was a well-muscled five foot seven, so most of what she took off the body fit over her lightweight blue delivery uniform. The boots were a bit large, so she tied them together and slung them over her shoulder.

The equipment check produced three weapons. There was a sword bayonet, an odd over/under two barreled rifle, and a spitting image of a Coult Walker revolver with a five-shot fifty caliber cylinder. Jasmine's former boyfriend had a replica of the pistol in .44 cap and ball, not shells as this pistol. The rifle was like nothing she had ever seen. The top barrel had a percussion cap under a half-cocked hammer, with the under barrel having a side-mounted hammer. The trigger had a long pull, and Jasmine surmised the first part of the trigger pull fired the top barrel and the second part the lower. Her grandfather would call the rifle a real

Rube Golberg affair.

"I am dreaming, or I have just proven the multiverse theory," said Jasmine. Whether she liked it or not, the Former Marine was back in the trenches again. She pulled the deceased off to the side of what looked to be a trail.

"Sorry, I can't bury you, troop, but I have to find out where the fuck I am. And who the good guys are."

She checked the man's shoulder bag and found a small powder horn, a flat tin with percussion caps, and a smaller coin bag with both coins and lead balls for the firearms. There was also some hardtack and old cheese. A little water bottle evened out the contents of the bag. She adjusted her load and began to walk up the slight slope. Jasmine thought that any self-respecting military unit would seize the high ground.

Jasmine walked for some ten minutes when a loud, deep voice called out.

"*Hey!* Slogger. Where do you think you're going?"

Jasmine watched as one of the largest men she had ever seen stepped from behind a boulder that barely hid him. The Former Marine estimated the stranger as about six feet six in height and ax handle broad shoulders. The man strode up to Jasmine adorned in splotchy colored full coveralls and a long-sleeved dark green sweater of some sort. Jasmine half raised her rifle.

"I'd feel comfortable if you stopped right there," she said. The man stopped and let out a booming laugh.

"A woman! Good. We could use someone nicer looking than the rest of us Sloggers. Where ya from?"

Jasmine jerked her head in a general direction over her left shoulder. "There."

"Northerner, I see. A bit of color from the bright sun on the tall peaks. I was there once. It was too bright."

"It can be—bright," Jasmine replied. She noticed the large man had an odd-looking revolving rifle in his hands and a bronze sword stuck in his belt. Both looked tiny compared to him.

"Well, come on ah—"

"Jasmine."

"Slogger Jazz. We need you up-front, and I need to get some eats. Being a Lancer, I get first pick on a new holemate. I just lost mine."

"You mean a Battle Buddy?"

"Yeah. That sounds kinda like it. We dig a hole, so when the shootin' starts, we don't get hit. Then we have to sleep in it—"

"No funny stuff, get it? What's your name?"

"Bull Knox. Lancer Bull to you. Bull because I'm as big as one, my Mam said I was big when she had me; I almost got stuck inside her"

Jasmine smiled at Bull. He seemed like a good

sort. Plus, having an oversized friend in this strange land would help her.

"Right, Slogger. No funny stuff. Schtuping, your hole mate, just causes problems. Like when you are supposed to be on watch—"

"Lancer Bull, did you say we were getting eats?"

Bull grinned wide. "Ah, a hole mate after my own heart. Thinks about eating. Come on to the supply cart and watch me. I'll show you how to scrounge real good."

Jasmine fixed the bayonet onto the end of her rifle. Scrouging may require some forceful persuasion.

Five minutes later, the new partners approached two carts hooked up to gigantic Llamas creatures. Close to a dozen soldiers (judging by their uniforms) were milling about, pushing, and shoving. Finally, a man with one more strip than Bulls three clambered up on one of the carts and began yelling.

"See these Stripes? I'm a Daggerman. I decide when you eat—"

"You're nobody but a rat-tailed skunk, Bernie," Bull bellowed. "You got that extra stripe hiding in the crapper while the rest of us fought, and Daggerman Willis died."

Daggerman Bernie's face blushed beet red.

"I'll put you on report, Lancer, you offspring of a wood ape and your mother."

Moving fast for a man his size weighed down with a backpack, Bull had Bernie by his throat before he could issue another threat. The next moment, the Daggerman flew through the air and made a hard landing in a mudhole the size of a small pond. Jasmine quickly decided this was the rainy season. At least she would not die of thirst.

Bull grabbed two large bags from the cart, paused, and added a long bedroll.

"Come here, hole mate Jazz, and help me carry."

Jasmine walked towards Bull, and two muddy Sloggers tried to block her path. Old habits took over, and she butt stroked the neared one in his groin, then had the bayonet poking the other under the chin. Bull laughed long and hard as Jasmine pushed her way to him.

"I knew you was a scrapper the moment I found you," bellowed the Lancer.

"You just knew I had a rifle, Lancer Bull. Nothing else."

Bull grinned. "A smart one too, I see. Here. Grab this bedroll and this bag. Time to find our hole."

Jasmine felt a long and hard object that felt like a rifle, but she said nothing. After ten more minutes of slogging through mud, and Jasmine understood how primary soldiers got their names in this place. Bull stopped in front of a depression with a busted stock rifle stuck barrel first into the mud.

"This will do. Gotta shovel, Slogger?"

"No, sorry, Lancer Bull."

"Wait here. And unpack our stuff, see what I grabbed."

The oversized human strode off, and Jasmine shook her head as she smiled. This place would be worse without Bull.

The Former Marine examined the two bags and found various foodstuffs. A sizeable smoked ham and a wheel of cheese told Jasmine they would be eating well for at least a day or two. She knew Bull's appetite must be astonishing. Loaves of bread, sausage meats, various tubers, and vegetables, and some tiny apples rounded out the eats and a handful of labeled in Old English cans. Jasmin then turned her attention to the bedroll. She unwrapped the object and whistled when she realized what it was.

The Sharps rifle looked like it had just fallen off a truck from some Hollywood film set. Jasmine checked it, figured out the action, and slipped what looked like a .45-.70 round into the breach

"Someone has kept excellent care of this," Jasmine whispered. She looked up and saw Bull walking back with a shovel in each hand. Jasmine slipped the firearm treasure back into the bedroll. Bull walked up and tossed one of the shovels to Jasmine.

"Start digging while I make a munchy," the big man ordered. Jasmine stepped over to the busted rifle and started to toss it away.

"Hold on, Jazz. That will make a good club."

Jasmine laughed.

"Yes, for a Samson like you."

Bull cocked his head in question.

"Samson?"

"A legend among my people. A strongman who fought for his family and people."

"Ah. That must be Mercus the Just. Same person, different name. Get to work."

Jasmine began digging, bringing back memories of Advanced Rifleman Training. The Former Marine never thought she would be doing this again.

"Ah. Special can. This bag came from an Overman, maybe an Upperman."

Jasmine glanced over with a shovel full of dirt. Bull held up a tin can that looked like an old beer from the World War Two era. Bull jammed the blade of his bronze sword into the edge of the drink.

"Come here, Jazz."

Jasmine tossed the shovelful of mud and soil out of the foxhole and stepped over.

"Junior Slogger gets the first slug." Bull handed the can to Jasmine, and she slurped some liquid from the container.

"Hmmm. Malt liquor. Nice." She handed the drink back to Bull. He toasted Jazz and then finished it off.

"Don't we have to worry about the Overman coming to snoop around?"

"You snooze, you lose. No one will come looking for a bag of food."

Jasmine paused, then stepped over to the bedroll.

"How about this?" Bull's eyes widened when he saw the Sharps rifle.

"Cover it. Once we have an attack from the Lowlanders, we can throw some mud on it and say they left it."

"You expecting an attack?"

"Tomorrow morning. It has been a week, so it is time. I have been here over a complete cycle of the moons. That is what they do."

Jasmine heard the reference to 'moons' and thought she might be on another planet entirely, not just an Alternate Earth. Jasmine kept digging for another ten minutes, and then Bull stood up.

"Here, catch." Bull tossed her what at one time would have been called a Dagwood Sandwich. Jasmine had to drop her shovel to catch the bread, meat, and cheese concoction.

"Sloggers need fuel. Eat."

Jasmine sat down and on the edge of the new foxhole and began to eat. She had not realized just how hungry she was until she bit into the sandwich. Halfway through it, between bites, Jasmine said, "You make a great sandwich, Lancer Bull."

The big man belly laughed and then replied between large mouthfuls of what appeared to be beer.

"A man my size learns how to feed himself early on. Otherwise, your stomach growls." Bull stood up and grabbed a spare shovel.

"Finish eating, then join me."

Five minutes later, Jasmine stuck a hunk of the remaining sandwich in her trouser pocket and joined Bull in digging. Trying to keep up with him was a chore in itself. An hour passed, and the two soldiers had a deep and halfway mud-free protective hole. Bull clambered out of their new home and strode off once again. Five minutes later, he came back with a handful of bags that looked a lot like Earthly sandbags.

"Fill," the Lancer commanded, and Jasmine helped him fill a dozen of the sandbags with dirt. Bull expertly arranged them at the top of the foxhole. He stood back with a satisfied grin.

"Now, *this* is a Slogger hole!"

"You're good at this, Bull."

"That is because I enjoy digging Slogger holes better than shoveling shite at my family farm. I left to be a Slogger as the farm work was so boring. Same thing, day in, day out."

Bull spat outside their new home, then pointed over to a clump of bushes and a couple of short trees.

"Over there is the shite hole. Take your blade with you, being a new Slogger. Someone may decide they like your looks with your trousers down."

"Who is in command here?" asked Jasmine.

"Whatever Overman or Upperman claims this area as his or hers. They only come by when an attack is a nay. The rest of the time, Lancers and Daggerman keep order. When we want to."

"So the Daggerman you belted—"

"Will say nothing, or others will brand a pure slime weasel."

Jasmine realized this group was no Marine Corps. It was more like a combination of a mercenary band and a militia.

"Okay, Lancer Bull. What's next?"

"We rest. You take first watch for the Lowlanders. If someone marches up in brown uniforms from that downslope, they are Lowlanders. Shoot them, for they will shoot you."

"Why the war?"

Bull looked at her and sighed. "Well, you are a Sky Stranger."

"What do you mean?" Jasmine felt like a stupid

question had just blown her cover.

"Come now, Slogger Jazz. I may be from a farm with twenty-one harvests under my belt, but I am not dense. You are not a Northerner; your skin is the wrong shade. The footwear you wear instead of those boots you carry is nothing from around here. You are not the first Sky Stranger I have met."

"So, what is a Sky Stranger?"

"People fall from the sky, like from a balloon or a glider. Many die or are badly injured. Our Thinkers and Smarties will not tell us why they fall, just that we are to report them."

"Are you going to turn me in?"

Bull grinned. "No. You will bring me Sky Luck. You are also a trained warrior. My previous hole mates were not and quickly got themselves killed."

"How many other hole mates have you had?"

"Three prior. I have spent many a day alone."

"And Sky Strangers?"

"One who fell and survived but spoke in some language I had never heard. You speak good, Upland."

"Any others?"

Bull grinned again. "A dead one a week ago with this."

Bull took a cloth-wrapped object from an inner pocket. Jasmine unwrapped it and cursed in surprise. "This is an M-9 Pistol. With a full magazine."

"It is too strange for me. I am not a Mechman or Tinkerer. I planned on turning it in for a bounty when someone visits from Capital City."

Jasmine worked the action and chambered a round.

"It was well taken care of by the previous owner. I could use this in the coming fight."

Bull shrugged. "Do that. I will take your large pistol in a swap. That I know how to use."

Jasmine made the swap and also checked out Bull's odd-looking revolving rifle. There was one loaded chamber, with the hammer cocked with a separate thumb ring. Jasmine lined up the last shot so that all Bull had to do cock the hammer, then pull the trigger.

"You must be a Tinkerer," said Bull.

"I knew a damn good one, which is how I dropped in on you."

"You will have to tell me that story sometime. The Daysun is setting. I will make us an evening meal, and then you will take the first watch."

Bull lit a small fire in a makeshift fireplace he constructed with stones into the side of the Slogger hole. Using a sizeable scavenged stewpot, Bull soon had a hot form of a goulash cooking. Jasmine soon discovered Bull must be a frustrated chef as she ate a bowl of very flavorful meat, cheese, and noodle concoction. Jasmine finished the remains of her lunch sandwich, stuffed.

"Some wine," said Bull as he passed her an animal skin. Jasmine took a swig and then gave it back.

"If I drink too much, I'll be knocked out."

"Suit yourself. I will relieve when the Nightsun rises high with the two moons."

Bull made a quick bed and was asleep in moments. Jasmine chuckled to herself as she established herself as comfortable as possible. The Nightsun was a very bright star that made shiny Venus look dull. The two moons were each about half the size of Luna and seemed to chase themselves across the heavens. The heavenly bodies provided more than the light of an oversized smuggler's moon. The Former Marine sat back and watched. Occasional bird or animal calls perked her interest. She saw a coyote shape lope across the slope leading to their Slogger hole.

The Nightsun was directly above her when Bull tapped on her arm.

"Go sleep. I will wake you when the Lowlanders attack."

Jasmine smiled as she went to her bed. Bull was so sure the attack would come. The Former Marine made sure the Sharps and the two barreled rifle were within easy reach and fell fast asleep.

A poke from Bull woke her up. "They come."

No sooner did Bull speak that a bugle sounded. *My God,* Jasmine thought, *the last time the enemy used horns was in the Korean War.* She moved into her supported firing position and peeked over the sandbags. Figures in the morning light moved back and forth on the slope. They all seemed to be in the brown uniforms Bull mentioned and carried long-barreled weapons. The Lowlanders' movements seemed disorganized and random. The one consistency was they kept coming towards Jasmine's and Bull's Slogger hole.

"Fire at will?" asked Bull.

"Here. Shoot mine first; I have a couple of hand bombs to throw. Once we shoot, hopefully, others will also."

Jasmine braced Bull's rifle on her sandbags. She cocked the weapon and let her breath out slowly as she pulled the trigger. The recoil was the slower push of black powder rather than the sharp recoil of smokeless. At some two hundred meters away, a figure dropped. In a surprise, Jasmine swore she had hit something with the unfamiliar rifle. Bull slapped Jasmine's back hard.

"I knew you could shoot!"

Jasmine grabbed up her two-barrel rifle and established a stable firing position. A scattering of shots zipped about from defenders and attackers. She fired again, and another figure fell. Jasmine then fired off the remaining barrel. This bullet ricocheted off a boulder, and a Lowlander ducked behind it. Jasmine laid aside that weapon and grabbed the Sharps rifle. The Former Marine established another stable Marine Rifleman prone position, the box of some two dozen 45-75 rounds in easy reach. The sights on the Sharps were superior over the other two more crude weapons; as she looked for another target, Jasmine heard a *'duh-duh-duh'* sounds of some slow automatic gun. From a low brush at the bottom of the hillside slope came flashes of simple tracer rounds. The target of the new weapon was a Slogger hole to their left.

"Crank gun," said Bull. "They are searching for you."

Jasmine wished she had a mounted scope on the Sharps, but she would have to make do. The Crank Gun, which sounded like a Gatling, chugged round after round as the weapons crew started to sweep the Upland positions. Jasmine focused on the muzzle flashes from the crew-served weapon. The snap of the recoil told Jasmine the Sharps was a modern smokeless powder replica, not an original historical example. Jasmine worked the action and chambered another round, fired again.

There was a secondary explosion in the brush.

"You hit the ammunition box!" bellowed

Lancer Bull.

A figure burst from the brush as he or she tried to beat out a flame on their left arm. A shot fired from another Slogger position knocked the Lowlander to the ground. Jasmine fired a third shell at the target area. Fireworks exploded in the brush, and bodies began to run in every direction.

Bull began to bellow out curses and encouragement. Jasmine looked at him in time to see him launch a hand bomb over a hundred meters down the ground slope. The bomb exploded and produced a massive cloud of black smoke. A Lowlander within the danger zone began to scream and roll on the ground. Suddenly, the rest of the attacking soldiers broke and ran. Bull began to pound Jasmine on her back.

"Hey, Bull! Don't break my body."

Within ten minutes, an Overman and Upperwoman appeared at the pair's position. Jasmine stashed the Sharps from prying eyes and stood at attention like a good Marine as the two officers grilled Bull.

"That was excellent shooting, Lancer Bull," said the beefy Overman, someone who had worked their way up from the enlisted ranks.

"It was Slogger Jazz here. She did the shooting."

The female Upperwoman looked at Jasmine. "You have an excellent military bearing, Slogger," said the woman. "You are not a recruit."

"I am a former Marine, ma'am," replied Jasmine. *You might as well tell the truth.*

"That explains it," the Overman said. "She spent time with our Mariners, shooting from moving decks. Judging by her dusky skin, down in the South Sea."

"Hmmm. We will keep you in mind, Upperslogger Jazz. We could use a few more like you in this Long War. Stay alive."

"Yes, ma'am."

The Overman handed Bull a bulging leather bag that clinked, then walked off.

Bull waited until the Officers were out of sight before he pounded Jasmine's back again. "We are rich now, Jazz. No trying to get the coin from the paymaster when they show up."

"You get paid regularly?"

"When they show up, the paymasters divide the money they have with whoever is still alive. If few are killed, we get little."

"How long has this been going on?"

"The war? Since I was born. Sometimes others besides the Lowlanders will fight Upland. We have many enemies."

"Why?"

"We have hard metals for weapons, the black goo that can burn and made by Mechmen and Makers into fuel as well as Blackburn rock which is used to melt the metals and for fueling Metalbeasts. "

It was beginning to sound more and more like a Steampunk nightmare. Only Jasmine's combat training as a Marine and her quick wit had enabled the Former Marine to survive. And, the luck of stumbling into Bull.

"Now what, my friend?"

"Why we go to town. The Lowlanders will not attack for another week. If they do, a few new Sloggers will be here. There is always new meat."

"Then we come back here?"

"For now, yes. But if you keep shooting like that, we will soon be moved to Capital City and be in a Hitter Unit. They always have the best fighters in the Hitter Units to protect Royalty. We might even have our hutch."

"Live together?"

"Just as hole mates. Unless, you know—"

"Lancer Bull, I like you a lot, but not that much."

Bull laughed. "Come, get the equipment you want to keep or sell in town. I will put our name on this Slogger Hole. Although someone may throw the sign in the shite hole."

"They have baths in town?"

"Yes. But why? It is not the new moons yet."

Jasmine laughed. "I think, my big friend, I will introduce you to the pleasures of slow, warm baths."

CHAPTER 10
SLOGGER TO DAGGERMAN

Jasmine followed Bull Knox to what he called Sloggertown. The story Lancer Bull told the Former Marine was similar to many an experience on Jasmine's Earth. The years-long war created a nearby town to support the military. Of course, the townspeople tried to relieve the Sloggers and others of their money and valuables. The population center had the well-worn main street; portions paved with a crude attempt at cobblestones. There were many side streets and lanes, many newly cut. Wooden planks served as sidewalks in some areas, with small boardwalks in front of the better establishments.

"Come, Jazz," said Bull. "We go first to the Moneyhouse to store most of our coinage."

"You mean you don't spend it on wine, women, and song?" Jasmine asked.

"I did that the first moon," said the Lancer with a

grin. "Then I was broke and remembered what my Mam said. You need a bundle-pouch, something to hold you over in bad times. This War will not be forever."

"Your mother is quite wise."

"Yes. When I have saved enough coins and riches, I will buy my leave and return home to buy land or a small shop near my family. Then I will raise a family."

"You buy your way out of the army?"

"Yes. You pay a gold piece for each harvest that passes. I am on my second harvest time. If you keep bringing me good luck, I will leave early."

"Where is home, Bull?"

"A moon's travel west. My family lives in the Western Hills, by Many Fish River."

"They have a farm?"

"Plants and animals, yes. Also, fruit trees. My Mam wrote to me, told me that since I left, they have a greater surplus. I guess I ate a lot."

Jasmine laughed. She may have bad luck falling through space and time to get here in—Warworld. However, Bull was good luck for her.

"So, Lancer Bull. Where is this bank, this Moneyhouse?"

"Just ahead, It is a nice stone building."

Five minutes later, the two warriors entered a large stone building with matching columns on either side.

Two beefy guards stood near the door with massive revolvers on their belts. Bull nodded to them as the Holemates entered, and the guards ignored the weapons the soldiers carried.

"They know you?" asked Jasmine.

"Yes. At least once a new moon, I bring money to place in my lockbox. I helped them once or twice deal with drunk Sloggers, so they appreciate my presence. Oh, and once I stopped a robbery."

Jasmine laughed. "You talk like it was no big deal."

Bull shrugged as he answered, "I used my sword to cut two throats. For my efforts, the Moneyman gave me a large gold piece for my lockbox."

The two soldiers walked up to a long counter at the back of an even longer and deeper entrance room. As Bull led the way, a comely dark-haired and fair-skinned young lady flashed a healthy-tooth grin at the oversized Lancer.

"Lancer Bull Knox," the lady greeted. "I am glad you survived the recent conflict."

"News travels fast, Aetna. May I introduce my new Holemate, Jazz Wright."

Aetna gave Jasmine a once over to examine the new competition, decided she was no threat, and smiled.

"Pleased to meet you, Slogger Jazz. Do you wish to open a pay line also?"

"She is now a Upperslogger. And yes, she wishes a lockbox also."

"Yes, please, ma'am," Jasmine added with a smile.

"I see Lancer Bull has been singing the praises of Hilltop Moneyhouse," Aetna replied. "We will have to give him another bounty for another new customer. Slogger Jazz makes six in total."

Jasmine gave Bull a sideways glance. *This man is far from a dumb farmboy,* thought Jasmine.

"I must tell you we lost one with a pay line last week, Aetna."

"That is most sad, Bull."

"What happens to money deposited here by a killed fighter?" interjected Jasmine.

"If we have no family on file, the coinage reverts to this establishment, except for a small silver coin. That goes to the person who collected the original bounty in hopes that they will bring in a replacement."

Jasmine's mind quickly went to the 'dark side' and thought a person could help someone die in battle and get some money for it. That bit of paranoia made Jasmine decide to press Bull a bit more about his past holemates. Aetna produced a grand printed form with a cartridge ink pen. Jasmine did some creative writing when filling out the form, but used her actual parents' names and street address, added to the South Sea.

Aetna perused the paperwork as she commented.

"I thought you had the darker skin of an Islander. Out of all the places on Twosuns, that is the one area I will visit before I die."

"If you passed away, my heart would shatter," Bull stated.

Aetna squeezed his arm as she smiled and licked her lips. Jasmine stifled a laugh as she watched the heavy-duty flirting. However, she had never asked what the inhabitants called this "Earth." Twosuns made sense with the night Sun and much bigger day sun.

"Please come with me, Upperslogger Jazz. I will find you a lockbox."

Jasmine decided that function was similar between the multiverses as the Moneyhouse back area containing the main vault and their version of safe deposit boxes looked like the interior of many a bank on Earth. Aetna found a lockbox within a couple of feet of Bull's. She handed Jasmine her key.

"I will leave you to handle your private transactions," Aetna said, then turned and walked back to the central bank area. Bull removed the bulging money bag and grinned. On a nearby small table, Bull displayed the contents.

"Since I am senior as a Lancer, I should take over half of the riches given us by rights," he said. "But, it is because of your luck and skill that we are here. And I wish to keep that luck and skill. Here, help me divide it in half."

The two Sloggers soon had stacks of coins evenly divided. Jasmine calculated her half would equal over a thousand dollars in the U.S. She stacked all but a couple of silver dime-sized coins into her lockbox, plus kept a few paper bills. She still had a small amount of money she had taken from the unfortunate Slogger who broke her fall as she fell down the rabbit hole.

"Aetna will give you a small book that will list the number of your box. Only if you put money into your general account will the book list an amount. You will put your mark and thumbprint on the inner cover."

Jasmine held up a few paper bills. "I take it since you have no bills in your box; this is not worth much."

Bull snorted. "It is good to wipe your bottom in a pinch. Much of it is fake, printed by the Lowlanders."

"I'll deposit it in my general account, with a few coppers I have. Will the silver coins get me a bath?"

Bull laughed. "I guess, Jazz, we must go to Mother Hubbards. There you can get a bath and someone to help wash your back if you are so inclined."

"Old Mother Hubbard?" Jasmine said with a smile and then caught herself. Bull Knox would not know the old nursery rhyme from Earth.

"She is far from old," answered Bull. "Her girls and guys are well known for entertainment. But first, we must rent a storage locker for our weapons."

Bull took them to a small warehouse on a side street and soon haggled with the owner for one tall storage locker. In went most weapons.

"I'll keep my M-9 pistol," said Jasmine. She also still had her delivery box cutter.

"Suit yourself, Upperslogger. I keep my bronze sword to cut my meat."

Ten minutes later and Jasmine undressed at Mother Hubbards Emporium, as a seminude young boy and girl filled an oversized wooden tub with hot water. Jasmine pulled a small end table near the tub. She folded her clothes as neatly as possible and concealed the pistol. Bull had gotten two private rooms at the boarding house portion of Mother Hubbard's warehouse-sized establishment. Jasmine slid into the hot water, with her panties and sports bra still on. It would do her good to have semi-clean underwear. She moaned with pleasure as she slid deeper into the bath.

"Does Mistress wish anything else—a bathing partner, perhaps?" the no more than thirteen-year-old lad asked as his female companion gave Jasmine a coy smile.

"No, thank you." Jasmine tossed some coppers their way, which they both caught handily, grinned, and left. "God, underage sex partners," the former Marine mumbled, feeling unnerved. "Not my idea of fun."

As she soaked, Jasmine sipped at a goblet of Sangria. Sloggertown had flavorful wines and beers, it seemed. The private rooms were "his treat," so Jasmine said he would take him out for a meal and drinks. However, he had to take a bath also.

"You twisted my arm," Bull answered with a grin and then let a comely lady wearing just a thong lead him to his room.

Jasmine laughed. Things were weird and surreal but could be much worse. The former Marine could be a slave, already raped, or left for dead.

"Improvise, adapt, overcome." Jasmine grinned. Those words may have come from a Clint Eastwood Movie, but they sure fit in Twosuns and Sloggertown.

A knock on the door made Jasmine realize she was dozing in the tub; not a good idea for a stranger in a strange land.

"Jazz, may I come in?"

Jasmine recognized the voice as belonging to Mother Hubbard, the namesake of the Emporium. Bull had introduced the statuesque blonde to Jasmine after she wrapped Bull in a massive bearhug. Jasmine's comrade got around, it seemed. Mother Hubbard gave Jasmine a firm handshake.

"You will want a bath, I bet," said Mother.

"Yes, ma'am."

The Emporium owner soon had staff up and running for the Jasmine's tub.

Mother Hubbard entered and shut the door behind her. "Here, young lady. Try these on."

Jasmine rose from the tub and accepted a set of brand new camouflage pants and shirts.

"Where did you get these?" Jasmine asked as she did a quick measurement against her body.

"From some Sky Strangers whose craft did not land well."

Jasmine glanced at Mother as she stepped from the tub. "So, you know."

"Yes, because ten years ago, or harvests as they count, I was in your position. This most recent conflict was just beginning after a pause for a year or two."

"So, you are from Earth."

"Amsterdam. I was in the sex trade, just past the Millenium when I fell through the sky. I landed in the nearby Muddy Waters Lake, so no broken bones."

Jasmine shucked off her wet underwear and began to dry herself off with a provided towel. "So, after you kept from drowning, Mother, how did you get here?"

"A squad of recruits brought me to Sloggertown. Back then, it was a few tents and a scrap-built hotel. I had some gold and jewelry on as I was meeting a high roller client. I spoke English with a Dutch Accent, but they understood me well enough as I dickered to sell some of my jewelry. The money kept me going long enough to set up my business. And I lost my accent."

"There was no cathouse here, to use an old term?" asked Jasmine.

"There were a couple of amateurs in a tent, being abused by their clients. I used my size, and Tae Kwon Do I learned from the Dutchman to set matters straight. A couple of small business owners who moved in became fans and helped me build the Emporium. I paid them off last year."

Mother Hubbard pointed at Jasmine's underwear. "I'll get you some replacements and spares. Plus, I helped develop some items for your menstrual cycle from local materials. My designs are quite popular in this—I think someone called it a steampunk world."

"How much?" asked the former Marine. "I have a budget."

"Gratis. We, strangers, need to stick together. And, you keep Bull alive, who is a favorite friend of mine."

Jasmine gave the woman a once-over before she spoke. "Pardon me while I look a gift horse in the mouth. Is there a catch?"

"No, ma'am," the tall, buxom woman replied. "Other than watch Bull's and my back. There are a bunch of various factions in Capitol City which keep this War going. Sometimes they jockey for position, and we little people get in the way."

"They are interested in us—Sky Strangers. Yes?"

"Some of us. There are Thinkers and Smarties, as they call them, trying to figure out Sky Strangers. So, some of us are grabbed for questioning and information we have about useful technology. By the way, however, we get here; time is not always linear. You came from Earth a bit later than I did, I wager to guess."

"Yes. Probably about twenty years later or so. However, there is one difference."

"What is that, Jazz?"

"I know exactly how I got here. It is because of a Game."

Jasmine took Bull to the connected restaurant and fed him the biggest steak she had ever seen. Mother Hubbard seemed genuinely surprised when Jasmine explained Grandpa King and his Game. The former Marine knew she had taken a chance by telling a recent acquaintance the weird story, but Jasmine also thought the people at Capitol City would come after her soon anyway. The Upperwoman who talked with her saw a difference.

Jasmine had a smaller hunk of meat, which Bull explained came from a creature like the American Bison.

"We have the bighorns which provide steaks like these. They still run wild in places. The woolies, the ones with the faces like large hoppers—" Jasmine figured hoppers were rabbits, "—we use their hair, like wool from sheep. Their meat is also flavorful."

Jasmine had surmised the Old English-based language brought many words to combine with whatever languages were native to Twosuns. Or maybe none were native. Someone or thing could be sucking humanoids and other beasts down the rabbit holes to populate the planet. Bull finally satiated, ordered some sweet liquor for both.

"I pay for this drink. Now, a toast. To good fortune with Upperslooger Jazz. Soon to be at least a Lancer if my instincts are right, which they often are."

The two comrades went to their respective rooms after Bull had bought a bottle of home-brewed beer for each of them. Jasmine sipped at hers, striped to her new skivvies, thanks to Mother, and lay down on the surprisingly soft bed. In moments she was fast asleep.

She awoke at Daysunrise, at first a bit disoriented. Then she remembered where she was.

"Well, I guess it is not all a dream," Jasmine said as she sat up and swung her legs over the edge of the bed. She sat for a moment, listening to the morning sounds. She heard a few birds singing, light footsteps down the hallway, and a far-off whistle similar to a steam locomotive. Jasmine stood up, stretched, then went to the bathroom. Bull had paid for indoor plumbing, a rarity in Sloggertown.

"Nothing too good for the best fighters in the Queen's Army," said the Lancer. That was when Bull finally explained the situation. They were foot soldiers for Queen Aurora in the Kingdom of Iron. The country's name derived from the Iron Mountain, which rose in the center of the kingdom. Large deposits of iron ore in the mountain and residues of other ore and precious metals abounded in the short mountain range known as the Metal Mountains. Tree Mountain had a massive old-growth forest and served as the home of the Royal Family of Maxim.

"The forest has rarely been harvested for wood," Bull said. "It is a massive hunting preserve for the Uppers."

"The upper class."

"Yes, Jazz."

"Is Capital City there?"

"No. It is on the backside of Iron Mountain. The Royal Family can see it from their vast home, and people claim they use large craft lense to watch the comings and goings of the Makers, Mechmen, the Recorders, the Overmen and Women, and the Senior War Lord. The Thinkers and Smarties sit scattered around the various smaller towns and cities, as are the Medicos and Alchemists."

Jasmine washed her face after relieving herself, contemplating all that she had learned. It sounded that the local scientists and intellectuals were working on the method Grandpa's Game used to send people to this world. Thus, there was always a chance she could finagle a trip back to her home. Until that possibility, it was improvise, adapt, and overcome. She was a former Marine and would not sit in the corner and mope. She would make the best of this strange new world, even if events forced her to live here forever.

She met Bull in the dining area, where they drank actual coffee. Someone had imported coffee beans to this area. As they drank coffee and ate some slices of cheese and bread, Bull told her some more of how the society in the area functioned.

"Most people come here to fight as there are little future and excitement where they lived. Here, at least, you can schtup someone if you have some coin, drink, grab what you can, and return to your village or town with good tales and a stake for some land or a shop." Bull slurped his coffee. "Or you can have a quick death, which solves any future problems."

"Why doesn't the Queen's Army go down and kick the Lowlander's ass until they are no longer a threat?" asked Jasmine.

"There is not just one group of Lowlanders. We lump all the people attacking us into one group, but the groups involved change. This War has Lowlanders from Lake Blue Rock, the Small Desert People, and Slagtown."

"They band together under one flag just to get the precious metals and iron they want? Why don't they trade for it?"

Bull guffawed. "They have nothing the Traders and the Royals want. Occasionally someone sells a beautiful woman for some coin, but other than that, we get all the slaves anyone needs from the Sloggers we capture or people sold because they cannot pay their debts. But in my mind, slaves are too much trouble."

"How so, Bull?"

"You have to feed them, watch them every minute, so they don't either slack off or run away or try to slit your throat in your sleep. Some Upper families and Royals keep most of the slaves. A few work with criminals in the mines. Metalworkers control the mines and usually have huge families who dig out the precious rocks and gems. Less thievery that way."

"So most people see no use for slaves."

"Just the Royals and such who want someone to wipe their behinds. They even get tired of that."

"No sex slaves?"

"Why? Anyone can find enough coin or locate some leftover shiny stuff in the slag heaps to buy a bedpartner. Why force someone?" He looked honestly perplexed.

Jasmine was about to point out the two thirteen-year-olds who wanted to bathe with her. Then she thought maybe that life was better than in their previous experience. The former Marine decided she needs to conduct more research before passing judgment on the Kingdom of Iron.

"So people attack the Kingdom for the metal and precious stones."

"Yes. Some people smuggle it to them."

"How do the Lowlanders pay if they do not have anything the people with money want to have?"

Bull shrugged as he answered, "I am not a smuggler, so I don't know what they want. Fewer questions and drink up. It is time to hit the Farmers Market. We will buy things we can use or resell to the new Sloggers who show up."

As they walked, Jasmine realized Bull had the mind of a beginning entrepreneur. He was always looking at a way to gain capital for future deals. A big dumb oaf he was not.

Bull bought some citrus fruit at the market that seemed to be a cross between a lime and an orange.

"Makes flavorful ditch wine." Jasmine figured that was like prison rotgut.

Bull also bought cans of fish that looked like

containers for sardines. "They keep forever. If we are stuck in our Hole, we will not go hungry."

Everything Bull bought was for a specific purpose.

Finally, Jasmine asked, "Bull, how long have you been here in the War?"

"I left home two harvests ago. I started fighting, and let's see..." Bull did some quick figures on a miniature abacus removed from some hidden pocket. "Eighteen moons ago, I arrived here. I talked to some older Sloggers in a beer place or two on my way here. My Mam and Paw always told me to think ahead and figure things out."

Jasmine realized the Gods of this Twosuns place had smiled on her when she met Bull. There was an excellent chance someone would lock her up for violating some local moray without Bull. Bull soon had her loaded down with various foodstuffs, local herbs, and a form of rubberized tarp material.

"We can line our hole with that; rainy season is coming."

"You mean this is not the wet season? Then why all the mud?"

Bull flashed her a quizzical glance just as a familiar voice called out, "Lancer Bull! We have a reckoning to arrange." It was Daggerman Bernie. With him were three other Daggermen, all in their cups from drinking the night before.

"Go away, Bernie. We have much business to attend to before the next attack."

"You will reckon with my friends and me *now!*" Bernie tried to bellow like Bull and failed."You have disrespected me for the last time—"

"Daggerman, sir," Jasmine said as she began to set her bundles and packages down. "A proper Non-Commissioned Officer knows better than to discipline troops while they have been drinking too much the night before. How about we all have some coffee and discuss things sober?"

The four Daggermen stared at Jasmine as if she had three heads. "Well, I tried Earth logic," Jasmine mumbled. She reached over to a nearby market stall and took a three-foot wooden rod used to smooth and roll out dough for various concoctions. While a Marine, Jasmine had received some riot training and knew which end of a baton to use. The long rod would work just fine.

"Go away, Bernie," said Bull. "You are drunk and need to sleep it off."

"You will both kneel and apologize for the disrespect you showed me the other day," demanded Bernie just as one of the other beefy Daggermen reached for Lancer Bull.

The large man moved quickly. A massive fist smashed the Daggerman in the face, pulping his nose.

Another of the Daggermen yanked a bladed weapon of some sort from under his tunic. He ate the end of Jasmine's makeshift baton, losing some teeth in the process. Using basic Koga Baton techniques, Jasmine used over and underhand thrusts to the chest and stomach of Bernie and the remaining Daggerman. The two men were soon lying in the mud and their vomit. Bull picked up the blade dropped by the man with the missing teeth and stuck it in his belt.

"Next person gets gelded," growled Bull. He grabbed his packages, and Jasmine recovered hers. As she did, she threw some coppers and nickels at the businesswoman whose roller she had borrowed.

"Thank you," Jasmine said to a grinning female face.

The two Holemates hot-footed it back to Mother Hubbards, where they locked their goods up in their rooms. Bull looked at Jasmine as they bellied up to the bar for a drink.

"'Where did you learn to stick-fight like that?" he asked.

"Riot Control Training, United States Marine Corps."

"These States Marines. Are they all like you?"

"Nah. Some are nastier."

Bull began to laugh, then slapped Jasmine's back so hard she almost dropped her beer.

The hole mates used some bread, meats, and cheese to make some sandwiches and ate in Bull's room. They swapped lies as Bull lubricated them with a bottle of ditch wine he had obtained at the market. Jasmine soon discovered it was sour and packed a punch.

"This shit will give me a head-busting hangover if I keep drinking it," Jasmine said after unpuckering her mouth.

"Then here, Blush wine to wash it down with."

"Mmm. That is better, Lancer Bull."

The oversized soldier looked at Jasmine and asked, "Do you have a mate in the States, is it?"

"Not yet, Lancer Bull."

"Why not? I know many men who would pay a bounty for your hand in marriage. You are pleasant to look at, tough as a bee-eater, intelligent, a hard worker, will produce healthy young—"

Jasmine began to belly laugh and almost spilled her wine.

"What is so funny, Jazz?"

"Is this a proposal? Or do you have a friend you want to set me up with?"

"I am just curious. I cannot marry until I have a bounty to offer a decent woman. You would have men piling bounty upon bounty in my area to get your hand in bonding."

Jasmine became serious. "You mean you have to

buy the right to marry a woman?"

"A man here has to show he has the metal to provide for a woman. If a woman runs off with men without metal, she shames herself and her family. If I tried to steal a mate, I would dishonor my family."

"So, that is why you came to this War?"

"Part of it. I wanted adventure, but I needed to make money also. My previous Holemates had no real metal, and the War quickly killed them. You are different. It is too bad you did not bring some sisters with you."

Jasmine smiled at the big man, then reached over and playfully punched him in the shoulder. "You are a good man, Bull Knox. You will find the woman right for you. I will protect you so you can one day find that woman. I ask you to help me survive, so maybe I can find a way to return to my Sky home. Deal?"

Bull punched her in the shoulder and knocked her off her chair. "Deal."

Bull pounded on her door right at Daysun's rise. "The bastard lowlanders are attacking early; we must respond."

Jasmine threw on her uniform fatigues as she asked, "What about all our extra things? We have no way to take them with us with this short notice."

"Mother Hubbard will keep them through the week. I slipped her another gold coin, to be sure. Now, we must run and recover our longarms. Come, Upperslogger. Time to earn your metal."

The hole mates were in the position within the hour. The word had gotten out not to mess with these two warriors, so their hole was undisturbed. Jasmine had the Sharps rifle out while wishing she had more ammunition. She had planned to go scrounging this day for the makings of at least black powder shells, but the broken pattern of enemy attacks had derailed that idea. So, as many a Marine had to do, you make do with what you have.

Bull had obtained what looked like an old single-shot breech-loading needle gun. He had a bag of cardboard-like shells, so at least he could throw a bunch of lead downrange. Some officer type had tossed him a bag of their version of hand grenades, and a Molotov cocktail magically appeared. Bull's legendary throwing arm attracted loads of bombs.

As the two secured their position, Jasmine heard an all too familiar sound.

"An enemy vehicle is coming."

"The mud will make it difficult to climb the slope. Jazz."

"Not if it has a tracked suspension. I'll explain later."

As Jasmine looked around, all the foxholes

seemed occupied. Many looked new, young, and scared. She cursed the people in this world who did not understand the necessity of having formal training and proper planning. She looked at Bull, who had a half-grin on his face. Jasmine was here for him, not the upper ranks. That was a story as old as warfare.

The source of the engine noise appeared. There were two four-wheeled armored cars with a reasonably long but smallbore cannon in a single turret. Jasmine estimated the bore of the weapon as 20 or 25 millimeters. They would soon find out if they were belt or clip-fed automatics. The metal beasts turned and began to ascend the muddy sloop. Then Jasmine saw the arcane manner the enemy planned to conquer the mud.

Over two dozen men and women came scrambling up the slope, laying wide wooden planks in front of the armored car. The tires of so-called Metal Beasts pushed the planks down into the mud. However, rough pieces of rubber and other materials on top of the planks gave the wheels something to grab. The tires pushed against the added plank material and provided a crude form of traction. Slowly the armored cars climbed the muddy slope.

"Shit," said Jasmine as she took a supported rifleman position on the edge of her foxhole. She searched for and saw the long front vision slit on the nearest Metal Beast. Her .45-75 bullet smashed into the vision slit, and pieces of glass flew. Jasmine quickly loaded another round into the rifle breech. A loud report reverberated as the front vehicle fired its main gun. Jasmine felt the passage of the shell about a foot above her head.No round followed it, so she assumed the cannon was a single shot. Jasmine aimed and fired another round at a range of some two hundred meters. It smashed into the front vision slit, and once again, glass pieces flew about.

From a small secondary opening to the right of the main gun came a burst of fire. The ratatat sounded to the former Marine similar to a pistol caliber submachine gun. The bullets still struck in and around the various fighting positions. Jasmine loaded a third rifle shell; she glanced to the side and saw the young soldiers in a near post raise to run away from the attacking vehicles. She yelled at Bull.

"Tell them to Hold, or I will shoot them!"

Bull bellowed as a burst of automatic fire struck one runner in the leg. Others hunkered down in their Holes.

"Just don't sit there, bighorn dung!" bellowed Bull. "Shoot back!"

Scattered shots ricocheted off the armored cars, and a couple of the plank carriers went down. Others scrambled up to take their places as Jasmine fired another bullet into the vision slit. A hole appeared, and a moment later, the submachine gun began to pepper Jasmine and Bull's position. Jasmine cursed, loaded another round into the rifle breech as she wished she had at least an M-1 Garand semi-auto. As the firing stopped, Jasmine popped up and put another shot into the vision slit of the lead vehicle. The armored car began to angle off the wood planks as more scattered bullets pinged off the Metal Beasts. Another Lowlander fell, this one in front of the second vehicle. Unable to see the fallen woman from the vision slot, the Lowlander shrieked as a wheel ran over her. Her voice was cut off in mid-scream as the wheel crushed her torso.

The first Metal Beast ran off the wooden plank roadway and sank sideways into the soft mud. Jasmine peeked over the edge of her foxhole and saw the first vehicle struggling to free itself as Lowlanders ran up to stick planks under its wheels.

"Think you can throw a bomb that far, Bull?"

The big man paused, then spoke. "It is over one hundred strides, but I think I can. Is there a hole in the front vision glass of that stuck Beast?"

"Yes."

"Okay. I will try the black oil bottle."

Jasmine did a quick demonstration of a football spiral throw, bottle bottom first. Bull grinned at her. "You think this is my first time? Light the fuze just before I throw it."

Ten seconds later, a lit Molotov cocktail spiraled towards the front vehicle. It would have made the NFL proud as it struck just in front of the vision slit, broke apart, and the flammable liquid ignited. Some slopped through the hole in the vision slit as smoke and flame rose from the damaged vehicle. A plank carrier Lowlander began to scream as some of the fiery liquid splashed on to him.

"Bull. Try a grenade, one of those hand bombs."

The large man's second throw bounced off the head of a Lowlander and exploded in the air. Shrapnel felled three plank carriers, and the armored car shuddered to a stop. A top hatch flung open. Figures began to climb out as smoke rose from the vehicle interior. Jasmine glanced over the edge of the foxhole and saw the escaping crew. A volley of shots rang down on the Lowlanders as the inexperienced Sloggers, catching the first Metal Beast aflame, found the courage to shoot more. The three escaping crewmembers fell to the sudden onslaught of fire.

The rear armored car began to back down the hill. Without Lowlander infantry to help guide it, it slid off the wooden planks and onto the soft muddy ground. Wheels began to spin helplessly as a general rout began. The main gun cracked, and a small explosive shell struck a fighting hole. Two Sloggers fell screaming as Jasmine bounced a rifle round off its turret. Bull threw a second grenade and watched it explode just short of the second vehicle. As the Metal beast worked to free itself, Jasmine looked at Bull.

"Want to try something crazy?"

"Sure, Jazz. Why not?'

Ten minutes later, with the help of a dozen Sloggers Shanghaied from their fighting positions, Bull and Jasmine had the crew of the second Beast captured after they threw a grenade under the vehicle and filled it with smoke and fumes. The rest of the Lowlanders ran, leaving all the road planks behind. Jasmine soon sat on the edge of their fighting hole with the crude but usable submachine gun from the second Beast.

Suddenly, Bull said, "Stand up, Slogger."

Jasmine looked up to see the same Overman and Upperwoman officers from a few days ago standing by their hole. Jasmine snapped to attention.

"You two seem to have set a new standard for fighting ability," said the Upperwoman.

"Do you agree, ma'am, they are being wasted here?" said the Overman.

"Yes, I do."

The superior female officer handed Bull and Jasmine the insignia of Daggerman and ornate pieces of paper.

"These papers are orders to report to Capital City

in a fortnight. Show them to anyone who gives you a hard time. The signature of the Supreme War Lord is at the bottom, so if anyone interferes, tell them they will be shot. Understand?"

"Yes, ma'am," Jasmine said at rigid attention.

The Upperwoman laughed. "I think you could teach our whole army a thing or two, Daggerman Jazz. See you both in Capital City." The female officer turned and strode off.

The Overman tossed Bull a bulging coin bag. "For expenses. Buy some dress uniforms. Mother Hubbard will know how to find them." The Overman turned on his heels and strode off.

Bull looked at Jasmine, slammed her on her back, then bearhugged her.

"You're crushing my ribs, you big oaf!"

Bull let her go and then began to laugh. "We will be rich, my Holemate, my friend. They will make us Hitters, at least. They know you are a Sky Stranger and will pay you well for your knowledge."

"You going to stay with me, Daggerman Bull?"

"Of course. You are my Sky Luck. I will always be there for you."

"Even if you find a mate?"

Bull shrugged. "She can live with us. After all, I will have a bounty few can match."

Jasmine laughed as she began to collect the gear

and weapons. If she could survive this Steampunk Warworld, she wondered if anyone would write a history of it.

She glanced at Bull as he collected his property. At least she had one hell of a friend. What was that Teddy Roosevelt said? *Bully!*

CHAPTER 11
CAPITOL CITY

Jasmine Wright sat next to her Holemate on the cart seat. Bull Knox had obtained a cart pulled by two oversized llamas for their trip to Capitol City. As the hours passed, Jasmine wished she protested the transportation beasts before they began the journey.

The llamas resembled their Earth cousins, but on steroids. The creatures had the camel-like disposition attributed to ones on Earth. Thus, they were willful, stubborn, prone to anger if you pushed them, and downright cranky. Sometimes the two white and brown beasties could be prodded to a trot. Other times, they would kick and spit if pushed much too hard and begin a slow walk. Thus, two days on their trip, and Jasmine felt they had made barely ten miles.

"Are you sure we will not be late, Bull?"

"For the tenth time, Jazz, no. The Upperwoman gave us eight days to report to Capitol City. It is two and a half days at a fast trot if we travel from first light to dark. That is twelve Uhr. The Upperwoman based our trip on us walking. I called in debt, and thus, we ride."

"What kind of debt?" Jasmine asked.

"We rolled the bones, and Bath lost."

"You'll have to show me these bones, Bull."

The huge man produced a cloth pouch and handed it to Jasmine. "Have a look."

Jasmine spilled the contents of the pouch into her hand and revealed seven four-sided long pieces of finger bone from a human hand. The four long sides had numbers of dots ranging from one to six. Unlike standard dice familiar to Jasmine, none of the seven bones matched another.

"Hmmm. So you throw these bones to achieve a certain pattern of numbers to win, yes?"

"You win by either adding up the total numbers of marks of the upsides or if you have multiple duplicate sides. If four bones land three marks up, you win, unless the next throw results in five bones showing three marks. Or four bones with four marks, each show. You would have more marks showing."

"What if you threw seven bones and one lands propped up on another, showing an end rather than a side?"

"You throw again."

"If you do that three times in a row?"

"You are thrown out of the game for having bad luck, which may rub off on the other players."

Jasmine chuckled. "So, do you bet on each throw?"

"You can. Or you agree that after five throws, the higher score wins the money on the table. I usually win those contests. My luck is good."

Jasmine contemplated the human obsession with games of chance. Every culture she knew had some form of gambling or game which involved chance or luck, even if no one wagered.

"We will have to play, Bull."

"When we do, Daggerwoman Jazz, do not cry if you lose your money to me."

As said in the local language—German influence?—a half Uhr later, chocolate-skinned and dark-haired Jasmine noticed a widening in the road. The two warriors neared the area in their cart, and Jasmine noticed several stone tables and campfire hearths. At one end of the clearing was a brightly covered wagon, with several hobbled horses grazing nearby.

"What is this place, Bull?"

"A Royal Rest Area."

"The Royal family of the Kingdom of Iron made this?"

"Queen Aurora's mother started building them.

Now, the eldest daughter is responsible for ensuring upkeep."

Jasmine paused for a moment, then asked, "Are there no Kings?"

"Why, yes, there are Kings. But Queen Aurora commands the Kingdom. King Gerald controls the warriors, the Makers, Thinkers, and Smarties who make our weapons to protect our country. The King also makes sure the metalworker families keep the mines open. Queen Aurora makes sure the people have food, and there are Medicos to treat the ill and infirm."

"So the Queen deals with the common folk."

"Everyone who does not report to the King is overseen by her. We have a saying here."

"What is that, friend Bull."

"We love the Queen. We respect the King."

Bull pointed over to the covered wagon.

"The colorful canopy of that wagon identifies it as a Traveler wagon. Watch yourself around them. They are known for stealing from non-Travelers, card tricks, drugged drinks, and fake money."

"If these travelers do illegal things, don't the Royals have a police force, people who enforce the law?"

"We have Sheriffs in various areas. Some towns have a Constable. People with money hire ex-warriors to enforce their rules on their lands."

"No court system? Who decides guilt, innocence, crimes, and punishment?"

"Queen Aurora for the common folk through her Lawgivers. People take their complaints to them. In those areas controlled by the King, the Warlords handle crimes involving warriors and fighters. All other problems have King appointed Lawgivers."

"The town you lived near; what did people do there with criminals."

Bull shrugged. "It depended."

"On what?" asked Jasmine.

"On the anger of the town members and surrounding landowners. The more anger, the more punishment."

Once again. Jasmine thanked her lucky stars she had bumped into Bull. What would have happened if she had landed in the middle of some angry town? She could be dead. "But the Travelers..."

"The Queen allows them to be who they are. Only the unwary fall for their tricks. Now, if they interfered with the King's metal mining—"Bull made the universal sign with a thumb of slitting a throat and the accompanying sound.

Bull maneuvered the cart over to an artificial pond. Jasmine helped him unhitch the llama team and water them. As the beasts drank, Jasmine noticed a couple of robed figures watching them from the wagon.

On a whim, Jasmine waved at the individuals, and they waved back. Bull grumbled.

"Now, they will think they can come over and steal."

"Not if I meet them in the middle of the rest area."

"Do not let them drug you with drink, Jazz. They will kidnap you and sell you into bondage."

"Well, you will just have to come to save me, partner. Right?"

Bull grumbled some more and began to unload items from the cart. "We will rest here, Travelers or not. I want to eat a good meal."

"Who's cooking?" asked Jasmine.

"Why, me, of course. I am a better cook."

Jasmine laughed. Bull was ever full of surprises.

As the sunset approached, two robed persons walked towards the Daggermen's camp. Jasmine kept her promise and met them halfway. The Travelers had removed some veils, and Jasmine saw women, one older and one younger. Jasmine met them with open hands to show she was unarmed. The older female began to talk fast in a language Jasmine did not recognize. As she did, the older woman made the universal 'devils horns' two-finger sign to ward off evil. The younger one began to scold her in the same unfamiliar language.

Jasmine laughed. "I am not a devil, ladies. Just a weary soldier."

"My mother says you are Sky Stranger. Thus, demons infest you."

"My name is Jasmine, young lady. May I ask yours?"

"Martinique. My mother will not give hers as then your demons may try to control her."

"I promise I have no demons or devils inside me. Your mother is quite observant to see I'm not from around here."

Jasmine saw Martinique as an attractive teenager who would have fit into any group of mall shoppers on Earth. She wondered how happy a life she had here on Twosuns.

"So, Martinique, what can I do for you?"

"We just wished to see who this woman warrior was. Women do not fight in Traveler families. At least, not as warriors. We will fight for our man, our family."

"I am a minority in my homeworld, although it is becoming common. Here, on Twosuns, it has kept me alive."

The mother began to pull on her daughter's arm. "I apologize, Jasmine. My mother thinks you will bewitch me with your words. It was nice meeting you."

"And I, you, Martinique. Have a nice Journey."

Jasmine walked back to a frowning Bull. "What's

they want, Jazz?"

"They were curious about me as a female warrior. The mother thought I have demons inside me."

"Sorcerors and spellcasters they are, not us. Sleep with an open eye tonight."

"Of course, Big Bull. Now, what is for dinner? I am getting hungry."

The small Nightsun rose in the sky as Bull and Jasmine shared a nighttime liquor. Bull explained to Jasmine that Sloggertown Moneyhouse had a branch location in Capitol City. Thus, they could access the riches they had already earned. The new Daggerman/woman placed a portion of the second bulging money bag they received from the Overman in their local accounts. The rest traveled with them. Bull set a small money chest in with the giant llamas.

"They are like mules and donkeys. They will raise a fuss if anything bothers them."

Jasmine spent some time before sunset servicing their firearms. The upper command allowed her to keep the Lowland submachine gun and the Sharps rifle. Jasmine kept the M-9 semiauto pistol hidden, so no one knew she had it. When Jasmine asked Bull about why the government in the Kingdom of Iron did not keep tighter controls of the weapons their warriors had, he had shrugged. "If a fighter is willing to supply a weapon," he said, "why should the leaders care? If he dies because it is rotten, it is that person's loss."

"So soldiers, fighters in the service of the King are rarely issued weapons?"

"Occasionally, some Leader or Senior Commander will obtain specific weapons for a group. Then they make sure the Sloggers who get them keep them at least until they are dead."

Now that the Nightsun had risen. Bull belched in a satisfied manner.

"Ah, this is the life: a full stomach, warm campfire, good comradeship, and a great liquor."

Jasmine grinned. "How about when we reach Capital City?"

"We will check in with the office of the Supreme Warlord. Some Upper Leader or Master Stripper will tell us where to go. I am positive we will be Hitters, the elite guards of the Royals, and the Supreme Warlord. That is why they wanted us to have dress uniforms."

"Are the Hitters for a show, or do they fight?"

"Mostly for show. But we also guard the Royals against assassination. It happens in history."

"So, we will get fat and soft, Bull."

"Never! Commanders expect us to keep ourselves fit and ready for combat. The Hitter Unit will provide exercise yards and fighting drills."

Jasmine chuckled. "Sounds as if you did some

research on the Hitters."

"As my Mam said, check what interests you. Find out what the position entails. Then, if it suits you, go at it with gusto."

"Your Mam is a brilliant woman."

"But of course, Jazz. She produced me."

An Uhr later and the short-cropped hair, Bull was snoring in his bed. Jasmine laid awake and stared up at the star clusters she could see after the Nightsun passed. The small moon named Chaser, as the legend was, chased the Nightsun, its mother, reflected the Nightsun's rays. Bull told her that there were very few dark nights on Twosuns. Darkness required stormy weather.

"Will I ever see my Moon again?" Jasmine whispered. She hoped the Tinkerer and others noticed her passing, as they had the King grandchildren. Jasmine knew the Game must have also transported them somewhere. The question was, where?

Jasmine began to doze off and was jerked awake by a loud female scream. The Former Marine bolted out of her bed and grabbed her pistol and the sword bayonet she had kept from the first rifle. The cry rang out again as Jasmine saw a second Traveler wagon had joined the first. A figure Jasmine identified as Martinique dashed from the wagons and towards the warriors' campsite. On her heels were two males yelling at her in their native language.

Jasmine took off like a shot as she half-heard Bull yell at her, "Don't!"

No way would Jasmine stand by while a young woman was in danger. The two males caught up with Martinique just as Jasmine angled into them. One knocked the young lady down, cursing. Then Jasmine bowled him over.

The Former Marine had hit the man by surprise, and he sprawled into the dirt. The second man responded with surprising speed and struck at Jasmine with a long and thick stick. Jasmine managed to parry the blow with the sword bayonet and then leapt back.

She heard Bull bellow behind her. "Do not interfere. It is a family business."

"Like *Hell*," replied the Daggerwoman. She circled the attacker as the man she had knocked down regained his feet.

Jasmine started to raise her pistol when Bull yelled something in the Traveler language and then bellowed at Jasmine, "*Do not start a Blood Feud! We will suffer it for the rest of our lives.*"

The big man strode up and stood between the two men and Jasmine.

"Hey, I can handle myself—"

"Quiet, Jazz. I will explain later."

Bull spoke a long sentence. Then he showed the

two men his short sword. An older man approached before there was any other conversation.

"That is my daughter," the man said in the local form of English. "What right do you claim to interfere with Traveler matters?"

"Jazz is a Sky Stranger and does not understand your ways."

With the mention of 'Sky Stranger,' all three men stepped back and made the 'devil's horns' sign to ward off her evil. The two younger men began to argue with the elder. The three ignored Bull and Jasmine as they squabbled. Martinique slowly stood up and then slid towards the Former Marine.

"Jasmine," said Bull, "you may need your coin purse."

"Why?"

"You'll see."

Finally, the father figure turned towards Bull. "Your woman struck one of my daughter's suitors. He demands satisfaction."

"So, he wants to die by my sword?" asked Bull. "Daggerwoman Jazz is under the protection of the Supreme Warlord, and he tasked me to bring her to him by the end of the seventh night."

The three Travelers conferred once again, then the father spoke. "My daughter has been bewitched by the Sky Stranger and is now no longer desirable. She will now never marry and will spend the rest of her days as a whore to survive. Your—Daggerwoman—owes my family for the disowner and the loss of a suitor bounty."

"Jazz, you need your coinage," said Bull.

Jasmine opened her mouth to argue, then realized she would have to kill all three Travelers and then the rest of the family if she ever wanted to sleep without a guard. Blood feuds were severe matters in many cultures and would go on for generations.

"Okay, Bull." Jasmine went and fetched her money pouch and then stood by Bull. Martinique stood behind her as Jasmine readied to pay.

"How much?" asked Bull. The father spoke an amount in his native tongue, and Bull growled.

"Do *not* try to abuse us with inflated monies. If I tell the Supreme Warlord you were harassing—"

"Okay. A quarter of that," said the father.

"Jasmine. Two gold coins."

Jasmine begrudgingly handed Bull the equivalent of old-time Pieces of Eight. The father took the money, spit towards his daughter, and the three men strode away.

"Now what, Bull?"

"Now you own a slave. And with her comes all the responsibility of slave ownership."

"Now wait a minute—!"

Bull ignored Jasmine and walked back to the

campsite. Martinique stood behind Jasmine and whispered, "I am sorry, Mistress. I will be a good slave—"

"No! I had ancestors who were slaves. You are *not* a slave."

"You—reject me?" The young woman, barely out of girlhood, stood with her jaw quivering.

"No, I accept you. I—oh *shit*! Come on; we'll make you a bed and talk about it in the morning."

Bull was soon snoring, and Jasmine felt a warm body pressed up against her back.

"God," she mumbled, "what have I gotten myself into?"

Pleasant breakfast smells woke Jasmine at daybreak. At first, she thought Bull had awoken early. Then she noticed the big man was only just standing up from his bedroll. Martinique stood by the campfire, stirring a pot as well as frying something in a pan. Bull laughed and called out.

"At least you picked a slave who can cook as well as me."

"She is not my—oh, never mind."

The young black-haired lady called out to Jasmine. "Mistress. Your meal is ready."

"Coming," Jasmine called back. She used a washcloth to wipe her face and hands and then approached the campfire. In a flash, Martinique handed her a plate of freshly fried near-potatoes, some form of bacon, and a ladle of stew.

"Oof, You will make me fat."

"No, Mistress. You will work it off. I know it."

Martinique then handed Bull an equally full plate. "There is enough for another serving, great Bull."

"Ah, a woman after my own heart," said Bull with a wide grin.

"Plate for you?" asked Jasmine after she swallowed a forkful.

"A slave does not eat with her mistress. It is disrespectful."

Jasmine stared at Martinique, then set down her plate. "Okay. Time for a discussion about new rules. Where I come from, slavery is a sin. Thus, you are *not* a slave."

The young woman frowned and then replied to Jasmine, "Then, what am I? You paid a marriage bounty, so you wish for me to be your wife? I have not bedded a woman, but if my Mistress wishes—"

Bull burst out laughing. "This not funny, Bull, dammit," Jasmine said through tight lips.

"Oh, my lucky Sky Stanger. This situation is amusing as it teaches a Sky Stranger with many more years of schooling than my eight years that she is still as ignorant in some matters as a newborn calf. As I said before, a slave requires much work by a master to keep his property fit and worthy. If you free her, what does she have? Her family rejected her. She could be a beggar or a whore. She is a good cook so that she might find employment there—"

"Oh, alright, Bull Knox. I get your point. I stepped into a pile of llama crap. Now, I am just trying to climb out."

Jasmine looked at Martinique. "Okay. First, you will be my servant, young lady. You are *not* a slave. You may stay with me as long as you wish, but you are free to leave at any time. I will arrange to pay you a wage to have money if something happens to me. Understand?"

"Yes, Mistress."

"And, since you are not a slave, you will eat with Bull and me. All I ask is that you follow my instructions as your—employer. Understand?"

"Yes, Mistress."

"And stop looking down when you talk to me. You are a human as I am. Look me in the eye."

Martinique met Jasmine's gaze with a hint of a smile on her lips. "Yes, Mistress Jazz."

"Good, as for you, Bull. I owe you a big debt for backing me up last night. I know I looked before I leaped—"

"One does not owe a debt to a friend and Holemate, Jazz. We are there for each other. We are there to also keep the other from doing evil. But no matter what, *We Are There.*"

Jasmine felt her eyes tear up a bit as it sank in how much of a friend Bull had become. "Thanks, Bull Knox."

The oversized man walked over to the campfire and loaded up a plate. Then he took it to Martinique. "Eat. You are too skinny."

The three broke camp an hour later. Martinique asked to handle the llamas and soon had them moving at a trot without usually spitting, complaining, and fussing.

"I think we have found our driver," said Jasmine.

"I have always had a way with animals, Mistress."

The trio made good time that day. They stopped for a late lunch to rest the beasts, and Bull showed them on a map where they were.

"We will skirt Tree Mountain here. The road then branches off to the North and Iron Mountain, and Capitol City. It would be best if you stayed alert near Tree Mountain as the number of beasts is many. Only Royals and Uppers are allowed to hunt the animals there, and thus it has become one large game preserve of all types of dangerous creatures."

"The result of your studies?" asked Jasmine.

"Yes. Again, following the advice of my Mam

serves me well."

Jasmine made sure the large-caliber Sharps rifle was loaded and close at hand. Martinique kept the llamas at a slow trot. They saw a few other carts and people walking on the road they were on.

"Not a lot of people will be traveling to Capitol City until harvest is over," said Bull.

"So, this is Spring changing into Summer?" said Jasmine.

"Yes. Within a couple of weeks, this road will be full of families and businesses transporting their goods to the major markets in and around Capitol City. People make money and exchange information, plus gossip."

Jasmine smiled at her Holemate as she spoke.

"You hide your knowledge and intelligence, don't you, friend Bull?"

Bull grinned at Jasmine. "People see what they want to. They see in me a huge oaf, long in muscle, short in brains. It gives me an advantage when people think they can take advantage of the farmer dolt."

The llamas suddenly pulled up short. The two white and brown hairy beasts began to fuss and spit.

"They have caught the smell of something they do not like," said Martinique. A distant horn broke the stillness.

"A Royal or Upper Hunt," stated Bull. "Watch for riders."

"And beasts," added Jasmine. The Former Marine picked up the Sharps rifle and positioned two spare rounds in a breast pocket. The llamas refused to move ahead, and the two warriors dismounted the cart.

"I don't like this," said Bull. Jasmine was surprised that the massive man exhibited a bit of fear for the first time since she met him. Jasmine brought the heavy rifle up to a High Ready position.

Suddenly a rider broke free from the surrounding forest. Jasmine saw it was a young girl, no more than twelve years of age. Three braids of long silver hair hung from beneath a silver helmet as her eyes met the gaze of the travelers.

"Ho, people," the young lady's voice rang out as she strove to control her black stallion. "Have you seen a—"

The llamas let out matching cries of a cross between a horse's scream and a camel's hoot as a massive 'thing' burst from the trees. Jasmine's mind told her it was a Hippopotamus with legs three to four times too long, supporting its enormous bulk. The beast slammed into the girl's stead, and massive jaws crushed the horse's head as the young girl was thrown free. A crossbow carried by the silver braided girl went flying one way as she tumbled to the other.

The stallion was dead in moments. Jasmine fired the 45-70 Sharps into the beast's skull and went into combat reload of the next shell. Bull let out a war bellow and charged the creature, slashing at the hamstring of the left rear leg with his bronze sword. The beast raised its head and bellowed. Jasmine fired the next round through the exposed throat and up into the lower skull. The four-legged nightmare twisted and snapped at an invisible threat, then shuddered and collapsed. All was silent save for the loud protests of the great llamas. Somehow, Martinique kept them from bolting.

Bull pulled his massive revolver from its holster, stepped next to the monster, and shot it in the right eye.

"Fuck!" said Jasmine. "That was close."

"I have never been that afraid, Jazz," said Bull. Then added, "Quick, the girl."

Martinique managed to wrap the llama's reins around the front wheels, so the most they could do was drag the cart. In a flash, she had corralled the young huntress and kept her from the beast and her dead horse. The silver-haired youngster cried tears of rage and sorrow about her stallion, Dark Star.

"Hey, young lady," said Jasmine. "I know it hurts, but you are lucky to be alive—"

Four large mounts with riders broke from the forest fifty yards down, saw the cart and deceased beast. Two lancers had their pig stickers inches from Bull as Jasmine yelled at them.

"Hey, assholes! We killed that damned thing.

Lighten up."

A fifth rider crashed from the forest at the attack spot of the beast. Bull's eyes widened, and he yelled, "Kneel before Queen Aurora!"

Jasmine saw a statuesque silver-haired woman, close to six feet in height, with a noticeable model's body even covered with light armor.

"Pull back your lances," her command voice rang out. "These three saved my daughter Atlania."

Jasmine tried to kneel as she kept the Sharps rifle ready. The Queen commanded, "Oh, stop with the kneeling. I should be kneeling before you as you saved my headstrong daughter."

The Queen slid off her horse with ease and walked towards her crying daughter. Martinique began to prostrate herself, and Aurora waved off the action.

"Stop that. Come here, my daughter."

Atlania wrapped her arms around her mother and sobbed. "Dark Star is dead!"

"Yes, my dear. Dark Star's death is why your headstrong actions must stop. Trying to earn your fourth braid at your young age must halt now. The competition you have with my younger self is not good."

"I just want you to be proud of me, Mother."

The Queen tilted Atlantia's head back and looked into her eyes. "You are too much like your mother, my sweet. Now, you must thank these strangers for saving you."

Queen Aurora removed her helmet, and Jasmine saw four silver braids hanging from four sides of the Royal's head. "So, what are the names of the three saviors?"

"Daggers Bull and Jazz, maidservant Martinique, my Queen," Bull bellowed out. Aurora examined each person in kind with a penetrating gaze.

"Hilden, attend me."

A muscular warrior dismounted and strode over to the Queen. He was large but still seemed average size next to Bull. "Yes, my Queen."

"Did we not receive a note about two unusual— fighters en route to Capitol City?"

"Yes, my Queen."

"I think these are they, plus one addition. We have a Sky Stranger, a Westman, and now a Traveler. If I were religious, I would say this is a portent of things to come. Jinanne!"

A female warrior stepped up to the group. "Yes, my Queen?"

Aurora nodded towards Jasmine. "This one needs a Royal Huntress braid. See to it. Her shot saved my eldest daughter."

"Pardon me, your Highness," Jasmine interrupted. "Without my Holemate Bull, I would have been dead days ago. And he finished the beast off."

Aurora looked at the Former Marine with renewed interest. "Hmmm. Your Highness. I like that term. And I see you and Bull here are quite the team." The Queen then gazed at Martinique. "Serve them well, maiden. They will bring you good fortune. I sense it."

The young lady nodded, unsure as to what to say.

Queen Aurora watched with a critical eye as Jinanne expertly braided strands of Jasmine's long dark hair into a thick braid on the right side of her head. Bull seemed on the verge of kneeling and kept checking himself from doing such. The entourage of hunters watched intently as a unique tableau unfolded. As Jinanne finished with Jasmine's new braid, the Queen spoke.

"Daggerwoman Jazz, henceforth, you are required to wear that braid as a unique identifier. You must also keep a higher level of honor in your actions as you are now a member of a select group of womanhood. You are a Royal Huntress. Understand?"

Jasmine snapped to Marine Corps attention and saluted. "Yes, ma'am!"

A grin formed on Queen Aurora's mouth, then she spoke. "You come from a warrior tradition, don't you, new Huntress?"

"United States Marine Corps, ma'am."

"Hilden, we must study these—Marines. I think they were superior warriors in their Sky Stranger World." Aurora turned her head and spoke to Atlania. "Daughter, you owe these three a special honor, yes?"

The girl's mouth formed an 'O' in surprised remembrance. Quickly she drew a dagger with a foot-long blade and advanced on the dead beast. With expert surgical precision, Atlania cut out three prominent tusks from the hippo-like creature. Then, she strode to Jasmine, Bull, and Martinique, handing each a bloody trophy as she bowed to them.

"You came to my aid, a stranger, when the Behemoth attacked me in a moment of inattention. These teeth will be forever reminders that I owe my life to you. Present them if you ever need my help in return."

"Well done, my daughter. Now, Hilden. The special pouch if you please."

In a few moments, Queen Aurora was handing a signet ring to each of the trios.

"When you report to the office of the Supreme Warlord, present the rings. I will also arrange with the King, someone to meet you who I believe will be interested in your unique skills and knowledge," The Queen paused and continued, "Being ordinary Hitters, I believe, will be a waste of your talents."

All three travel mates acknowledged the Queen's instruction as Aurora extended her arm and helped her daughter mount behind her. In a flash, the Queen spun her horse around and galloped down the road. The entourage peeled off and followed. Hilden paused long enough to toss a coin purse to Jasmine.

"A drink on me for saving the young one. I owe you."

Then he spurred his horse and galloped away.

Jasmine stood almost stunned. Everything had happened so fast.

"It's like a damned fairytale," said Jasmine.

"You saved our bacon, Jazz," Bull stated,

"Hey, you helped me get the killing shot, my friend."

"I was almost frozen with fear, Jazz. I have never been that afraid before. I feel—dishonorable."

"Bull, you don't think I was scared? My training just took over."

"I am rarely scared, Jazz. This feeling is much too strange to me."

"A wise drill sergeant told me something once."

"What was that?" asked Bull.

"Fear tells you that you may have just done something stupid. Then, it gives you a kick in the butt to help you survive if you learn how to use that fear. Only the foolish and the crazy have no fear."

Bull nodded in agreement. "This drill sergeant

was a wise man."

"A wise woman. We had female trainers." Jasmine looked at the remains of the Behemoth and the horse. "Speaking of saving bacon, you think we can salvage some steaks from those animals? I hate to leave it all to the scavengers."

"A Holemate after my own heart, Jazz. Let me use my short sword—"

The two soldiers looked up and saw Martinique had beat them to the task, using Jasmine's sword bayonet to hack hunks and steaks from the Behemoth.

"I told you, Jazz, you picked a good slave."

"A servant, Bull. Not a slave."

The rest of the trip was uneventful. Just over two days later, they came to a three-story-tall set of entrance gates to Capitol City. Off to one side was a stone building with a massive sign proclaiming 'SUPREME WARLORD.'

"I guess he controls the comings and goings, Bull."

"It makes sense, Jazz. He is in charge of the warriors and what you call the military."

"Well, my large friend, time to check in and see what the future holds."

Bull and Jasmine left Martinique with the cart and llamas and walked into the substantial office. Behind a front counter was a bored clerk, who became quickly unbored when he saw the signet rings. The man dashed to the rear and brought back a well-fed middle-aged man with grey striped hair and beard. The man dressed in pressed and cleaned tailored coveralls stopped and examined the Bull and Jasmine before speaking.

"You must be Jazz, and you Bull, yes?"

Jasmine picked up the still noticeable Scottish brogue. "You are not from around here, are you, sir?"

"Michael MacLintok, formerly of Her Majesty's Royal Marines. The Queen here says you are a former U. S. Marine, a Sky Stranger like me."

"How long have you been here?" asked Jazz.

"Twenty Harvests. I am now a Senior Maker and sometimes Thinker, fancy names for someone who tries to design and fix things in the godforsaken world of Twosuns."

"What has that to do with us, sir?" asked Bull. "I am no Thinker or Maker. I am but a poor—"

Jasmine began to laugh, and Michael chuckled. "Well, you are not poor nor stupid, Bull Knox. I have already checked you out. You have a sharp mind, as does Jazz. I don't know how I got here in Twosuns, but at least I have a job that keeps me fed, clothed, and not bored." The Maker paused. "I understand you have a servant who is a good cook also."

"Yes. Martinique," replied Jasmine. "She

is outside.”

"Bring her in. She will be a member of our happy family as we try to build things."

Jasmine started to fetch Martinique and then stopped. "One thing in clarification, my Royal Marine. You said you do not know what brought you here."

"Huh. Does anyone, Jazz?"

"Call me, Jasmine. I know what brought me here?"

"Really? What?"

"A Tinkerer and the Game."

CHAPTER 12
CAPITOL CITY: PART 2

Jasmine Wright, a former U.S. Marine and Dagger Woman, stood at an extended workbench and perused the item before her. As a new member of the Kingdom of Iron (shorthand was the Iron Kingdom) Royal Armory, one of her tasks was to examine things that had fallen from the sky. Such things came from alternate worlds/universes, just as Jasmine had weeks ago. If they appeared to have value as a weapon, the object stayed with the Armory. If it did not, Jasmine passed it on to whatever Thinker or Maker she or her Boss, former British Royal Marine Michael McClintock believed, could use the item.

Jasmine's former Holemate and battle buddy Bull Knox did much the same, although he often used his great strength to bend something back into what was believed its natural shape or pull something apart for further examination. Bull did not have the others' formal education, but he had an innate intelligence and feel for what was right in the world of Twosuns.

Jasmine frowned at the soccer ball-sized object in front of her. It was smooth and well machined, with two flashing orbs which alternated in the light show. She was always leery of something with flashing lights as she immediately thought, *bomb*. Thus, Jasmine had no desire to try and disassemble it. As she stared, a friendly voice with a bit of a Scottish brogue spoke from behind her.

"For once, Warrior Thinker Jazz is perplexed."

Jasmine turned and smiled at her Boss, Michael, who was now more of a friend than a supervisor.

"The shape and flashing lights say 'bomb' to me, so I would just as soon get it out of here. Where was it found?"

"A farmer on the edge of Capitol City found it in his gardens. That was some two days ago local time, and it has not exploded yet."

From Jasmine's time on Earth, Michael had arranged a new title or classification for Jasmine and Bull. Warrior Thinker meant that Jasmine and Bull were not only excellent fighters but also of a higher intellect. "Time to make the Royals and Uppers think in new ways," Michael said.

Queen Aurora and King Gerald agreed. The Queen had already met the two former Sloggers when they stopped her daughter Atlania from being killed by a

Behemoth on a hunt gone wrong. Thanks to that, Jasmine was also a Royal Huntress, required to wear a particular hair braid denoting her status. Jasmine's servant Martinique made sure the braid was in its proper condition at all times.

"Is there any way to check for radiation?" asked Jasmine.

"No one has built a Geiger Counter yet, but we have a natural way of measuring radiation. A form of uranium and radium does exist here."

Michael stepped away to another room in the Armory Section, part of the Supreme Warlord large complex of buildings. Other Thinkers, Makers, Mechmen thought the Armory Section was unfairly large. When Michael, the Senior Maker, and Thinker had offered to send explosives and other possible dangerous items to the complainers in exchange for giving them some of his space, there was suddenly the sound of crickets.

A few minutes later, he returned with a jar full of some worms. Jasmine looked at them and saw they had long setae at the fore-end and tail.

"The locals call these rock worms. If you place them next to a suspected source of radiation, their death rate will give you a rough estimate of the radioactivity of the rock or other substance."

"Well, let's set some near this object in a small cabinet. This object may be a weapon, or maybe, a beacon."

"A beacon for who?" asked Michael.

"Maybe the beings who keep dropping us Sky People on top of the inhabitants in Twosuns."

"I could pry that apart, Jazz," interjected Bull.

"Let's see if there is anything dangerous first. I would hate to blow us all up or poison us."

The three investigators placed the soccer ball object in a lead-lined safe with the rock worms. Thus, if the worms died by the morning, they would know it was from the object's proximity, not from external radiation. Jasmine's turn was to obtain something for Martinique to prepare for dinner, so she left the Royal Armory offices and laboratories for shopping in Capitol City. The City was vast and a combination of medieval, early industrial Europe and areas which resembled 20th Century America. Steampunk fit the local culture. One moment you had people and items all leather and steel. The next block had row houses from the 1950s with petroleum alloys and plastics included in manufacturing; then steam power as a means of locomotion mixed in with petroleum-fueled engines on the various streets and thoroughfares. Jasmine walked to one of the many open-air markets which served as conduits for fresh food and prepared dishes. There were a handful of the equivalent of supermarkets and the beginning of a 20th Century shopping mall. However, Jasmine liked the feel of the street-level small shops, which reminded her of street fairs near her hometown.

Jasmine used some of her newfound influence (a Royal Huntress was a big deal) to limit the sale of 'bushmeat' mixed in with live farm stock. After explaining the Coronavirus in her world and its alleged origins, Royal Health Officials cracked down on sanitation and food preparation regulations. The people of the Kingdom of Iron were far from uneducated or ignorant. Queen Aurora supported a public education system that served as a model for many communities.

Thus, Jasmine strolled the streets and byways as she collected fresh foods, spices. Sweetmeats and the local version of sushi and sashimi. Many merchants knew her or knew of her and did their best to get Jasmine to open her purse. As the former Marine smiled and greeted the shopkeepers and street vendors, she noticed a set of young eyes fixated on her. Jasmine smiled at a red-haired girl of about five years of age. The young child kept staring at Jasmine, so she stepped up to the redhead with a smile.

"Hello, young lady. You look at me as if you have a question."

"You are a Royal Huntress," the young girl stated.

"Yes, I am. Jasmine Wright at your service."

"You are not from around here, are you?" asked

the young girl. "Your skin is darker than most people in Capitol City."

"Yes, I am from a place far from here. You know my name. May I know yours?"

"Oneida."

"That is a nice name, Oneida. Are you here with your family?"

As Jasmine spoke, a young woman, no older than Jasmine, bustled up with a young child on her back in a carrier much like a papoose. She called Oneida's name and began to lecture her about wander off. She then cast her eyes to the ground and performed a half curtsey.

"I am sorry, milady. My daughter must learn not to bother those with important lives and jobs."

"She was not a bother ma'am. May I ask your name?"

"Olivia Redfern, milady. Again, I apologize—"

"Olivia, may I ask you to look me in the face, as your daughter does?"

Olivia jerked her eyes up to look at Jasmine. "I mean no offense, milady."

"None was taken. May I ask you to walk with me and help me with my shopping? I can tell you, and your daughter knows the ins and outs of this marketplace much better than I. Could you help prevent the local vendors from taking advantage of me?"

Olivia paused in reply until Oneida tugged on her dress. "Please, Mother. May we help?"

Olivia's mouth formed a small smile as she nodded in the affirmative.

"It would be rude not to render aid to a—stranger in town. Especially one of great import."

Jasmine took one of Olivia's hands in hers. "Trust me when I say being a good mother is one of the most important jobs around. Without my mother, I would have been a lost soul."

The not-shy Oneida grabbed Jasmine's shirt sleeve and gently tugged on it. "Mother was about to buy us a sweet drink. Do you want to join us?"

"I'd love to if you allow me to buy. I have some old coins I must get rid of before they become worthless."

The three females soon sat at an open-air café, sipping some unique liquid concoctions Bull had not ever mentioned.

"These are great, Olivia. Thank you for introducing me to them."

"My husband, Olander, and I make similar drinks from our fruit trees and local berries. It is not hard to do, mi—Jasmine."

"You have a farm?"

"Yes. We have fields and an orchard we work with his brother and his wife. We came to Capital City as an odd flashing ball fell in our fields. We brought it to the Royal Officers for a reward they offer for Skythings."

Jasmine realized some odd fate had connected her and this family. She watched as Olivia nursed her son, Tuck, and mused how it would be nice to have a simple life like this family. Yet, even they had complications from objects falling from the sky. Jasmine could imagine, if she fell into their fields, the shock a Sky Stranger would bring.

"Have objects fallen into your fields before?" asked Jasmine.

"Not ours, but our neighbors. A body fell once. My husband's brother says it is the work of demons who enjoy causing hate and discontent." Olivia smiled at her nursing son. "Then I look at my son and daughter and know that no demons can upset our lives if we do not allow it."

"And we have a Royal Huntress' like you to protect us," stated Oneida with a five-year-old conviction.

Jasmine laughed. "I appreciate your confidence, young lady."

There was a loud, popping noise that interrupted the conversation. Then a sizeable furry shape crashed into the near table. People screamed as an oversized feline lunged to its feet and let out a loud screeching growl. Jasmine was on her feet in a flash, displaying her sword bayonet.

"Get behind me," Jasmine commanded as she stepped in front of Olivia and her children. Jasmine swore as she wished she had carried a firearm since coming to Capitol City, despite being told it was outside of cultural norms. The large feline predator growled and spit, displaying long twin dagger-shaped canines. Jasmine saw a creature that looked like an American Cougar, the rear legs more massive than the front. The overlong teeth reminded her of a Sabre Tooth Cat from Earth's ancient history.

The great cat gathered itself to spring, and Jasmine lifted a restaurant chair: used it to jab and distract, as seen in many an old circus epic. Temporarily taken aback, the predator slapped at the chair instead of leaping.

"Take off, kitty," Jasmine yelled as she tried to make herself look as large and threatening as possible. She remembered reading somewhere that cougars and such would hesitate if the prey looked like it could do some damage. Unfortunately, this feline demonstrated it was not like an Earth-style cougar/mountain lion: it lept straight at the former Marine.

The cat slammed into the lifted chair and propelled Jasmine to the restaurant floor. As the chair came apart, Jasmine thrust her long blade into the creature's innards. The Royal Huntress grabbed at the attacker's throat to keep the extra-long fangs from her face, but in a split second, she saw she would fail.

Some force grabbed and lifted the cougar on steroids, flinging it across the room. Through hazy vision, she saw it was Bull. Her Holemate went after her attacker with a speed which belied his size, grabbed the beast, and snapped its neck as he bellowed some Westman warcry.

"Mother, Jasmine is hurt!" cried Oneida. At that moment, the Former Marine realized she was leaking some claret and thought, *Where did that come from?* Then everything faded to black.

Jasmine awoke in a Medico's office, with the Kingdom of Iron's medical staff hovering over her. Jasmine's eyes focused, and she saw Oneida's head and shoulders above everyone else. Then she realized the young girl was sitting on the impossibly broad shoulders of Bull Knox.

"It's about time you awoke, Jazz," Bull said in as stern a tone as possible. "You think you can force your work at the Armory on me while you relax in a medico bed? I should say not."

"Was I the only one hurt?" Jasmine asked.

"Thanks to you, yes," replied Olivia as she lifted a flask of some liquid to her mouth. Jasmine did not realize how dry her mouth was until she sipped the cool water.

"My family owes you a debt we can never

repay," Olivia said with teary eyes.

Jasmine smiled at the friendly faces and tried not to laugh at the vision of Big Bull giving Olivia the ultimate horsie ride on his shoulders. Her immense friend attempted to present the gruff exterior of a battle-hardened warrior yet had a soft heart a mile wide. Again the former Marine thanked Fate and the Gods for the fortune of being found first by Bull.

"I was just doing what anybody would—"

Loud voices interrupted Jasmine's response. Above the hubbub, Jasmine finally made out the words "Queen Aurora! Make way for Queen Aurora!"

And then the statuesque silver-haired monarch was in the hospital room. Bull tried to kneel, which brought Oneida's young, wide-eyed face down to the Queen's level. The Royal burst out laughing.

"I see Great Bull has a new job as a royal mount for a young princess," Aurora said, then fixed her gaze on Olivia.

"You must be the proud mother of the young lady who can tame such a mount as Great Bull."

Olivia tried to kneel with young Tuck in her arms, and Aurora reached out for the male babe. "May I hold your child? I have a weakness for young children."

"But of course, my Queen."

Aurora soon had the young Tuck giggling and cooing. As she handed Tuck back to his smiling mother, another royal personage burst into the room.

"My wayward daughter, Atlania, finally arrives."

"Sorry, Mother. I was on the far side of the Capitol when you sent the message."

"Well, my daughter. I will let you do the honor this time."

The younger image of the royal mother walked up to Jasmine's bedside and began to comb and separate her jet black hair.

"It is my privilege to weave your second braid into your hair, Royal Huntress Jazz. Once again, you have demonstrated the qualities of an outstanding Huntress."

"Please, Queen Aurora, it was Bull who saved this family and me. I was flat on my back when he broke the beast's neck."

"But you stopped the attack on the innocents, which is one of the many tasks of a Royal Huntress. But, of course, I have not forgotten Great Bull."

Queen stepped in front of the still kneeling Bull Knox and grinned at Oneida, still sitting astride his neck and shoulders."

"Young lady, could you please help me place this about Great Bull's neck?"

"My God," said Olivia. "It is the Star of the Protector."

Queen Aurora's voice resonated throughout the area of the medical center.

"From this day forward, Bull Knox is henceforth known as Great Bull, Protector of the Realm, Savior of the Kingdom of Iron. May he save many an innocent from the likes of the unknown beast."

As a blushing Bull accepted the star-shaped silver amulet on the equally silver chain, Jasmine interjected.

"Pardon, Queen Aurora, did you say unknown beast?"

"Yes, Huntress. The large cat is similar but is not a member of our breeds—another surprise from whoever feels the need to drop people, beasts, and objects into our realm." The Queen presented a sly smile to Jasmine. "I believe you and your fellows will be looking into the matter of this great cat."

Jasmine heard an order concealed as a suggestion. She knew there was no rest for the wicked, even someone in a hospital bed.

Two days later, Jasmine was back at her workstation. There was a medical dressing that the Medicos told her to change at least once a day. In actuality, Martinique, technically a servant but more like a sister to Jasmine, demanded that task.

"We Traveler women are all taught the medical skills to deal with wounds," Martinique said as she first changed the dressing. "Most Medicos think we are beneath their care."

The Twosuns version of Gypsies had to deal with much the same prejudices as those on Earth. Jasmine would admit that the culture that made women into commodities for sale also brought problems onto its members.

"The Medicos said some rear claws of the beast came close to dealing my womanhood area a lethal blow." Jasmine sighed. "I guess my days of wearing a bikini while showing off my natural suntan are over."

Martinique frowned at the supposed mistress/employer. "Bikini, suntan? What are these? I am confused, Mistress."

Jasmine spent a few minutes explaining the varieties of Earthly beach and mating culture as Martinique replace the dressings.

"You have no worries, Mistress Jasmine, for I am here. There are many salves made from unique plants, berries, and soils, which reduce scaring. "

"So, Travelers have similar—problems?"

"I mentioned women would fight for their men in Traveler camps. We fight like this great cat that attacked you, clawing, biting, and tearing. Traveler women learned over the years to repair such damage so our men would find us desirable after such fights."

"Why fight over a man, Martinique? If a man is attracted to you, why would he expect you to fight for him?"

The young woman looked at Jasmine as if she had three heads. "Why, for the family honor. Traveler women must show they are willing to fight for their family, their tribe, as the men are. We must be tough to survive."

Jasmine realized such cultural norms were part of why the young woman had attached herself to Jasmine so readily. Jasmine was a warrior, so Martinieque saw her as being in a position of honor.

"Well, while you are living with Bull and me, please check with us before you decide to fight someone for a man. I think he and I can find you the right candidate for a mate and marriage."

"Like Great Bull?"

Jasmine saw Martinique's previous glances, where a woman sizes up a potential male partner when Bull was not looking. Jasmine made sure she did not smile when she answered, "We'll cross that bridge when we get to it, my dear. Now could you make Bull, me, and Michael one of your soon-to-be-famous lunches? My healing body requires extra food."

As the four ate lunch on the second day from the giant cat's attack, they discussed the 'beacon' ball object. The item did emit a small quantity of radiation based on the death of a few rock worms. Thus, now was the question as to why.

"I still say you let me tear it in half to see inside

it," said Bull in between large bites from a tender roast Martinique prepared.

"And if you release some poisonous vapor or destroy some unique mechanism inside, what then?" replied Michael. "There are only one of these ball objects, so even if it does not contain anything dangerous if you destroy it, then no further useful study."

"Someone needs to invent the X-ray machine or MRI," interjected Jasmine, "then we could examine it without Bull tearing it in half."

"Thinkers and Makers are even now creating vacuum tubes and possible transistors," Michael replied. "It will take a while to create these complicated machines."

Great Bull snorted. "Whenever you two start talking about all those complicated inventions from your Earth, I am glad I was born here near the Kingdom of Iron." The man of immense size and appetite grabbed half a fruit pie and began eating it. In between bites, he continued with his dissertation.

"My desires in life are simple. Enough gold and silver to purchase land or a small business. Then, I have a wife who will bear me healthy children that will produce grandchildren to spoil in my later years. So simple as opposed to creating possible monstrosities of metal."

Jasmine could not withhold her laughter before

she spoke. "My great friend Bull. That is one of the most prolonged and most profound speeches you have made since we met."

"I have to agree," interjected Martinique. "You have expressed my desires also."

"See? The young Traveler expresses the truth of *this* world. We would be better off without all the interference created by Sky Strangers and other things falling from the sky. Current occupants and friends at this table are exempted, of course."

"Well, my large friend," replied Michael, "just as soon as Jasmine and I can find a way to return to our portion of the sky, we will be waving goodbye. No offense meant."

"None is taken, Boss Michael. Now. May I ask our excellent cook for some of those sweets Jazz calls donuts? I see you have improved on someone's idea, as usual."

Jasmine saw Martinique present Bull with a smoldering, come hither look as she quickly obtained the desired pastries. She wondered if Great Bull, as designated by the Queen, realized he was the object of the young lady's desire.

They are going to have to work that out themselves, Jasmine thought.

After a long day and a shared aperitif provided by Michael McLintock around a fireplace, Jasmine excused herself and went to her bed. Of course, Martinique had turned down the clean bedcovers. Jasmine knew that if Martinique decided to leave and start a family, Jasmine could no longer be spoiled like this. Well, she had been a Marine, where no one had anyone turning down their beds for them. Jasmine would gladly give up a servant in exchange for a trip back to her Earth apartment.

The former Marine was fast asleep.

A scream from Martinique on the ground floor had Jasmine leaping from her bed. She grabbed the semi-automatic pistol she obtained by trade from Bull and bounded down the stairs from her quarters to the main floor.

Framed by a weird light stood a large being holding Martinique by her long black hair and throat.

"Let her go, motherfucker!" Jasmine ordered as she sighted in on the humanoid's head. Then her peripheral vision saw—a small humanoid.

"Where is the spy ball?" the small being demanded. "It is in this building. Present it, and the girl will be released."

"How about I blow your brains out instead, shorty? *Let her go!*"

"The object was not meant for—"

A thrown battle ax split the skull of the being imprisoning Martinique. An enraged Great Bull followed the thrown weapon, bellowing as a Berserker on Earth must do. He scooped up the small person and had their head and throat in his massive hands.

"No!" Michael yelled as he appeared. "Keep him alive, Bull. We need to question him."

"You are ever so lucky, little man," hissed Bull. "If Martinique is hurt, you will suffer ten-fold."

The small man tried to reach his belt, and both his hands were engulfed in one of Great Bull's hands.

"Reach for a weapon again, and I will rip your arms off, rodent turd."

"Take his belt off, Jasmine," said Michael. "I bet you there is a device there which allows him to return to his place in the sky."

"Gotcha."

Ten minutes later, Martinique was being comforted by Bull Knox as the Little Person was bound to a chair, totally nude.

"Must you kill my Biggun servant?" The small man spoke as he seemed to ignore his dire situation.

"He was hurting Martie," Bull replied as the young woman clung to his broad bare chest. Jasmine could not help but think the two young adults would soon leave for a more normal life on Twosuns. At that moment, Queen Aurora and King Gerald burst into the Armory with a full company of armed soldiers. Jasmine and the others started to kneel or bow, and King Gerald barked, "Stop that. When did all this bowing and scraping become so damned important?"

Queen Aurora smiled. "About a hundred Harvests ago, my husband."

The statuesque ruler walked up to the bound smaller being and towered over him.

"So. We finally have one in our custody who keeps dropping things and people on our heads."

"You must be the Queen," said the prisoner.

"And your name is?" Aurora replied.

"Ion Prime. Senior Thinker of Alderon. And we are not the ones who drop things on you. Well, at least not the only ones."

"There is more than one group who can do this?" asked the King.

Ion Prime nodded towards Jasmine. "Ask her how she came here. It was not we Small Ones who brought her."

It was a long night. As the sun rose, Queen Aurora walked with Jasmine out into the courtyard. "Do you have pretty sunrises on this—Earth, your home?"

"Yes, ma'am. But we have only one Moon and one Sun."

Aurora sighed. "How I wish things were simpler. Sky Stangers and such began in earnest some one hundred harvests ago. At least, that is when they happened enough to cause a lot of record-keeping."

"I believe my people will come looking for me, Queen Aurora. I was sent here by accident."

"Ion Prime came here on purpose."

"Yes, ma'am. I, for one, hope we can use his devices to send me home."

"Did you have a mate waiting for you, Huntress Jazz?"

"No, ma'am. I was kind of working on that when—I fell down the rabbit hole."

Aurora laughed. She placed her hand on Jasmine's arm. "You will always be welcome here, Jasmine Wright. You and Great Bull saved my daughter and seemed to be in the right place at the right time on more than one occasion. Capitol City will sustain a loss when you leave." The Queen grinned. "Although in Bull's case, it will be due to love. I cannot fault that fact."

Queen Aurora looked into Jasmine's eyes. "If you all choose to remain, it would be appreciated. This Kingdom needs people such as you."

"Well, Queen Aurora, I doubt we will be leaving anytime soon. At least Michael and I will not. Even with Ion Primes technology, finding the pathway to my Earth will not be easy."

The Queen looked back at the Armory. "No matter what occurs, as the saying goes, what happens will be quite interesting."

"Where I come from, there is a saying, often

stated as a curse."

"And what is that, my friend Jasmine Wright of Earth?"

"May you live in interesting times. And in this case, interesting worlds and kingdoms."

The two women, both Queens in their rights, went to share breakfast as the local Daysun rose on a new day in Twosuns. As they did, Great Bull and Martinique discussed their future.

All involved would live in exciting times, which is not always a curse when love and friendship are involved.

Jasmine Wright finished the diagram of the Game as she remembered. The man nicknamed the Tinkerer had created a device capable of sending people into different universes and worlds by accident.

"There. The best I can remember. My friend John King built this Game, which turned itself on and snatched me up. Then, I fell into a mudhole here in Twosuns."

The Former Marine pushed the oversized piece of art paper to the small being—who looked much like someone with dwarfism on Earth—who referred to himself as a Small One from someplace called Alderon. Ion Prime resembled an actor Jasmine knew from a famous Earth television series, down to speak with a voice comfortable in the theater

Ion spent a full minute examining the drawing before speaking.

"There must have been a connection to universal forces and energies we Small Ones are only now coming to grips with and understanding. We used a fundamental connection with what we call the Ether Power. I do not know if you have the necessary Thinker or science background to understand—"

"You mean Dark Matter or Dark Energy? I may not understand the math, but I read enough to know the basic concepts, just like in the Star Wars Universe. There is the 'Force' the Jedi Knights tap into when they need something powerful."

Ion frowned as he replied, "The Force? Knights? And what is this Universe you mentioned?"

Jasmine laughed then explained, "Fantasy concepts we used for entertainment on my world. However, their base is on mathematical, scientific theories."

"You Bigguns use complicated theories for entertainment? And I thought our Bigguns had strange thought patterns."

"Well, I guess we'll have to figure out if all we Bigguns come from the same place, the same universe."

"Well, we did have a strange Biggun appear not long ago. Plus, we had a most unusual Biggun disappear from our world, some of what you would call years ago."

"Who was this person who left? Did he have a name?"

"It was a female. Her name was Yeleanah Moon. She was born on Alderon. At least that is what we know."

"And the person who appeared in your world?"

"This was a male Biggun. His name was Maxwell King."

Bull Knox, Jasmine's Holemate/Battle Buddy, and Michael McClintock, their boss, and a senior technician or Maker and Thinker to the Royal Family, had to go to some lengths to prevent Jasmine from forcing answers from Ion. And force was Jasmine beating the Hell out of Ion. They discovered the reason was Maxwell King was Jasmine's first Battle Buddy. She was personal friends with the King family and now had a chance to *find* him, maybe return him to his family. If that meant using extreme pain against some short guy from another universe, so be it.

"Please," pleaded the Small One, "this Maxwell was a mistake. We were trying to discover the process which sent Yeleanah away from us. She helped to defeat an evil being who came to us from the sky, from another world. That in and of itself was fantastic, a Biggun having the mental capacities to do what we Small Ones could not."

"Methinks we have a midget bigot in our midsts," said Mike.

"I am used to such prejudgments," said Bull. "Many look at my size and see me as a giant oaf."

"So tell me exactly what happened. How and when did Max wind up in your world."

Ion's eyes went from one of so so-called Bigguns to the next. "I only understand part of it as I was not the one managing the experiment."

"Then why are you here?" demanded Jasmine. "Why is not the one who snatched Maxwell not here trying to make things right? Why did you come looking for the probe?"

Ion paused, then finally answered, "Because I was the one in charge. The Small Ones worked for me. So, our ruling council stated I must attend to the matter."

"Which resulted in the death of your Biggun servant," said Jasmine.

Ion shifted uncomfortably in his seat. "I miscalculated," Ion said in a subdued voice.

"Alright," said Jasmine, "tell the story, the truth, the whole truth, so help you by whatever you Gods you believe in."

"I will tell you what I know. I have no reason to lie."

"You'd better."

Bull laughed. This situation could be interesting for his comrades and painful for the Small One. Great Bull would soon see the next chapter to this story.

CHAPTER 13
SMALL ONES AND BIGGUNS

Maxwell King, Marine Corps Sergeant, was hauling ass in a HUMVEE across Afghanistan's rough terrain. Private James Sloan was in danger of dying of a burst appendix if Max did not take him to a medical unit at Warp speed. The field hospital was some eight-klicks distance that was not far if it were a paved road. However, this was not the United States.

As he dodged another pothole, he heard Private Sloan groan.

"We'll be there very soon, Marine. Hang in there."

Another moan answered Max.

"Goddamn no Air Evac," mumbled Max. Some wiseacre had said eight kilometers did not warrant a helicopter pick up unless during some combat operation. Max wished he could force the decision-maker to have appendicitis and see how he would like a rough vehicle ride in that condition.

Max dodged another pothole. Then there was a bright flash.

Max thought he hit a landmine and instinctively ducked. He was ready to be thrown from the HUMVEE. Instead of potholes, he is driving through a field full of tall grass and strange flowers. The Marine slammed on his brakes, and the HUMVEE slid to a stop. Max glanced around and tried not to let his mouth fall open in surprise.

"Where the Hell are we?" he said as Sloan groaned. Max grabbed the vehicle radio microphone and began yelling, trying to reach anyone. Static was his reward. Max swore and grabbed his military Lensatic compass and tried to obtain some form of orientation. He heard a loud human bellow from behind his back as he tried to use the small flip-up eyepiece and the sighting wire. Max grabbed his rifle and spun around towards the sound. This time he could not stop his mouth from dropping open.

An oversized humanoid with horns on his forehead rode towards him. The four-legged mount resembled a cross between a jackass and a zebra. Max remembered from some cable television show an Okapi from Africa, but this version was at least twice the size. The rider brandished a massive broadside.

Max swung his weapon up and fired a three-round burst at the feet of the oversized Okapi. The mount shied and reared, the horned rider clearly cursing in his native language as he fought to bring it under control.

"Stop right there, buddy!" yelled Max as he aimed in on the warrior. As he did, Max realized the horns emanated from the humanoid's head, not a helmet. What was going on?

Over the nearby hill came a mass of other humanoids. The males looked like cousins to the first one, with some slender and shorter females driving carts filled with possessions and children bringing up the rear. The Marine NCO realized he had fallen into a world of shit, outnumbered with a wounded man in his care.

"God, I hope someone calmer is in charge," Max mumbled.

A much smaller being was operating an ATV type pulled in front of the carts and mounted warriors, yelling into a bullhorn. This action brought a mounted warrior festooned with various golden armbands and neck chains to the show. The horned humanoid bellowed and pointed at Max as the small one put down the bullhorn and began to speak in a much calmer tone to the recognized leader. Max stood and watched, calculating if he should haul ass in the HUMVEE. But where would he go? The Marine had no idea where he was, what direction was west

The small human-looking being rode slowly up on the ATV as the warrior leader grumbled and cursed. Max thought those actions were a show for his people, to show he was ready for a fight. The rider Max shot at was sitting off to one side on his now controlled mount. The local ATV engine sounded like an electric golf cart. Max watched as the smaller being dismounted from his machine.

The Small One stepped towards Max, gave a short bow, and then began speaking in an unknown tongue.

"Sorry, mister. I don't understand a word you're saying," said Max. The Small One stopped, motioned in a universal sign to keep speaking.

"As I said, that was not English; my Pushtah and Arabic are limited, although my Spanish is pretty good."

The reduced statue being paused then spoke. "You—speak—Outlander?"

"We call it English."

The short individual drew himself up to his full diminutive height and spoke. "I am Gonn, Thinker Second Class on Alderon. You are?"

"Maxwell King, Sergeant United States Marine Corps. I have a wounded man here who needs medical attention."

"You need a Medico?"

"Yes. Private Sloan is dying from appendicitis.

Where am I?"

The being named Gonn yelled back at the horned warriors in their language. There was much internal yelling, and then a slighter-built female in silk-like robes came walking up carrying what looked like an Earthly doctor's bag. She smiled at Max, who noticed her Elfin-shaped ears and tiny forehead horns. He watched the female as she examined the injured Marine. Then the Medico called to Gonn, who yelled instructions back to the now very curious humanoids. In a flash, more females appeared. The males sat on their mounts, spitting, belching, and passing some drinking skins around: they acted like nothing unusual.

The Medico spoke to Gonn in the odd combination of sing-song rhythms mixed in with harsher guttural sounds. Max's fleeting thought this language would give many a linguist a headache. In minutes the females, assisted by some older children, had a tent set up next to the HUMVEE. The beings moved Private Sloan carefully to a long and sturdy table. Surgical instruments appeared from cases and leather bags.

"So they are going to cut on him, take out his appendix?" Max asked Gonn. "By the way, what are these people called?"

"They are Leafkin warriors and nomads. Their wives are referred to as pixies, although they are not of that race. A resemblance to actual pixies led so-called early Thinkers to mislabel them. Lord Kalvane is the leader of this group, which I believe is the largest among the Leafkins."

"You have other races, species of people here on—Alderon?"

"We have numerous civilized groups and countries. You will also find uncivilized groups. We Small Ones classify all these large oafs as Bigguns. The smaller the being, the larger their intelligence is the result of our studies."

Max smirked. "Then how do you explain a large person like myself, operating complicated machinery?"

Gonn shrugged. "There are often exceptions to many a rule and finding."

The Medicos were swift and efficient. Sloan was soon resting comfortably on a bed of thick furs and comforters. The senior female Medico explained to Gonn what they did, and he translated the information to Max.

"She removed the swollen organ, although the Medico stated it was unlike anything in a Leafkin body. Leafkin pixies are very intuitive with their medical treatments and are nearly as efficient as we Thinkers in medicine."

"How do I repay them for saving Sloan from a burst appendix, Thinker Gonn?"

"You don't. The Leafkin females are bound to help all creatures. Except for Dark Pixies, who they deem beyond help."

Max pointed to the sizeable Leafkin warrior whose mount he shot at when first met.

"That man has been giving me a 'stink eye' since we first met."

"You challenged him by shooting near him, scaring his mount. You thus disrespected him in front of the other warriors. He may demand a—duel is your word, I believe."

"Well, no time like the present, I guess," said Max as he walked towards the mounted warrior. His fellows began to laugh and chant some phrase which no doubt translated as *'fight, fight, fight'* as in schoolyard days.

The offended Leafkin slid from his saddle and towered over Max. The Leafkin leader, identified as Lord Kalvane, called out to his warrior, and the male grumbled as he removed his broadsword. Max was a solid six-footer, but the Leafkin had a good six inches on him and built like an NFL lineman. The Leafkin stepped up in front of him and spat at his boots. Hoots came from the body of warriors. Max grinned at the body of warriors, then at the Leafkin in front of him.

The Marine then discovered the male humanoids' testicles were in the exact location as Earth humans. Max kicked to the family jewels, followed up with a three-punch combination, and the warrior collapsed in the grassy meadow. His fellow warrior roared with laughter as Max retrieved his assault rifle.

The Small One Thinker frowned at the Earthling as he spoke. "Why you Bigguns are so violent is a mystery to me. It must be some inherent racial characteristic."

"How about telling your Leafkin friends that if they want a fight, I'll do it if it means protecting Sloan."

Gonn snorted. "Lord Kalvane is not a friend. We Small Ones provide them with trinkets, new medicines, and mechanical toys for the children. It helps to preserve the Long Peace."

Lord Kalvane spurred his mount and rode up to Max as the Marine recovered his weapon. The Leafkin warrior slid from his horse-like creature and extended his right hand as he laughed. "You are a warrior," Lord Kalvane said in passable English/Outlander.

"Join us at our tables for food and drink, stranger."

"Thank you, Lord Kalvane. That sounds like an excellent idea as my friend recovers from the surgery."

"Your comrade is safe with our women. Unless he tries to place his hands where they don't belong."

"I doubt he'll want to do that after being cut open."

The Leafkin warriors recovered their unconscious comrade as Lord Kalvane escorted Max to a long table the females had quickly set up. Some young lady set a tall tankard in front of Max along with some odd-looking cooked tubers. Max tasted the drink and decided it was a form of mead with a kick. He'd have to keep his wits about him as he tried to figure just what had happened to him and Sloan. Of course, the warriors wanted to examine his weapons, so Max unloaded his rifle and pistol and allowed them to be passed around. If these men wished him harm, he would have been dead by now. Lord Kalvane pointed to his combat knife/bayonet, and Max handed it to him.

The Lord nodded his head in appreciation. "Excellent metal. Your metalworkers are nearly as good as ours." The Elfin Leader fixed him with an examining gaze."So, Max, as you are named, where is home? You are not from anywhere near our forests."

Max sipped the mead drink then answered, "From here, I don't know, Lord. One minute I was transporting my comrade for medical treatment, the next moment, we are here. By the way, where is Gonn? "

Kalvane laughed. "Our warrior's tables unsettle him. He is examining your metal wagon. Gonn acts as if those around him, those he calls Bigguns, are of no consequence, yet he tries to ingratiate himself with us."

"What is this Long Peace he mentioned?"

Kalvane sneered. "Something which a strange being broke many cycles ago. The Small Ones still profess that they have restored the Long Peace after this male—*creature*—shattered it. "

The Leafkin Lord waved his hand, and more drinks arrived as Max munched on the fried tubers. The Marine's weapons came back to his chair, and several of the warriors raised their new filled tankards in appreciation. Max raised his drink as a toast in reply, and then the Leafkin Max flattened approached.

"Oh shit," said Max as he rose from his chair.

"Stay seated, warrior Max," said Kalvane. "We Leafkin know when we are bested in a fair fight. Arovane, my cousin, thought he would knock you down with ease. He was wrong and will admit it."

The linebacker Leafkin stood a yard back from Max and gave a slight bow. "You fight well, strange one. What group or family do you claim?"

"United States Marine Corps, my large friend. And how do all Leafkin warriors speak my language?"

"Outlander? Because we Leafkin travel where we wish, which is everywhere. Only Frontier Traders travel as much."

"The Small Ones see we Leafkin as stupid oafs because we don't have this desire for all things metal and mechanical," interjected Lord Kalvane. He held up his greatsword. "Metal is best in blades and weapons, not mechanical toys to entertain children. Too many machines make people weak."

"How about weapons of war?" asked Max.

"Mechanical mass destruction led to the First Long Peace," replied the Leafkin Lord. "Then this—Ceipher came down from the heavens. And once again armies marched." Kalvane gulped down his drink, belched, and bellowed, "Meat and drink! Now, women!"

A humongous roast appeared, and the smaller women bustled about refilling the numerous steins and glasses. It was not long before Max had an alcoholic buzz on, but since he did not desire to drive anywhere, no harm, no foul. Soon the younger Leafkin males were demonstrating various feats of strength, agility, and weapons usage. Max assumed it was to impress both males and females, but the Leafkin soon dragged him into the fun. His knife and ax throwing ability surprised the warriors. They had no way of knowing he had spent summers in his youth around Northwest Loggers, who still throw axes and such for fun.

Then Kalvane stood on the table and bellowed everyone into silence. He raised his mead stein high in salute. "Today, we meet a non-horned warrior from a far-off land. This Marine Corps member shows us that there are still males not of Leafkin clans with strength and honor. There is help for this world of Alderon still. I toast Max King as a new member of our Leafkin family. What say you all?"

The roaring shook the surrounding trees and

bushes. The Max was lifted and passed around in the Leafkin version of a rock and roll concert audience body surf. Then the Marine was unceremoniously dumped into a chair between two giggling Leafkin pixie maidens. They smelled and felt like any Earthly female he had known, with his manhood responding as such. Max tried to hide his erection, but the maidens soon spread the fact in their local language. This communication led to more bellowing laughter and another forced crowd body surf. Max plopped down into his original seat as Kalvane shoved another tankard into his hand.

"Drink up, Max. The night is young."

Hours later, Max managed to stumble to where Sloan was resting. The Leafkin female Medico met him with a smile.

"He rests," the Medico said in Outlander.

"Thank You, MiLady," Max answered, feeling like he was at a Renaissance fair. He took her hand and kissed it, watching the Medico blush.

"I am Kalvane's younger sister. You are very welcome. I spoke through Gonn before as we did not know if you were a person of honor. We know now you are."

"I try to be, young lady."

"You succeed." The female kissed him, then stepped back.

"What is your name?" asked Max.

"Divinity."

Max smiled. "Nice name and it fits you. Will I see you again?"

"Yes. You stay here with your friend tonight, as will I. Come to bed, please. I must make a medical examination as the maidens claim about your—size."

Later in the night, Max arose from the bed of thick furs to relieve himself.

"When in Rome…" he mumbled as he undid his fly. Apparently, a Lord could send his sister to pleasure some new impressive stranger. Max could tell that Lord Kalvane was a commensurate politician in this world, and Little People underestimated him. Max chuckled. What a turnabout, small-statured people, looking 'down' on much larger beings. Max was refastening his fly when he thought he saw a darkened figure sneaking into the camp from the surrounding trees and brush. Max kept his Marine KA-BAR knife near him at all times, and he had it in his hand before he realized it. The Marine moved to intercept the strange figure, years of experience and training taking over.

The figure was slender like Divinity but shorter. Even this being was taller than Gonn. Max stalked the shape, and he thought the Leafkins could do with some dogs if they did not post guards. As he neared, he saw the head of the intruder snap towards him.

"Shit," he cursed, knowing his presence was noticed. "Hello, there," he called out. "Who might you be—"

Max's combat reflexes enabled him to flatten just in time to dodge an arrow. The figure was up and running back the way it came, and Max went in hot pursuit as the camp arose. The slender figure was quick and lithe, knew the area, so Max was having trouble keeping it in view. The large moon of Alderon and the distant binary world gave off a lot of ambient light, so Max saw the figure whip around towards him. Again, he flattened out as a projectile zipped overhead.

"Goddammit, I just want to talk, you asshole," he called out.

Something significant and spinning came from the darkness behind Max and hit the fleeing figure. He heard a feminine scream as the shape dropped to the ground. A Leafkin warrior dashed past the Marine, and Max ran to catch up. On the ground tangled up in some form of a bola was a dark-skinned person clad in furs and leggings. The warrior bellowed in his language then repeated in Outlander.

"A Dark Pixie! Rouse the camp! Danger is neigh."

The Dark Pixie spat and spit like a cat as she struggled to free herself. The Pixie was female, as her struggles revealed a naked breast. The Leafkin, whom Max recognized as Arovane, raised an ax to strike, and

Max stopped him.

"I'd like to talk with her first, Arovane. Your bola throw has stopped her ability to flee or fight."

Arovane grunted and lowered his weapon. "You will be lied to, Max of the Marines. However, I think that will be an education for you about Alderon."

Max knelt next to the Dark Pixie just out of her reach should she break free.

"Do you speak Outlander, young lady?"

"Of course I do. I am Pixie. We are smarter and quicker than all others, especially Small Ones and Leafkins." She paused her struggles for freedom and examined Max.

"You are neither, Biggun. You are a stranger from—somewhere else. I think not Alderon."

"Very perceptive, I see. Now, can you tell me why you are nosing around this camp at night?"

"My people heard that something strange had appeared. After the one named Ceipher appeared and caused so much trouble, any odd occurrence attracts us. Dark Pixies are attuned to disturbances in our environment."

"That is because you practice the dark arts." The comment came from Lord Kalvane as he approached. "Did this one injure you, Max?"

"Nah. She is a bad shot."

If the Dark Pixie's eyes could have physically shot

daggers, the blades would impale Max many times over.

Lord Kalvane laughed. "You have stung the pride of this Pixie, Max the Marine."

"By the way, young lady, what is your name?"

"Star Dark."

The name caused Kalvane to whistle. "A member of the Dark Pixie royal family. What are you doing running around at night without an entourage?"

"We Dark Pixies need no servants and body men to assist us. We take care of matters personally."

Why do I feel like I fell into a Tolkein novel? thought Max King. He looked at Lord Kalvane.

"Now what? How do Leafkin usually deal with Dark Pixies?"

The Lord snorted and replied, "After the attacks instigated by this Ceipher and his wispy creatures, we killed many of them. The Small Ones claim a reinstituted Long Peace and stopped future violence. I find that hard to believe until I see some proof." Kalvane glared at Star Dark. "Pixies sneaking into our camps at night is not proof of peaceful intentions."

"I told you, Leafkin, I was investigating this— Max person. I don't ask Leafkin for permission to take care of business as I see fit. Especially Leafkin males."

"This Ceipher character sure stirred things up," interjected Max. "Where did he come from, and where did he go?"

"We Dark Pixie have information he was created by a failed Small One's breeding experiment. A Biggun Thinker, one of the few, helped to exile him to some other realm."

"Who was this Thinker who got rid of him?"

"A female named Yeleanah."

"What happened to her?"

"When Ceipher was destroyed, Yeleanah was yanked to another realm. Where we do not know."

"Hmmm. Yanked and pulled like my fellow Marine and I were, I bet."

"If so, stranger, you coming here may be a portent of trouble to come."

After a short discussion, Max convinced Lord Kalvane to release Star Dark.

"I was the one she tried to stick, so I should be the one who complains or does not complain."

"Hmmm. Warriors logic. If you have no desire for satisfaction as in a duel, then I have none. Arovane demonstrated what happens to those who skulk around our camps."

Star Dark cursed in some arcane language under her breath. The Dark Pixie then stood as tall as she could in front of Maxwell. "I accept your warrant and release. I see a form of honor in you not often demonstrated in Alderon. Your tribe or people must be a superior breed."

Max grinned as he answered, "United States

Marine Corps prides itself on a long history of honor. It rubs off on its members."

As the Dark Pixie prepared to leave, Gonn walked up.

"Of course, the Small One appears when the danger is past," Kalvane said sarcastically.

"The noise just awoke me," the Small One Thinker replied in a huff. "I see the Dark Pixie is now leaving us."

"Had I realized a Small One is about, I would have left earlier," sneered Star Dark. She nodded at Max.

"Well met, strange warrior. Sorry about the arrows and darts."

Max shrugged. "No harm, no foul. See you later, young lady."

The Pixie flashed a quick smile at the Marine, then seemed to melt into the surrounding forest.

"Best be careful with those Pixies," said Gonn. "They can bewitch and bewilder Bigguns. They were in league with the Dark One, Ceipher."

"I keep hearing about this boogeyman called Ceipher. Did he cause that much trouble?"

"He was pure evil. Ceipher killed many, caused many to kill others. We are lucky the Biggun Thinker Yeleanah, with help from Senior Thinker Ion, was able to find an ancient science that enabled her to banish Ceipher from our world."

"Young Star Dark said Ceipher was a creation of some Small Ones, which slipped from their control."

"Lies and fables spread by those who wish to discredit we Small Ones. Certain people, like Dark Pixies, wish to reassign blame."

Maxwell grinned at Gonn's indignation, which told the Marine there was some truth to Star Dark's comments. The little person protested too much.

"Well, where I come from, there is the story of Doctor Frankenstein and his creation which slipped from his control and then viewed as a monster."

Gonn sniffed in disdain and then spoke. "Must have been Bigguns involved, not Small Ones."

Lord Kalvane roared with laughter. "Ever the conceit of small people equals big brains. Come friend Max, let us break out fast with a morning meal."

"Ah, I must tell someone I will not be back to bed."

Kalvane laughed some more. "My sister is wise about the ways of men, especially warriors. No need to worry about offense, especially as you are *my* guest. Come, we eat."

Again, the morning meal was an all-male affair, the female Leafkin waiting on the warrior's hand and foot. Some children darted around, sneaking glances at Max. Tall Biggun males with no forehead horns must be a rarity. Max decided to pump Kalvane for some information about Alderon and its people.

"Our horns were the result of our warrior heritage," said Kalvane after taking a long drink of warmed spice wine; Coffee was not a drink of Alderon.

"The Great One deemed us, warriors, so we received horns, along with our great size. My Grandmother said everyone and things have their place, and every place has its people and things. This is how the world of Alderon is kept orderly and sane."

"Until beings like Ceipher show up."

Lord Kalvane sneered and spat. "He was a stain on this place. Now, we Leafkin attempt to live by the old ways and leave others alone, expecting them to leave us alone."

The giant Leakin warriors slapped Max on his back. "But no more depressing talk. Eat, enjoy my table and remember Leafkin are your friends."

After the Leafkin version of a Farmer's Breakfast, Max went to see if James Sloan recovered. He found Divinity spooning some thick broth into Slaons's mouth. The Leafkin met Max with a warm smile and spoke as she continued feeding the young Marine. "Your fellow is recovering well, Max. The question is, where will you take him from here?"

"Since I have no map or knowledge of Alderon, that is an excellent question."

"Where are we, Sergeant?" asked Sloan.

"That is the sixty-four thousand dollar question, James. We fell into a fantasy novel as far as I can tell."

"Max, we Leafkin are traveling towards Alderdale, the principal city for leagues around. There we will trade with other people and share the news from far-off places. I imagine my older brother Kalvane would be happy to have you travel with us. He enjoys your company, likes your mettle."

"Is that where Gonn is from?"

"Yes. There is a prominent Thinker Hall of Knowledge located there. Gonn and his fellow Small Ones will love to question and prod you Marines to discover how you came to Alderon.

"If prodding means taking pieces from us, they will wish they hadn't tried. One operation on Sloan is enough.

Divinity's laugh was an enjoyable feminine tinkling of bells. Maxwell had to admit traveling with her would be delightful. "Until Private Sloan here is recovered from his operation, traveling with you Leafkins would be best."

"You are right, Max, to be watchful of the Small Ones. They look down on others and are often are not truthful to those they see as inferior."

"Short Men's Complex. I have dealt with it before. Now, Divinity, I will escort you to your tent if I may."

"But of course, my friend."

"Take a nap, Sloan. I'll be back shortly."

"Yes, Staff Sergeant," said Sloan with a knowing grin.

As Max walked beside Divinity, he said, "About last night—"

Divinity laughed. "Rest your fears, Max of the Marines. Last night's congress between us is basic selfishness on we Leafkin. New seed from fertile males helps keep our clan alive and healthy. Though I was also determining if my companion maidens were exaggerating about your physicality."

"Well, did they exaggerate?" replied Max.

Divinity smiled and took the Marine's hand. "No, they were very accurate. Months from now, if I can give birth, there will be rejoicing. It is the younger daughters and sisters' task to help increase our numbers with new births."

"You don't feel—used? Just an object of desire?"

Divinity laughed. "Men can't have children; we females can. It is nature, not a burden forced on us. New births are joys, not dreads."

Max thought he had a lot to learn about the various cultures in this unusual world. However, the primary mission was a way back to Earth for the Marines

Lord Kalvane was joyful Max planned to travel with the numerous band. The Marine realized in Alderon, having an oddity in your camp may be a form of higher social status. As long as no one tried to put him and Sloan in a display case, it did not bother Max that he was a possible carnival attraction. Kalvane arranged to tow the HUMVEE with some of their oxen-like creatures. This action saved the limited fuel reserves of the vehicle. Gonn crawled over the HUMVEE, then tried to pick Max's brain about its operation. Finally, Max said," Gonn, when we get to your Hall of Knowledge in Alderdale, I promise I will help you diagram every inch of my transport. Of course, there will be a fee."

"Oh yes? And what will that be, Biggun Max?"

"Working to find how Sloan and I came here and how to return us home."

Lord Kalvane and his Leafkins were in no hurry to arrive at Alderdale. The warriors went hunting and practiced with their weapons as the female 'Pixie' Leafkin drove the carts with the children's help, set up meals, produced craft items for sale to Alderdale, as well as supplied medical aid to all who asked. Along the road, non Leafkin peoples would approach and ask the Medico Leafkins for assistance, given under the warriors' bored gazes. However, Max soon learned the boring sitting on their oversized Opaki mounts was just a front. The warriors always watched over the children and women.

Max rode a spare mount next to Lord Kalvane when a child's scream echoed from the edge of the forest. The mounted Leafkin warriors exploded into action in a heartbeat.

"Daggercats!" someone yelled out. Max tried to keep up with the galloping Kalvane as they breached the forest edge. Some children had stumbled into the Alderon version of a pride of lions. As Max reined in his beast, he saw a half-dozen cougar-type large felines arrayed in a line as some younger cats retreated deeper into the firest. The daggercats had long dagger-shaped teeth protruding from their upper jaws and lower jaws but were not Sabre Tooth Tigers. Whatever the genus in the world of Alderon, one had a ten-year-old maiden pinned to the ground. The warriors were hesitant to use their bows, spears, and oversized revolvers for fear of hitting the child. The daggercat had the young girl's head in its mouth as if to say *'back off, or she dies.'*

Max slid off his mount with his rifle in hand. Max's marksmanship skill meant he received a Designated Marksmanship Rifle in .308 caliber on Earth, with an improved optical and laser sight. Sloan, recovering from his operation, rode in a cart with his assault carbine in .223. Even if James were in position, his .223 was not suited to take on a large feline.

The Marine went to a kneeling position, used the optical sight to draw a bead on the threatening creature, and put a round through its right eye. The cat's head exploded in a red mist as the high-velocity bullet entered the creature's head. The child's head slipped from the lifeless jaws as the rifle's loud report stunned the other daggercats. A young Leafkin warrior charged on foot towards the girl child and scooped her up as arrows and other projectiles drove the rest of the felines back into the forest.

Within moments, Leafkins crowded around Max and the young rescuer. As Leafkins rushed the young lady to the Medicos, Max and the warrior named Dragondane were hoisted on shoulders and paraded about. The Marine saw the Leafkin accolades for actions they decided were honorable and heroic were never half-hearted. Lord Kalvane gave a short speech and pounded Max on his back. Later, the Leafkin leader made Max give him a private demonstration of his shot. Afterward, Kalvane was in profound thought.

"Maybe more complicated machines are suitable for warriors," Kalvane mumbled.

After the evening meal and more accolades, Max walked towards Sloan's wagon when an adult female approached, leading the now head bandaged rescued victim. The mother bowed low, and the child knelt head bowed.

"She and I owe you, strange and great warrior," the mother said with a quivering voice. "She is now your body servant to do for and obey you."

Shit, thought Max. *How do I get out of this without insulting Leafkins?*

The Marine clasped the hands of the mother and looked into her eyes. "In my home, we do not use body servants nor expect payment for doing what is right. Saving a child from harm is always right. Please, take your daughter and raise her to be an honorable person. That I will take as payment."

The rescued girl hugged him as she cried, and Max tried to keep the lump in his throat under control. After all, tough Marines don't cry in front of others. Well, maybe their fellow Marines, but not in front of the public. The mother and daughter Leafkin walked back to their wagon, and Max went on to check on Sloan. The young Private was healing well and was allowed to move around a bit from his bed. Divinity gave strict orders about not opening up his stitches.

"How are you doing, James?"

"Fine, Sergeant. Have you figured out where we are yet?"

Max smiled. It was hard enough on Max, but Sloan had joined right out of high school and even left a sweetheart at home. This assignment was his first tour of duty, and now he was in God knows where. "If you read science fiction, it looks like we are in some alternate universe or world. As for the unasked question, I am still working on how we get home."

"This city we are traveling to, you think they may have some answers?"

"I hope. This Gonn character says there is a Hall of Knowledge where their scientists study such subjects. So, we can hope."

"What if they can't?" asked James Sloan.

"Then we find someone who can. There are several civilizations on this planet. One of them must have some answers. Until then, we stay together and survive. Got it, Marine?"

"Yes, Staff Sergeant. At least Divinity is helpful and nice to look at."

"Yes, on both counts. Now, get some rest. Tomorrow is another day."

Divinity allowed James to join the communal morning meal under Max's watchful eye. Lord Kalvane assured Max he would ensure none of his warriors tried to involve James in any of their roughhousing until fully healed. Max also limited the young private's warmed spiced wine intake, knowing Divinity had the Marine on some light painkillers. The Leafkin warriors did prod James about his combat experience and once again passed around the man's unloaded weapons. After seeing Max killing the daggercat with one shot, the worth of Marine firearms took on a different meaning.

At the end of the meal, the horned warriors

welcomed James into the Leafkin fold with a formal toast but no body surfing. As Max and James stood talking to Lord Kalvane, Destiny walked up.

"Lord Kalvane, my brother. May I borrow Max for a few moments?"

"But of course, my sister. I will escort young James back to his resting area." Kalvane winked at Max as he walked off with Sloan, talking about Marine Corps Training.

"And how may I help my favorite Medico, Destiny?"

"Maxwell King is your formal name. Yes? Please understand your very noble and kind words to the young girl you saved from the Daggercat have had some far-reaching effect. The Leafkins will enter the name Maxwell King into a book we call The Book of Honor. We females are responsible for the upkeep of such records and references. Females have the final say of who is included." Divinity smiled at Max. "As I believe it is similar in your world, females wield power behind the veils, while males posture and bellow."

Max laughed. Divinity was a power to be reckoned with and a natural intelligence well above the norm. He wondered if the gene pool was close enough between Leafkins and Earthlings that there was a chance she carried his child. That would be a happy occurrence if Max were stuck on Alderon for the rest of his life.

"I am honored by your Leafkin actions, but my efforts are based on my upbringing and Marine training. My parents and the Corps stressed doing what was right and not expecting personal rewards."

Divinity kissed Max on his cheek. "We will always welcome you and yours into my family's tents and homes."

"And I owe you for saving James Sloan's life."

Divinity smiled. "Like you, we do what is right, not what is profitable."

Max wished he could spend more private time with Divinity but understood there were social mores here on Alderon different than from Earth. He must tread carefully as Max and James needed to have help to return home. Max rejoined Lord Kalvane as the Leafkins struck camp. The prominent male leader grinned at the Marine.

"I see my younger sister has an interest in you."

"If I may be blunt as a guest, Lord Kalvane, and ask some questions about your lifestyle."

"After saving the child, Max the Marine, you may ask most anything. Leafkin children are our pride and joy."

"So, I am a so-called Biggun here, as the Small Ones also call you as such. So, are Leafkin and Earthlings—compatible in personal relations?"

Kalvane laughed. "We Leafkins know all of the Bigguns came from the same stock. The Small Ones like Gonn spread myths and tales under the guise of scientific study. We Leafkin refer to the Great One as the being who created us all. That is our religious beliefs. Despite Gonn thinking that we Leafkins are violent oafs, we know how creatures reproduce through sexual coupling. The Dracon Frontiers people, the Winterdyne clans, the female-controlled Skylendahl, we all interbreed. You seem related to us somehow, have the same shapes and very similar organs. All except that appendix, I think you called it. "

"How about breeding with the Small Ones?" asked Max.

Kalvane spat on the ground. "That idea is almost obscene. No Leafkin would stoop that low."

"So if James and I are stuck here for the rest of our natural lives, there is a good chance for raising families."

"Yes, my new friend. And you two Marines are objects of talk among all the female Leafkin. As my sister told you, we Leafkin are open to expanding our bloodline without formal bonding. So, be warned. Many may want to bed you and see if our peoples are compatible for offspring."

"What can I expect in Alderdale?"

"Word is spreading that we have a stranger with

us, from some unknown place. Because of Ceipher, some people will be on edge and afraid. The Small Ones will want to poke and prod you. Since You are now an adopted Vane Clan member, we will keep them from abusing you. Small Ones look at all others as potential study subjects, not equal to Small Ones."

"Thank you, Kalvane, for all your help and fellowship. Without it, James and I would be dead."

Kalvane laughed. "I doubt it. Your Marine Corps produces excellent warriors."

Two days later, the train of people, carets, and other beasts reached the outskirts of Alderdale. A uniformed official backed by armed soldiers and customs officials met the band. The stories about Max and James preceded the group, and the local government seemed on edge. The official in the resplendent uniform stepped forward to meet Kalvane and Max. The Marine noticed the beefy man had a complicated mechanical hand and arm replacing the natural right one. As the man neared, Max glanced around and immediately thought, *steampunk.* Everywhere, there was a combination of leather and steel, machines and animals with some electronics powered with traditional steam power. Max thought once again what he fell into when the HUMVEE came to rest in the field.

"Ho, Lord Kalvane," said the official in

Outlander, the universal trade language. "I see by the size of your band that life has been good."

"Yes, Commissioner General Ymesh Moon. The Vane Clan has much in trade goods."

"You also have some—strangers with you? From an unknown land?"

Max decided they would not talk about him in the third person. "United States Marine Corps Staff Sergeant Maxwell King at your service, General Ymesh. Private First Class James Sloan and I are here on Alderon not by choice but by accident. I believe Thinker Gonn has a report on the matter."

Ymesh twisted the ends of his large handlebar mustache as he examined Maxwell.

"So, Maxwell King, Thinker Gonn will be en route to the Hall of Knowledge to file a report with Director and Senior Thinker Ion. However, being responsible for peacekeeping and enforcement of customs laws, I must ask you to surrender your weapons—"

"I think not," interrupted Kalvane. "No Leafkin warrior is asked to surrender his weapon. You have always accepted peace bond from us."

Ymesh frowned. "These outsiders are Leafkin clan members?"

"Marines King and Sloan are full-fledged Leafkin warriors and will be protected by us." Kalvane flashed a feral grin at General Commissioner. "You know we believe in all for one, even from a different family group. Leafkin take insults on one of us as an insult on all our people."

Ymesh paused and looked at Kalvane. Then he smiled. "I will accept your assurances, Lord Kalvane, based on our past peaceful relationship. Marine King, I hope you will not demonstrate your weapons prowess here in Alderdale. Your reputation with the daggercat proceeds you here."

"Of course, sir. I wish peace until Sloan, and I can return home."

"He is not a Ceipher in furry fisher clothing, my friend Ymesh," said Kalvane. "We saw to that."

"A Dark Pixie reported as such, Lord Kalvane," replied Ymesh. "She spoke quite highly of Max King, which is unusual for a Dark Pixie. They are short on compliments for non-Pixies."

"See, Max, you already have a growing group of friends," said Kalvane. "So, may we enter now, Ymesh?"

"Of course. Just have someone deliver a peace bond at the customs office."

Lord Kalvane led his people to a large clearing near some stockyards. As the group passed the city, Maxwell kept his head on a swivel. Most store owners and merchants gave scant attention to the Leafkins passing. A few shouted greetings while others ran up to present minor signs announcing some item's sale. Above the streets was a colossal Jumbotron television screen broadcasting both information and entertainment. Steam and electric vehicles mixed with beasts of burden. Some new entrepreneur tried to sell a gasoline-powered car in a side street as the Leafkins passed.

"Steampunk," Max mumbled. "Pure steampunk." He watched a goggled and leather-clad young Biggun dickering with a merchant over some odd-looking fruit. None of the Biggun people approached the size and statue of the Leafkin Warriors. Yet, no one paid them any attention. Leather-clad Frontier Folk rubbed shoulders with Winterdyne travelers carrying their fur coats in the warmer clime of Alderdale. The only people who seemed a bit standoffish were a gorgeous chocolate-skinned woman walking with an entourage of nearly naked muscular males.

"Who is that?" Max asked Kalvane.

"Her? Queen Onaleaha, of Skylyndahl. The females rule in that highland area. Males are traded and sold as the rulers please and are warriors alongside the females, with female commanders. In the past, Leakin and the Skys, as we call them, fought wars. The last great fight before Ceipher appeared involved our two peoples."

"That was the war that led to the Long Peace?'

"Yes. Over forty cycles of no wars, no fights

other than occasional duels." Kalvane sniffed. "It was boring."

"Huh. The Queen is beautiful."

"She is a tease who does not want a true male, a warrior. She wants to be the dominant one, wishes she has the phallus."

Max grinned. "So, it sounds like you—"

"She is a tease. That is the end of the matter."

Max tried not to laugh. Kalvane was a Lord, so public embarrassment was not a good idea. Max decided to let sleeping dogs lay.

Just as the Leafkin band reached the chosen clearing, Max heard a shout. Both he and Kalvane turned at looked for its origin. The Leafkin male frowned. "It is Queen Onaleaha. She saw you enter the city."

"Well, Lord Kalvane, do we ignore her?"

"No. That is rude, and then we appear to be weak and afraid of the Queen's attention." Kalvane gave Max a stern look. "Be warned. She is slippery and not to be trusted."

The Queen walked straight towards Max and Kalvane as one used to command and going where they wished. Max followed Kalvane's lead as the Leafkin Lord did not dismount; Max immediately surmised he was about to observe some royal one-up-manship (or up woman ship) activity. Max saw just how attractive the Queen was as she neared. Her dress or flowing robes shifted and flowed as she walked, threatening to reveal the feminine bits all men want to see. Then, just as quickly, the thin silklike material would close about the object of desire. Max felt a familiar stirring in what fantasy stories would call his loins.

"She has that effect on all males, and she knows it," said Kalvane.

"That obvious?" asked Max.

"Yes."

Several yards from Max, the semi-nude males ran in front of the walking Queen and formed a flesh stairway up to Max and Kalvane. The Marine noticed the final two body servants raised the Queen to eye level with the mounted Kalvane.

"So Lord Kalvane of the Leafkins, the stories are true. You brought a strange warrior to our midst."

"Why yes, Queen Onaleaha of the Skylyndahls. He is now an accepted Leafkin warrior."

The Queen's pretty mouth displayed a sly smile. "I see Lord Kalvane acts quickly to give a possible advantage, as always."

"There was no arcane plan, Onaleaha. He performed acts which warranted his Leafkin Warrior status."

The Queen fixed Max with an examining gaze. "What say you, warrior? Were you honored as a warrior or as a new servant?"

Kalvane's jaws began to tighten at the veiled attempt to call the Lord a liar. Max saw it was time for him to speak.

"Maxwell King, Staff Sergeant, United States Marine Corps."

Onaleaha smiled at Max and pushed back a lock of her raven-colored hair. "Is it true you killed a daggercat with one bolt from your weapon? That you saved a young female's life?"

"Of course, Ona, my friend. Would I lie to you?" The statement came from Divinity as she walked up. The Skylendahl ruler let out a very unqueenlike squeal and clambered down from her humanoid stairway. The two women were soon hugging and talking in some other language. Max looked at Klavane, who shrugged.

"Fate willed they met as children during the Long Peace while attending school. They have been fast friends ever since."

The Queen and Divinity walked over to Max, arm in arm. The Marine saw this as a chance to dismount without making anyone 'lose face' in this land.

"My, he is large for a non-borne Leafkin," said the Queen. "I heard rumors that he also is large—"

"Shall we not insult my new fellow warrior with talks about his personal items?" Kalvane said. "You females can discuss such matters in private."

Onaleaha laughed at Kalvane. "Come down off

of your high mount, Lord. Our families have known each other for many cycles."

Kalvane slid off the giant Okapi and stood by Max.

"Does being a Marine has something to do with the sea?" asked the Queen.

"Yes, ma'am. Marines are warriors in, on, and from the oceans where I live."

"This United States. It is a state, a land?"

"It is a series of States, joined together by a sacred document we call the Constitution."

"Do you have Kings, Queens, Lords who rule you?"

"No, ma'am. We vote, elect citizens who represent us. Though they sometimes think they are our Lords."

"Pixies of old had such institutions. Now, we have Queens; the Small Ones have Directors. The Leafkins have powerful Lords like Kalvane, who can resist even females like me."

Lord Kalvane seemed to blush a bit as he spoke. "We must set up camp, Queen Onaleaha. My people have business to do, items to sell, and trade. I could arrange for a place at one of our tables with Max—"

"And watch childish males trying to impress all the females around?" replied the Queen. "Instead, I will ask that you allow your newfound friend and warrior to meet me at my quarters. I promise I will not steal him away."

"Only if I can bring my comrade, James Sloan," interjected Max.

"And I can attend as a chaperone," interjected Divinity.

"Done and done," replied the Queen with a laugh. "Tomorrow, shall we say?"

Kalvane sighed. "I know when to agree. I will accept your words as a guarantee you will not attempt to place these Marines in someone's breeding pool."

Onaleaha cocked an eyebrow as she spoke. "I have an idea no one could keep these Marines against their will."

Divinity laughed at that statement and escorted Onaleaha back to her entourage. Max followed the Queen as she walked.

"That lady has parts in all the right places of just the correct amount," said Max.

"Onaleaha is a temptress of the first order," replied Lord Kalvane.

"So, why didn't you two hook up, as we say in my world?"

Kalvane laughed long and hard. "It would be a constant battle as to who would be on top in all things. It would lead to another war between Skys and Leafkins. Our people are too different."

Max saw that Leafkin warriors would not allow groups of half-naked male body servants waiting on women's hands and feet.

Max helped do the required 'males work,' which was part of the camp's setup. This work mainly consisted of hauling or lifting if it would take too many females to complete. That and letting some of the young children crawl over them, giggling. As fierce as the Leafkins acted, they were doting parents on all the children.

As the Leafkins finished with the camp set up, trumpets sounded. Max looked up and saw a group of Small Ones approaching behind a Biggun holding a flag pole. Suspended on the staff was a banner proclaiming 'Hall of Knowledge.'

"I think Gonn's boss approaches," said Kalvane. Max noticed that Commissioner-General Ymesh seemed to be tailing the group at a distance.

"The man wants to see what is going on unnoticed," mumbled Max.

Lord Kalvane strode out to meet the small band. Max stayed behind as he sensed there was a definite protocol between all the people and various authorities. Leafkin were temporary visitors and not residents of Alderdale but demanded some dispensations. Unlike Gypsy types on Earth, there was no Sheriff with a desire to keep them moving along. Roving groups of various peoples seem the norm on Alderon rather than the exception.

After some conversation, Lord Kalvane waved Max over. He slung his rifle and sauntered over with what he thought was typical Leafkin ego.

"This is Maxwell King of the Marines. The Leafkins, our Vane Clan, officially accepted Max as a member and a representative of his Marine Corps. Treat him with due respect."

A Small One dressed in a fine suit stepped forward, a monocular device over one eye. Max realized he resembled a well-known actor on Earth, and when he spoke, the voice was also a match.

"I am Director Ion Prime, Senior Thinker, and the leader of all in the Hall of Knowledge. I understand you and a fellow—Marine appeared unexpectedly near Lord Kalvane's clan. And, you brought an unusual machine with you."

"All true, Director. I have hope you Thinkers can help Sloan and myself return to our homeworld—Earth."

"Pardon us if we Thinkers are disturbed by your arrival. But I imagine Lord Kalvane has informed you about the beast known as Ceipher, who appeared from out of the Heavens and brought death and destruction with him."

"Unfortunately, my family and I on Earth are well experienced with the adverse effects of war and conflict."

"So you men of Earth have had no Long Peace."

"Not for a couple of centuries. However, those who have suffered in war are the last people who want to start a conflict. You have nothing to fear from us Marines."

Ion paused for a moment, then spoke. "But you are quite proficient with weapons."

"As are all Leafkin warriors," interjected Lord Kalvane. "And we kept the Long Peace until Ceipher upturned the brown tuber cart."

"I mean no offense, Lord Kalvane. You lost your twin brother in an early battle caused by Ceipher and his wispy minions. I appreciate that you have learned again to live with the Dark Pixies."

"So, Small One, can we end this conversation? Maxwell is due at the warrior's table."

Ion looked at Max. "May I extend an invitation to some conversations with the other Thinkers at the Hall of Knowledge? Tomorrow—"

"Is out, Ion," interrupted Kalvane. "Queen Onaleaha has a prior invitation for tomorrow. We must follow protocol to keep the New Peace."

Max saw Ion's jaw tightened. The Small One was used to getting his way, was power in Alderon. The Director gave a slight bow to Kalvane and Max.

"Then I will leave you in the capable hands of Lord Kalvane and Queen Onaleaha until the day after tomorrow. Then I will ask for a complete examination—of your machine."

"I look forward to it, Director," replied Max.

Max watched as the line of Small Ones marched out behind their banner.

"Ion does all the talking for the Small Ones, doesn't he?" said the Marine.

Kalvane sneered then spit. "Ion tries to run all of Alderdale. There is a City Council with a Director, but Ion tells him when to squat and when to speak."

"Why is that, Lord Kalvane?"

"Too many Bigguns think the Small Ones are so smart, they are afraid to confront them. Some think the smarties need to tell all us dummies what to do. I think Small One would love to rule all of Alderon. Over my dead body!"

"I think the Queen would agree."

"She did back me when I swore a blood death for the death of Trevane. I will always honor her for that."

"If I may ask, what happened?"

"It is easier to show you the spilled blood and death by Ceipher."

Upon request, Divinity produced parchments and news sheets made in Alderdale and other cities. Most were in the local language, not Outlander. The odd mixture of technologies in the Steampunk world resulted in high-quality photographs reproduced in the scandal sheets. In them, Maxwell saw the dead bodies of Leafkin warriors, their neo-Pixie wives, and many children. Some of the bodies looked like pincushions from all the arrows and darts. There were gruesome photos of Dark Pixies' missing heads and limbs. One photograph in a Winterdyne periodical showed a line of Dark Pixie heads on stakes, lining a road.

"Shades of Rome and Vlad Dracul," said Max.

Divinity gave him a questioning look.

"People on Earth did much the same thing to their enemies. At least you can say you had a Long Peace." Max glanced over at Lord Kalvane standing across a field, bellowing directions. "Your brother does not like these pictures."

"We keep the ones of dead Trevane locked away. He was my brother also, but as a keeper of the records, I must ensure our history is complete." She looked away. "It is recorded that evil Ceipher regaled in the sight of such death and blood. He was truly a monster."

Max gently touched her shoulder. "I'm sorry."

"You have seen much death also, Maxwell. I can tell. You understand the pain."

Max gently hugged Divinity, and she hugged back. "Maybe we can keep things on an even keel, as they say. It would be nice to say, 'No more war.'"

Max took a short stroll after the typical Warriors meal to walk off the food and drink.

"I am going to get fat if I don't have more exercise," Max said as he walked. He would have to see about working out with the Leafkin warriors, even if most did tower over him. James Sloan could soon exercise with Max, the stitches to be removed tomorrow. Max looked for and saw the laid-out male latrines on the edge of the camp. The females had the equivalent of horse-pulled RVs with self-contained septic tanks, easily emptied. Again, a confusing mix of technologies and services.

"I wonder if someone is behind this cultural confusion," Max said as he undid his fly.

A figure approached from the shadows, and Max called out a greeting to the supposed warrior. He caught a whiff of an odd scent—then darkness.

Max awoke in a semi-dark room with an ether headache. Some Medics and EMTs had told him over the years that early mixtures of ether and anesthesia left patients with bad hangovers. Now he knew they were not fooling.

Max slowly rose, and found two animal skins hanging on a nail on a wall. He drank the water from one and spat out the sour wine from the other. He knew the old tome of the hair of the dog, but this surely did not apply.

He saw the door in the dim light, then looked up and saw the so-called ceiling was a series of metal bars. Max was in some dungeon or Alderon version of Devil's Island.

Max stepped to the barred window of the door and yelled out, "Hey, assholes! You know this is kidnapping, right?"

His yelling brought a pair of Bigguns to the door.

"How's it like to be ordered around by a bunch of midget motherfuckers?" Max sneered at the two men. They were not Leafkin, that was for sure. And Onaleaha never needed to kidnap males; they came to her like bees to honey. Thus, it must be the Small Ones. Dark Pixies would have dragged him from the city.

"You must not yell," one of the jailers said in Outlander. "It upsets the Thinkers."

"Oh yeah? Well, what will happen if I don't shut up? No egg in my beer?"

"You'll be put to sleep again, which is not healthy," the second Biggun answered.

"Well, come on in and try. At least this time, I can fight you. No knocking me out as I piss."

The two Bigguns stepped back and conferred in some other dialect. Then the first one said, "We summoned a Small One. You can complain to him."

"Good, I hope it's Gonn or Ion. I'd love to put a

boot up their asses."

The two jailers disappeared, and Max examined his cell. He reached up and grabbed the ceiling bars and pulled himself up. This lockup was for a smaller person judging by the low ceiling. As he climbed across the high bars like a Marine Corps obstacle course, he quickly noticed there was rust everywhere. One corner had a barred access door secured by a very rusty lock. Some pushing and moving showed Max with a little bit of time; he could break the lock. This cage had not been used for a long time, and the upkeep sucked.

Max heard footsteps and voices and quickly dropped down to the cell floor. Moments later, someone unlocked the door, and three weapon barrels pointed at the Marine. As his eyes adjusted to the changing light, Max saw Gonn and Ion standing with four Bigguns, three with long arms.

"So, you have guns. So much for peace."

"We have limited weapons for defense, especially after Ceipher," replied Ion.

"He sure gets blamed for a lot."

In the reduced lighting, Max could see Ion's face flushed with anger. "You have no idea, Earth Biggun, the destruction he brought. Now, I am sorry we had to use a gas gun on you to bring you here, but we must be sure now, not days from now, you are not another Ceipher."

Max guffawed. "You don't think Kalvane and

company wouldn't notice? They seem to hate Ceipher as much if not more than you."

"Leafkins intelligence is limited. They may miss salient clues. Now, enough talk. Come with us to our laboratory for some tests and examinations. You may come voluntarily, or we will force you. It is your choice."

Max shrugged and replied, "Lay on McDuff. I'll come quietly."

Max walked down a dark corridor following the Small Ones with the Bigguns nervously pointing weapons at him. After a couple of turns the group arrived at a massive combination lock door. Gonn worked the combination, and the Biggun without a weapon helped the Small One swing the door open. Max stepped in and immediately thought, *mad scientist late-night movie.*

"Victor Frankenstein would love this," said Max.

"If this Frankenstein is a scientist, I agree," replied Ion.

"You know the Leafkin will notice my absence, Ion."

"Bah. Kalvane and the others will run around like the large children they are, posturing and bellowing until you return. Or, if you are a minion of Ceipher—"

"Hey, Homey. Do I even look like this Ceipher asshole?"

"Ceipher was a shapeshifter so that you could be

a member of his species."

"I heard a rumor you Small Ones helped create him."

"Lie!" spat out Gonn. Ion stood silent.

Something shook the laboratory. Max thought it felt like a massive shape charge detonation.

"Do you little people have earthquakes a lot?" Max asked.

Gonn grabbed a communication tube and yelled into it, speaking some other languages. There was a further rumbling as the tube communication continued.

"Termites? Moles?" Max asked with a wide grin.

"Be quiet," commanded Ion.

"Well, it's been fun, but—"

Max used the distraction caused by the possible explosions to slam a military boot into the nearest guard as the Marine twisted the longarm from his hands. Max did not waste time figuring out how to fire the weapon but instead used it to butt stroke the second armed guard and then clubbed the third. When the fourth grabbed ahold of the rifle-like weapon, Max punched him twice in the face. The Marine then turned towards Gonn and Ion.

"Let's see if I can get this thing to shoot," said Max as he aimed the weapon at them.

Some large object slammed into the thick entrance door.

"I think someone is knocking on your door, people."

Max thought he heard a humming and electrical discharge coming from the door area. Then, the combination lock flew into the laboratory. Seconds later, Leafkins and Skies burst in, led by Lord Kalvane and Queen Onaleaha. Private Sloan dashed forward and shoved his M-4 Carbine into the faces of the two Small Ones.

"You okay, Staff Sergeant? Want I should off these two pieces of shit?"

"Nice to see you are recovering, Marine," Max replied. "Keep them alive. We need some answers."

Kalvane strode forward and slapped Max on the back.

"I see you were freeing yourself, Max King. Our efforts may seem wasted."

"Hell no, my friend. You provided the distraction I needed. By the way, who provided the explosives and fried the door."

"Skylendale did, Max," said Queen Onaleahe, holding a long rod with an enormous crystal in the end. "We developed energy crystals long ago, even though the Small One's think we are large oafs and stole the knowledge."

"Cutting tools and lasers, cool," said Max.

"We Leafkins had explosives years ago. After the

war that led to the Long Peace, we went more for the traditional personal weapons after a distrust for large mechanized weapons."

"How'd you find me?" asked Maxwell. "These Thinkers believe you were too slow to find me before they had interrogated me to determine if I am a new Ceipher."

Kalvane bellowed in some arcane language. "I should rip their heads off for such insults," Kalvane continued in Outlander.

Maxwell looked at Ion and Gonn.

"Instead, I think we obtain from them a pledge to help Sloan, and I return home." Max stepped up to with inches of the two Thinkers. "Yes? You agree?"

"Yes," replied Ion."I pledge our help."

"Good. Let's make like sheep and get the flock out of here."

Kalvane and Onaleaha gave Max quizzical looks.

"I'll explain the expression later."

Divinity met the large rescue party on the steps of the Hall of Knowledge.

"Commissioner-General Ymesh approaches with a large number of troops."

"I need to talk with that man," said Maxwell. He pushed his way to the front of the Leafkins and Skies and strode down the main thoroughfare. As Divinity had said, Yemesh was leading columns of troops towards the Hall of Knowledge. The high official halted the marching column upon seeing the Marine. Ymesh walked towards the approaching Marine and called out.

"I was told there was a battle in the streets."

"Just my friends rescuing me, Commissioner-General after Ion kidnapped me."

"Kidnapped? What do you mean?"

"I mean you, as a ranking official, cannot let these so-called Thinkers push you around. They knocked me out and kidnapped me for some examination to determine if I was Ceipher's offspring. Either you or the City Leaders run this place, or you don't."

Ymesh looked down as he spoke. "I owe my life and this wonderous mechanical arm to the Thinkers. They rescued me from the battle that led to the Long Peace after my father's death."

"Well, the concept is being warped and abused, General. Where I come from, Generals lead, not kowtow."

Ymaesh stood in thought, then replied, "I think you speak the truth, stranger. I'll talk to Ion and ensure none such unilateral action is taken again."

"Please do that, sir. Now, if you will excuse me, it has been a long night."

Maxwell snapped a sharp salute to Ymesh, who returned it with a surprised look. The Marine walked back and explained what happened to the others.

"We Leafkins can stay for business and trade but eventually leave. We are not city folk," explained Kalvane.

"Nor are my people tied to Alderdale," added the Queen.

"Well, I must stay with Sloan to push for a way home," said Max.

"I will stay with you, Max," Divinity said quickly.

Her older brother frowned at her. "A Leafkin female alone in this pit of depravity?"

"I will grab the warrior Dragondane, the young one who ran to rescue the child. He admires Max King and would like to help keep him safe as a personal bodyguard."

Kalvane paused in thought. "Fine. It is done. Divinity will be my personal representative as my sister. Dragondane will stay here and learn some new ways as a young male. His courage needs to be used and appreciated."

"Anyone ever tell you that you are a wise lord, my friend?" said Max.

Kalvane laughed and slapped him hard on the back. "It is nice to be appreciated by one such as yourself. Queen Onaleaha, you will leave a representative also?"

"Yes. I think these Small Ones have become

swell-headed. We need to remind them intelligence comes in large bodies also."

Back at the Leafkin camp, Max spoke alone with Divinity. "When Earth is mentioned, Ion does not seem surprised. He knows about our world."

"Then, the Small Ones may have pulled you here to Alderon?"

"Yes, and by damn, they can send Sloan and me back." Max looked at Divinity and smiled. "I am glad for your company, Divinity."

The young neo-Pixie linked arms with Max. "I am glad for yours—Maxwell King of Earth. My brother Kalvane respects you and trusts you with me. So if we share sleeping quarters—"

"I thought you'd never ask."

Jasmine Wright fixed Ion with a stony stare on the world of Two Suns where she was stuck.

"So I was yanked from Earth, it seems by Max's father's game. But you extracted Max to Alderon while trying to find out about this Yeleanah and Ceipher. Right?"

"That seems to be the situation. That is the truth as I see it."

"Great. Well, Ion, start working. You either need to send me to help Maxwell King, my Battle Buddy or get everyone back to Earth. You're not leaving here until you do."

"It is a series of accidents. Why must I be punished by exile here?"

"Welcome to the club of unintended consequences, Ion. Now, get to work."

Bull Knox whispered to his soon-to-be-betrothed Martinique as they watched the interplay between Ion and Jasmine.

"This King Family of Earth are people not to be trifled with nor bothered. Even their friends like Jasmine are willing to fight and die for them."

"Such love and loyalty should be emulated, Great Bull," replied Martinique.

"Yes, and passed on to one's children."

"So, Bull, would you want children with one such as me?"

Bull looked at Martinique then kissed her.

"Hey, get a room!" called out Jasmine. "I need to find Max and Earth."

Bull Knox grinned. "Yes, Jasmine. As you wish."